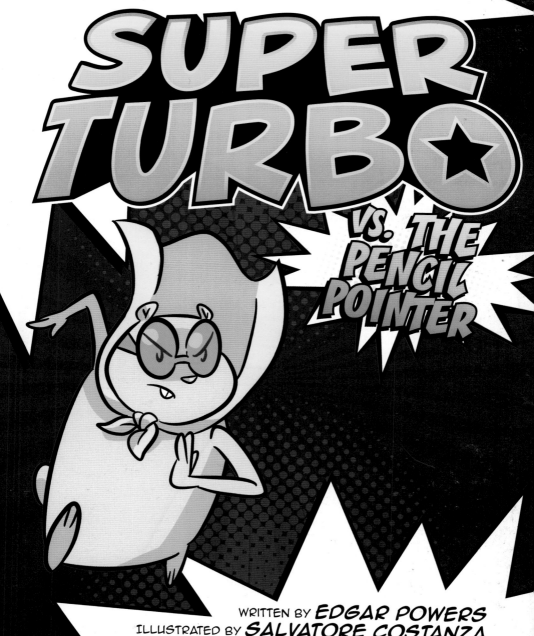

SUPER TURBO ★

vs. THE PENCIL POINTER

WRITTEN BY **EDGAR POWERS**
ILLUSTRATED BY **SALVATORE COSTANZA**
AT GLASS HOUSE GRAPHICS

LITTLE SIMON
NEW YORK   LONDON   TORONTO   SYDNEY   NEW DELHI

LITTLE SIMON
AN IMPRINT OF SIMON & SCHUSTER CHILDREN'S PUBLISHING DIVISION
1230 AVENUE OF THE AMERICAS, NEW YORK, NEW YORK 10020
FIRST LITTLE SIMON EDITION JUNE 2021 * COPYRIGHT © 2021 BY SIMON & SCHUSTER, INC. ALL RIGHTS RESERVED, INCLUDING THE RIGHT OF REPRODUCTION IN WHOLE OR IN PART IN ANY FORM. LITTLE SIMON IS A REGISTERED TRADEMARK OF SIMON & SCHUSTER, INC., AND ASSOCIATED COLOPHON IS A TRADEMARK OF SIMON & SCHUSTER, INC. FOR INFORMATION ABOUT SPECIAL DISCOUNTS FOR BULK PURCHASES, PLEASE CONTACT SIMON & SCHUSTER SPECIAL SALES AT 1-866-506-1949 OR BUSINESS@SIMONANDSCHUSTER.COM. THE SIMON & SCHUSTER SPEAKERS BUREAU CAN BRING AUTHORS TO YOUR LIVE EVENT. FOR MORE INFORMATION OR TO BOOK AN EVENT CONTACT THE SIMON & SCHUSTER SPEAKERS BUREAU AT 1-866-248-3049 OR VISIT OUR WEBSITE AT WWW.SIMONSPEAKERS.COM. DESIGNED BY NICHOLAS SCIACCA * ART SERVICES BY GLASS HOUSE GRAPHICS * ART AND COLOR BY SALVATORE COSTANZA * LETTERING BY GIOVANNI SPATARO/GRAFIMATED CARTOON * SUPERVISION BY SALVATORE DI MARCO/GRAFIMATED CARTOON * MANUFACTURED IN CHINA 0421 SCP * 2 4 6 8 10 9 7 5 3 1 * LIBRARY OF CONGRESS CATALOGING-IN-PUBLICATION DATA NAMES: POWERS, EDGAR J., AUTHOR. | GLASS HOUSE GRAPHICS, ILLUSTRATOR. TITLE: SUPER TURBO VS. THE PENCIL POINTER / BY EDGAR J. POWERS ; ILLUSTRATED BY GLASS HOUSE GRAPHICS. DESCRIPTION: FIRST LITTLE SIMON EDITION. | NEW YORK : LITTLE SIMON, 2021. | SERIES: SUPER TURBO, THE GRAPHIC NOVEL ; BOOK 3 | AUDIENCE: AGES 5-9 | AUDIENCE: GRADES K-4 | SUMMARY: "SUPER TURBO AND THE OTHER SUPERPETS FACE OFF AGAINST A MYSTERIOUS NEW FOE THAT SEEMS TO BE TRYING TO BURY TURBO ALIVE IN PENCIL SHAVINGS!"— PROVIDED BY PUBLISHER. IDENTIFIERS: LCCN 2020027925 (PRINT) | LCCN 2020027926 (EBOOK) | ISBN 9781534478381 (PAPERBACK) | ISBN 9781534478398 (HARDCOVER) | ISBN 9781534478404 (EBOOK) SUBJECTS: LCSH: GRAPHIC NOVELS. | CYAC: GRAPHIC NOVELS. | SUPERHEROES—FICTION. | HAMSTERS—FICTION. CLASSIFICATION: LCC PZ7.7.P7 SVP 2021 (PRINT) | LCC PZ7.7.P7 (EBOOK) | DDC 741.5/973—DC23 LC RECORD AVAILABLE AT HTTPS://LCCN.LOC.GOV/2020027925 LC EBOOK RECORD AVAILABLE AT HTTPS://LCCN.LOC.GOV/2020027926

CONTENTS

CHAPTER 1

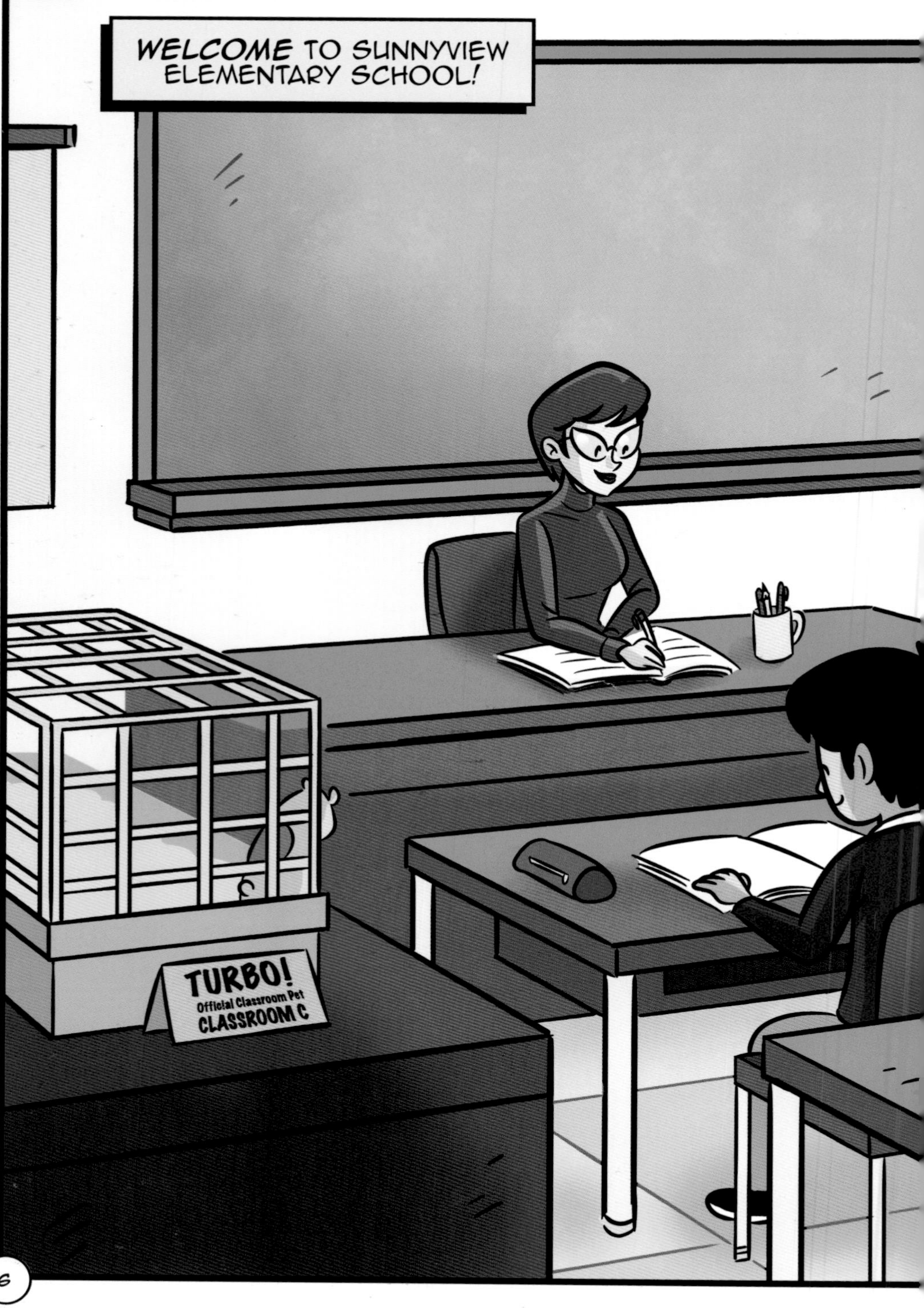
WELCOME TO SUNNYVIEW ELEMENTARY SCHOOL!
TURBO!
Official Classroom Pet
CLASSROOM C

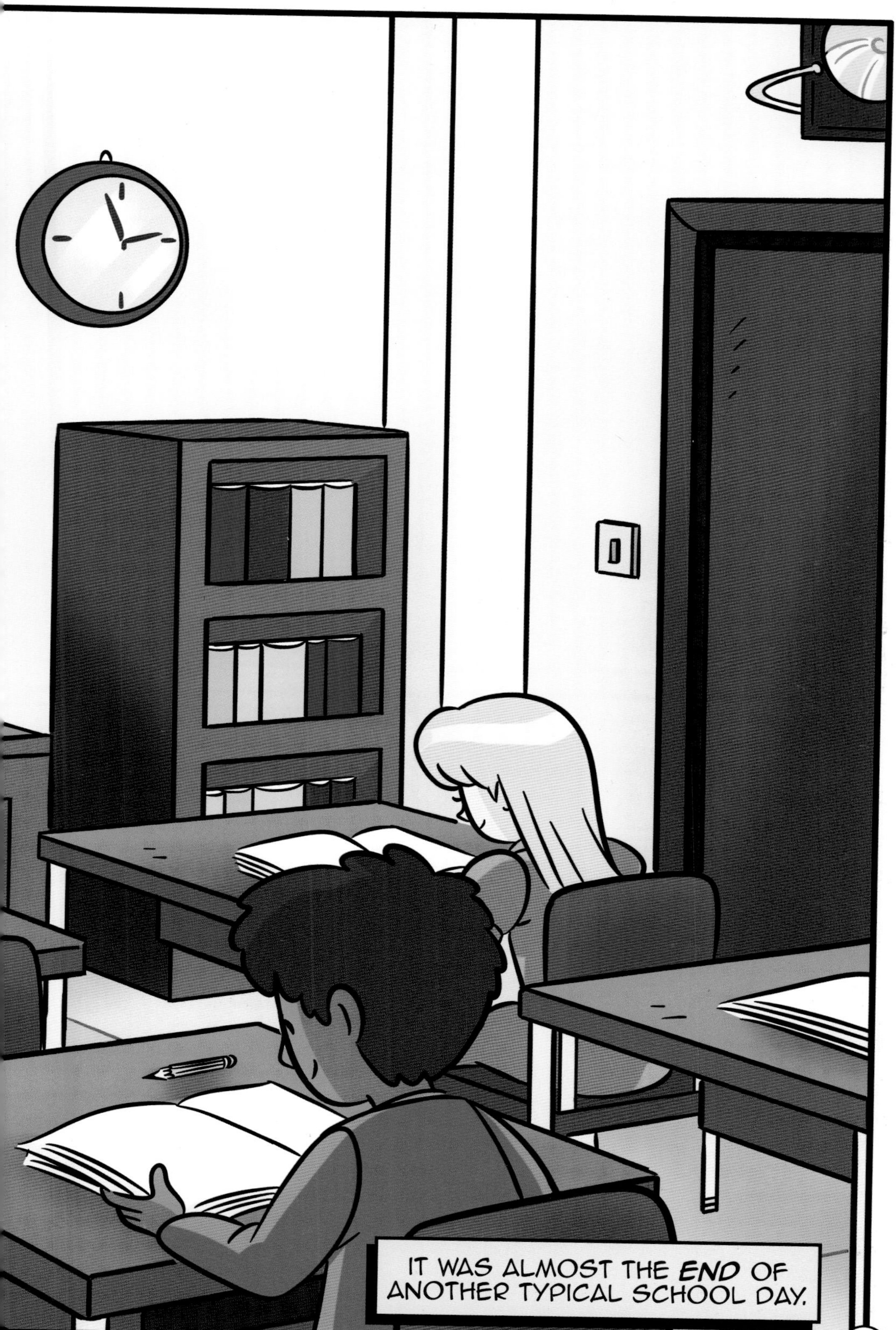
IT WAS ALMOST THE *END* OF ANOTHER TYPICAL SCHOOL DAY.

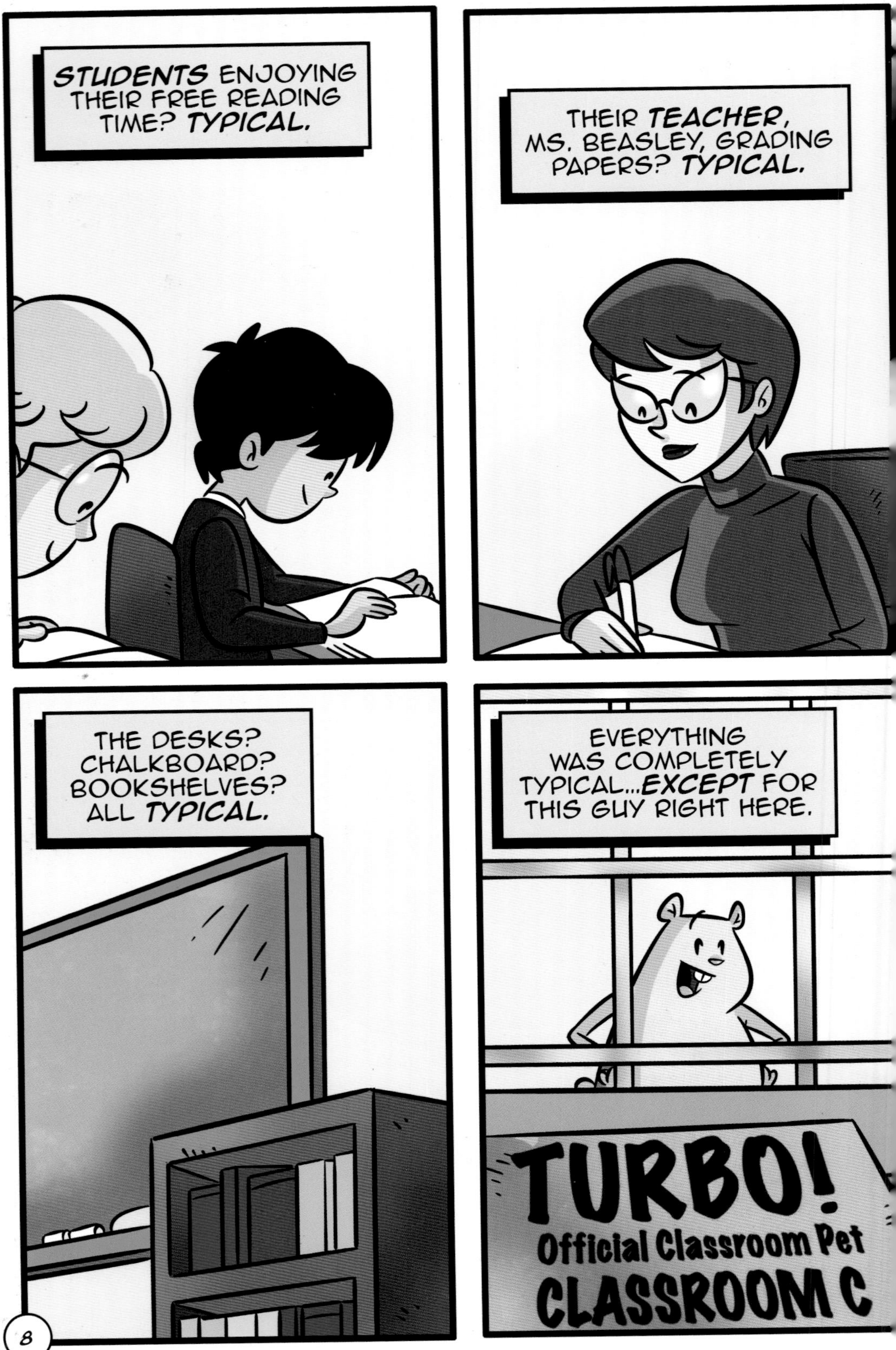
STUDENTS ENJOYING THEIR FREE READING TIME? TYPICAL.
THEIR TEACHER, MS. BEASLEY, GRADING PAPERS? TYPICAL.
THE DESKS? CHALKBOARD? BOOKSHELVES? ALL TYPICAL.
EVERYTHING WAS COMPLETELY TYPICAL...EXCEPT FOR THIS GUY RIGHT HERE.
TURBO!
Official Classroom Pet
CLASSROOM C

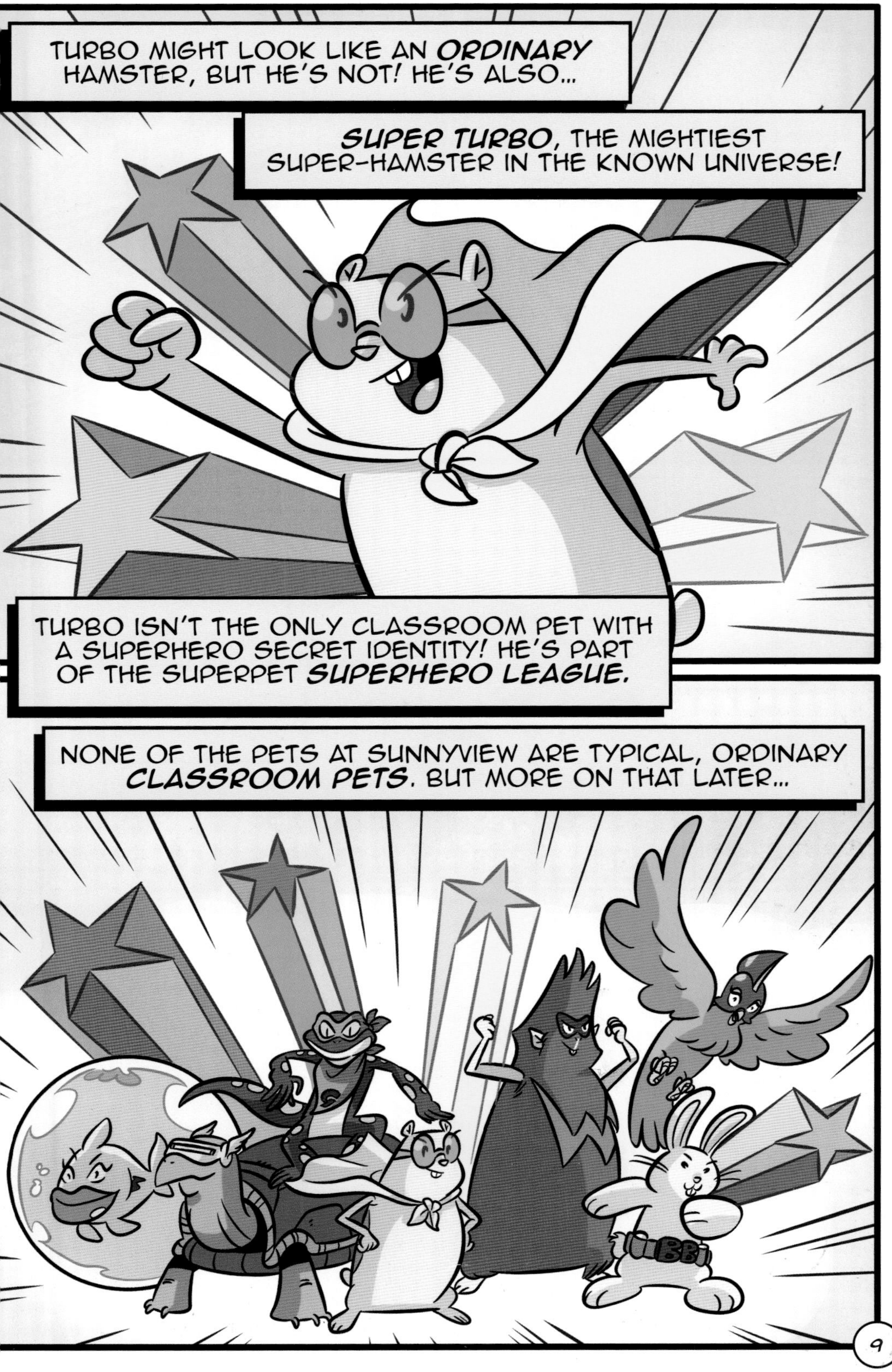
TURBO MIGHT LOOK LIKE AN *ORDINARY* HAMSTER, BUT HE'S NOT! HE'S ALSO...
SUPER TURBO, THE MIGHTIEST SUPER-HAMSTER IN THE KNOWN UNIVERSE!
TURBO ISN'T THE ONLY CLASSROOM PET WITH A SUPERHERO SECRET IDENTITY! HE'S PART OF THE SUPERPET *SUPERHERO LEAGUE.*
NONE OF THE PETS AT SUNNYVIEW ARE TYPICAL, ORDINARY *CLASSROOM PETS*. BUT MORE ON THAT LATER...
BB

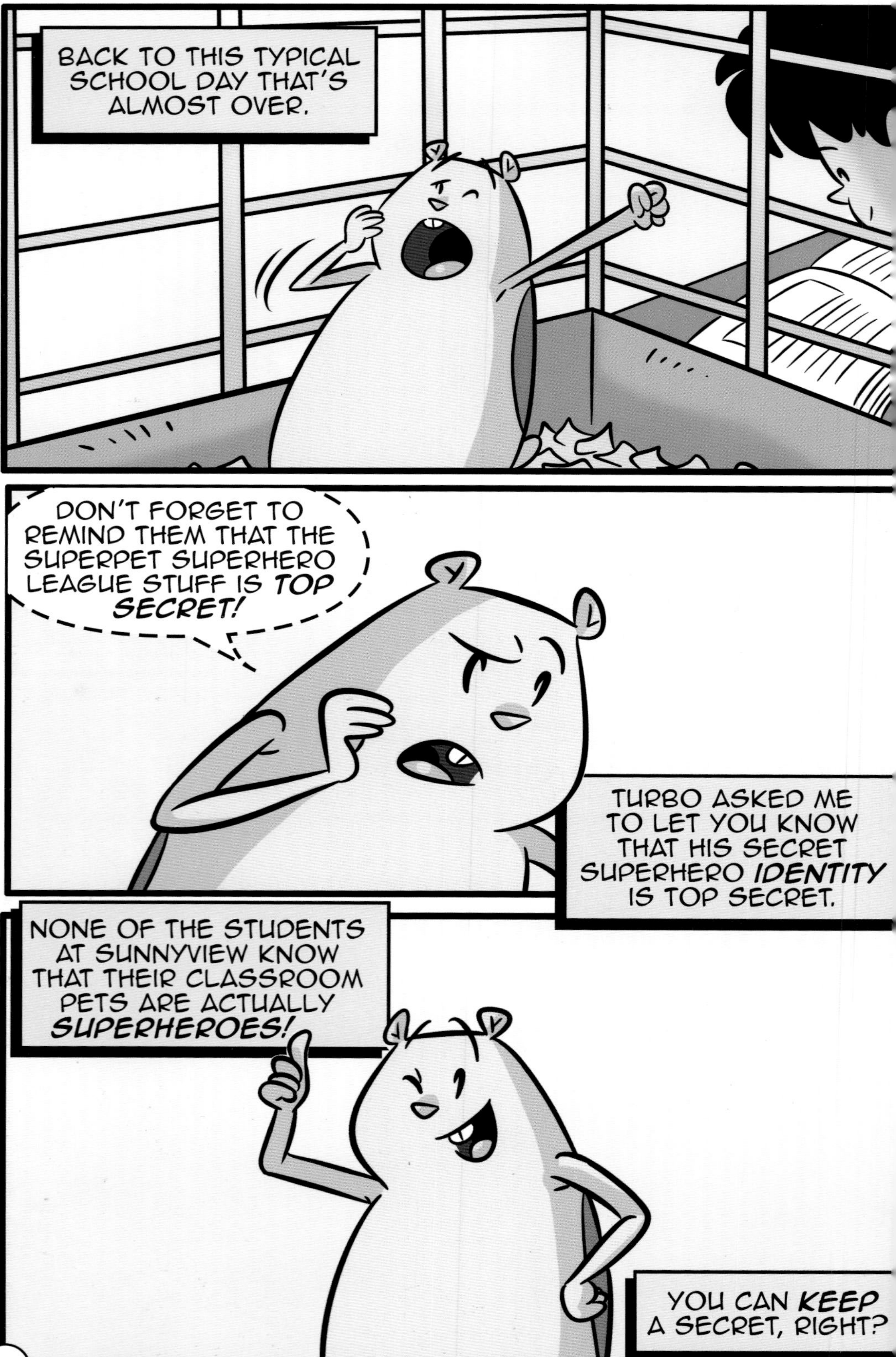
BACK TO THIS TYPICAL SCHOOL DAY THAT'S ALMOST OVER.
DON'T FORGET TO REMIND THEM THAT THE SUPERPET SUPERHERO LEAGUE STUFF IS *TOP SECRET!*
TURBO ASKED ME TO LET YOU KNOW THAT HIS SECRET SUPERHERO *IDENTITY* IS TOP SECRET.
NONE OF THE STUDENTS AT SUNNYVIEW KNOW THAT THEIR CLASSROOM PETS ARE ACTUALLY *SUPERHEROES!*
YOU CAN *KEEP* A SECRET, RIGHT?

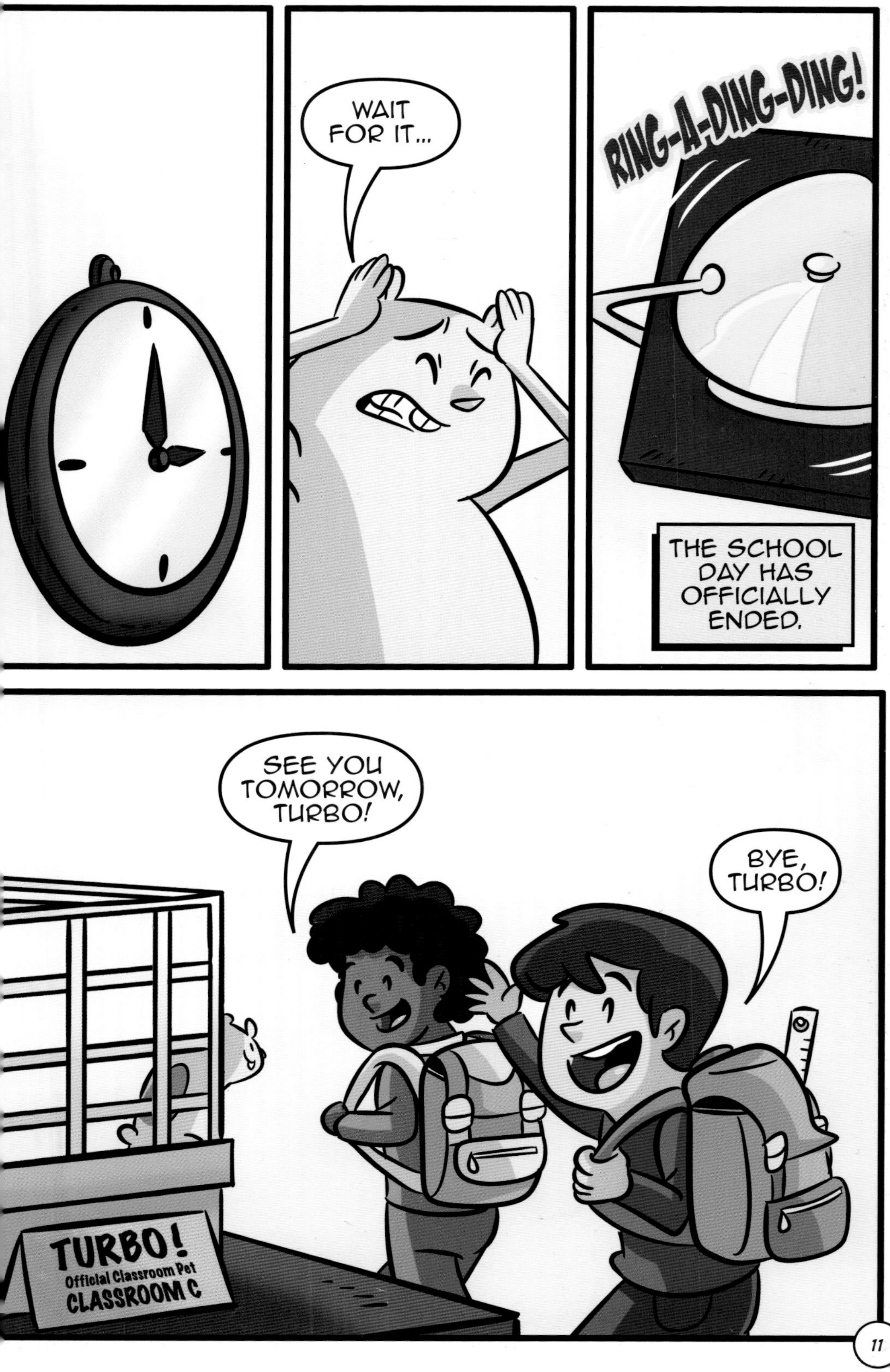
WAIT FOR IT...
RING-A-DING-DING!
THE SCHOOL DAY HAS OFFICIALLY ENDED.
SEE YOU TOMORROW, TURBO!
BYE, TURBO!
TURBO!
Official Classroom Pet
CLASSROOM C

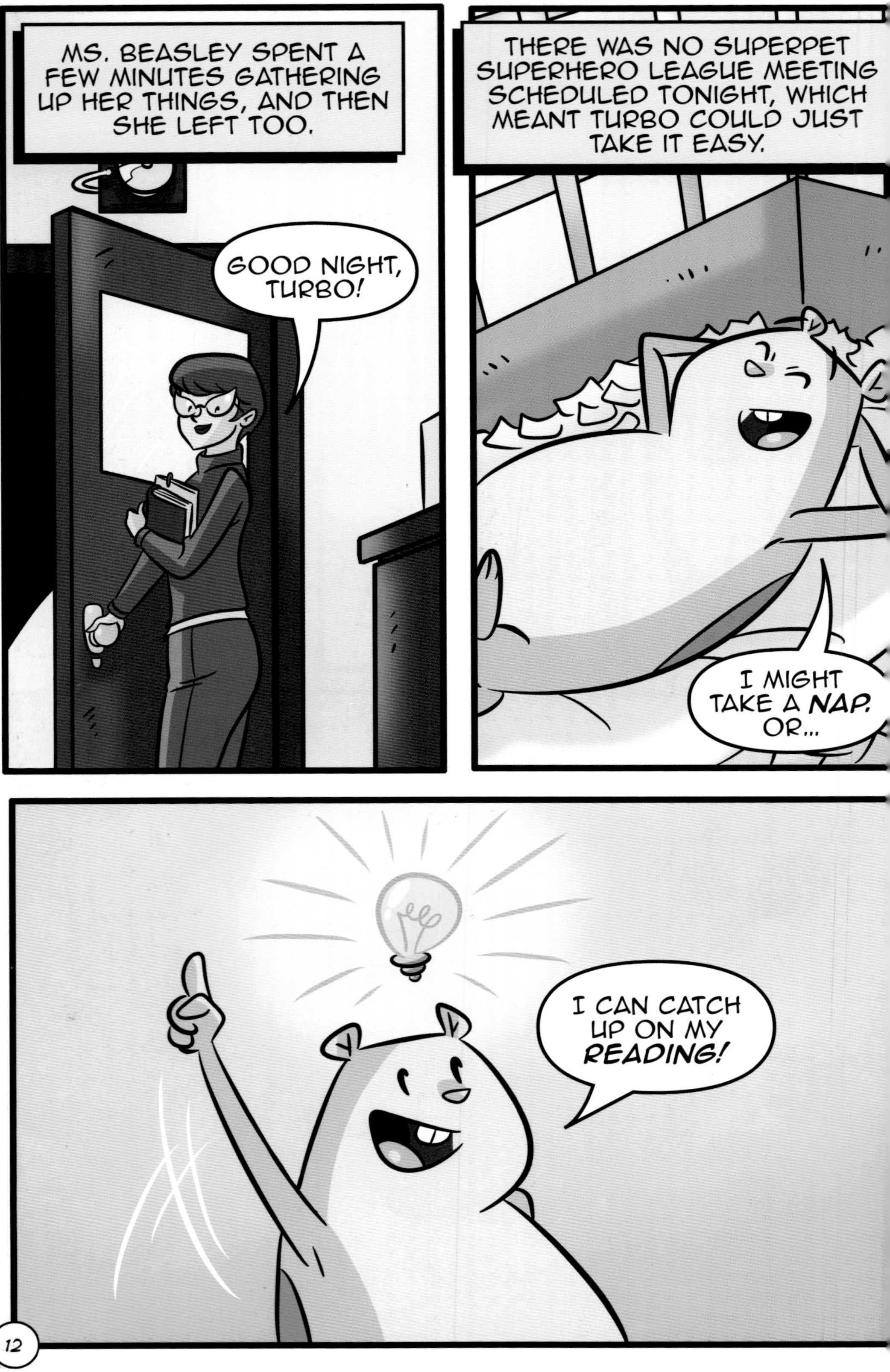

MS. BEASLEY SPENT A FEW MINUTES GATHERING UP HER THINGS, AND THEN SHE LEFT TOO.
GOOD NIGHT, TURBO!
THERE WAS NO SUPERPET SUPERHERO LEAGUE MEETING SCHEDULED TONIGHT, WHICH MEANT TURBO COULD JUST TAKE IT EASY.
I MIGHT TAKE A ***NAP.*** OR...
I CAN CATCH UP ON MY ***READING!***

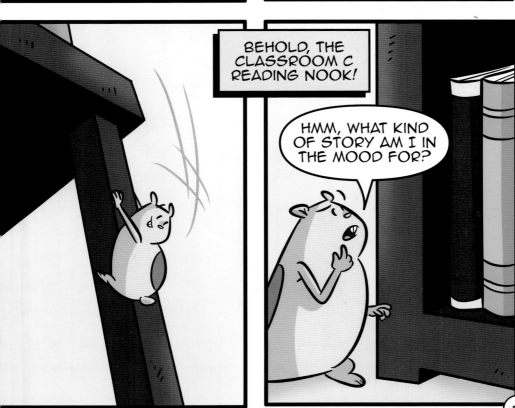

BEHOLD, THE CLASSROOM C READING NOOK!

HMM, WHAT KIND OF STORY AM I IN THE MOOD FOR?

TURBO WAS JUST ABOUT TO BEGIN READING THE DETECTIVE STORY HE HAD CHOSEN WHEN **SUDDENLY**...

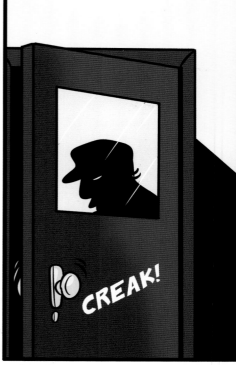

CREAK!

OH NO! SOMEONE'S COMING! I NEED A HIDING SPOT!

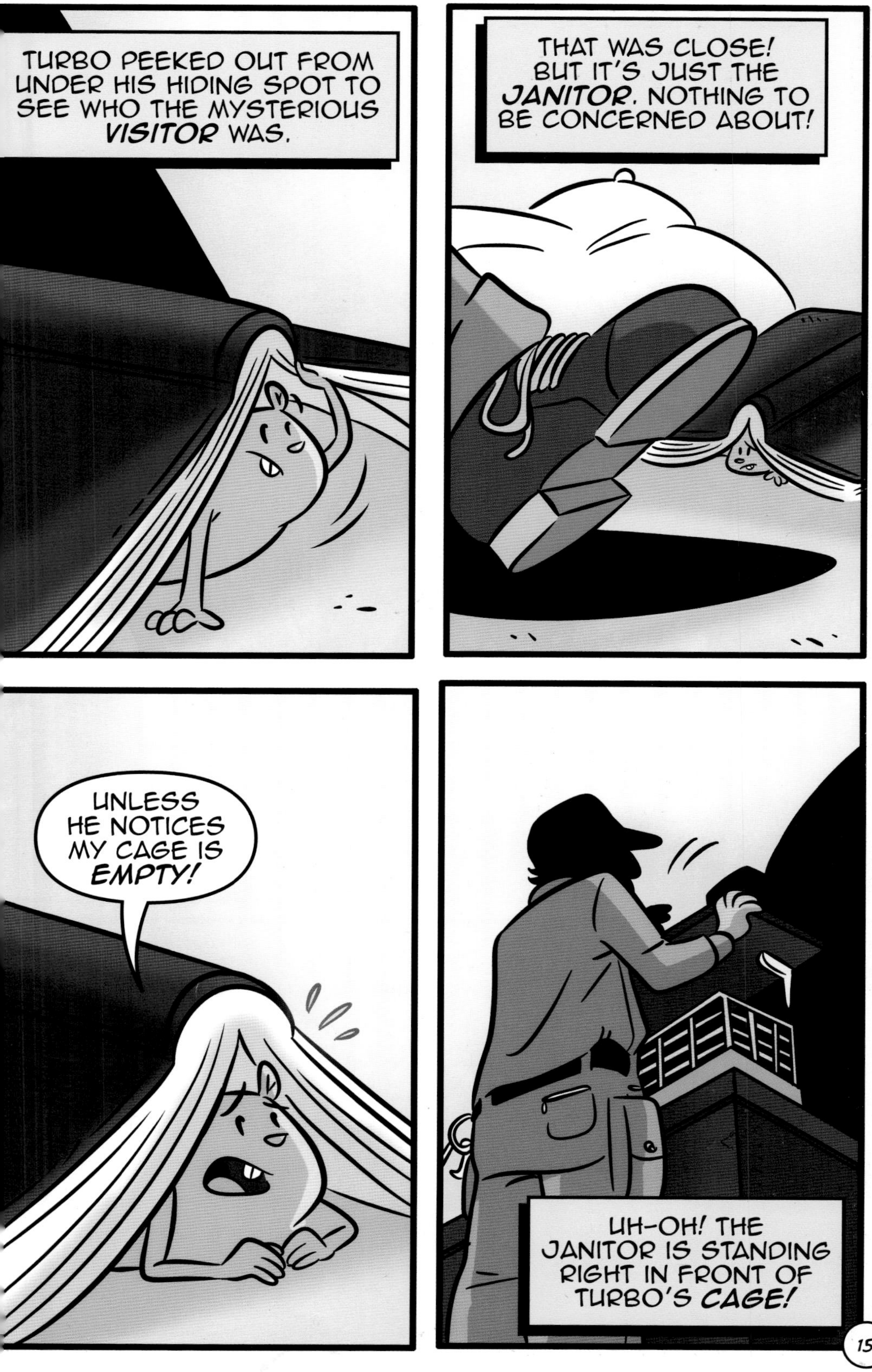

TURBO PEEKED OUT FROM UNDER HIS HIDING SPOT TO SEE WHO THE MYSTERIOUS *VISITOR* WAS.
THAT WAS CLOSE! BUT IT'S JUST THE *JANITOR*. NOTHING TO BE CONCERNED ABOUT!
UNLESS HE NOTICES MY CAGE IS *EMPTY!*
UH-OH! THE JANITOR IS STANDING RIGHT IN FRONT OF TURBO'S *CAGE!*

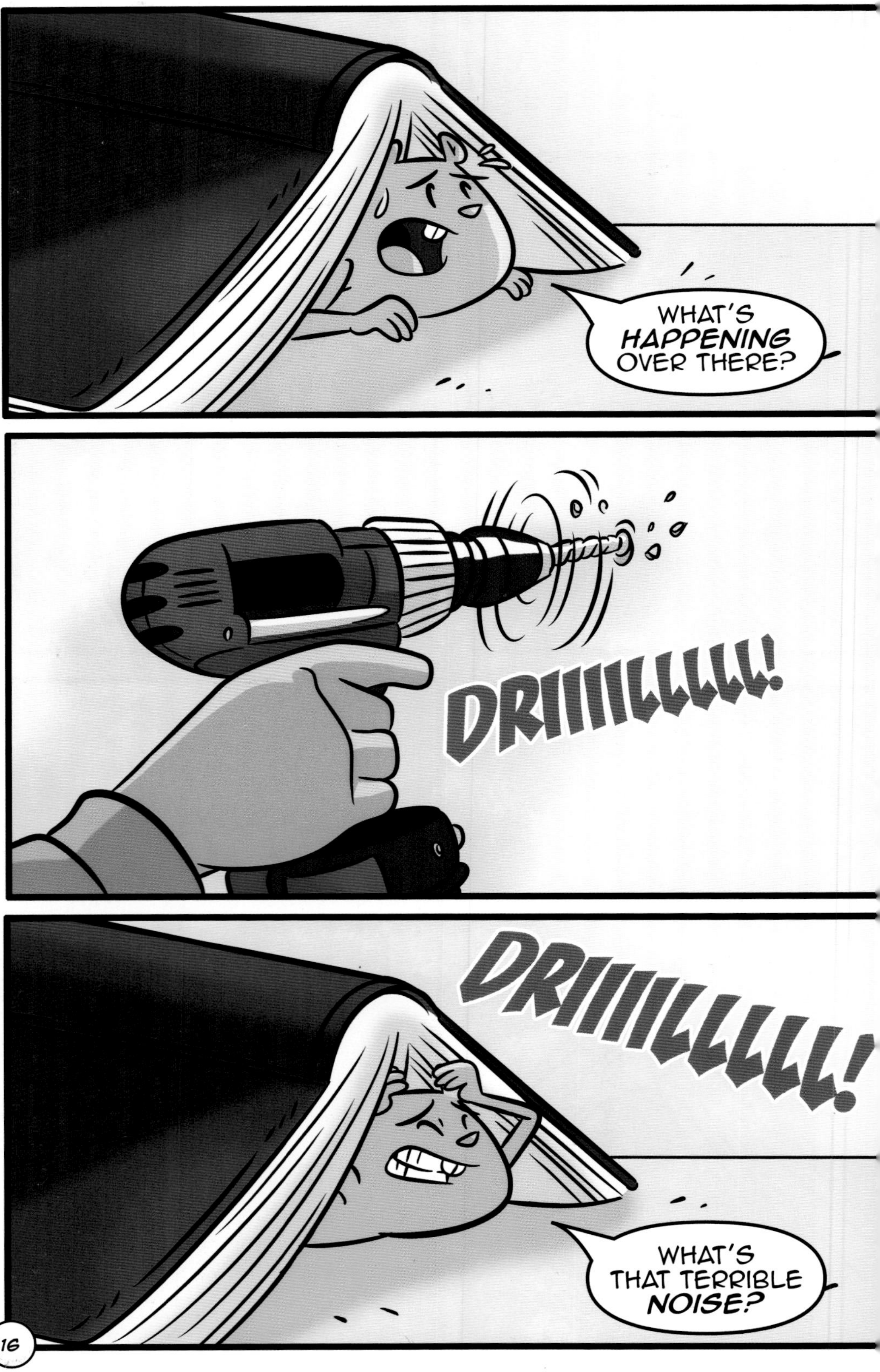
WHAT'S HAPPENING OVER THERE?
DRIIIIILLLLL!
DRIIIILLLLLL!
WHAT'S THAT TERRIBLE NOISE?

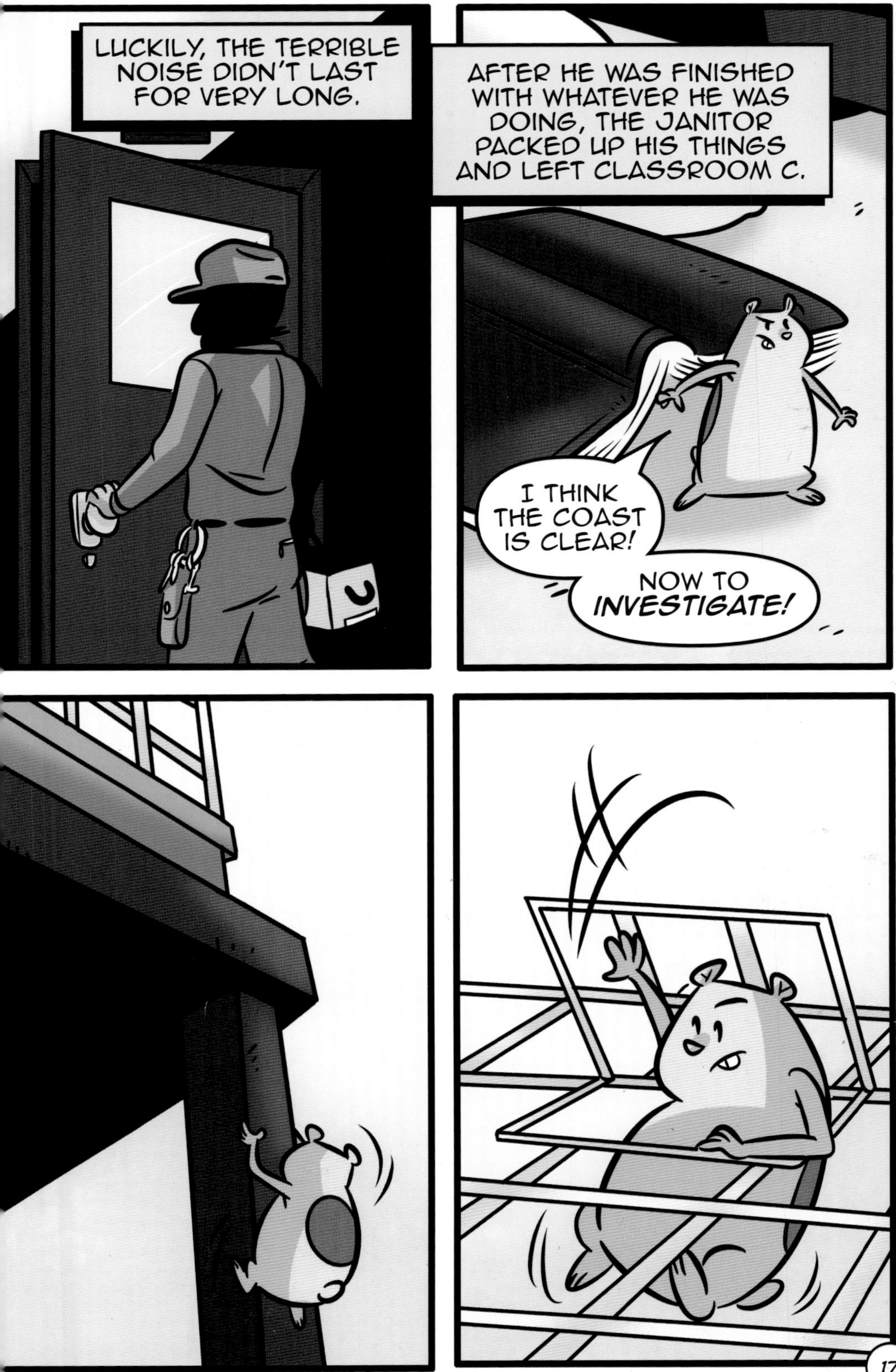
LUCKILY, THE TERRIBLE NOISE DIDN'T LAST FOR VERY LONG.
AFTER HE WAS FINISHED WITH WHATEVER HE WAS DOING, THE JANITOR PACKED UP HIS THINGS AND LEFT CLASSROOM C.
I THINK THE COAST IS CLEAR!
NOW TO *INVESTIGATE!*

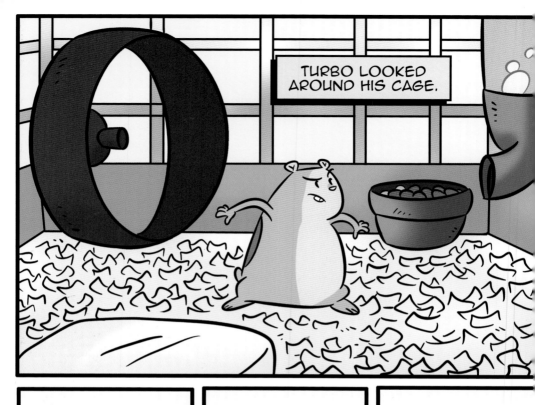

TURBO LOOKED AROUND HIS CAGE.

NOTHING SEEMS TO BE *MISSING!*

MY EXERCISE WHEEL LOOKS THE *SAME.*

MY BED LOOKS THE *SAME.*

SPEAKING OF TURBO'S BED...

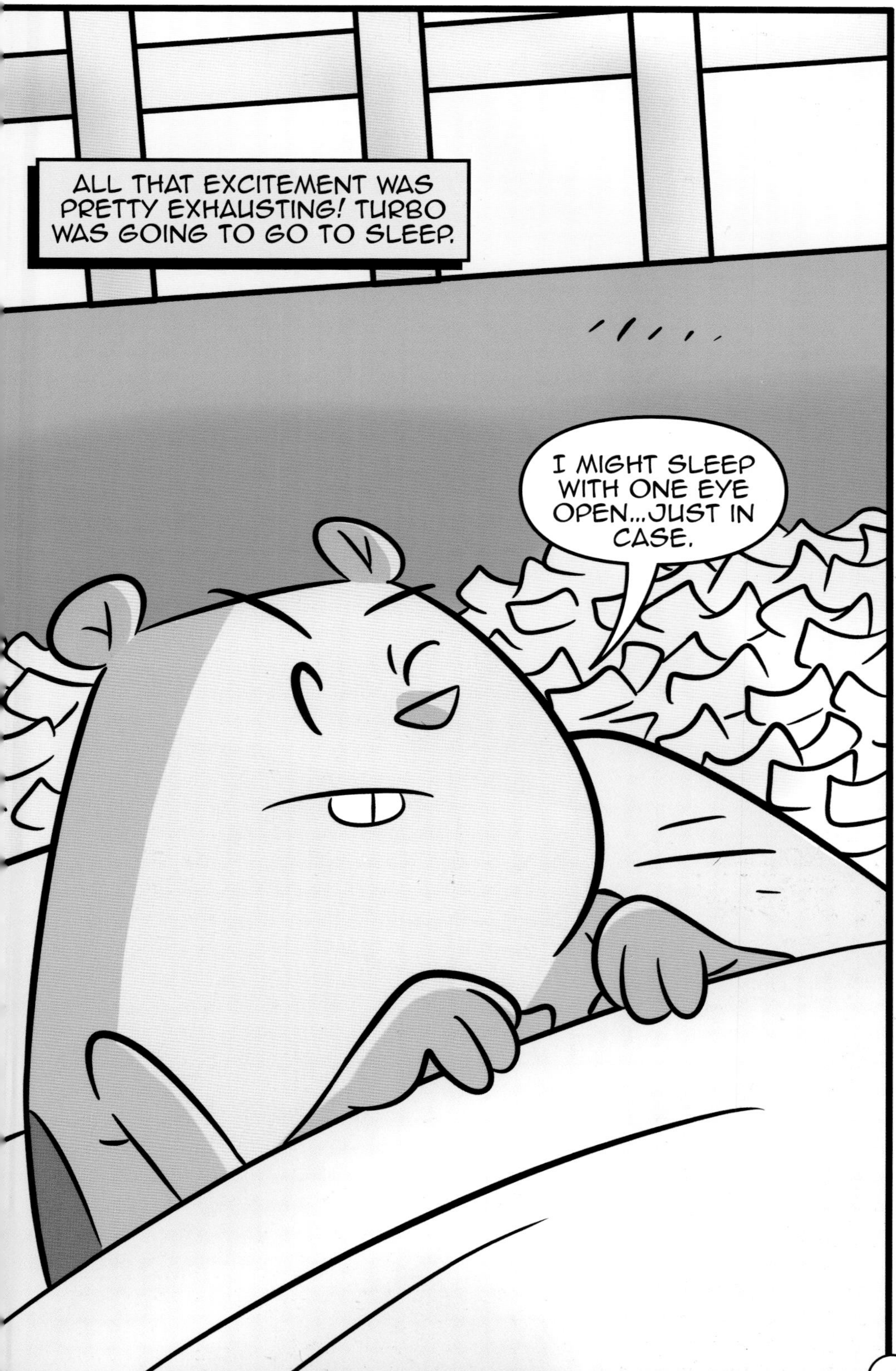
ALL THAT EXCITEMENT WAS PRETTY EXHAUSTING! TURBO WAS GOING TO GO TO SLEEP.
I MIGHT SLEEP WITH ONE EYE OPEN...JUST IN CASE.

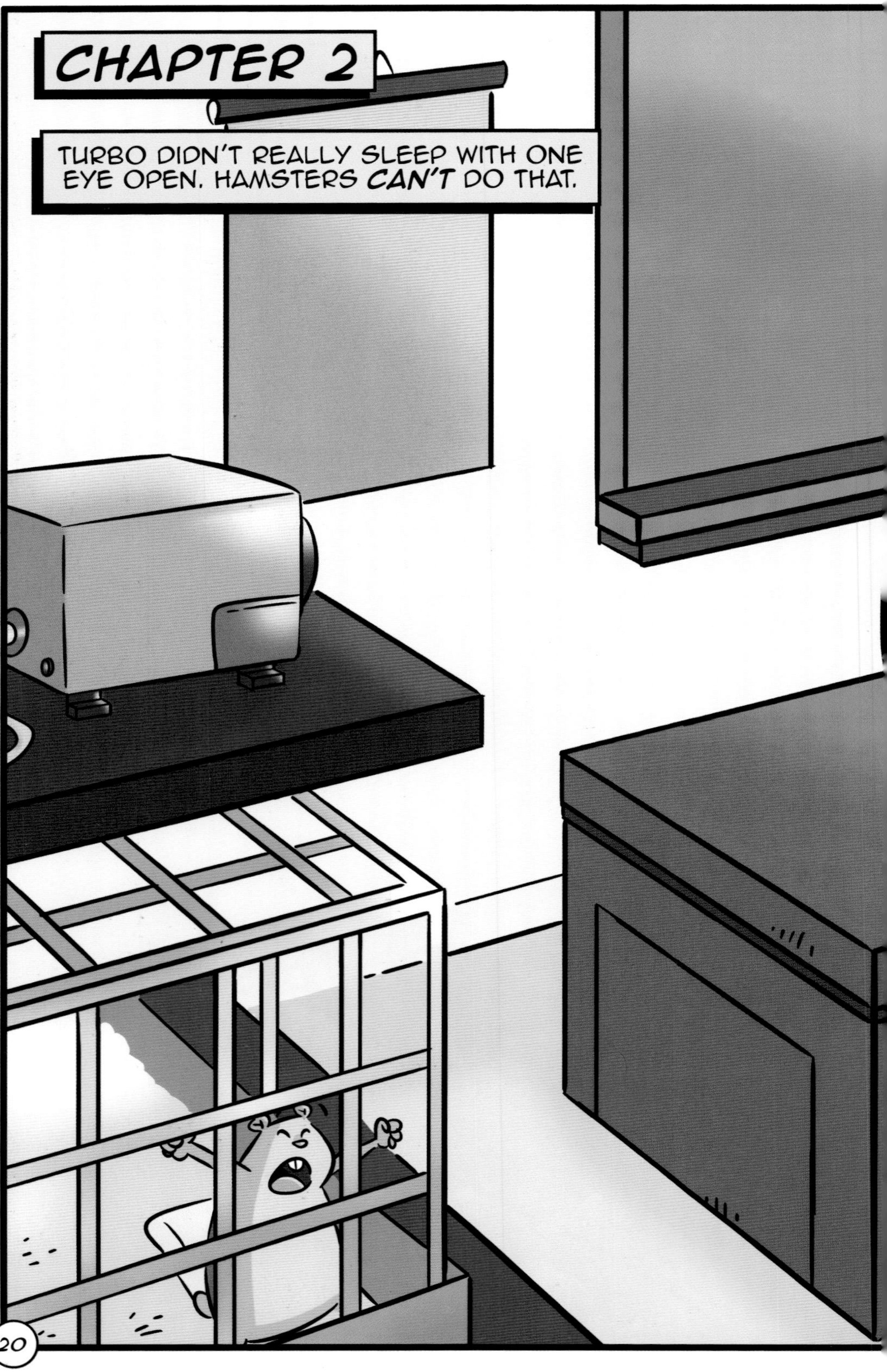
CHAPTER 2
TURBO DIDN'T REALLY SLEEP WITH ONE EYE OPEN. HAMSTERS CAN'T DO THAT.

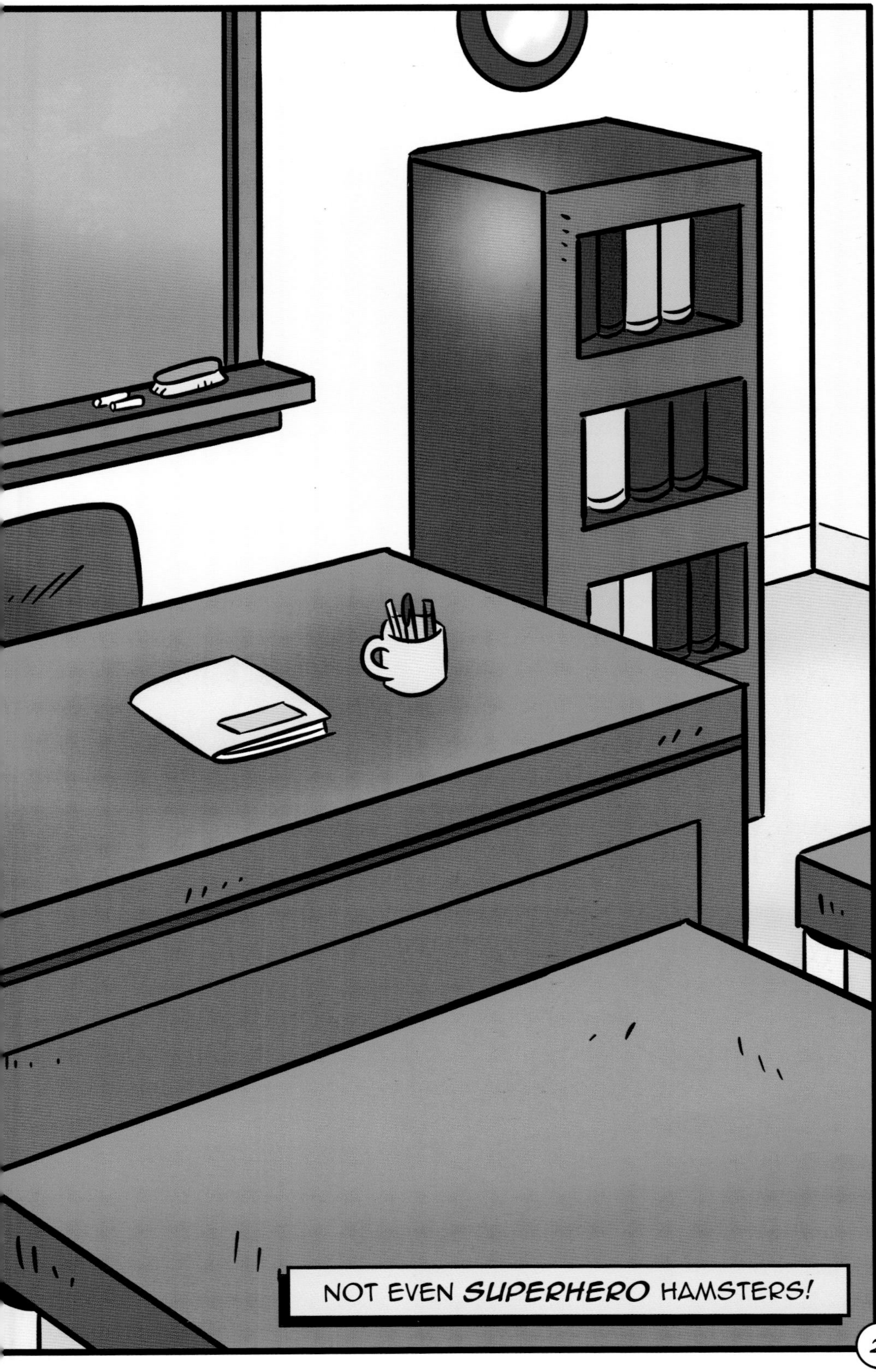
NOT EVEN *SUPERHERO* HAMSTERS!

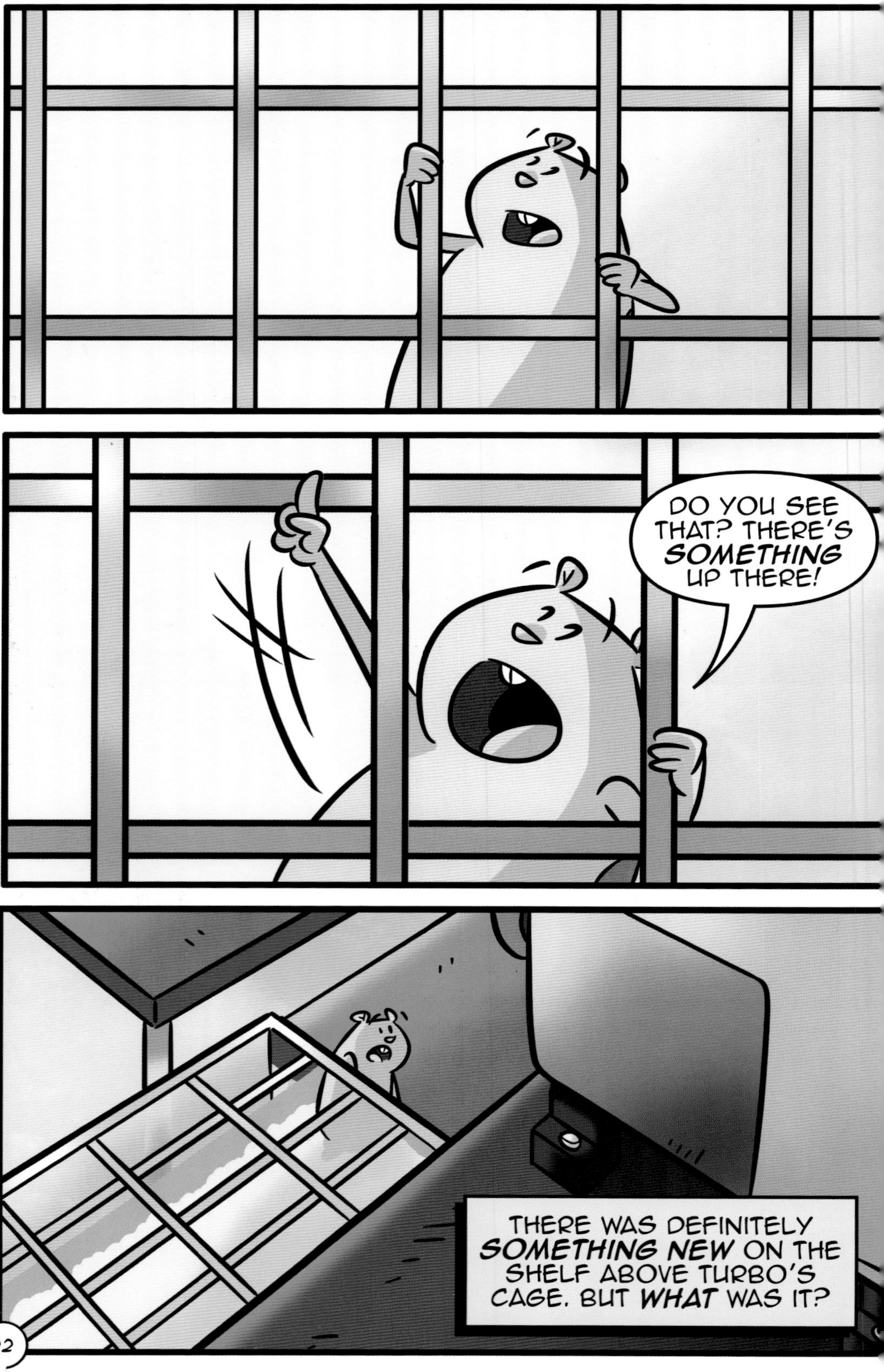
DO YOU SEE THAT? THERE'S *SOMETHING* UP THERE!
THERE WAS DEFINITELY ***SOMETHING NEW*** ON THE SHELF ABOVE TURBO'S CAGE. BUT ***WHAT*** WAS IT?

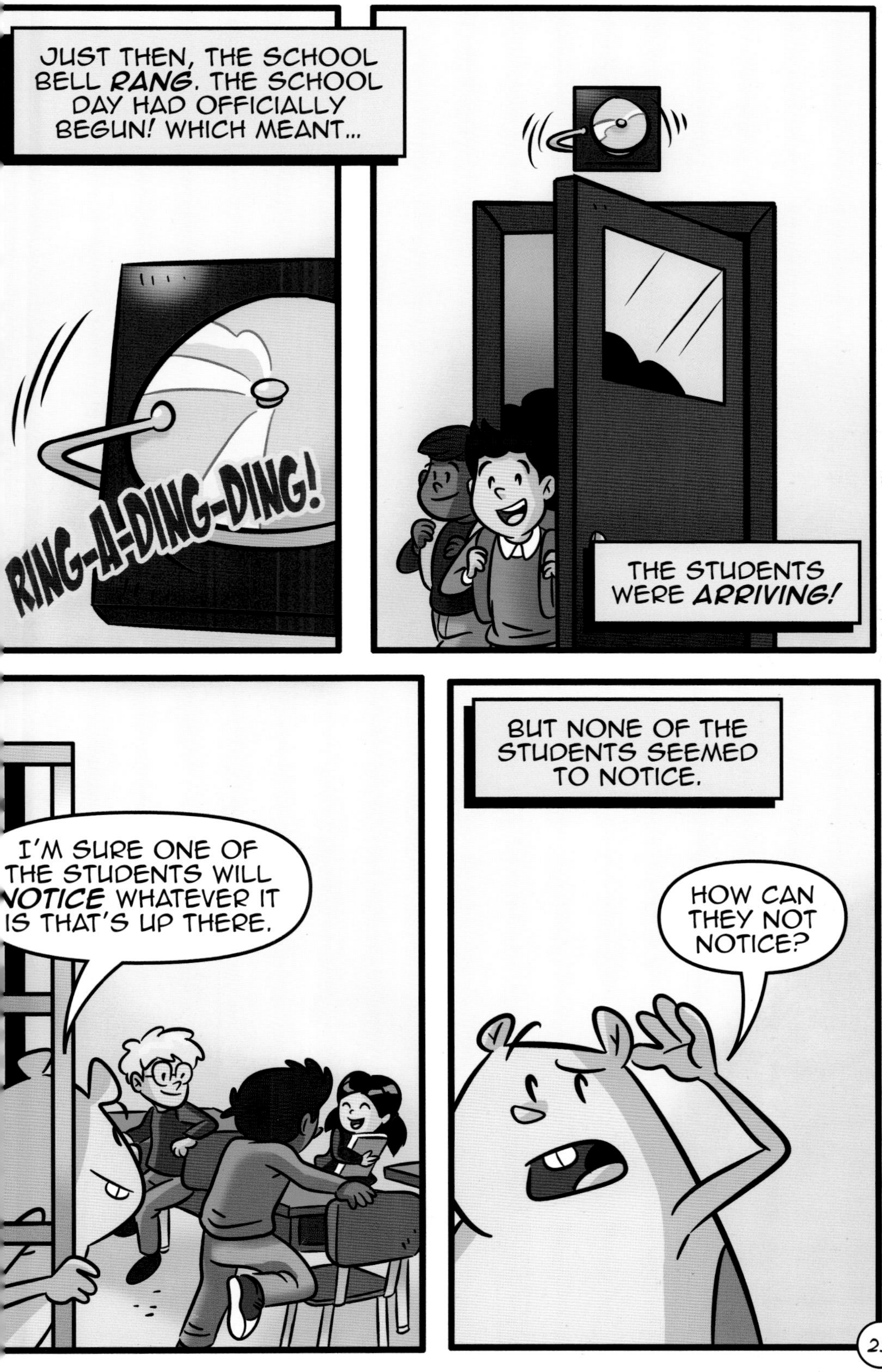
JUST THEN, THE SCHOOL BELL RANG. THE SCHOOL DAY HAD OFFICIALLY BEGUN! WHICH MEANT...
RING-A-DING-DING!
THE STUDENTS WERE ARRIVING!
I'M SURE ONE OF THE STUDENTS WILL NOTICE WHATEVER IT IS THAT'S UP THERE.
BUT NONE OF THE STUDENTS SEEMED TO NOTICE.
HOW CAN THEY NOT NOTICE?

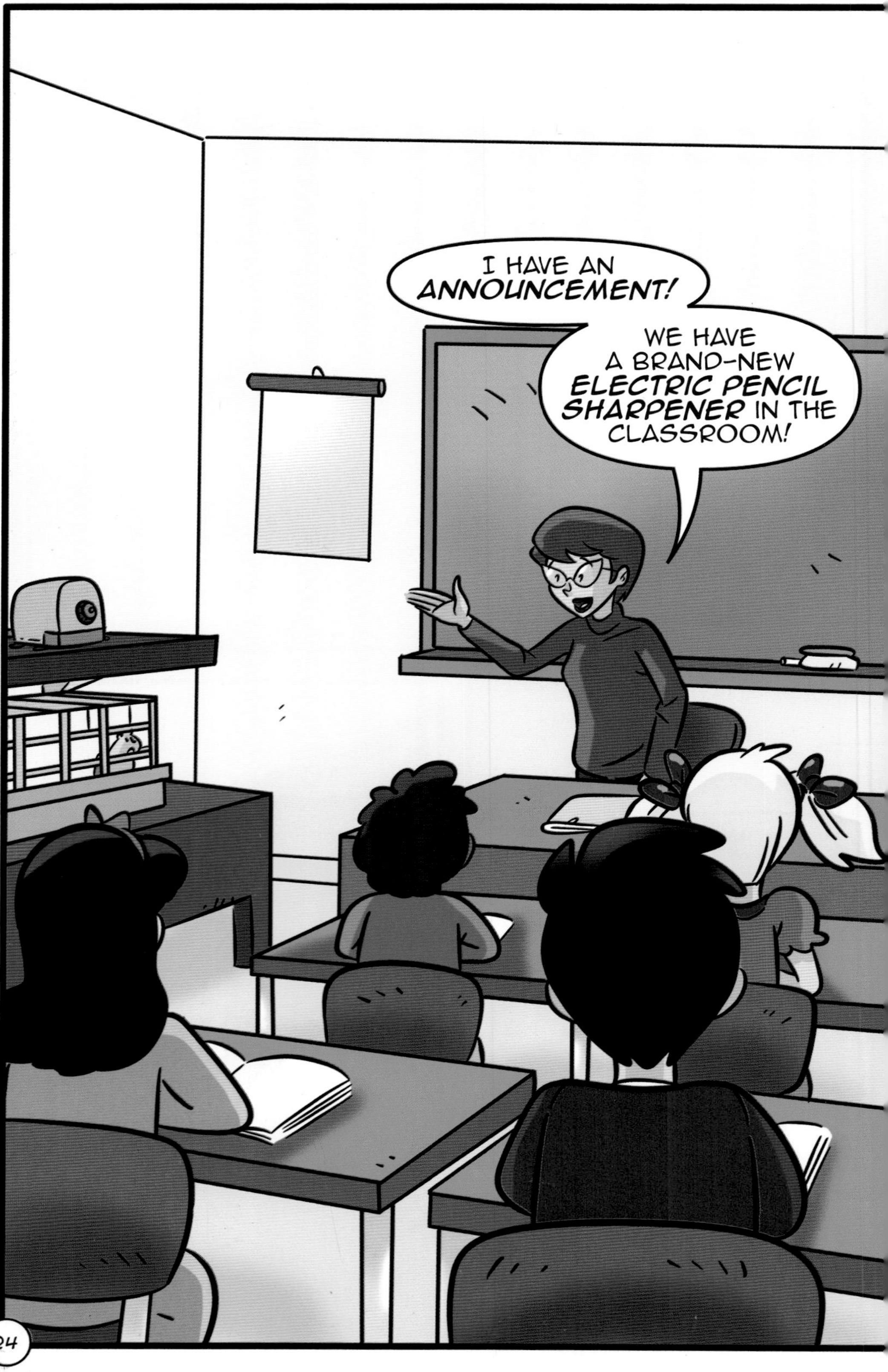
I HAVE AN ANNOUNCEMENT!
WE HAVE A BRAND-NEW ELECTRIC PENCIL SHARPENER IN THE CLASSROOM!

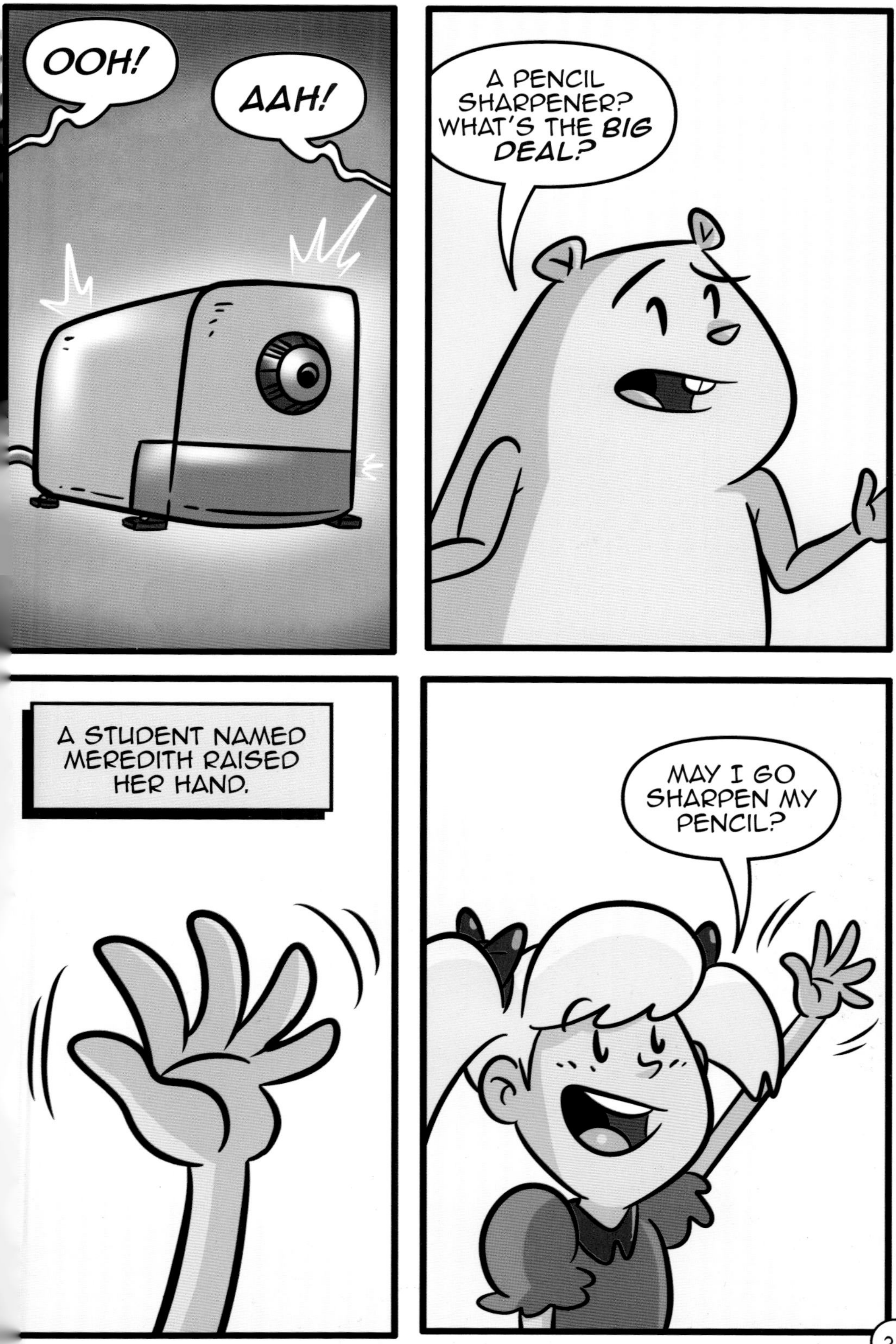
OOH!
AAH!
A PENCIL SHARPENER? WHAT'S THE BIG DEAL?
A STUDENT NAMED MEREDITH RAISED HER HAND.
MAY I GO SHARPEN MY PENCIL?

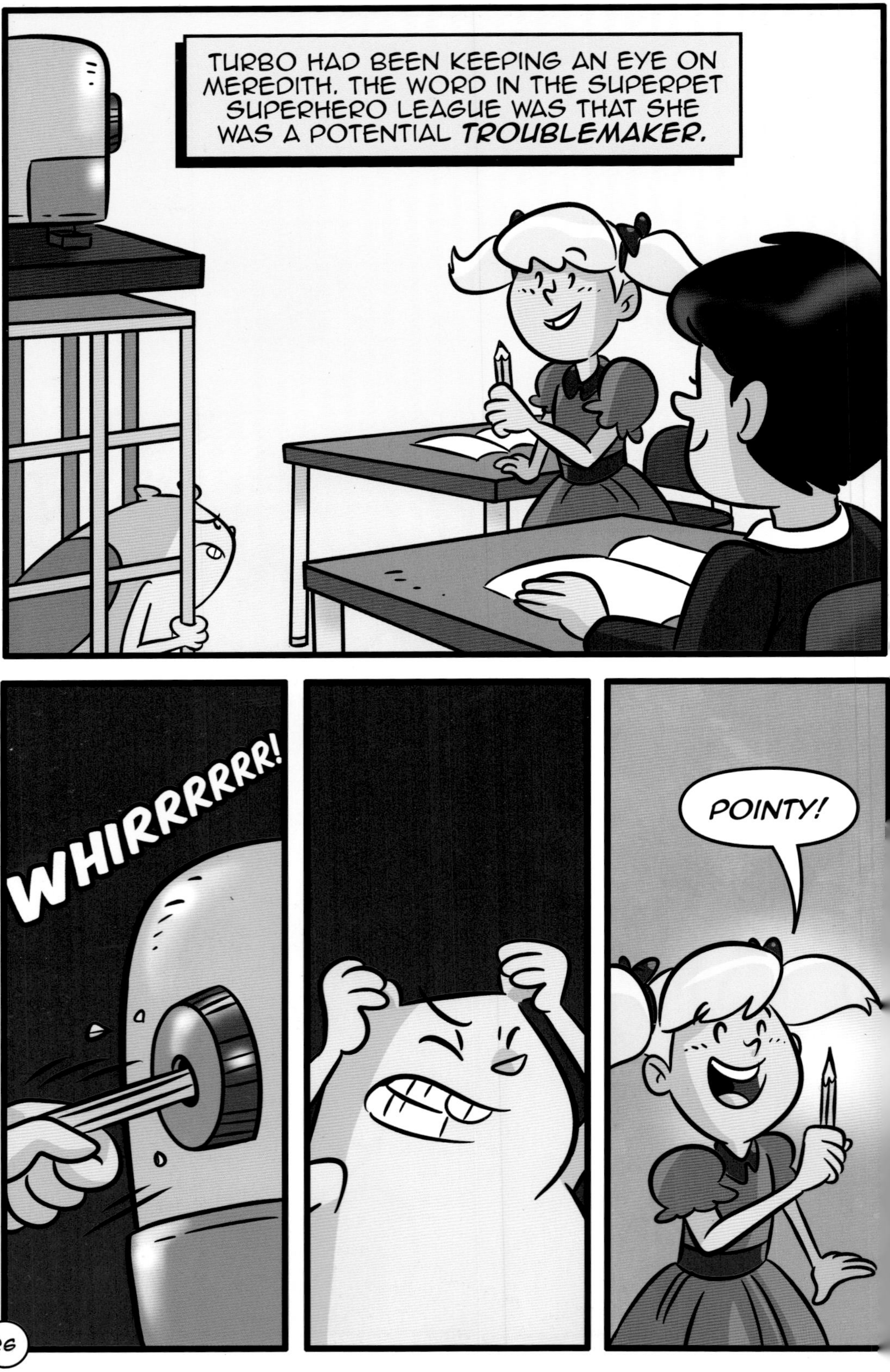
TURBO HAD BEEN KEEPING AN EYE ON MEREDITH. THE WORD IN THE SUPERPET SUPERHERO LEAGUE WAS THAT SHE WAS A POTENTIAL *TROUBLEMAKER.*
WHIRRRRRR!
POINTY!

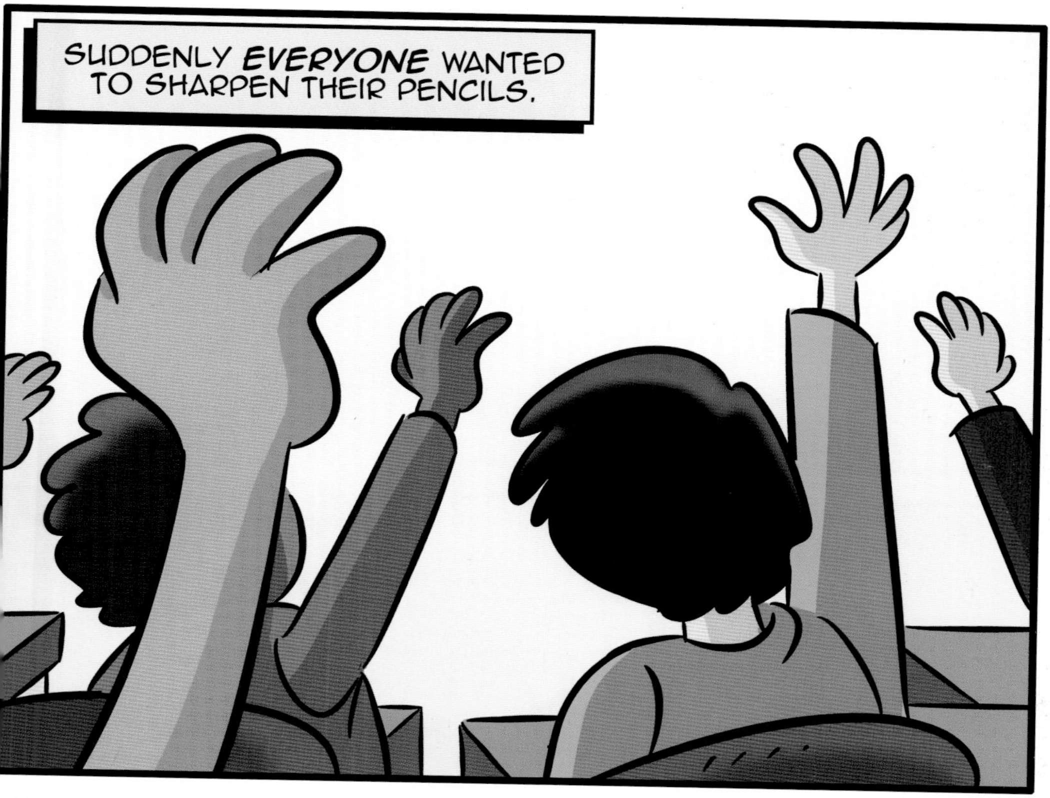
SUDDENLY *EVERYONE* WANTED TO SHARPEN THEIR PENCILS.

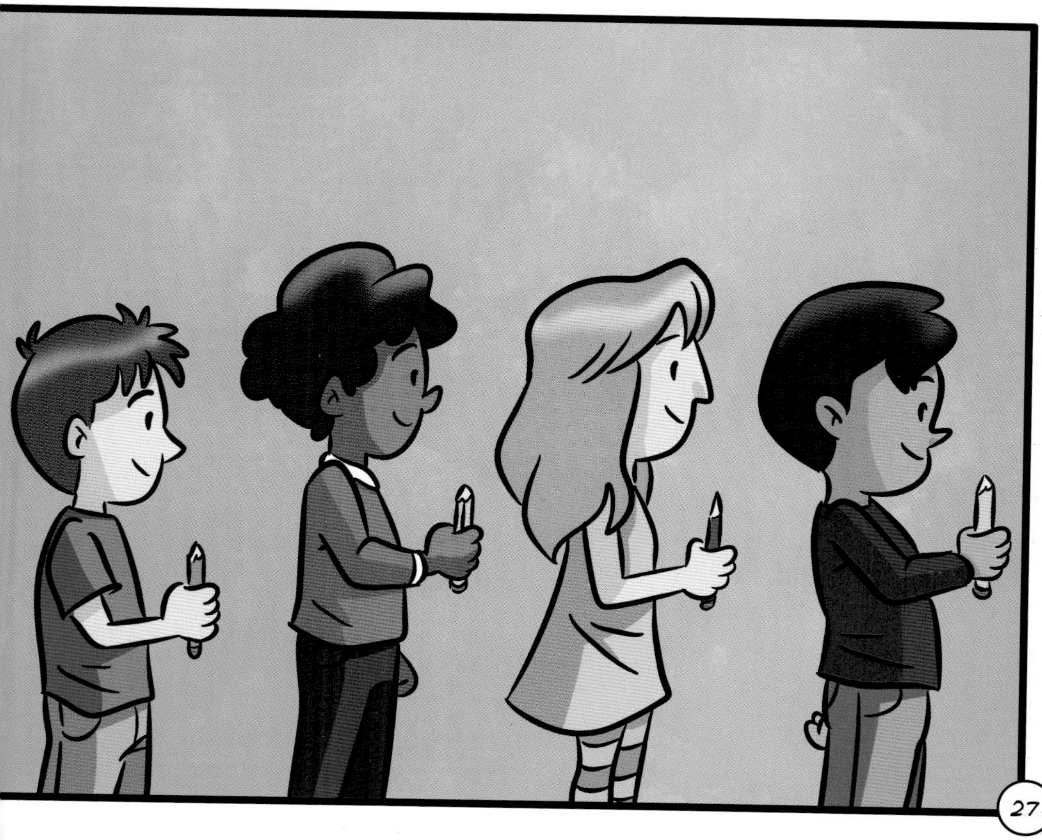

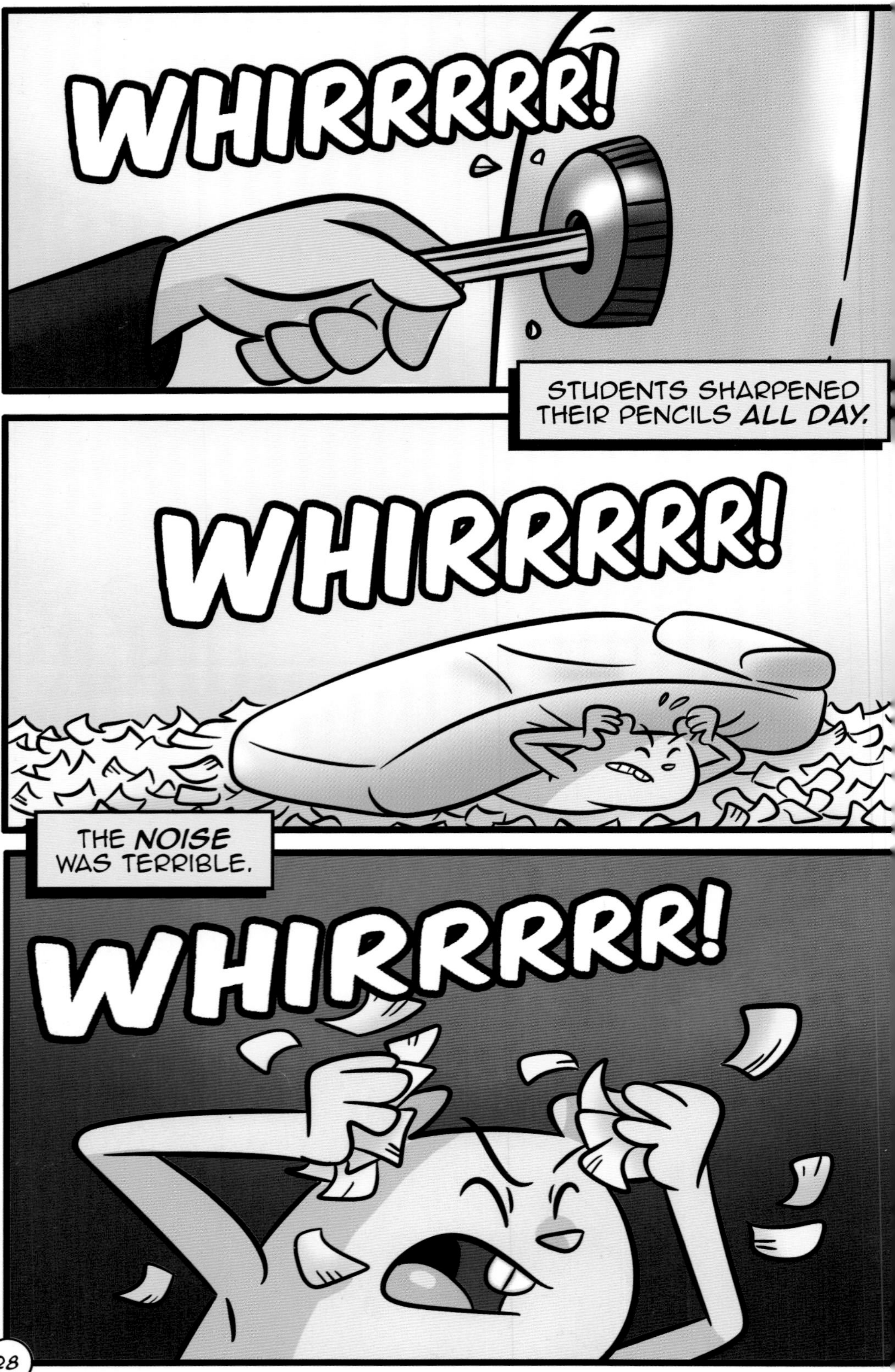
WHIRRRRR!
STUDENTS SHARPENED THEIR PENCILS ALL DAY.
WHIRRRRR!
THE NOISE WAS TERRIBLE.
WHIRRRRR!

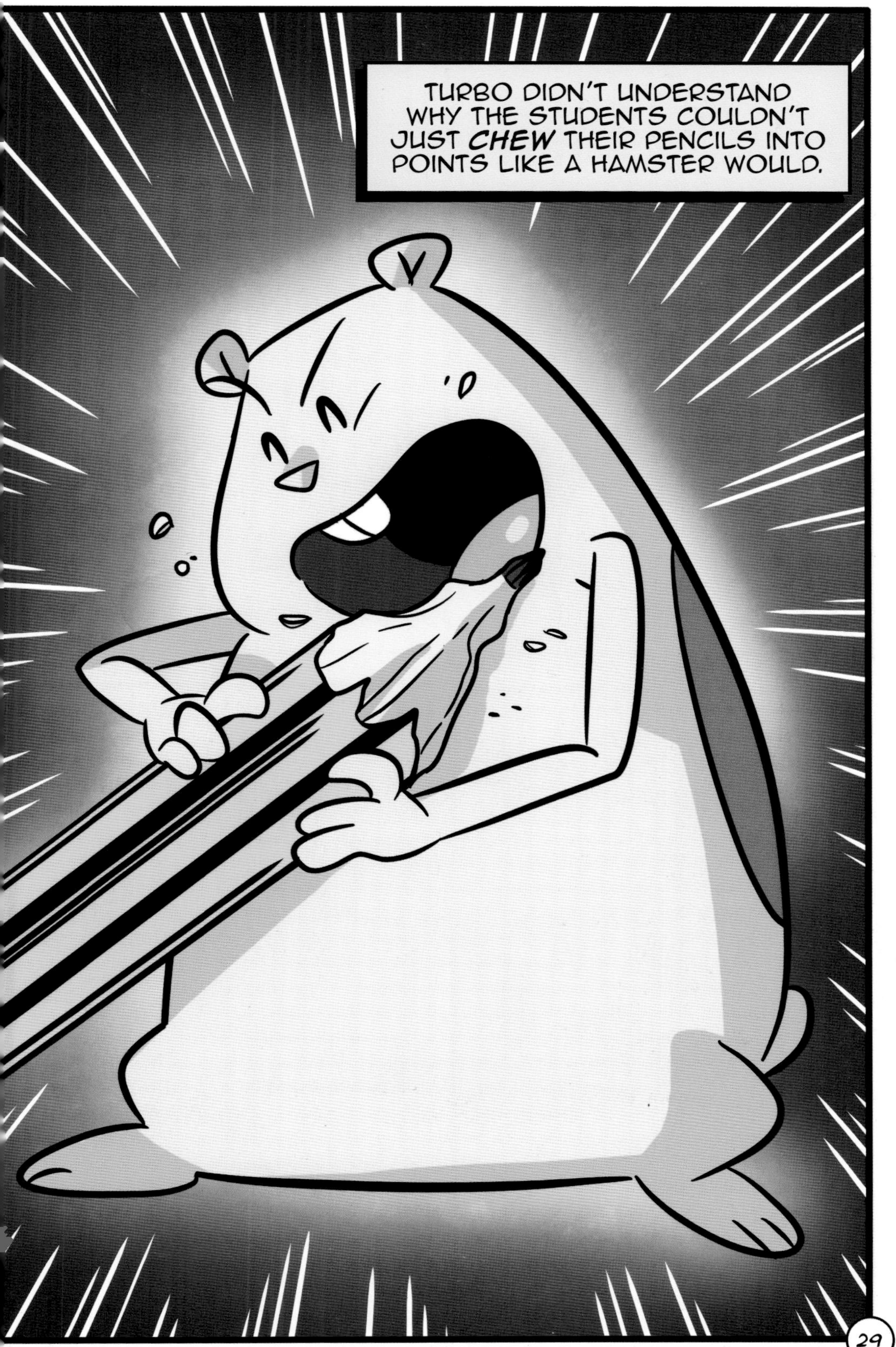
TURBO DIDN'T UNDERSTAND WHY THE STUDENTS COULDN'T JUST *CHEW* THEIR PENCILS INTO POINTS LIKE A HAMSTER WOULD.

WHY IS EVERYONE SO *EXCITED* ABOUT A PENCIL SHARPENER?

BUT THE *SOUND* WASN'T EVEN THE *WORST* THING ABOUT THE NEW PENCIL SHARPENER...

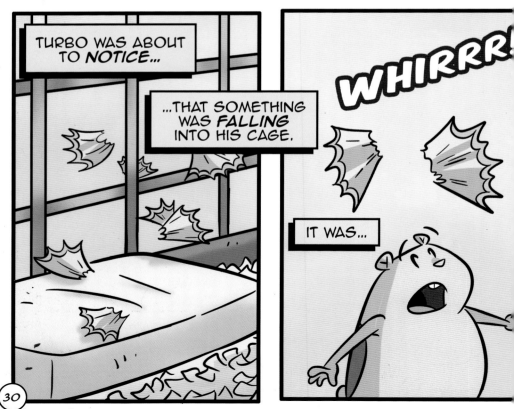

TURBO WAS ABOUT TO *NOTICE*...

...THAT SOMETHING WAS *FALLING* INTO HIS CAGE.

WHIRRR!

IT WAS...

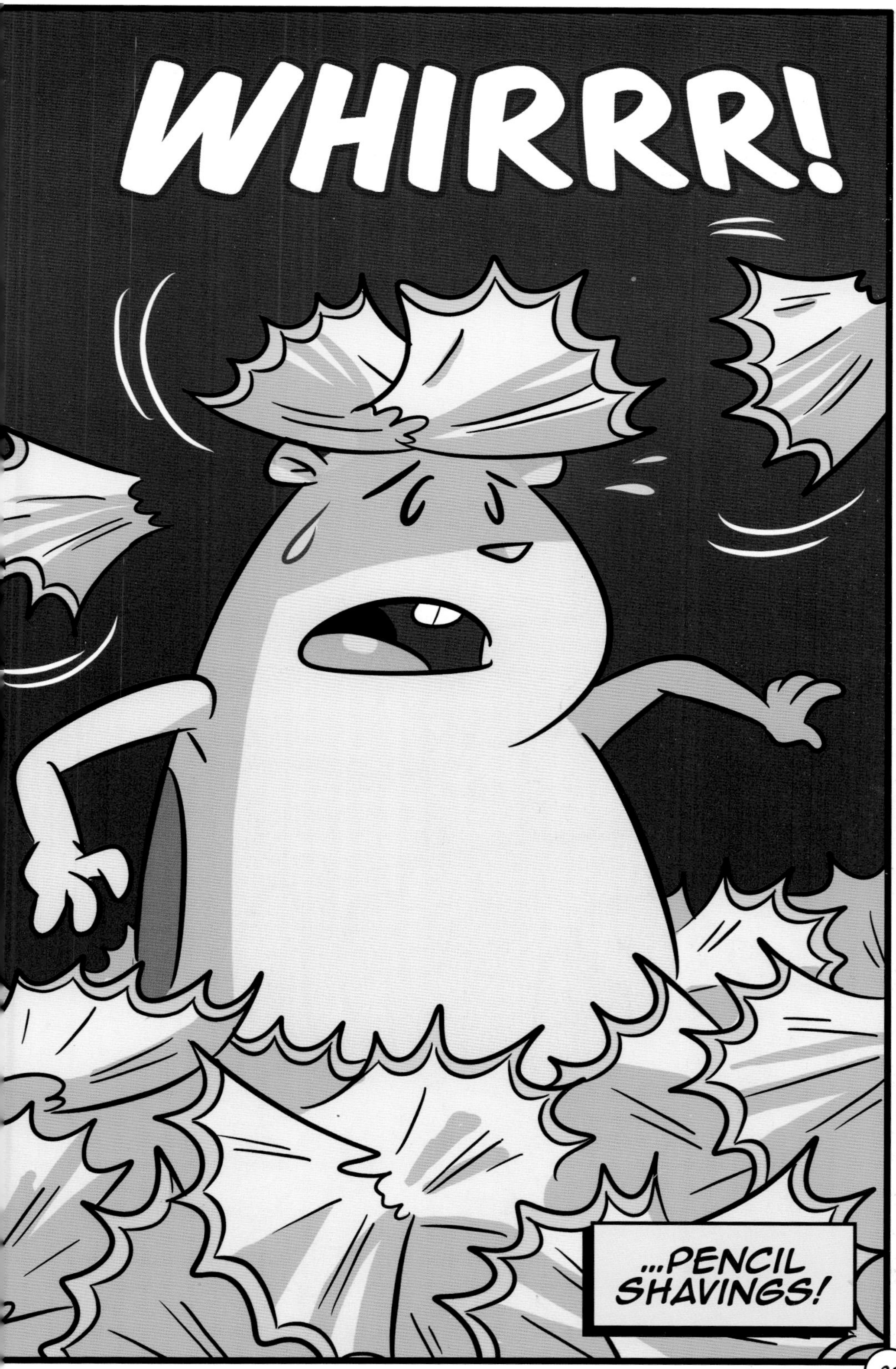
WHIRRR!
...PENCIL SHAVINGS!

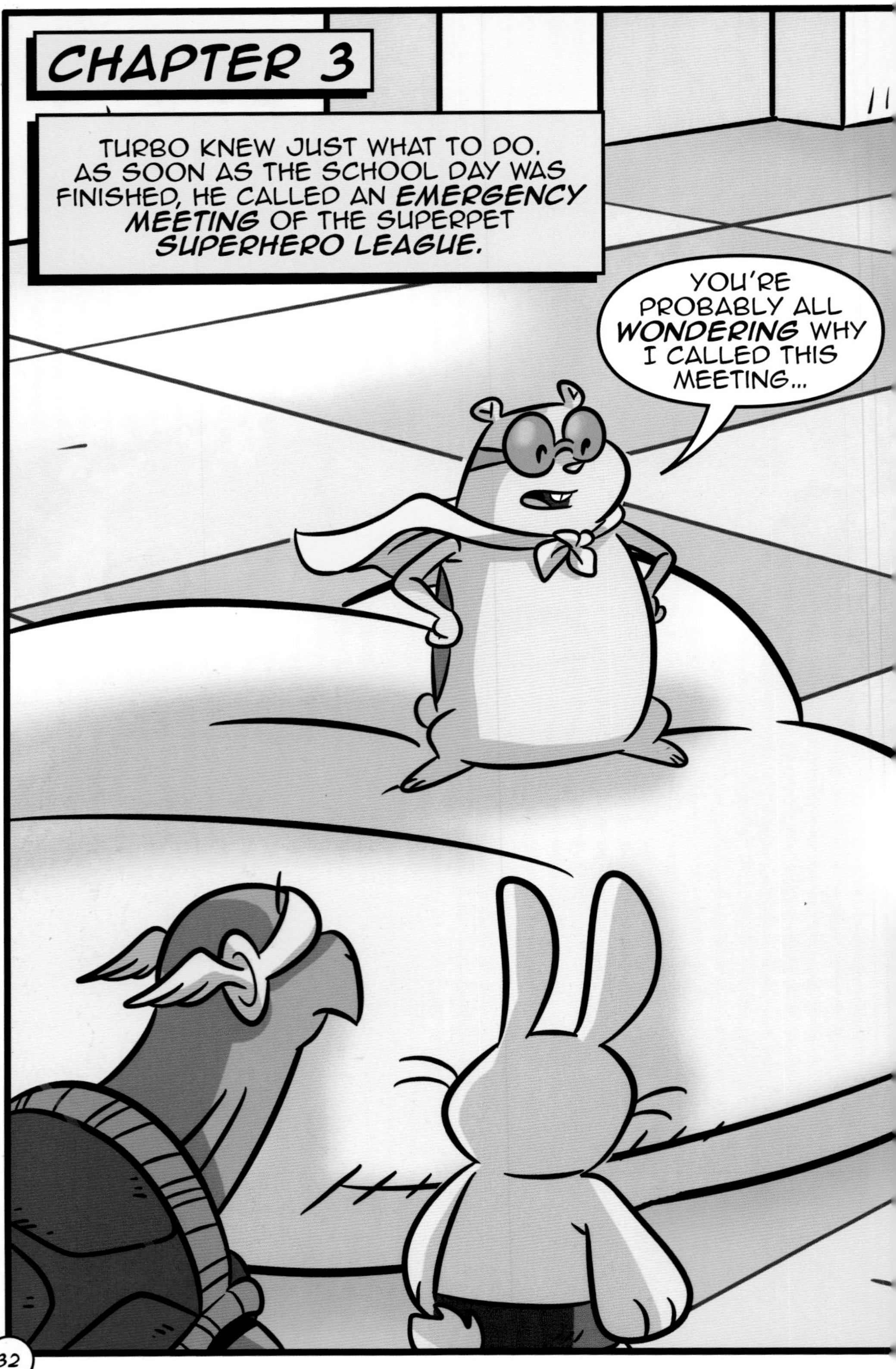
CHAPTER 3
TURBO KNEW JUST WHAT TO DO. AS SOON AS THE SCHOOL DAY WAS FINISHED, HE CALLED AN EMERGENCY MEETING OF THE SUPERPET SUPERHERO LEAGUE.
YOU'RE PROBABLY ALL WONDERING WHY I CALLED THIS MEETING...

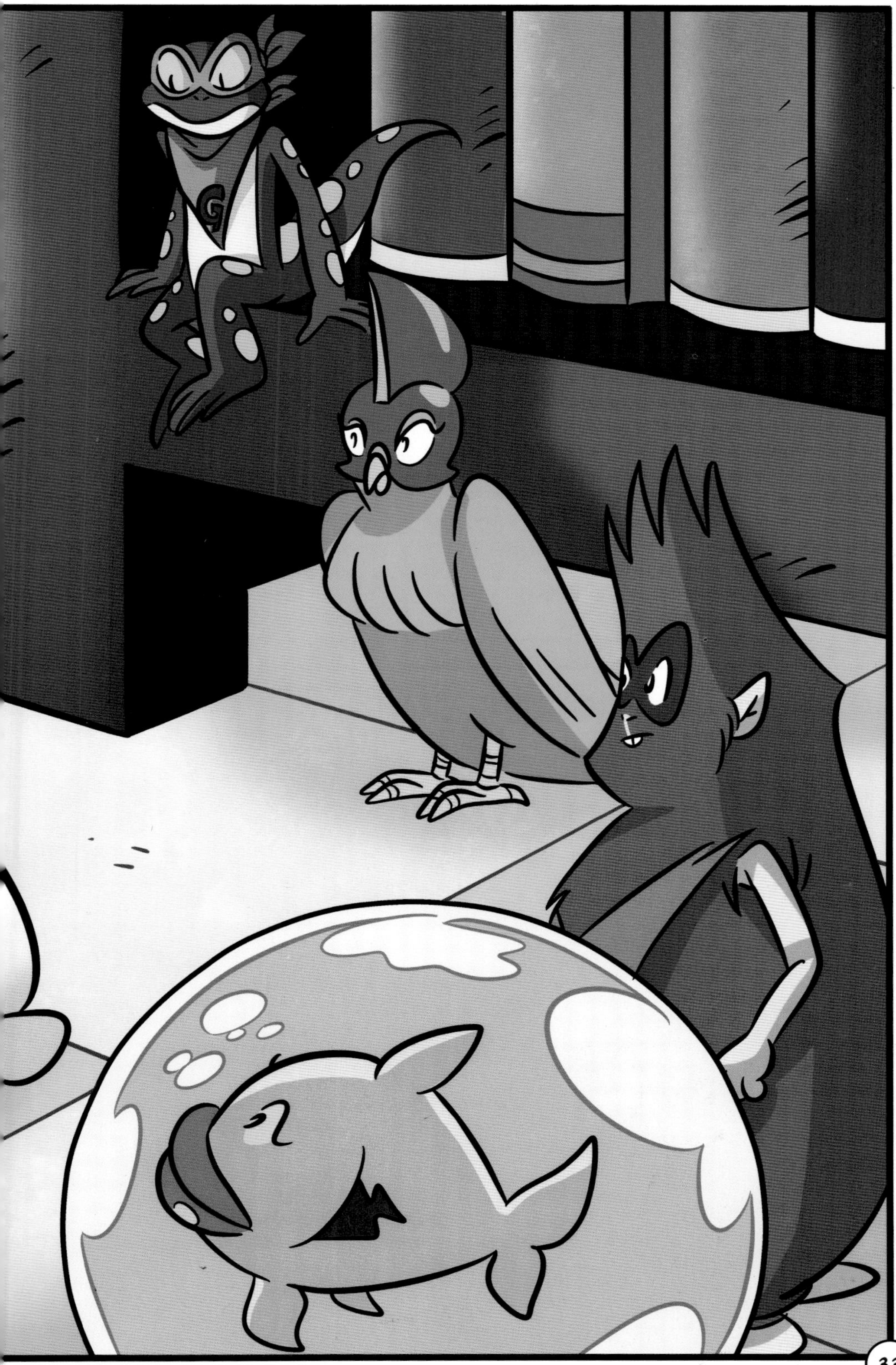

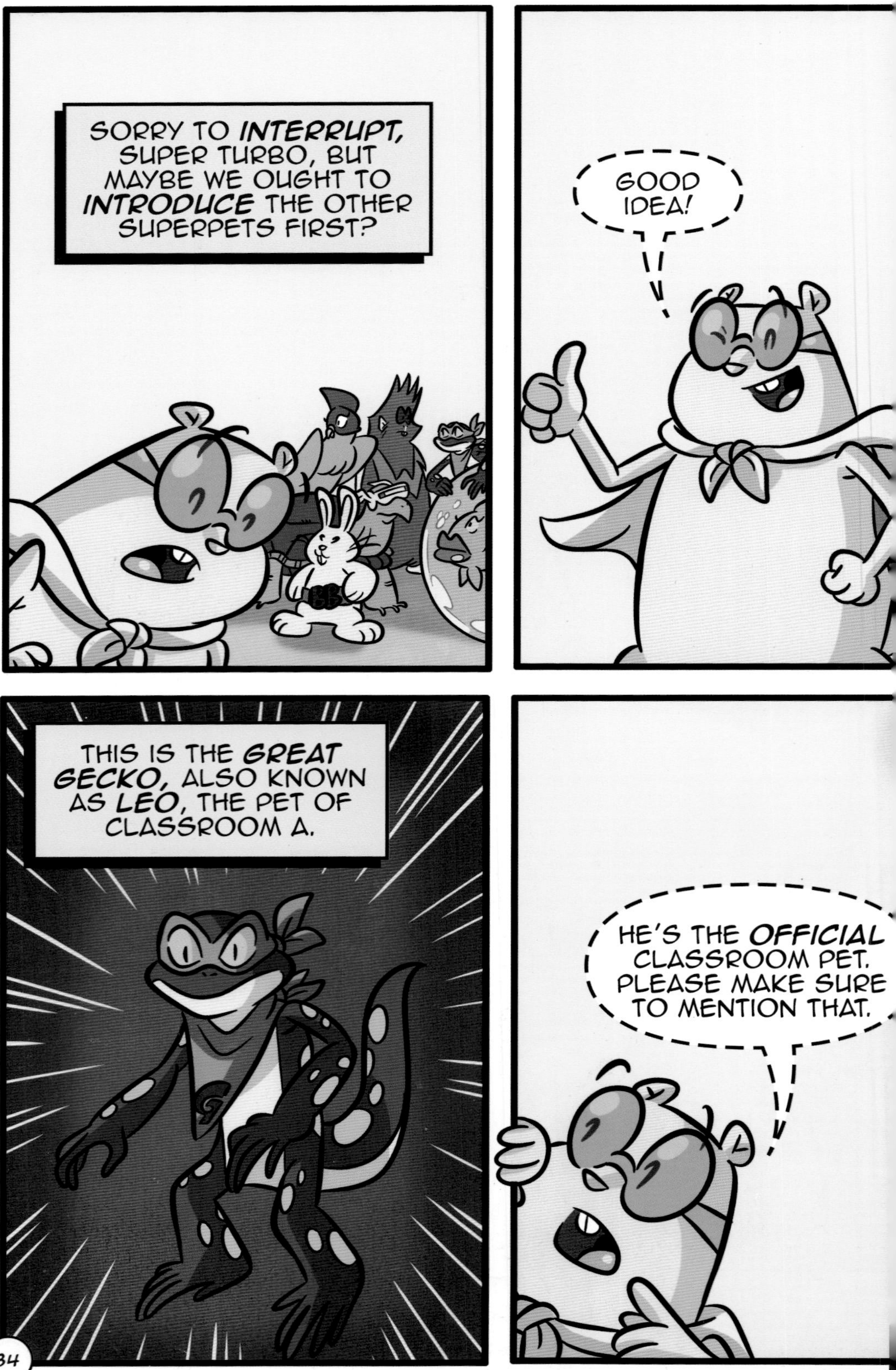
SORRY TO INTERRUPT, SUPER TURBO, BUT MAYBE WE OUGHT TO INTRODUCE THE OTHER SUPERPETS FIRST?
GOOD IDEA!
THIS IS THE GREAT GECKO, ALSO KNOWN AS LEO, THE PET OF CLASSROOM A.
HE'S THE OFFICIAL CLASSROOM PET. PLEASE MAKE SURE TO MENTION THAT.

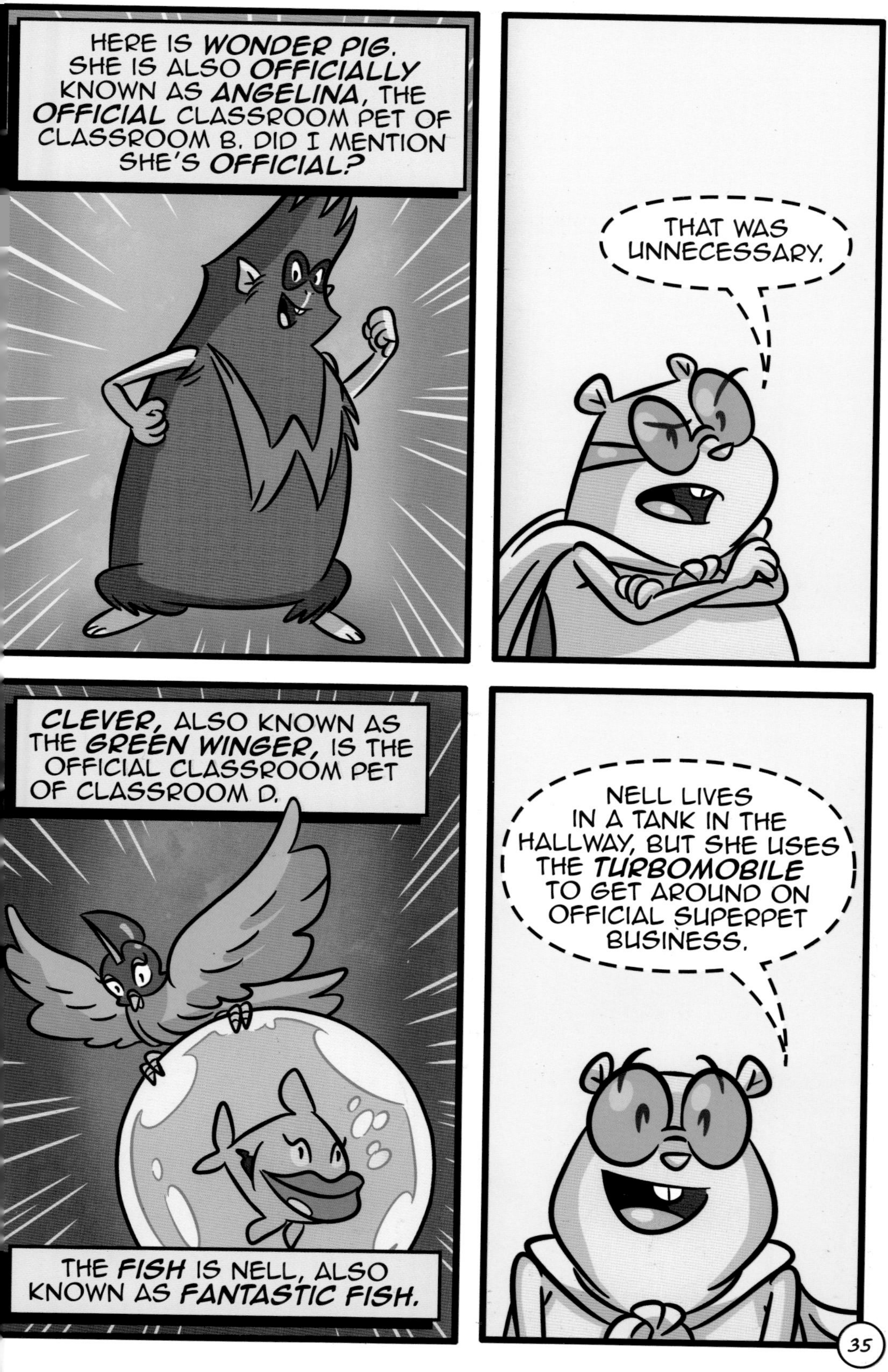
HERE IS WONDER PIG. SHE IS ALSO OFFICIALLY KNOWN AS ANGELINA, THE OFFICIAL CLASSROOM PET OF CLASSROOM B. DID I MENTION SHE'S OFFICIAL?
THAT WAS UNNECESSARY.
CLEVER, ALSO KNOWN AS THE GREEN WINGER, IS THE OFFICIAL CLASSROOM PET OF CLASSROOM D.
THE FISH IS NELL, ALSO KNOWN AS FANTASTIC FISH.
NELL LIVES IN A TANK IN THE HALLWAY, BUT SHE USES THE TURBOMOBILE TO GET AROUND ON OFFICIAL SUPERPET BUSINESS.

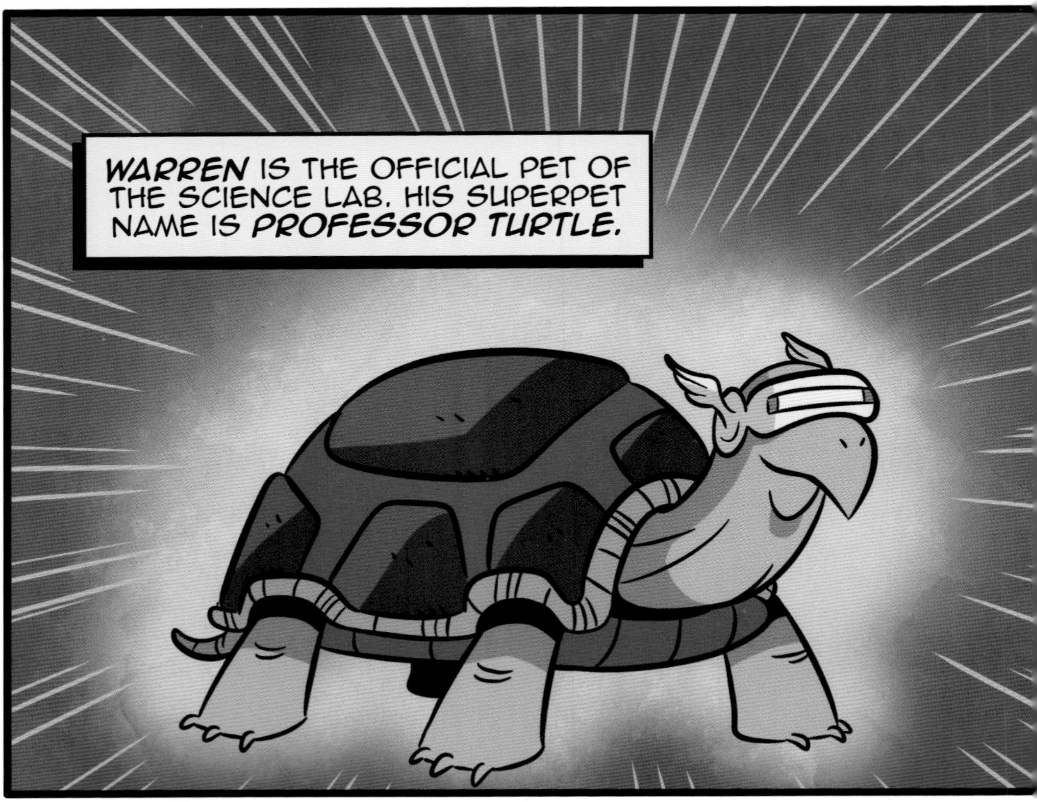
WARREN IS THE OFFICIAL PET OF THE SCIENCE LAB. HIS SUPERPET NAME IS PROFESSOR TURTLE.

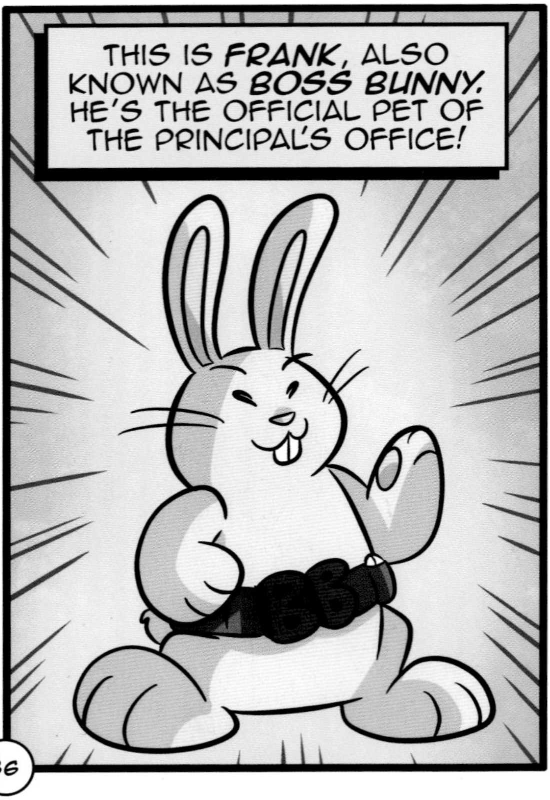
THIS IS FRANK, ALSO KNOWN AS BOSS BUNNY. HE'S THE OFFICIAL PET OF THE PRINCIPAL'S OFFICE!

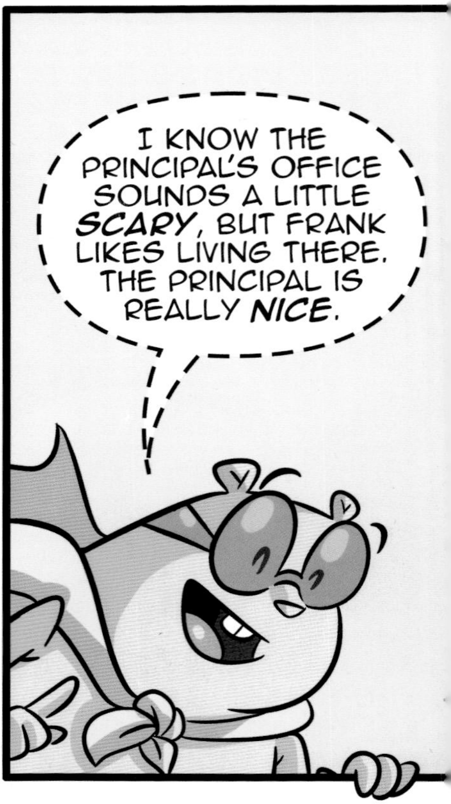
I KNOW THE PRINCIPAL'S OFFICE SOUNDS A LITTLE SCARY, BUT FRANK LIKES LIVING THERE. THE PRINCIPAL IS REALLY NICE.

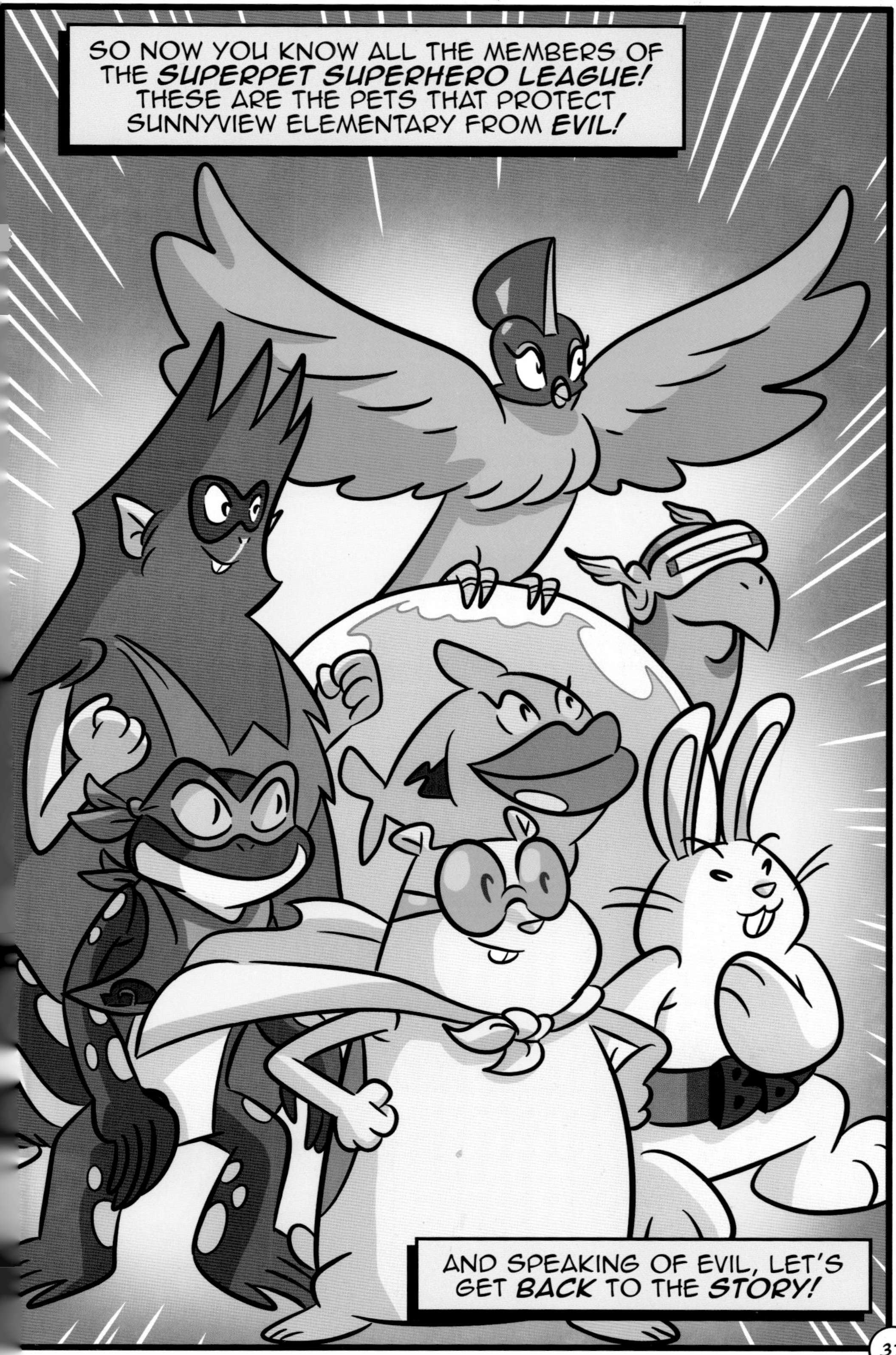
SO NOW YOU KNOW ALL THE MEMBERS OF THE *SUPERPET SUPERHERO LEAGUE!* THESE ARE THE PETS THAT PROTECT SUNNYVIEW ELEMENTARY FROM *EVIL!*
AND SPEAKING OF EVIL, LET'S GET *BACK* TO THE *STORY!*

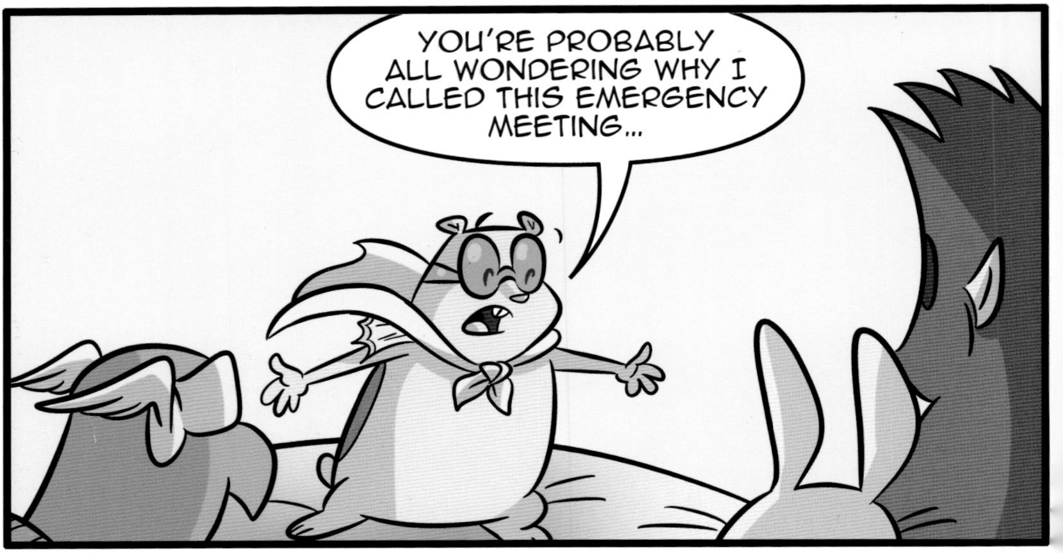
YOU'RE PROBABLY ALL WONDERING WHY I CALLED THIS EMERGENCY MEETING...

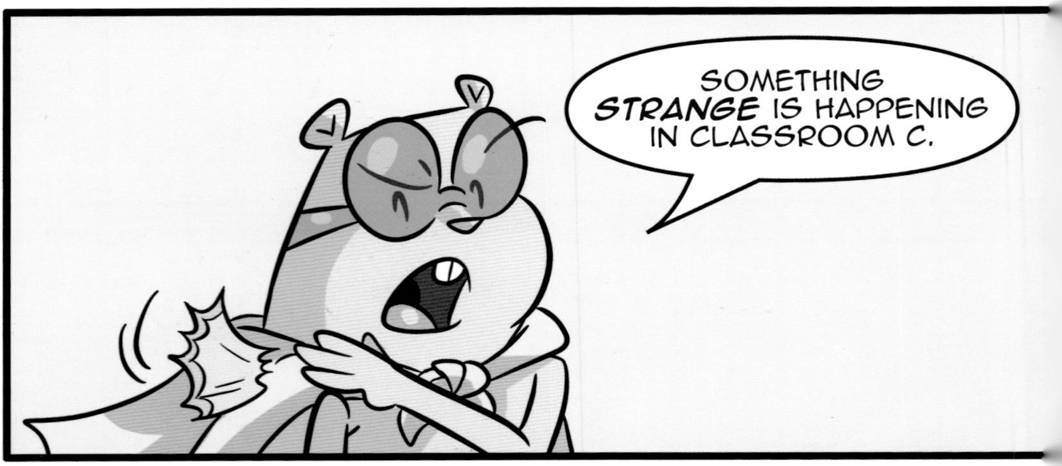
SOMETHING **STRANGE** IS HAPPENING IN CLASSROOM C.

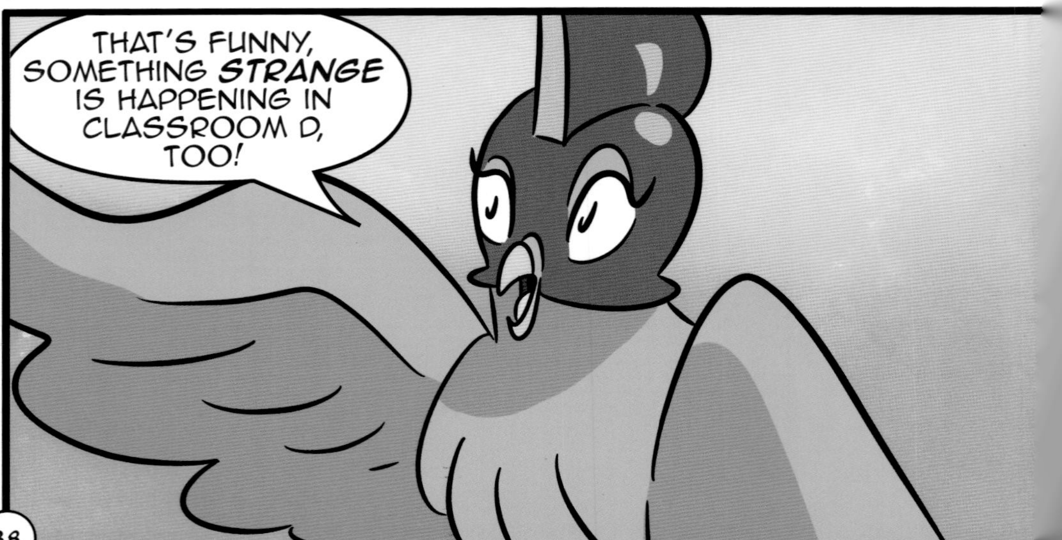
THAT'S FUNNY, SOMETHING **STRANGE** IS HAPPENING IN CLASSROOM D, TOO!

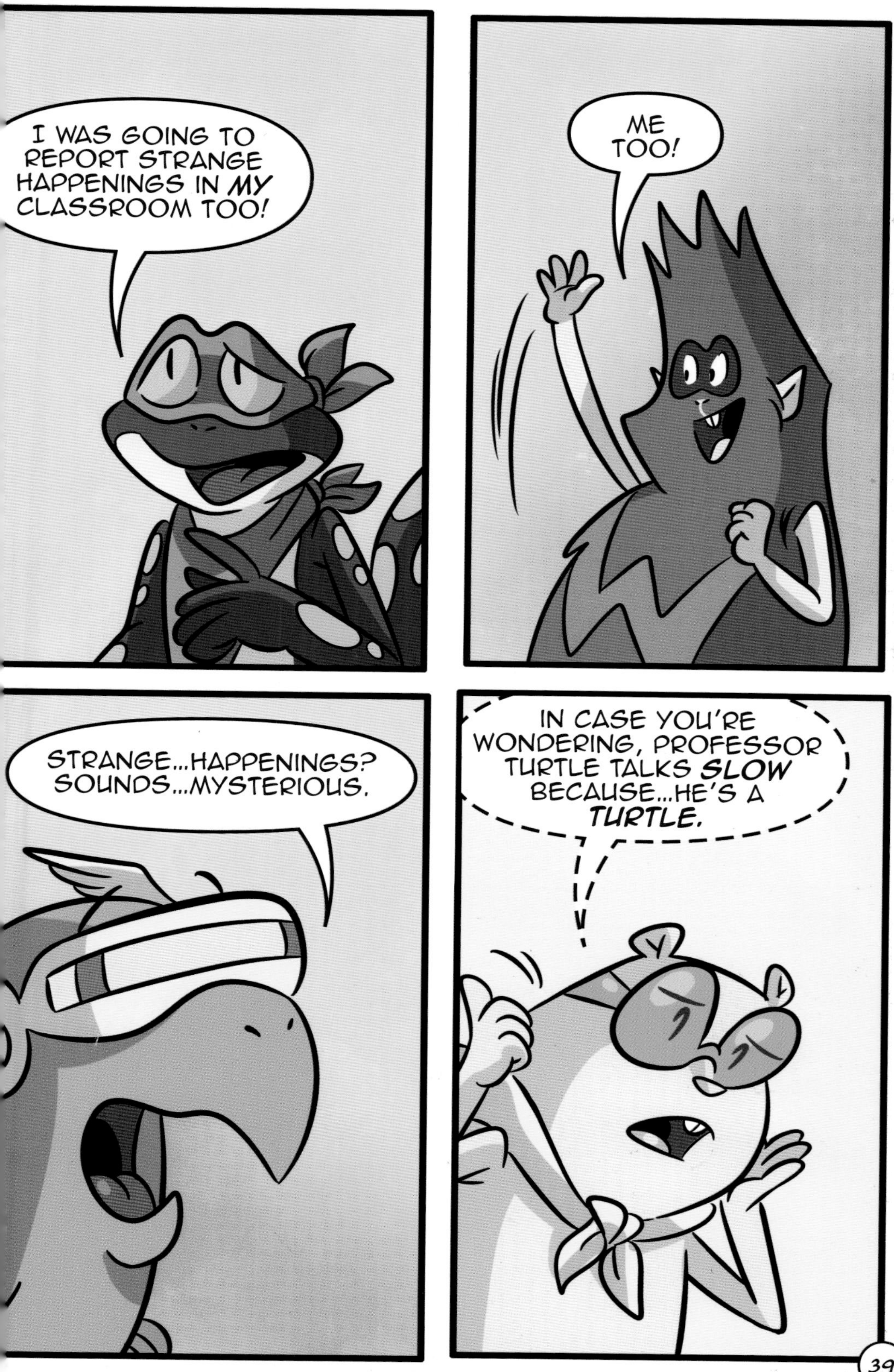
I WAS GOING TO REPORT STRANGE HAPPENINGS IN *MY* CLASSROOM TOO!
ME TOO!
STRANGE...HAPPENINGS? SOUNDS...MYSTERIOUS.
IN CASE YOU'RE WONDERING, PROFESSOR TURTLE TALKS *SLOW* BECAUSE...HE'S A *TURTLE.*

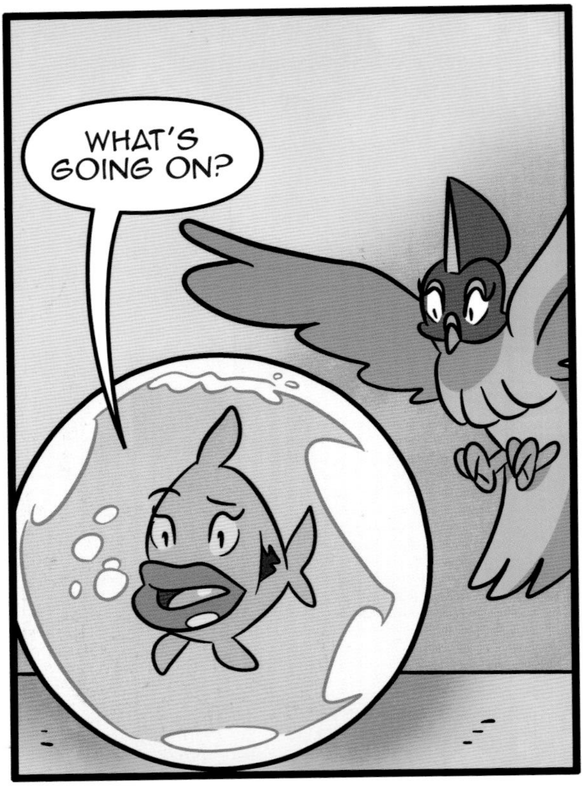
WHAT'S GOING ON?

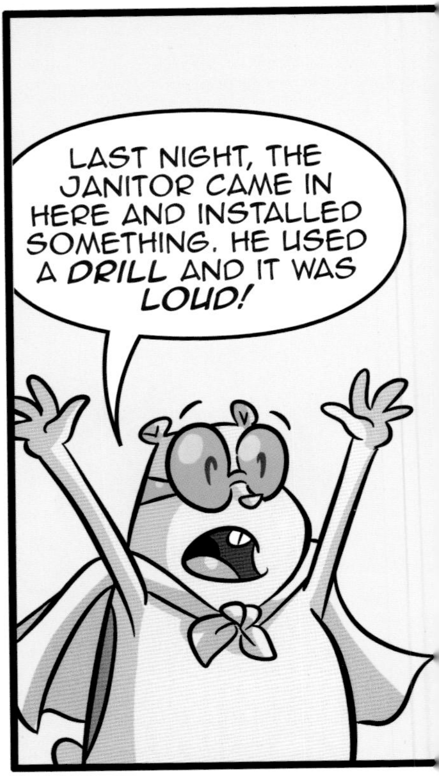
LAST NIGHT, THE JANITOR CAME IN HERE AND INSTALLED SOMETHING. HE USED A *DRILL* AND IT WAS *LOUD!*

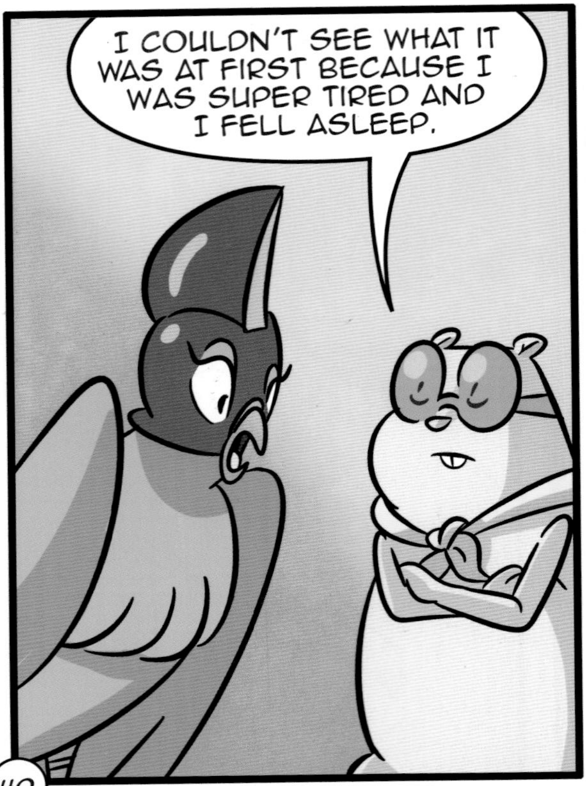
I COULDN'T SEE WHAT IT WAS AT FIRST BECAUSE I WAS SUPER TIRED AND I FELL ASLEEP.

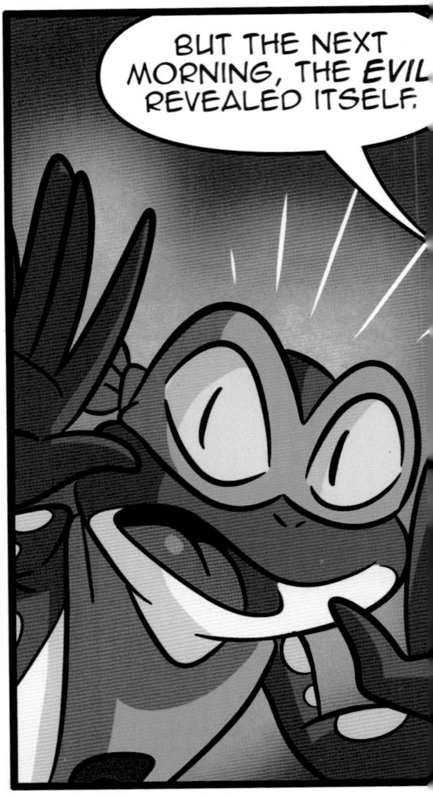
BUT THE NEXT MORNING, THE *EVIL* REVEALED ITSELF.

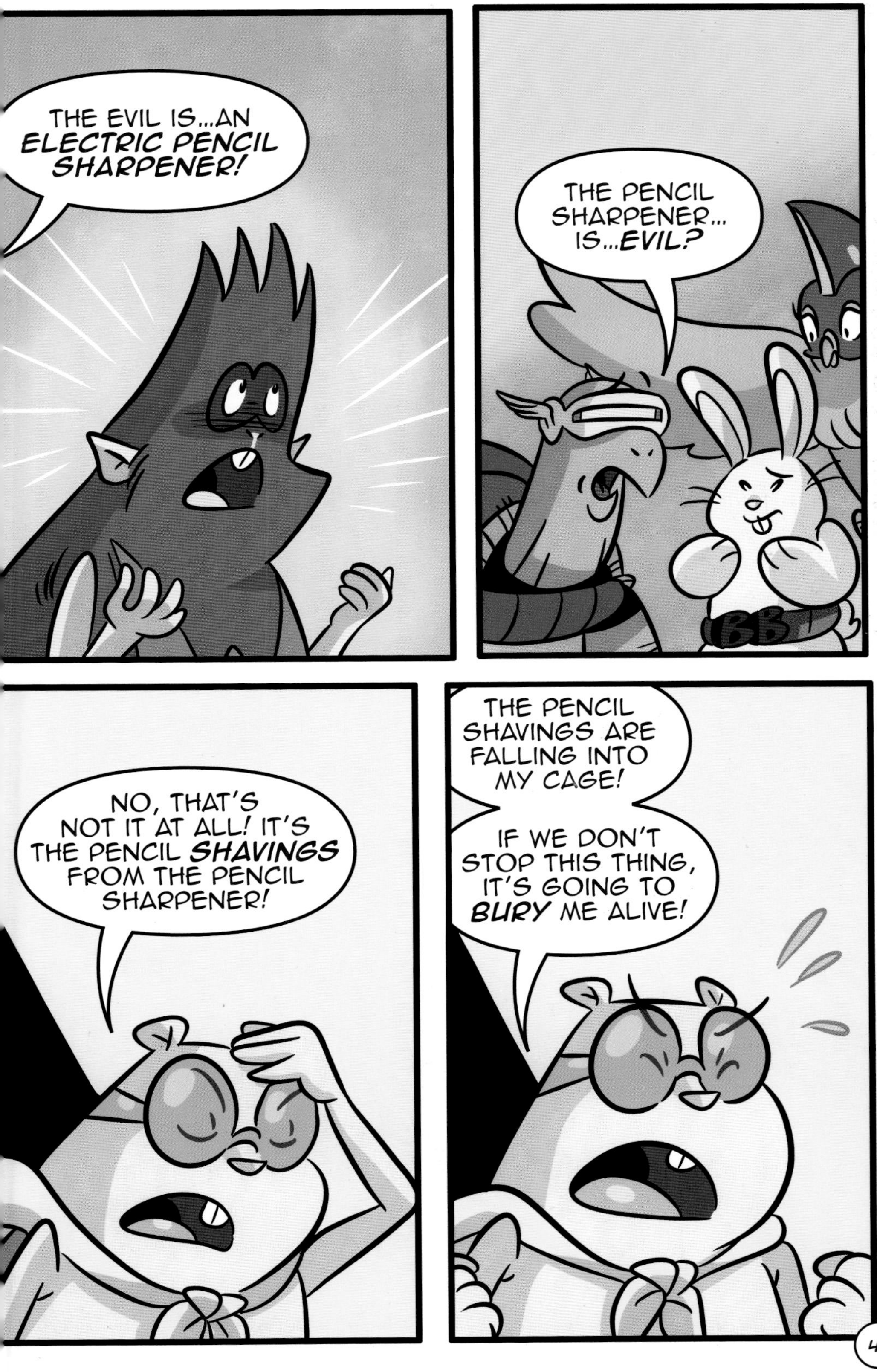
THE EVIL IS...AN ELECTRIC PENCIL SHARPENER!
THE PENCIL SHARPENER... IS...EVIL?
BB
NO, THAT'S NOT IT AT ALL! IT'S THE PENCIL SHAVINGS FROM THE PENCIL SHARPENER!
THE PENCIL SHAVINGS ARE FALLING INTO MY CAGE!
IF WE DON'T STOP THIS THING, IT'S GOING TO BURY ME ALIVE!

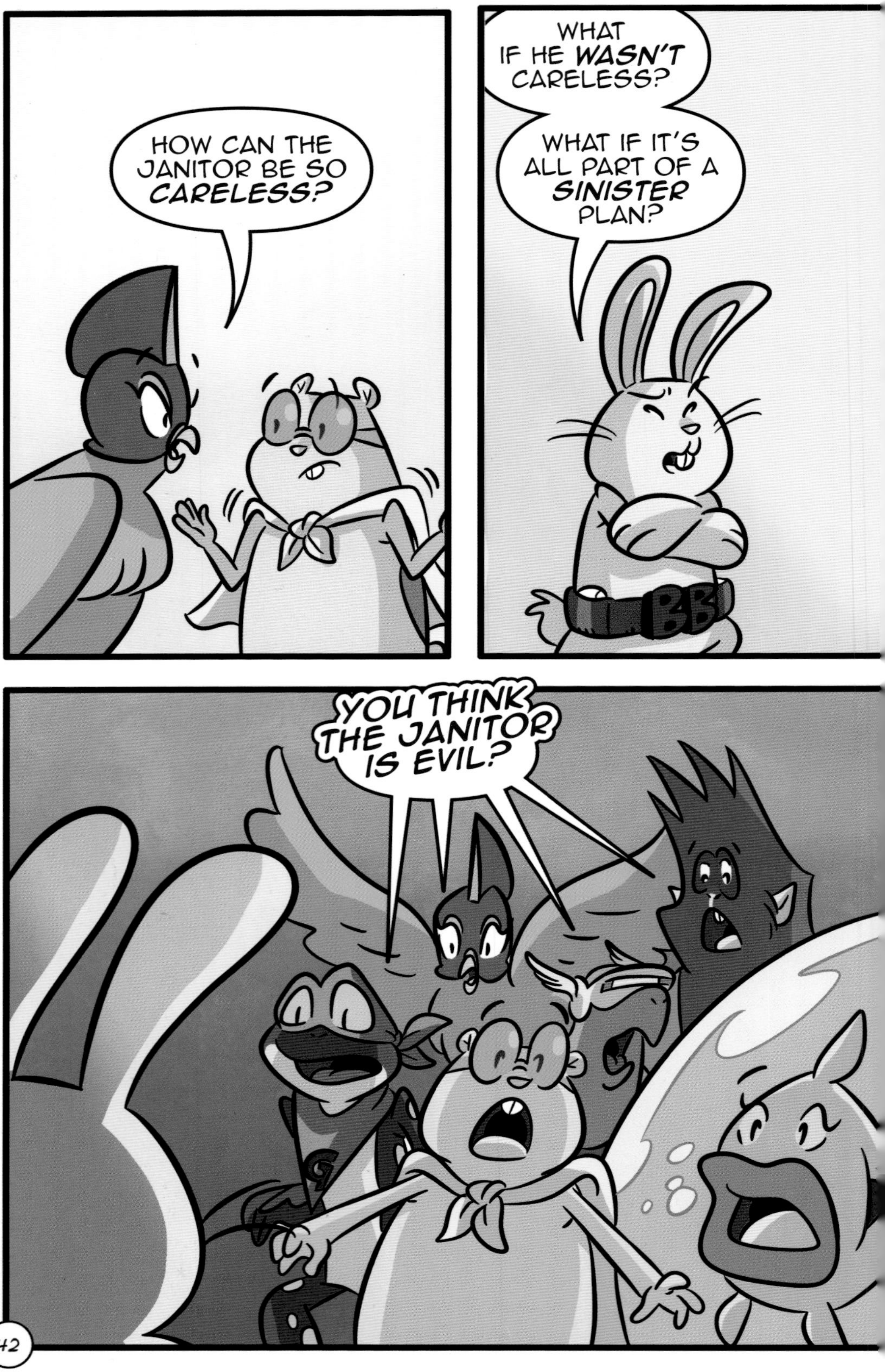
HOW CAN THE JANITOR BE SO CARELESS?
WHAT IF HE WASN'T CARELESS?
WHAT IF IT'S ALL PART OF A SINISTER PLAN?
BB
YOU THINK THE JANITOR IS EVIL?

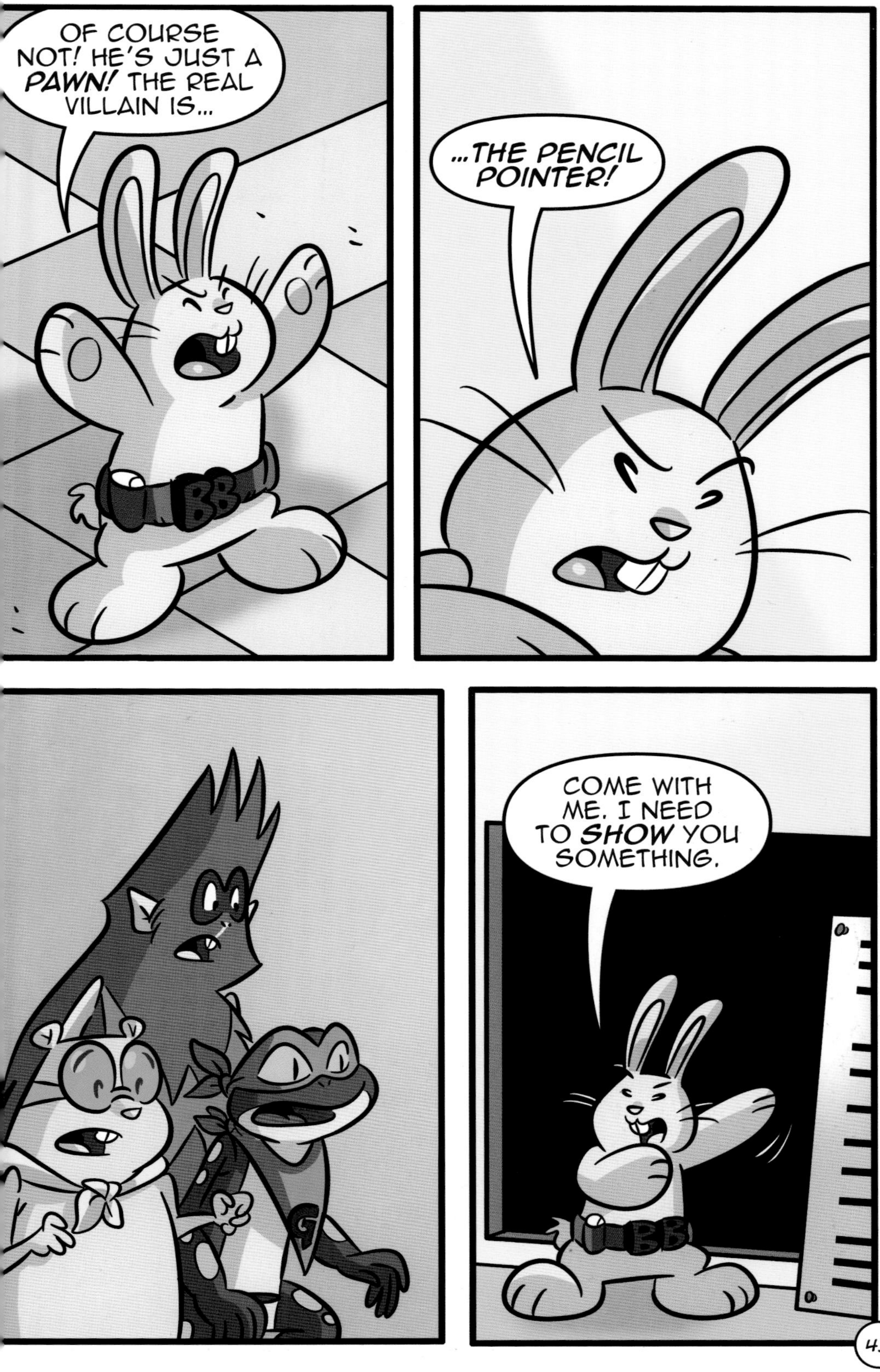
OF COURSE NOT! HE'S JUST A *PAWN!* THE REAL VILLAIN IS...
...THE PENCIL POINTER!
COME WITH ME. I NEED TO *SHOW* YOU SOMETHING.

CHAPTER 4

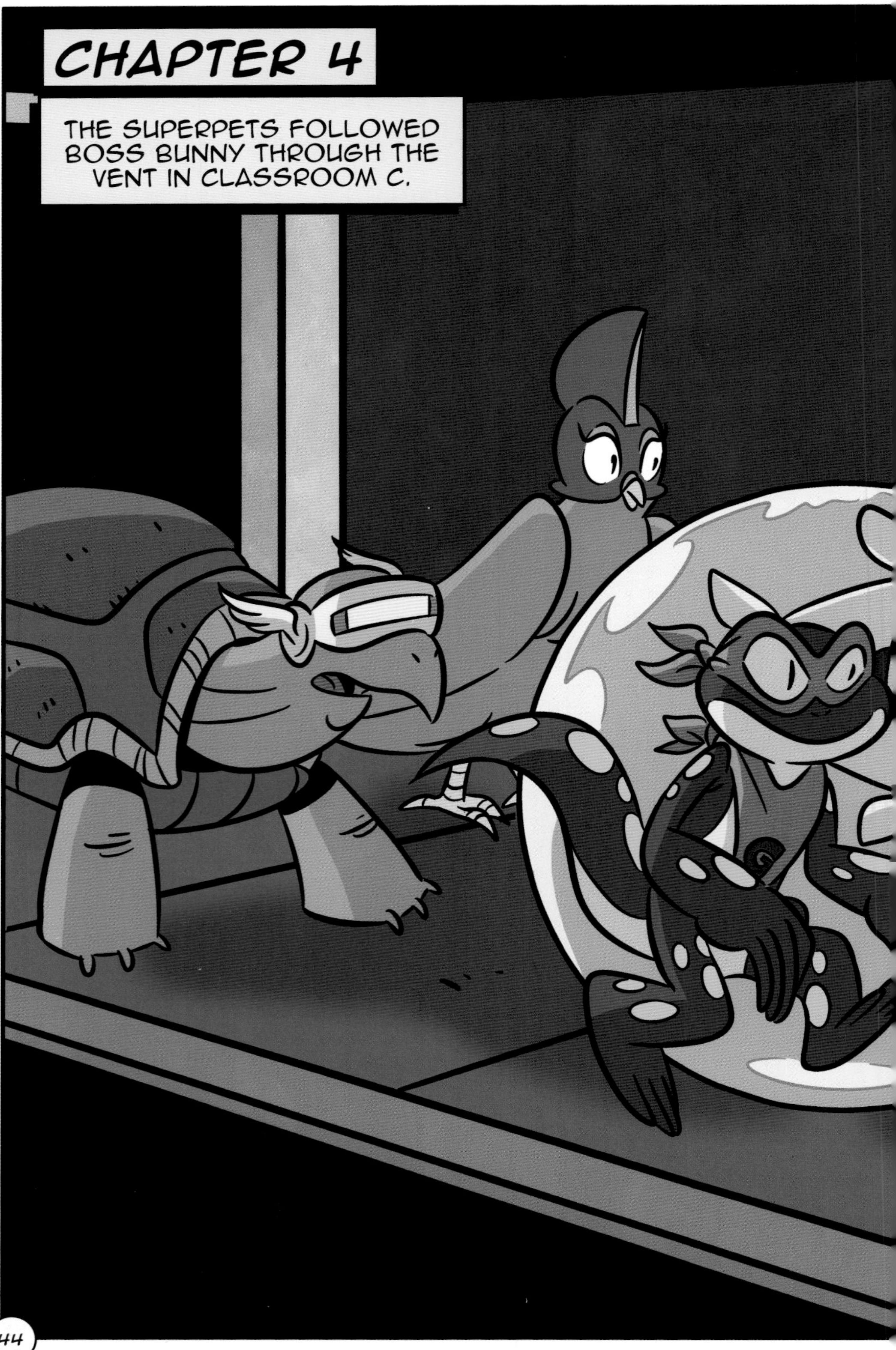
THE SUPERPETS FOLLOWED BOSS BUNNY THROUGH THE VENT IN CLASSROOM C.

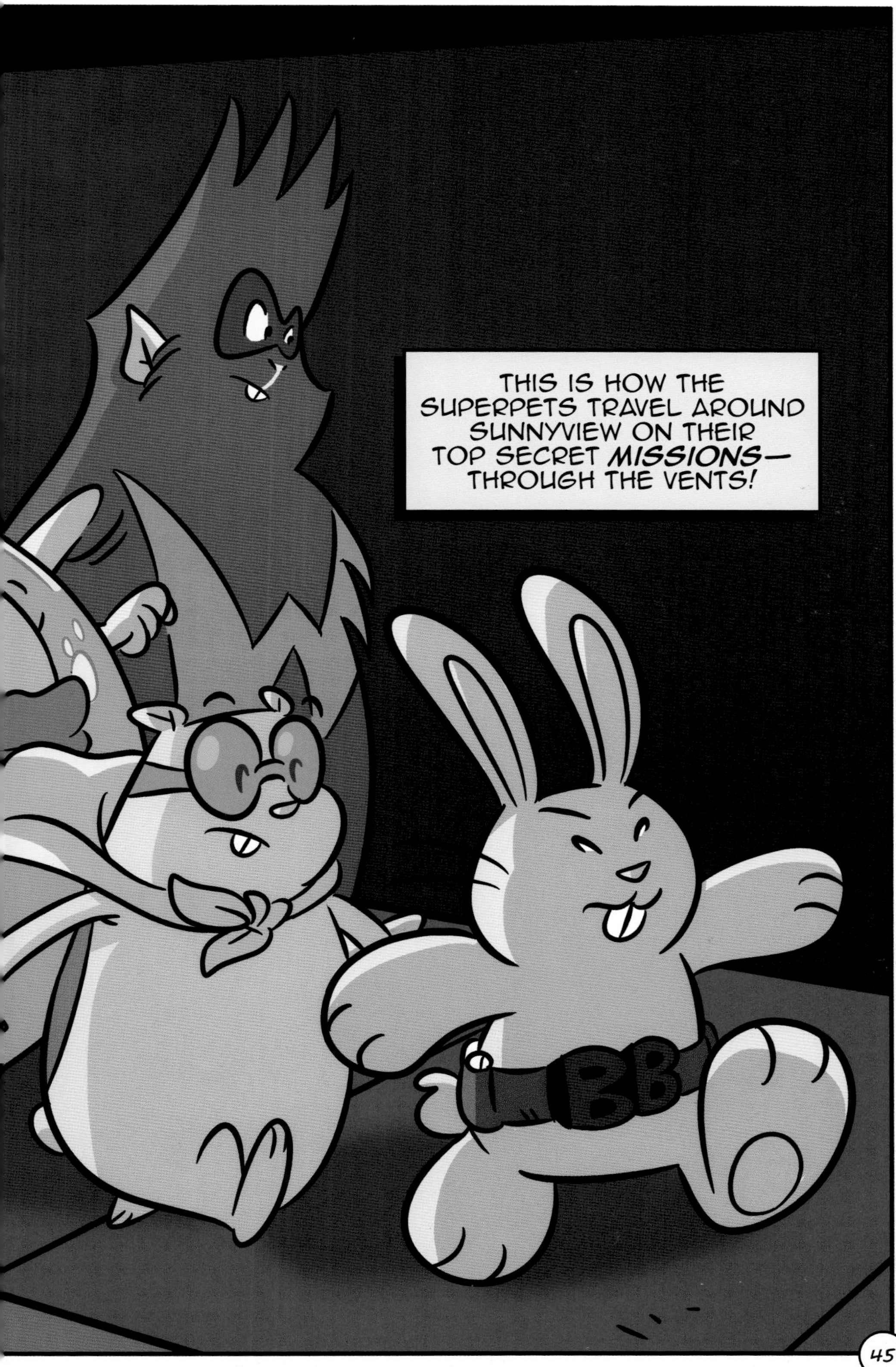
THIS IS HOW THE SUPERPETS TRAVEL AROUND SUNNYVIEW ON THEIR TOP SECRET MISSIONS—THROUGH THE VENTS!
BB

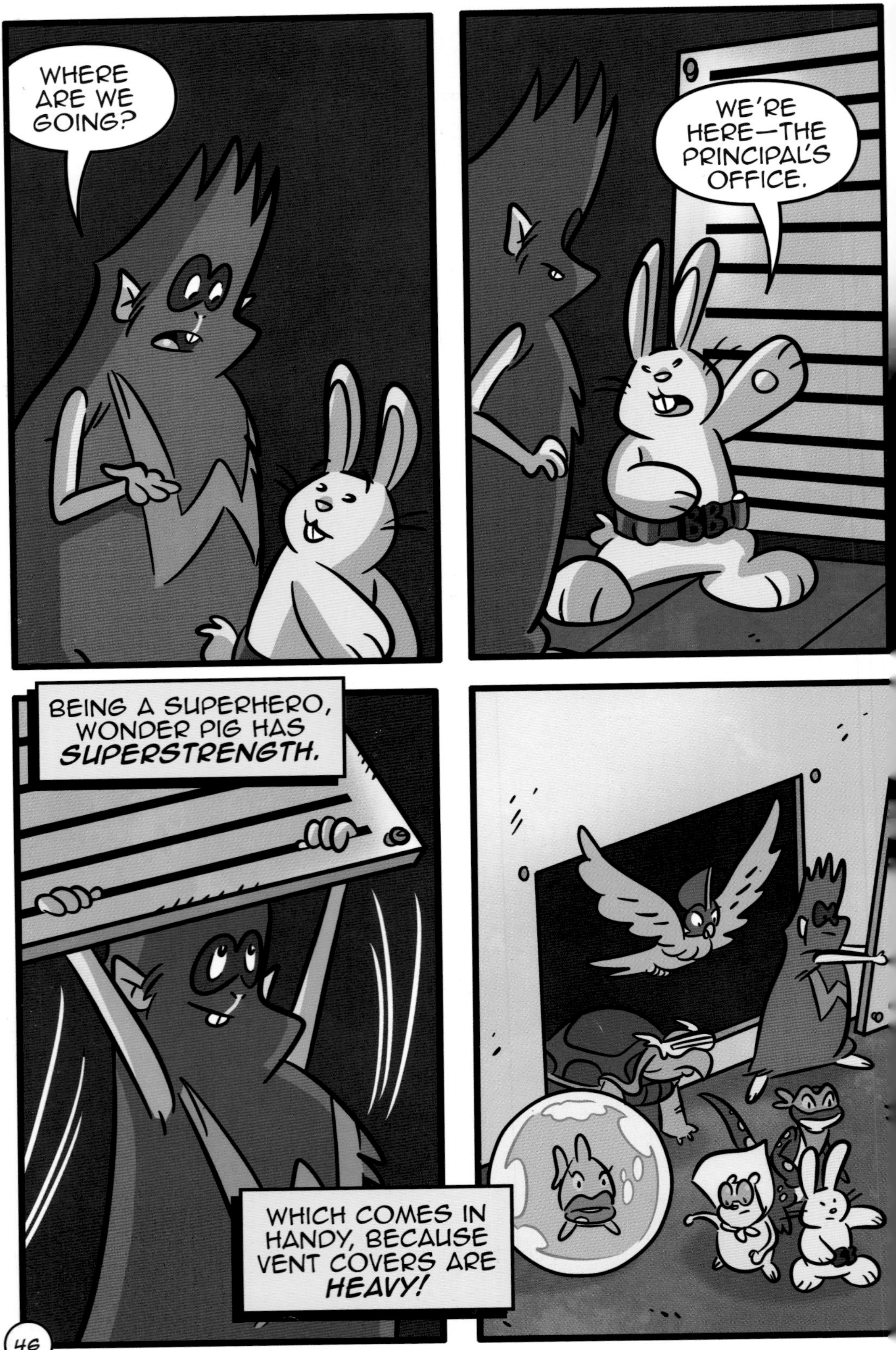
WHERE ARE WE GOING?
WE'RE HERE—THE PRINCIPAL'S OFFICE.
BB
BEING A SUPERHERO, WONDER PIG HAS *SUPERSTRENGTH.*
WHICH COMES IN HANDY, BECAUSE VENT COVERS ARE *HEAVY!*

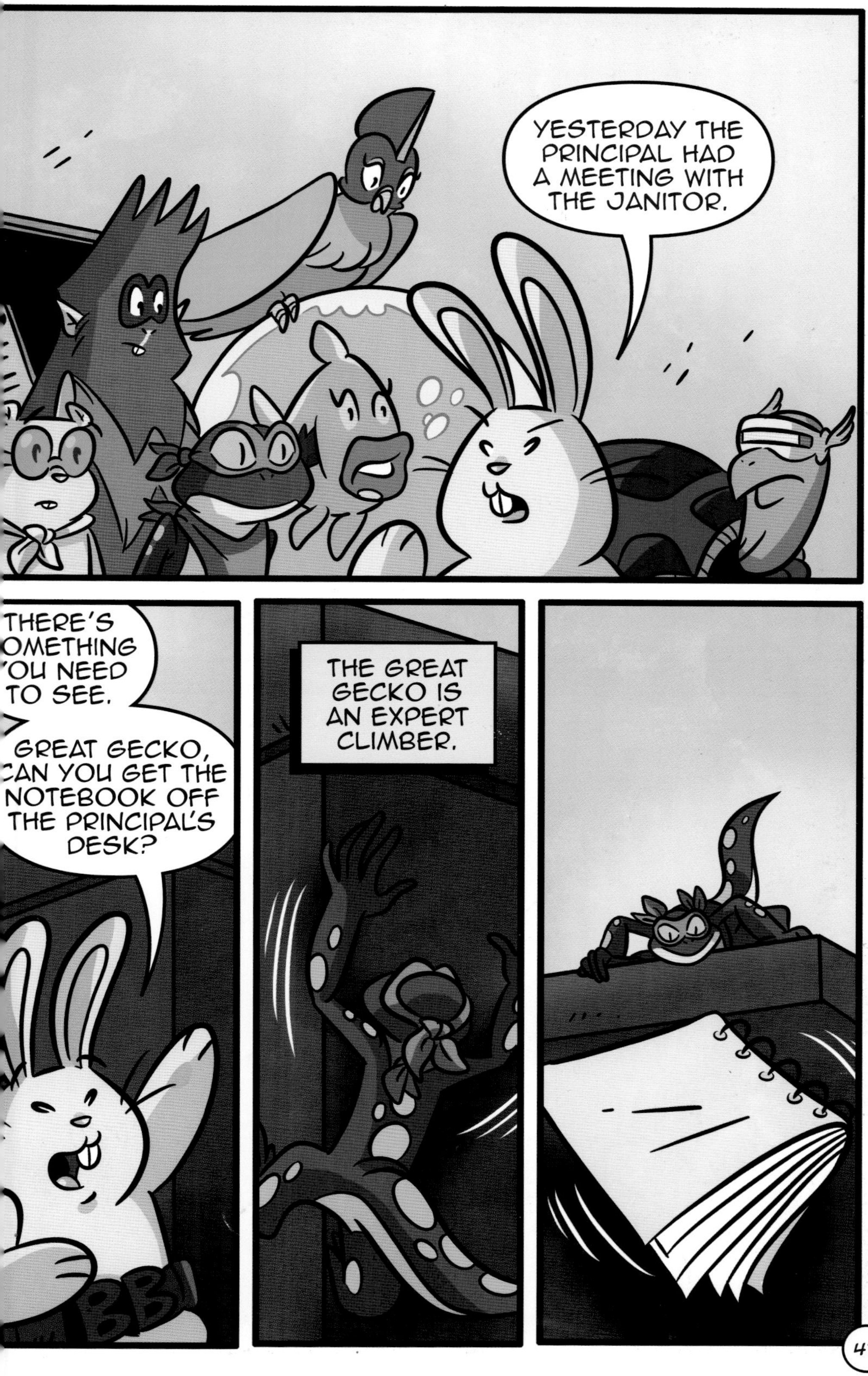
YESTERDAY THE PRINCIPAL HAD A MEETING WITH THE JANITOR.
THERE'S OMETHING 'OU NEED TO SEE.
GREAT GECKO, CAN YOU GET THE NOTEBOOK OFF THE PRINCIPAL'S DESK?
THE GREAT GECKO IS AN EXPERT CLIMBER.
BB

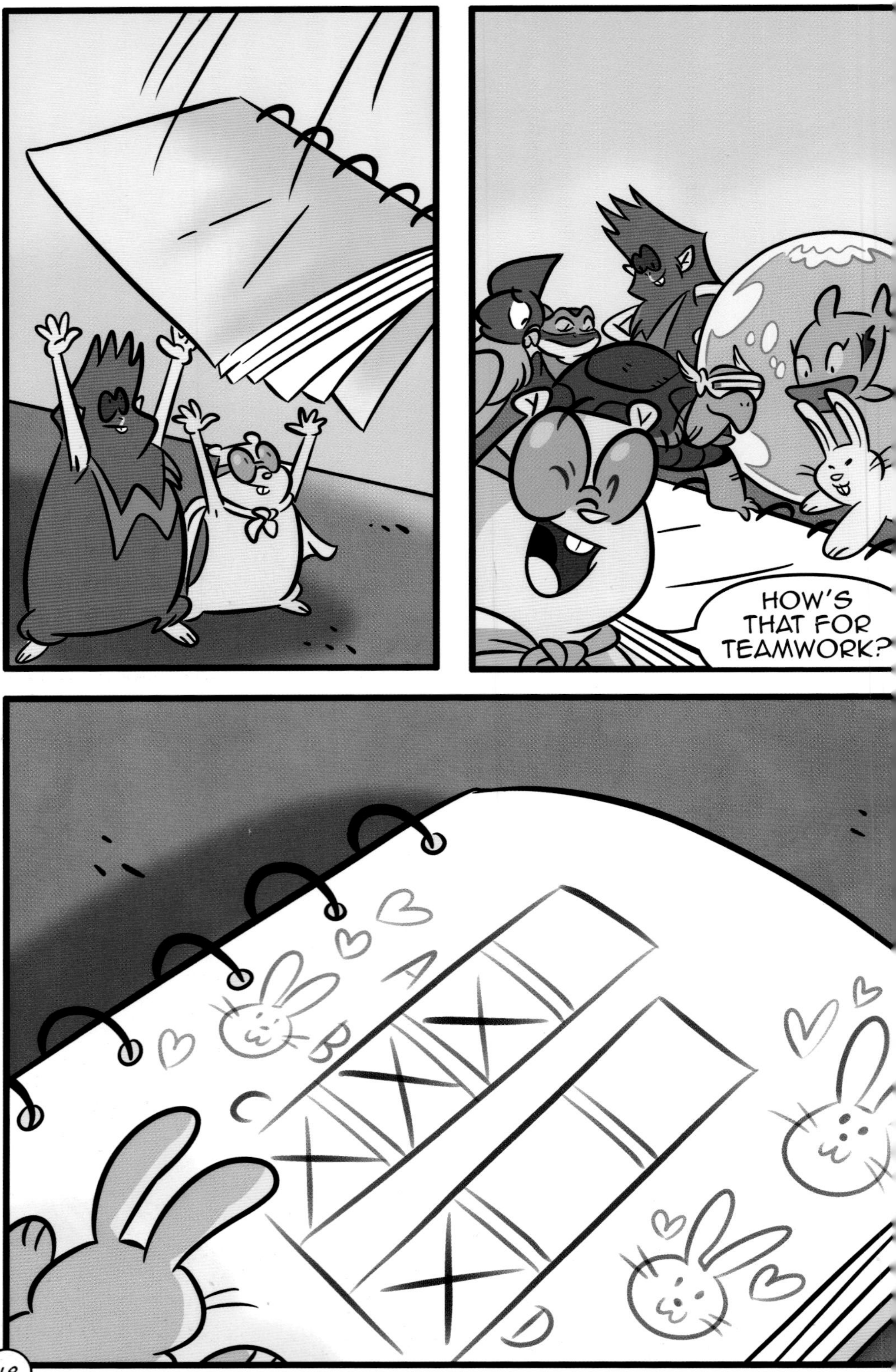
HOW'S THAT FOR TEAMWORK?

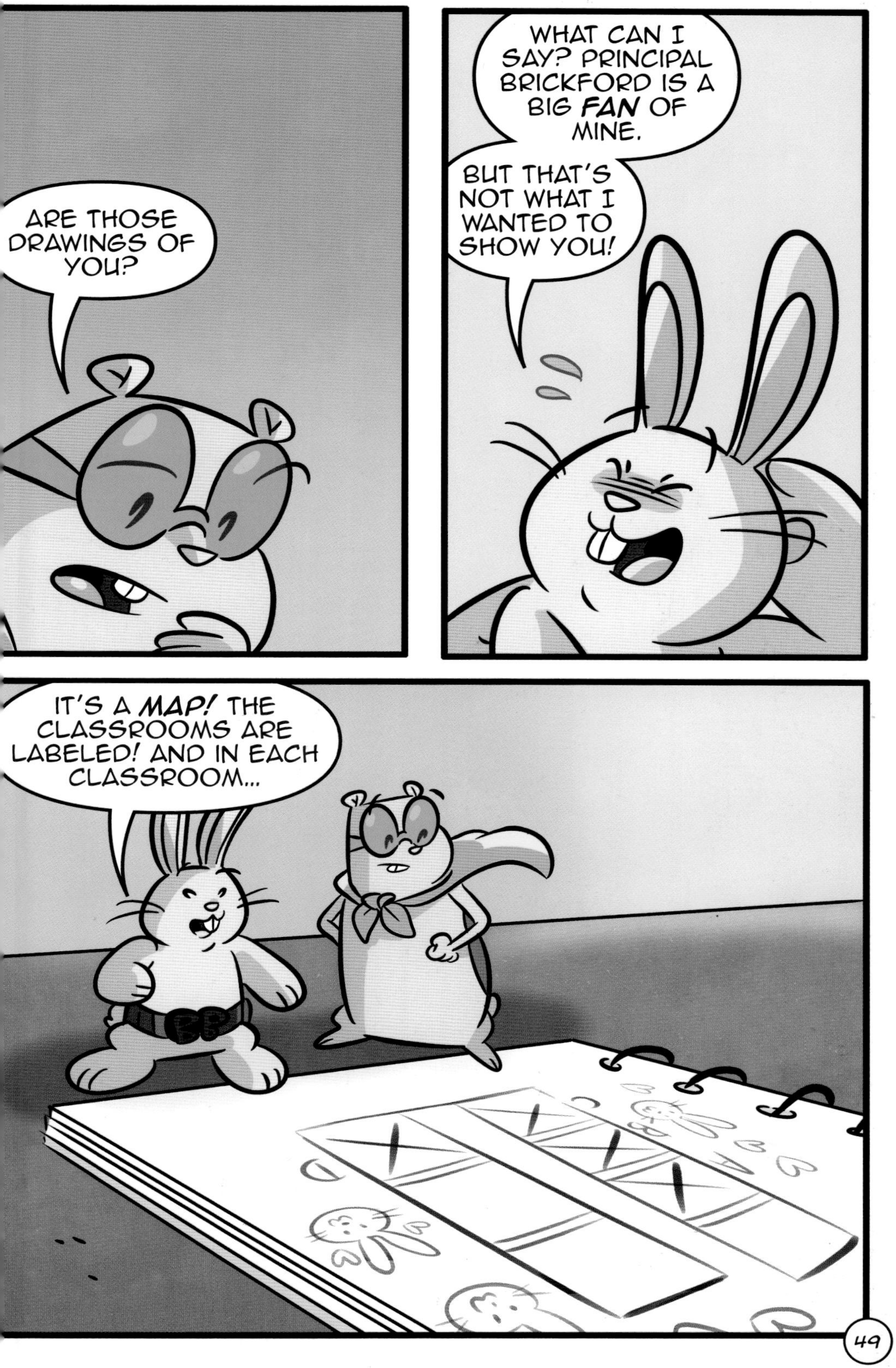
ARE THOSE DRAWINGS OF YOU?
WHAT CAN I SAY? PRINCIPAL BRICKFORD IS A BIG FAN OF MINE.
BUT THAT'S NOT WHAT I WANTED TO SHOW YOU!
IT'S A MAP! THE CLASSROOMS ARE LABELED! AND IN EACH CLASSROOM...

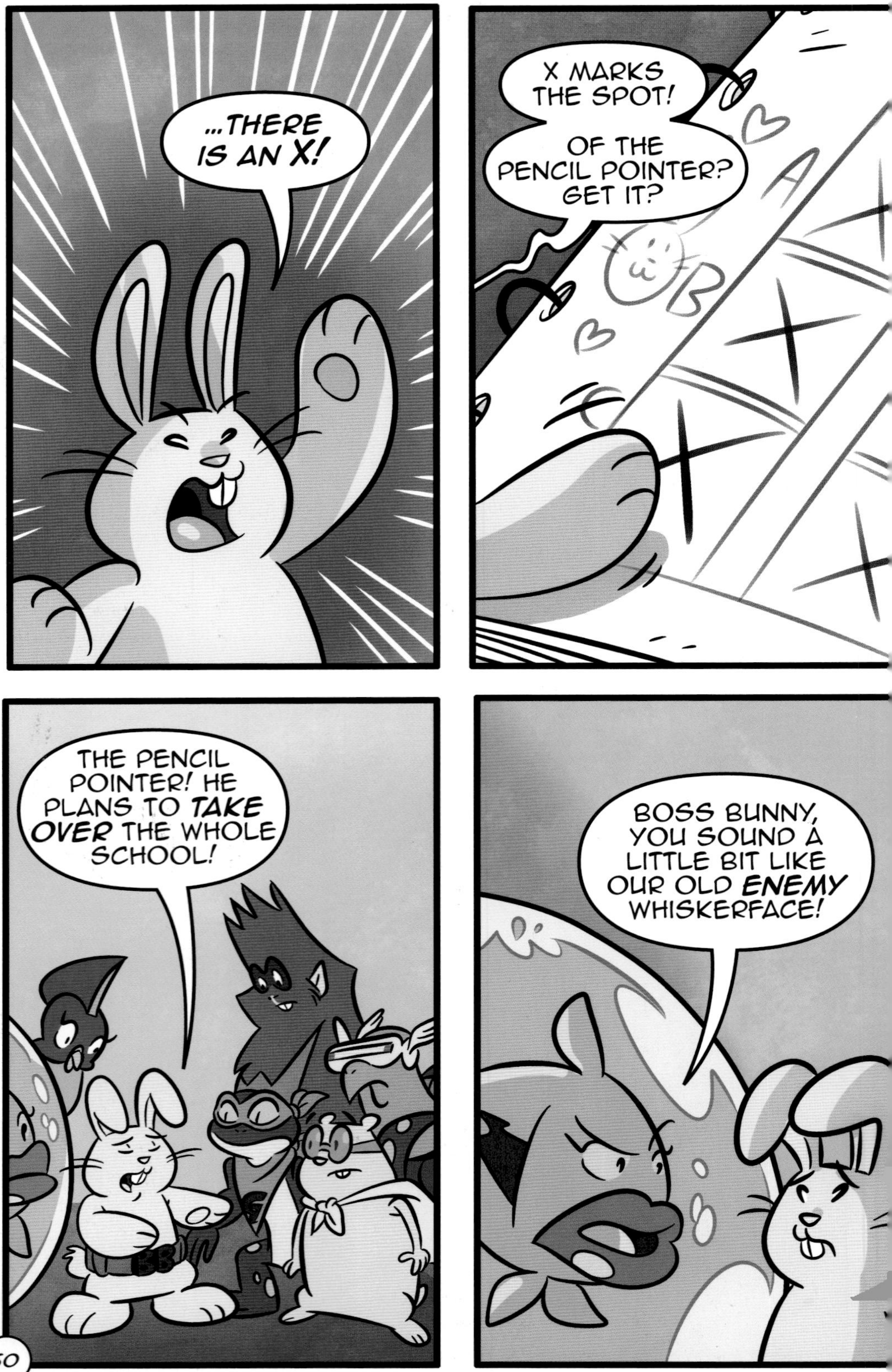
...THERE IS AN X!
X MARKS THE SPOT!
OF THE PENCIL POINTER? GET IT?
THE PENCIL POINTER! HE PLANS TO TAKE OVER THE WHOLE SCHOOL!
BOSS BUNNY, YOU SOUND A LITTLE BIT LIKE OUR OLD ENEMY WHISKERFACE!

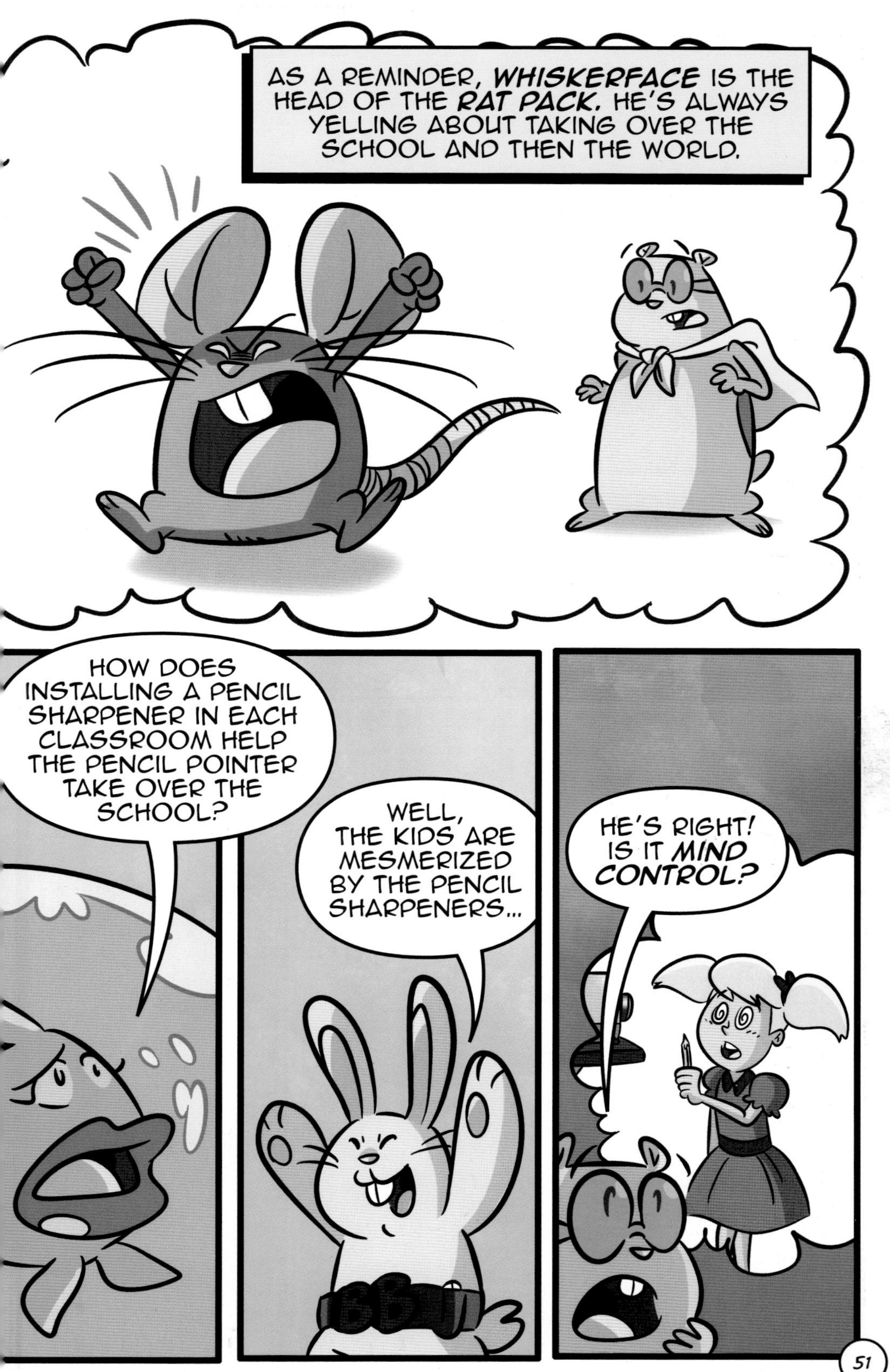
AS A REMINDER, *WHISKERFACE* IS THE HEAD OF THE *RAT PACK.* HE'S ALWAYS YELLING ABOUT TAKING OVER THE SCHOOL AND THEN THE WORLD.
HOW DOES INSTALLING A PENCIL SHARPENER IN EACH CLASSROOM HELP THE PENCIL POINTER TAKE OVER THE SCHOOL?
WELL, THE KIDS ARE MESMERIZED BY THE PENCIL SHARPENERS...
HE'S RIGHT! IS IT *MIND CONTROL?*

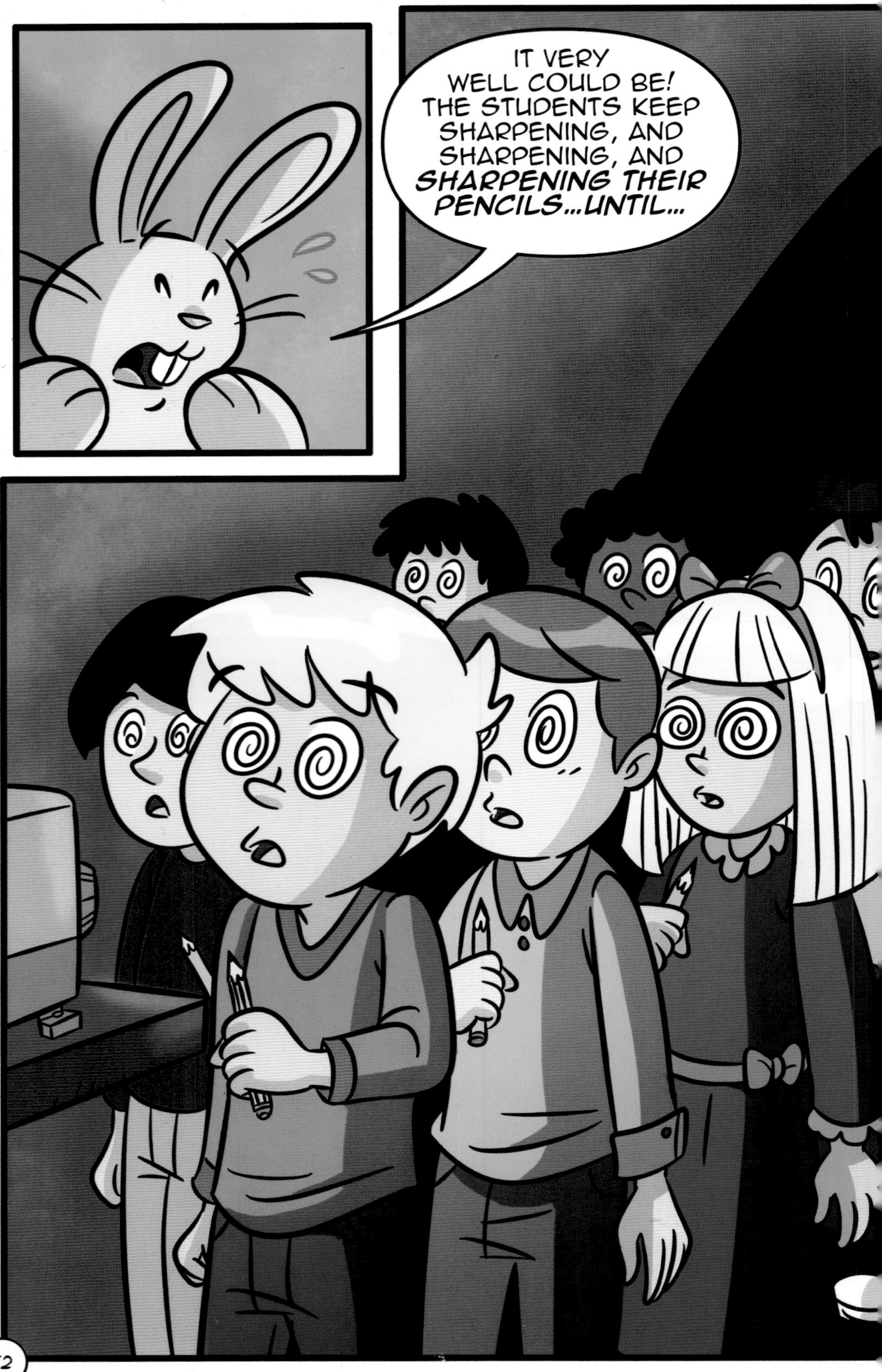
IT VERY WELL COULD BE! THE STUDENTS KEEP SHARPENING, AND SHARPENING, AND *SHARPENING THEIR PENCILS...UNTIL...*

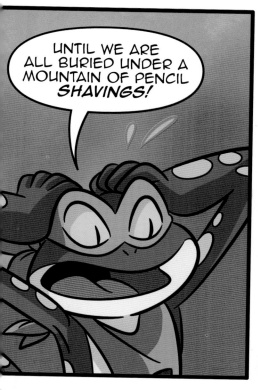

UNTIL WE ARE ALL BURIED UNDER A MOUNTAIN OF PENCIL *SHAVINGS!*

AND THEN THERE ARE NO SUPERPETS TO *PROTECT* THE SCHOOL!

EXACTLY.

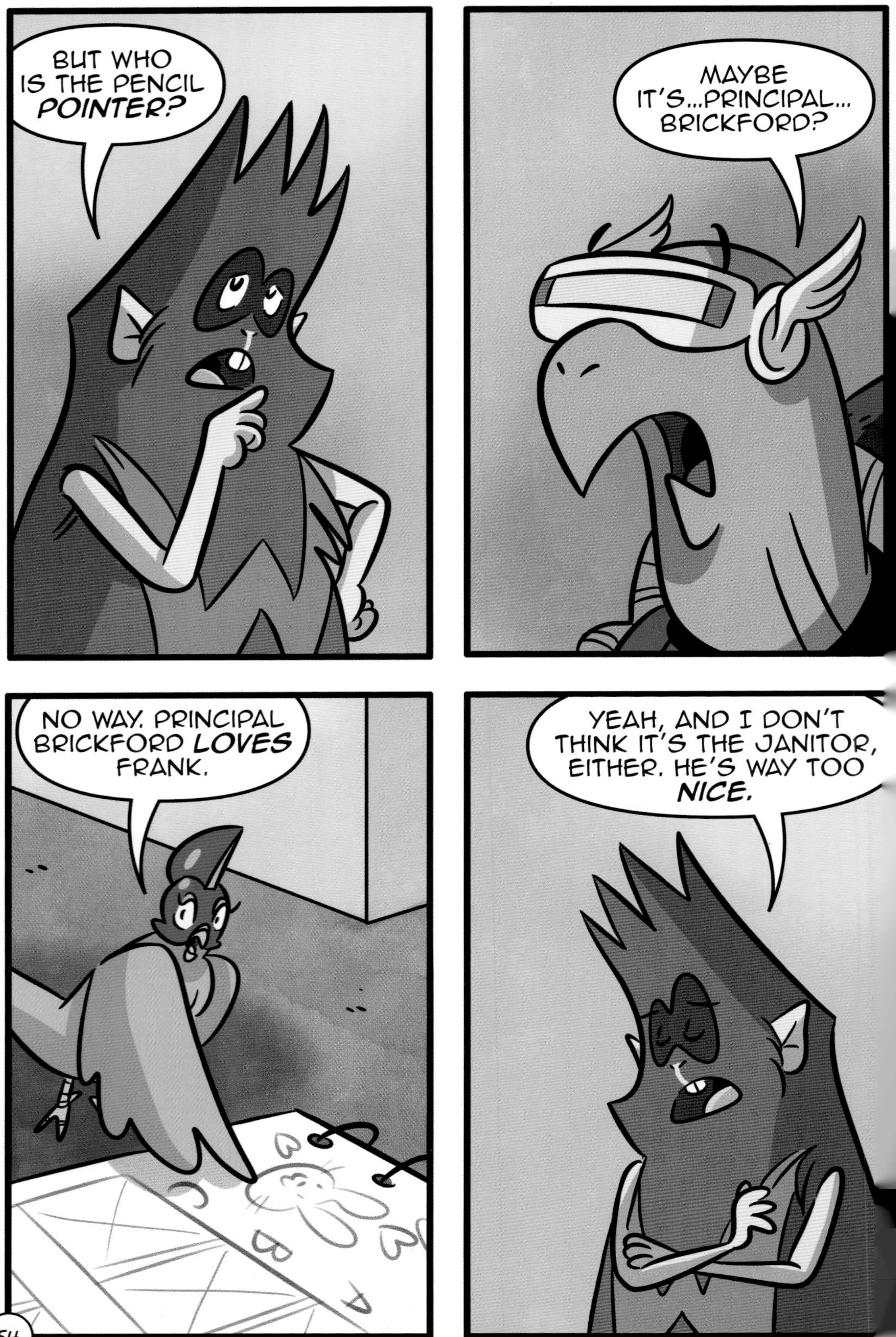
BUT WHO IS THE PENCIL POINTER?
MAYBE IT'S...PRINCIPAL... BRICKFORD?
NO WAY. PRINCIPAL BRICKFORD LOVES FRANK.
YEAH, AND I DON'T THINK IT'S THE JANITOR, EITHER. HE'S WAY TOO NICE.

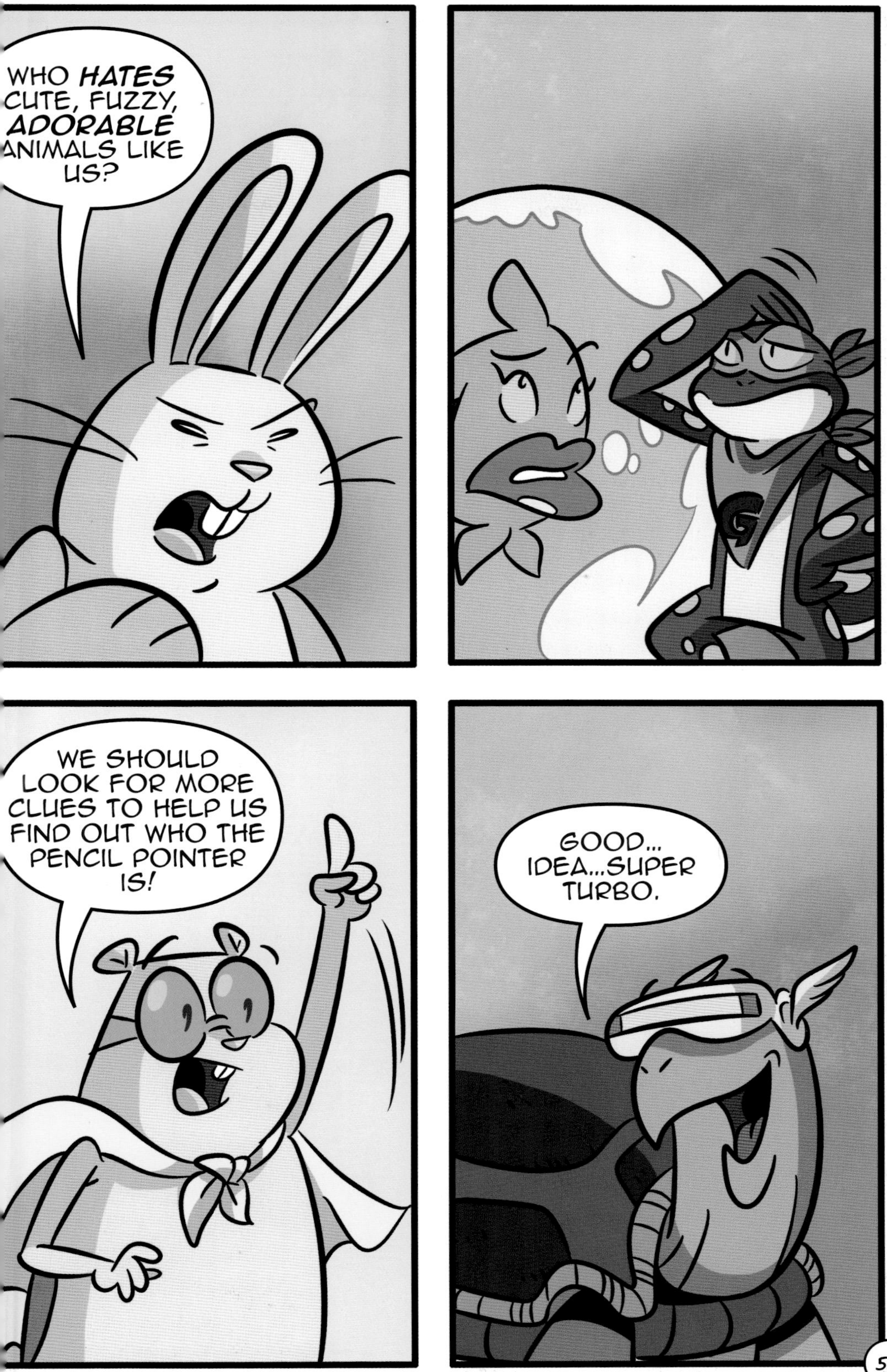
WHO HATES CUTE, FUZZY, ADORABLE ANIMALS LIKE US?
WE SHOULD LOOK FOR MORE CLUES TO HELP US FIND OUT WHO THE PENCIL POINTER IS!
GOOD... IDEA...SUPER TURBO.

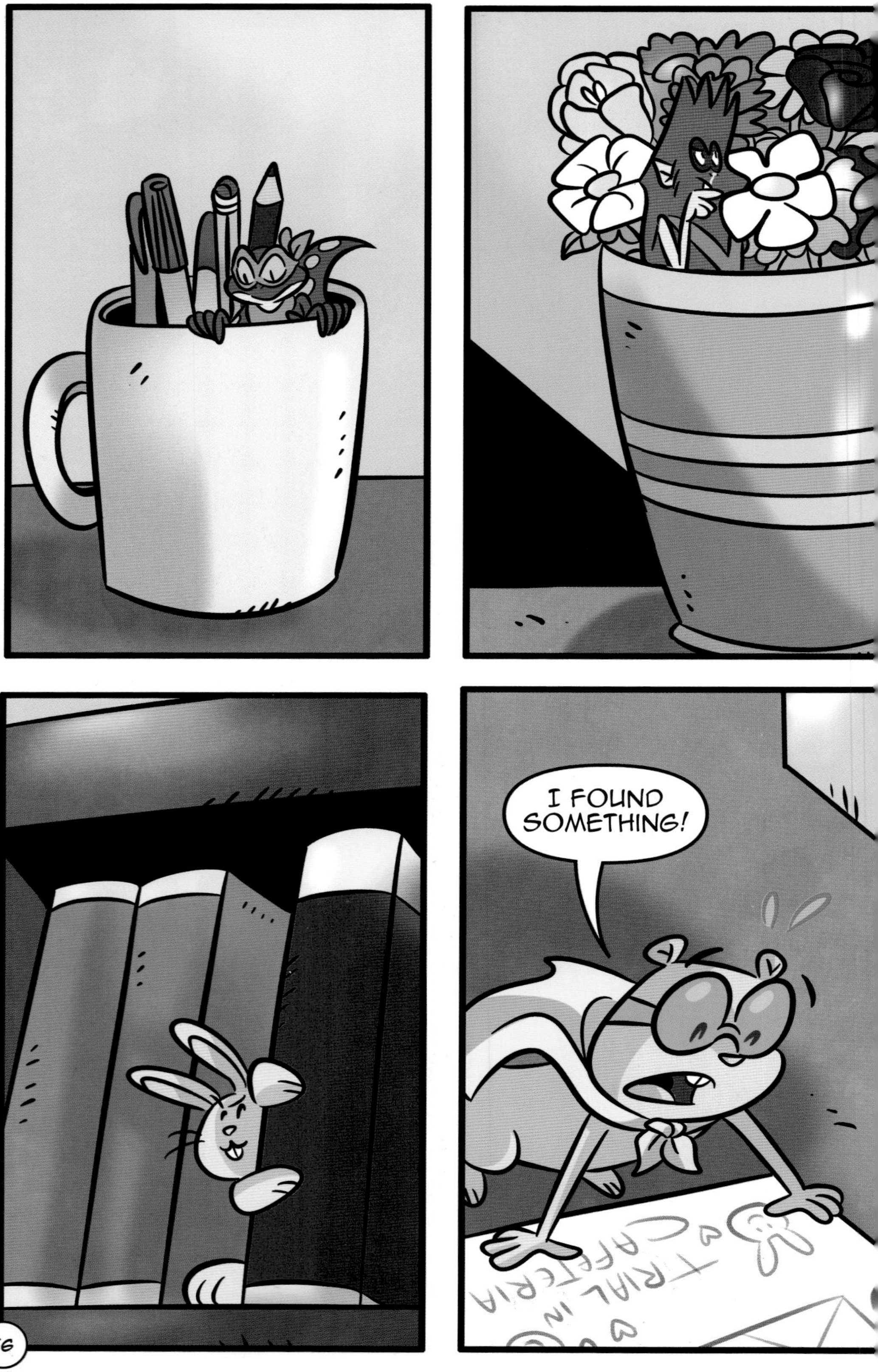
I FOUND SOMETHING!
TRIAL IN CAFETERIA

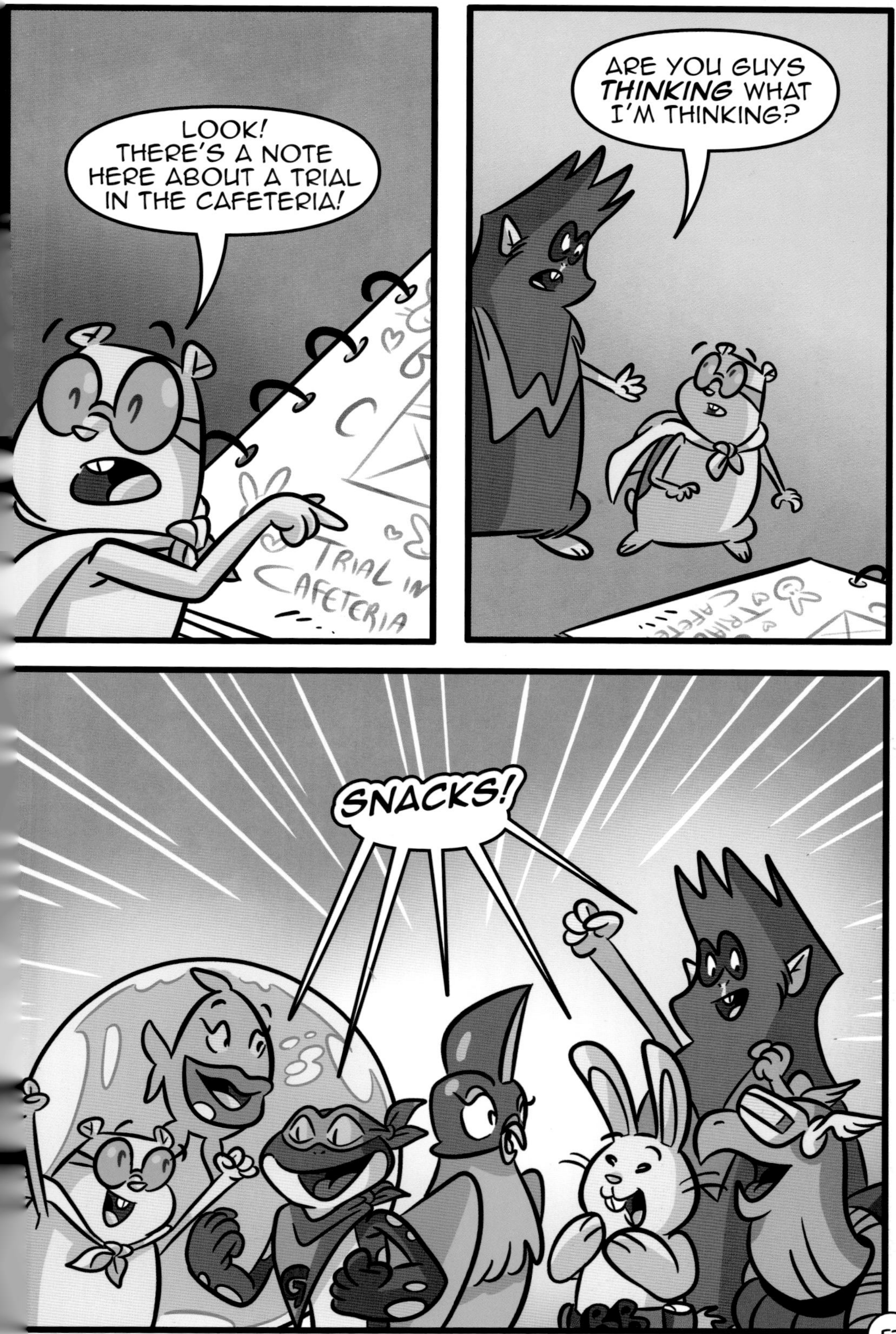
LOOK! THERE'S A NOTE HERE ABOUT A TRIAL IN THE CAFETERIA!
TRIAL IN CAFETERIA
ARE YOU GUYS *THINKING* WHAT I'M THINKING?
SNACKS!

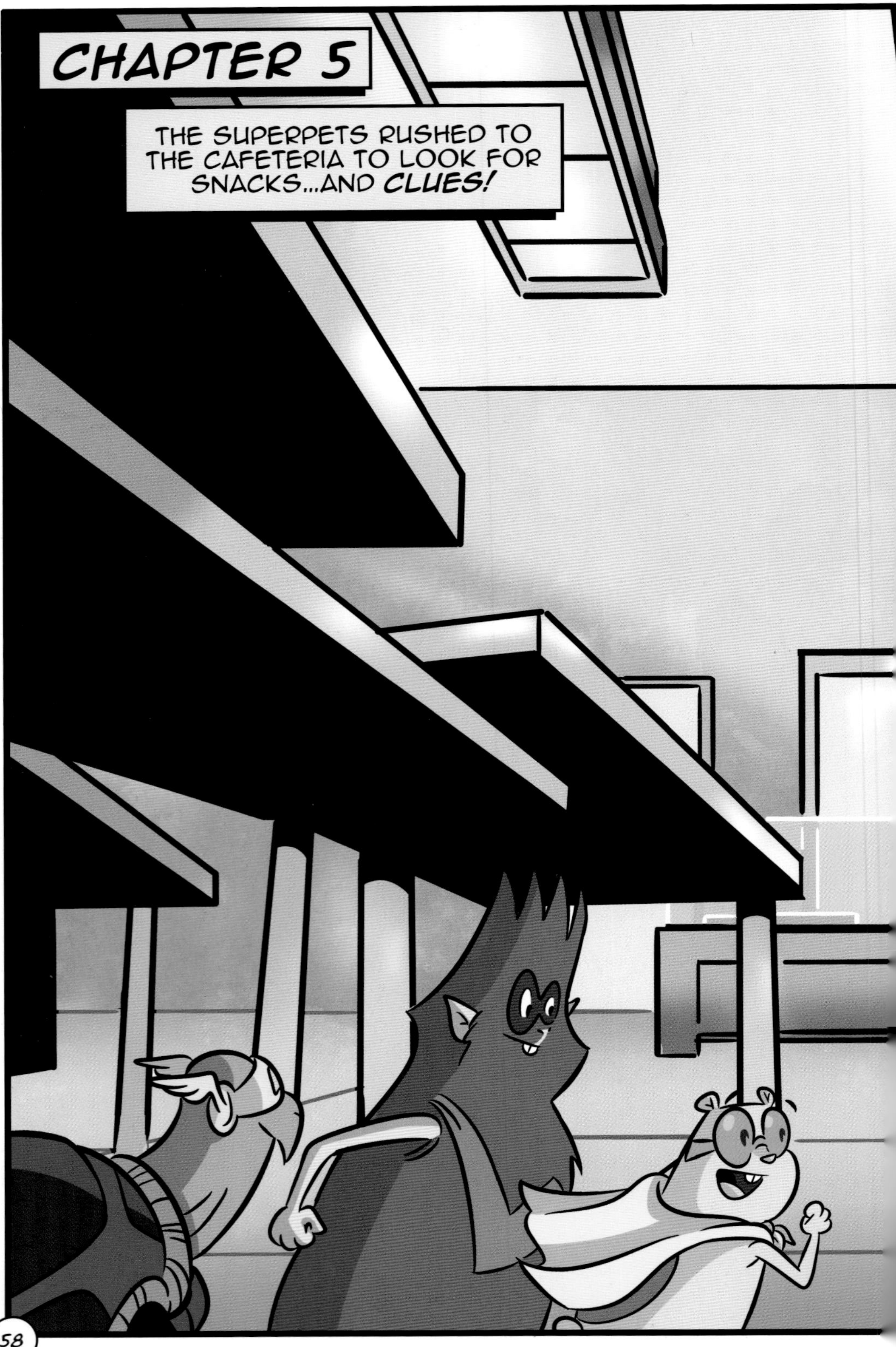
CHAPTER 5
THE SUPERPETS RUSHED TO THE CAFETERIA TO LOOK FOR SNACKS...AND CLUES!

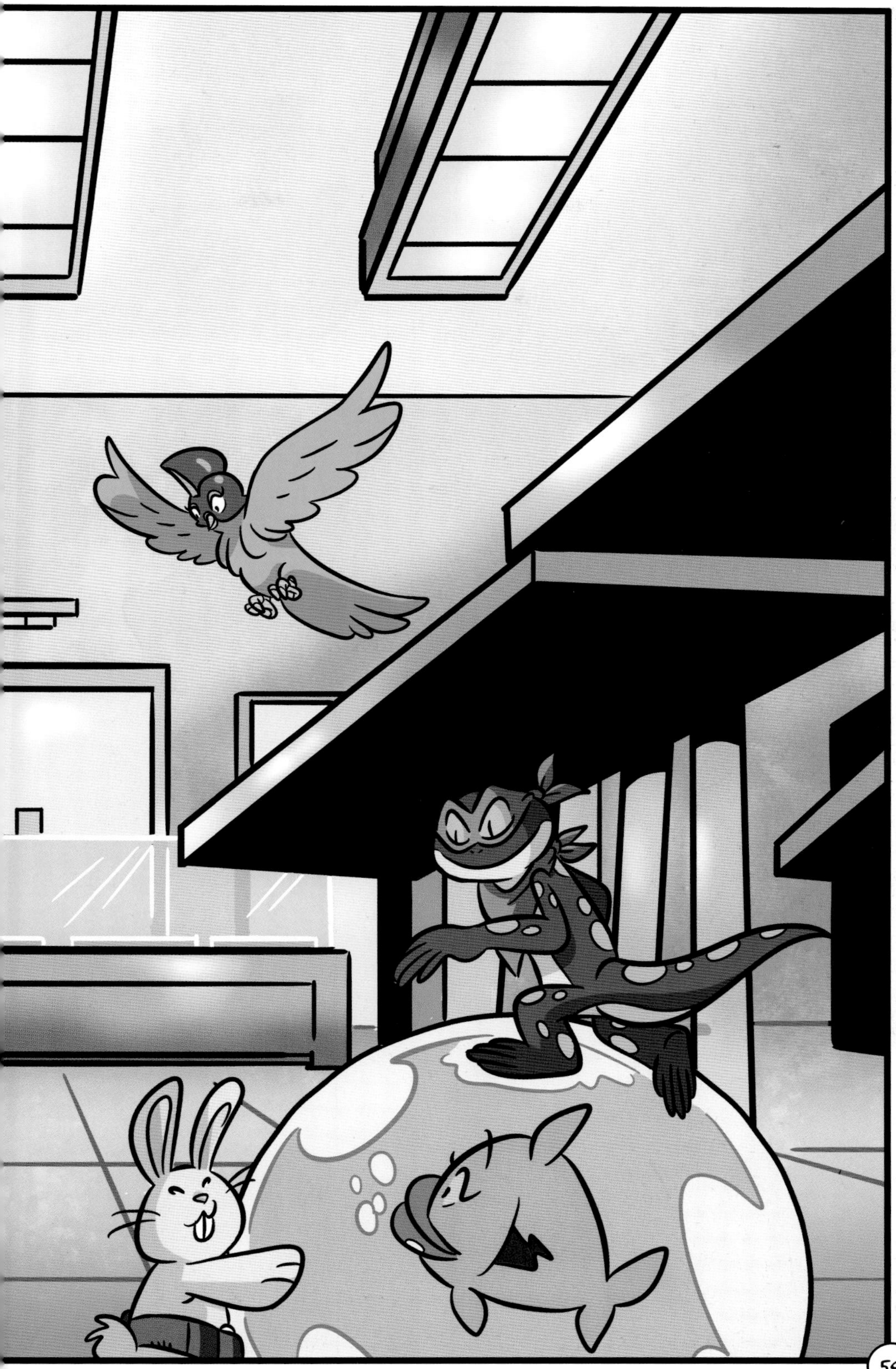

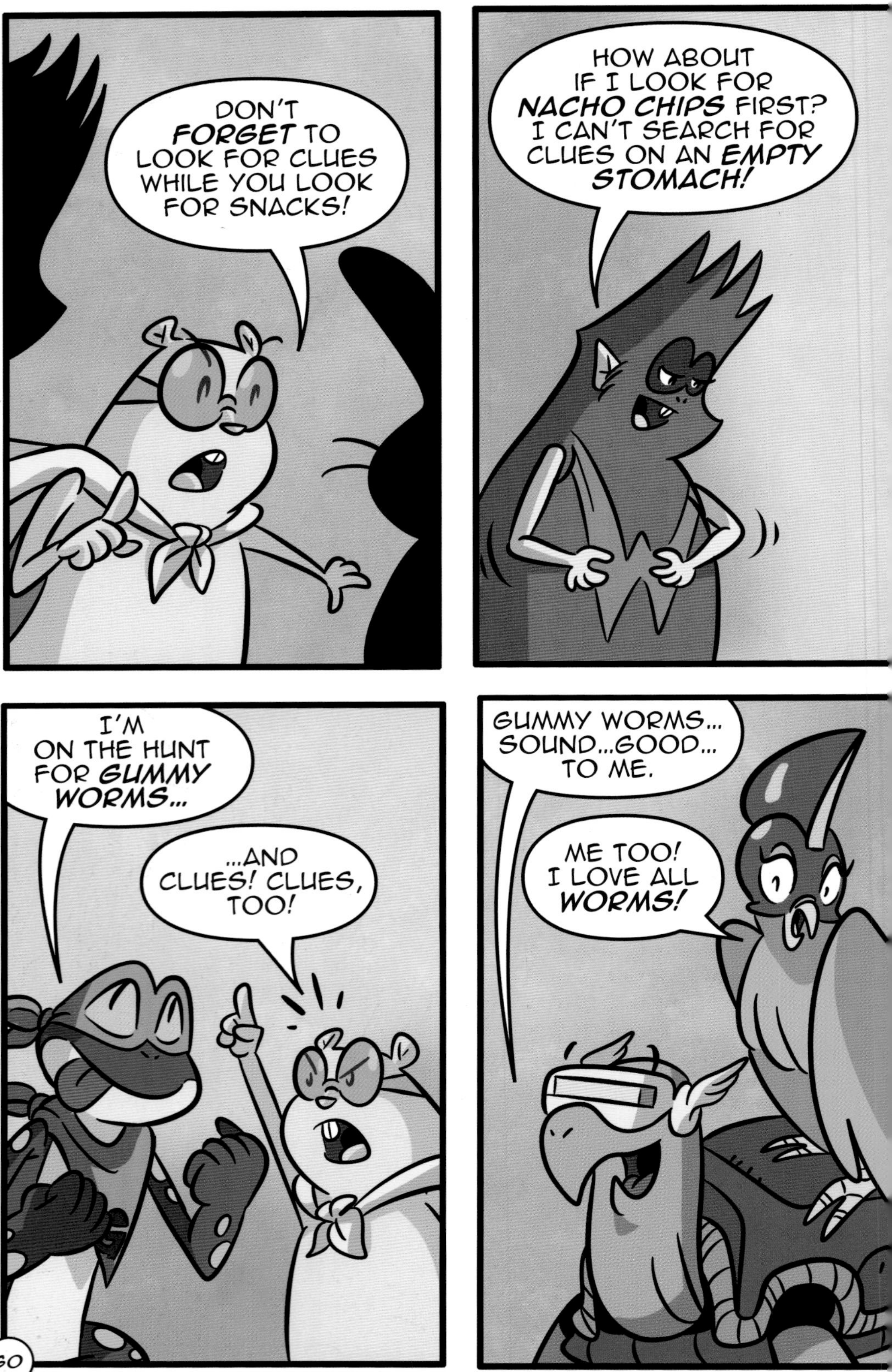
DON'T FORGET TO LOOK FOR CLUES WHILE YOU LOOK FOR SNACKS!
HOW ABOUT IF I LOOK FOR NACHO CHIPS FIRST? I CAN'T SEARCH FOR CLUES ON AN EMPTY STOMACH!
I'M ON THE HUNT FOR GUMMY WORMS...
...AND CLUES! CLUES, TOO!
GUMMY WORMS... SOUND...GOOD... TO ME.
ME TOO! I LOVE ALL WORMS!

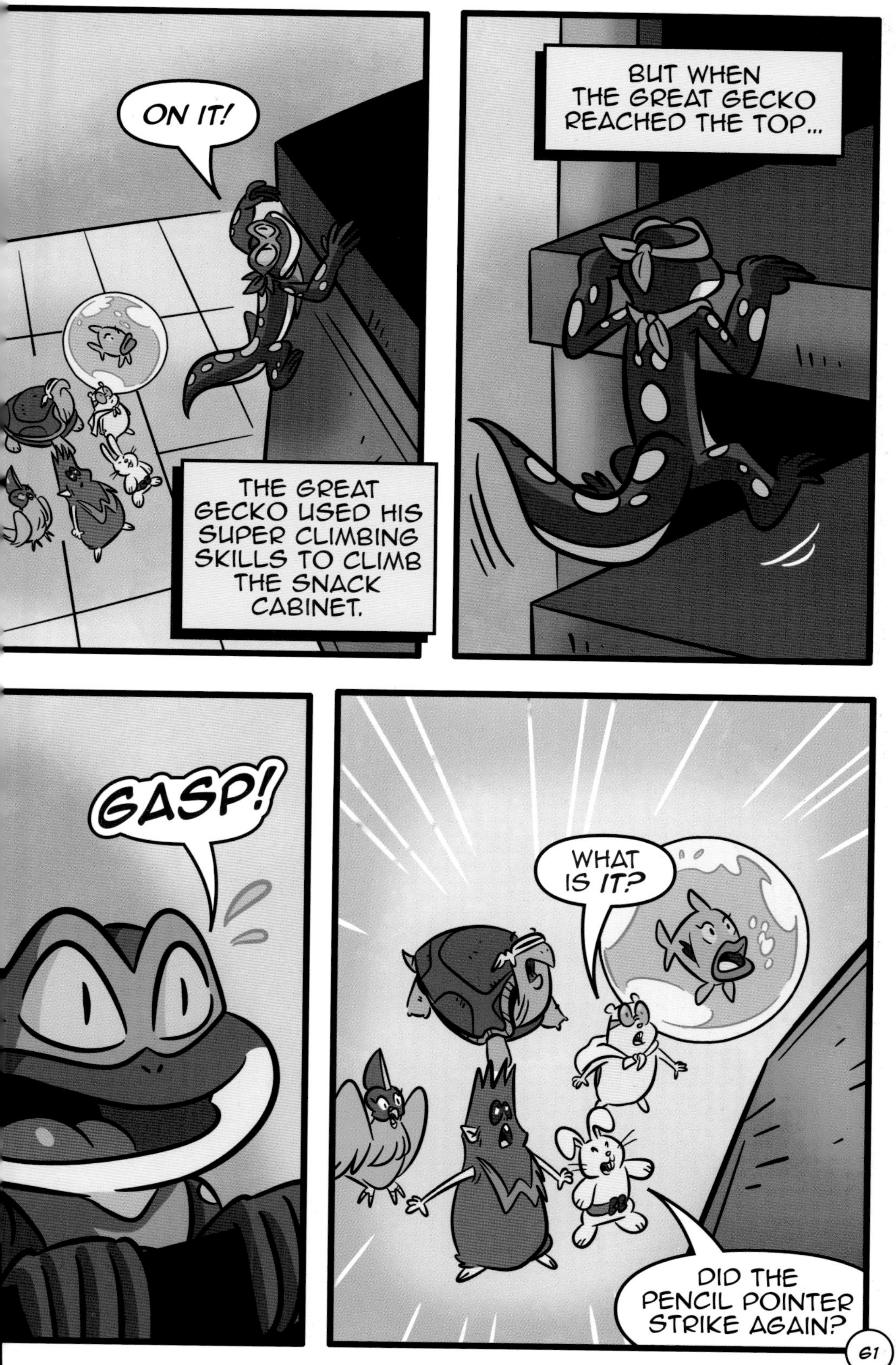

ON IT!
THE GREAT GECKO USED HIS SUPER CLIMBING SKILLS TO CLIMB THE SNACK CABINET.
BUT WHEN THE GREAT GECKO REACHED THE TOP...
GASP!
WHAT IS IT?
DID THE PENCIL POINTER STRIKE AGAIN?

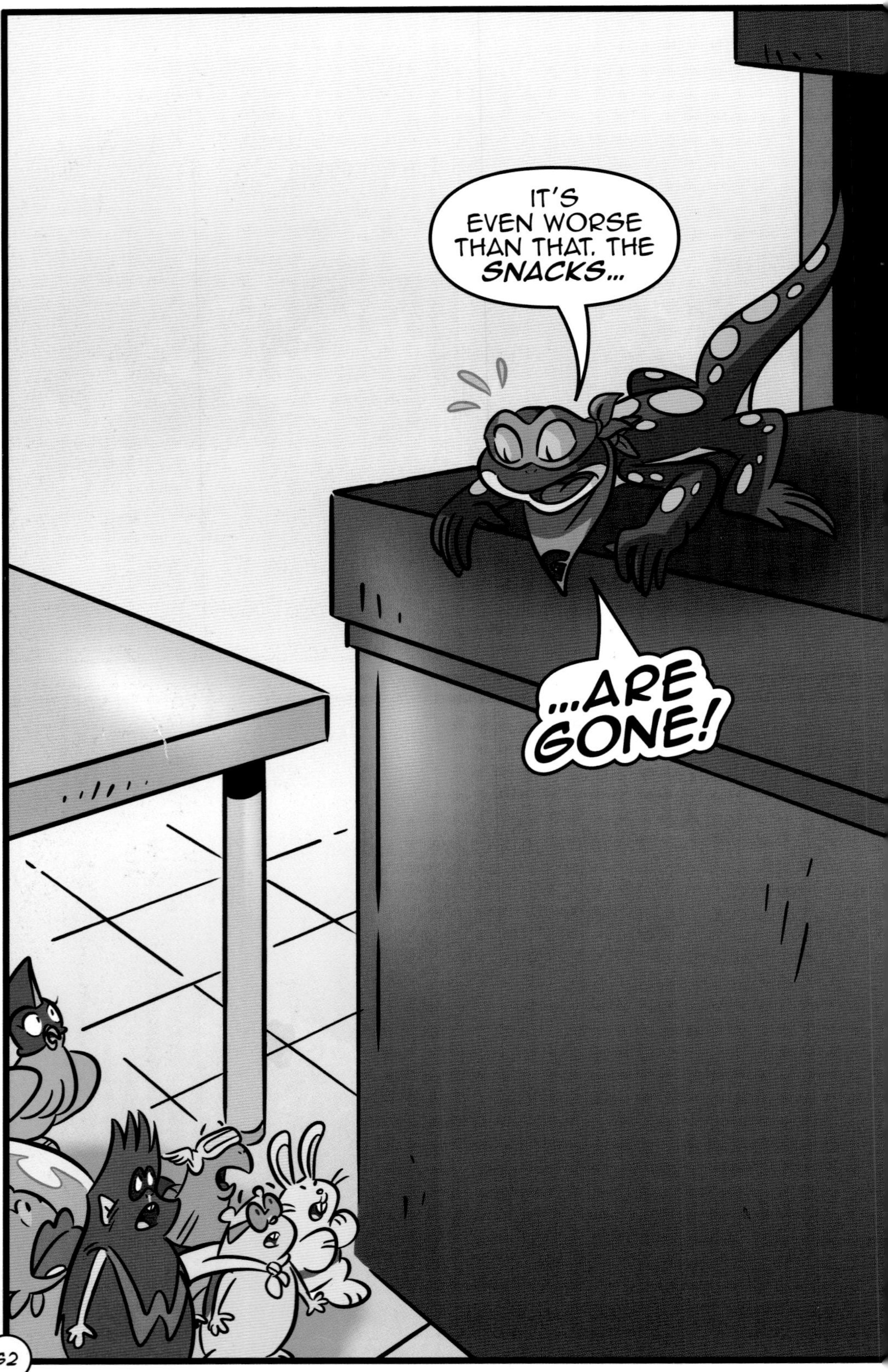
IT'S EVEN WORSE THAN THAT. THE SNACKS...
...ARE GONE!

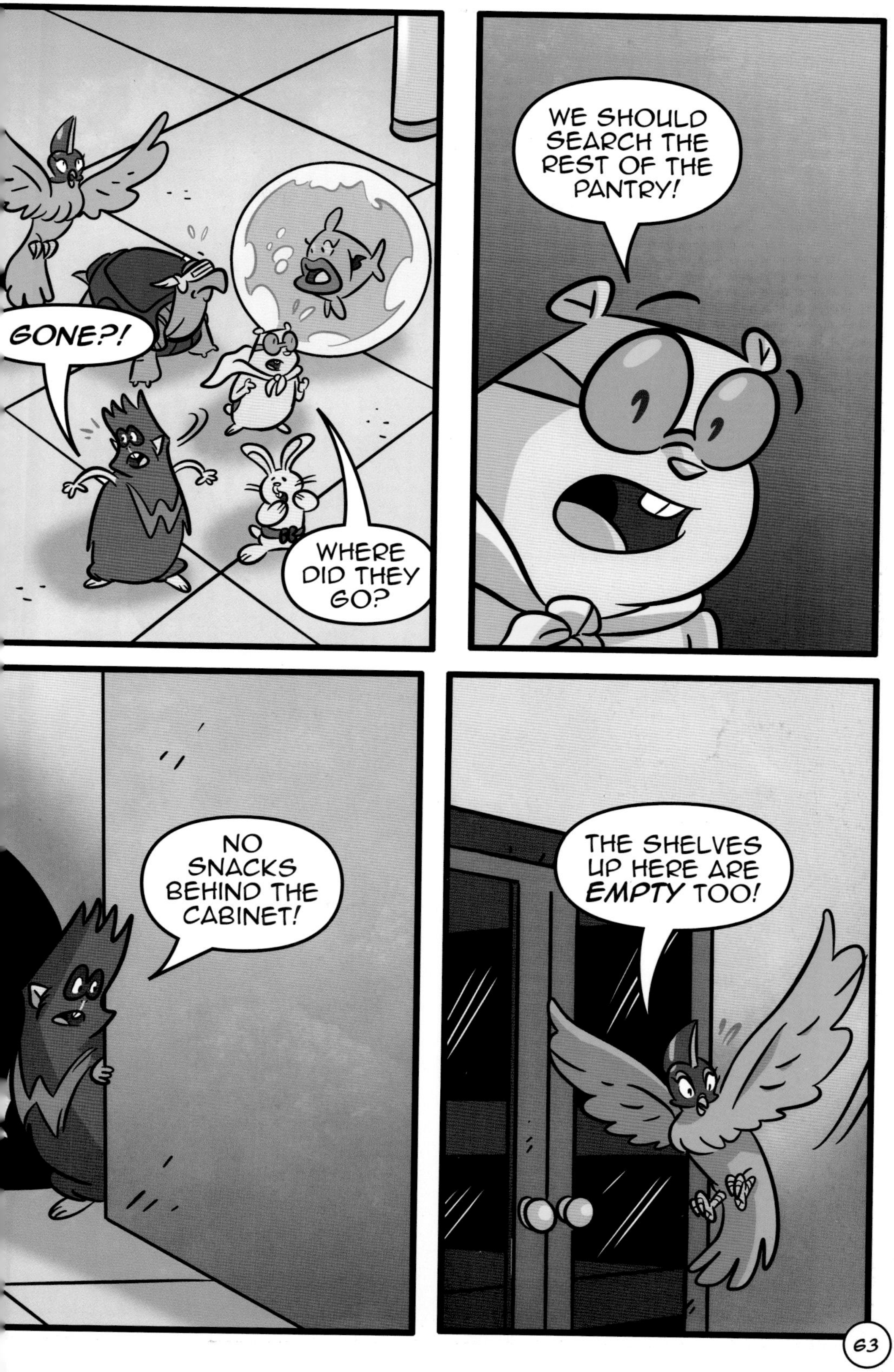
GONE?!
WHERE DID THEY GO?
WE SHOULD SEARCH THE REST OF THE PANTRY!
NO SNACKS BEHIND THE CABINET!
THE SHELVES UP HERE ARE *EMPTY* TOO!

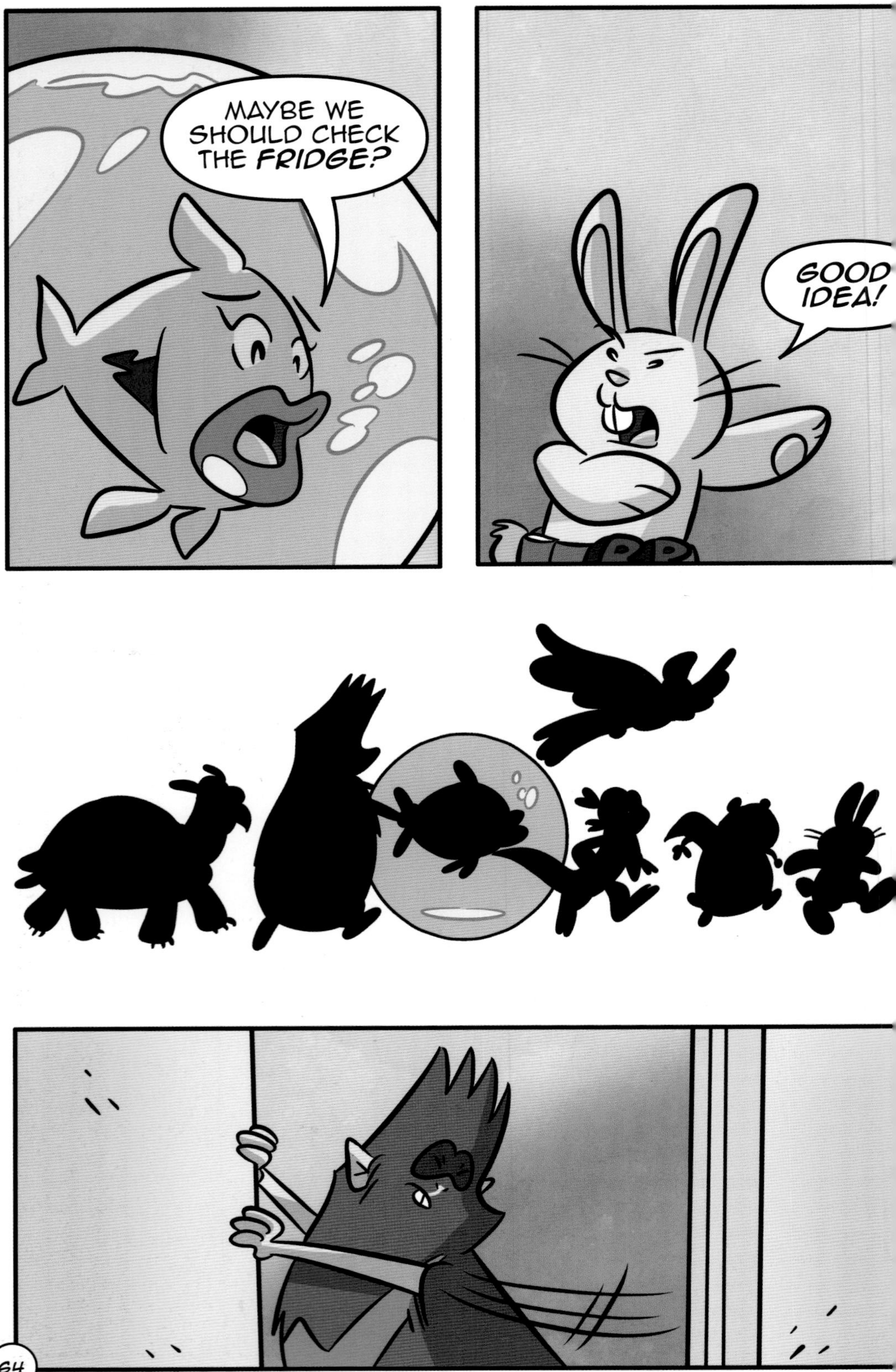
MAYBE WE SHOULD CHECK THE *FRIDGE*?
GOOD IDEA!

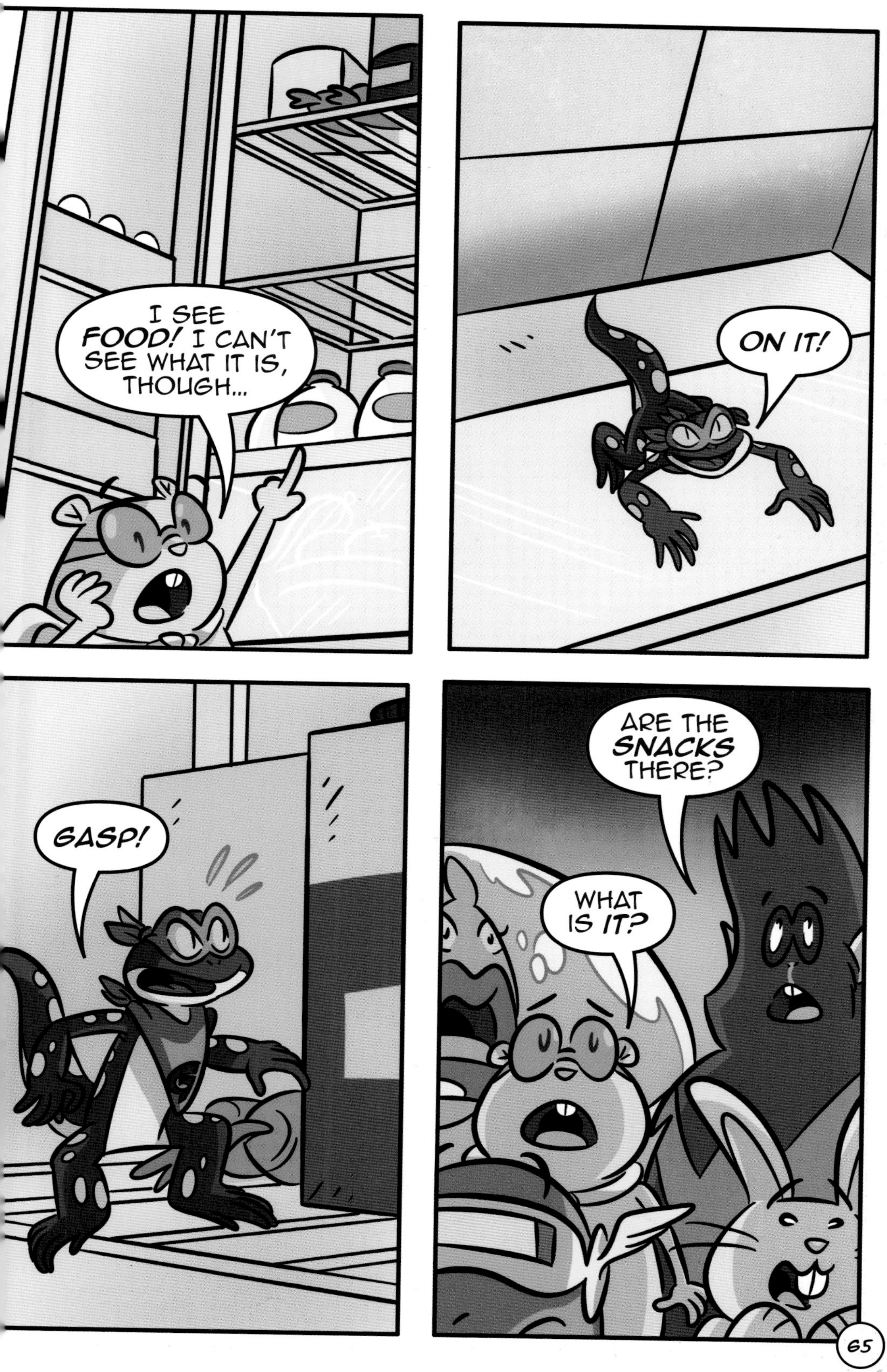
I SEE FOOD! I CAN'T SEE WHAT IT IS, THOUGH...
ON IT!
GASP!
ARE THE SNACKS THERE?
WHAT IS IT?

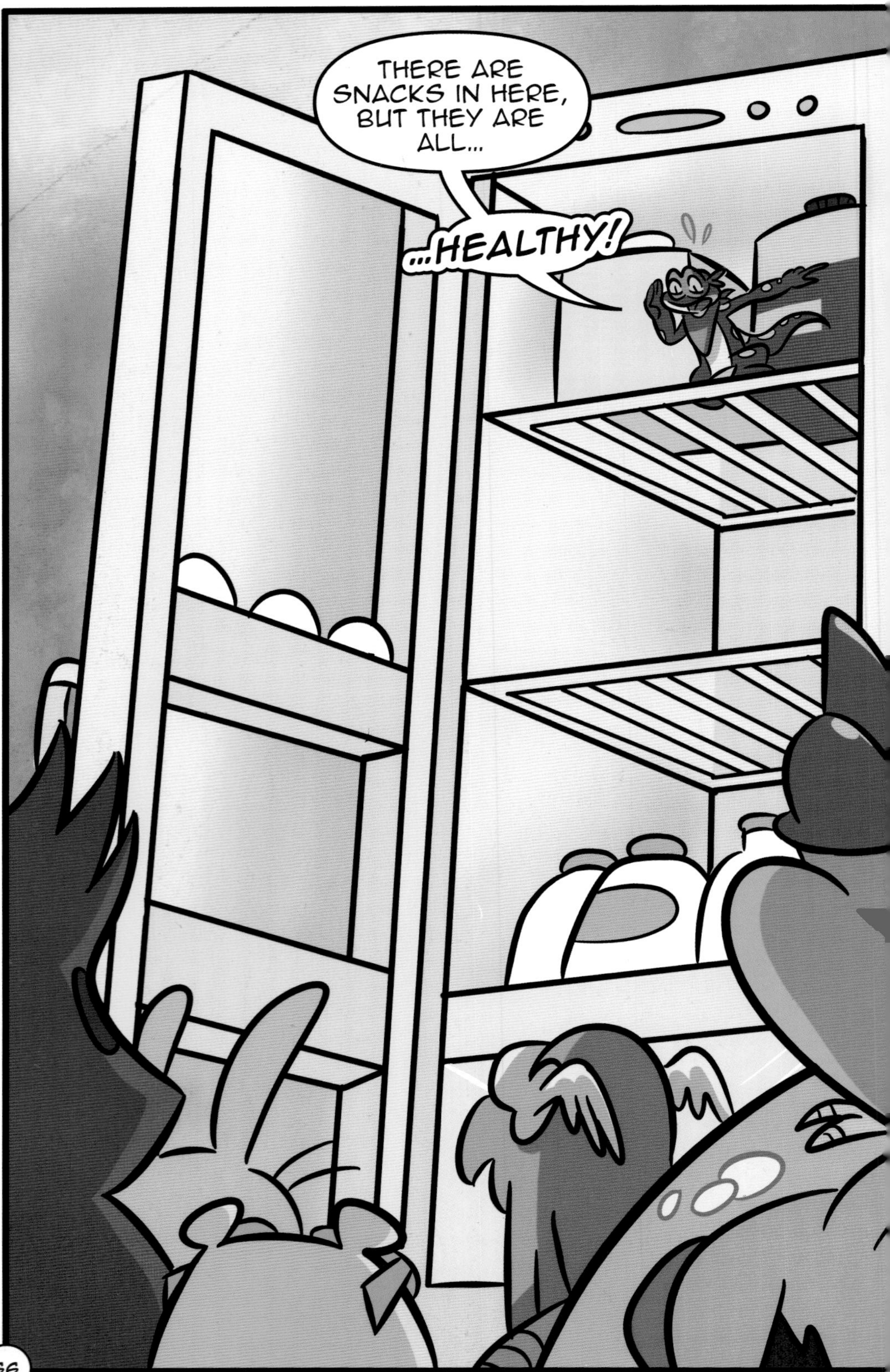
THERE ARE SNACKS IN HERE, BUT THEY ARE ALL...
...HEALTHY!

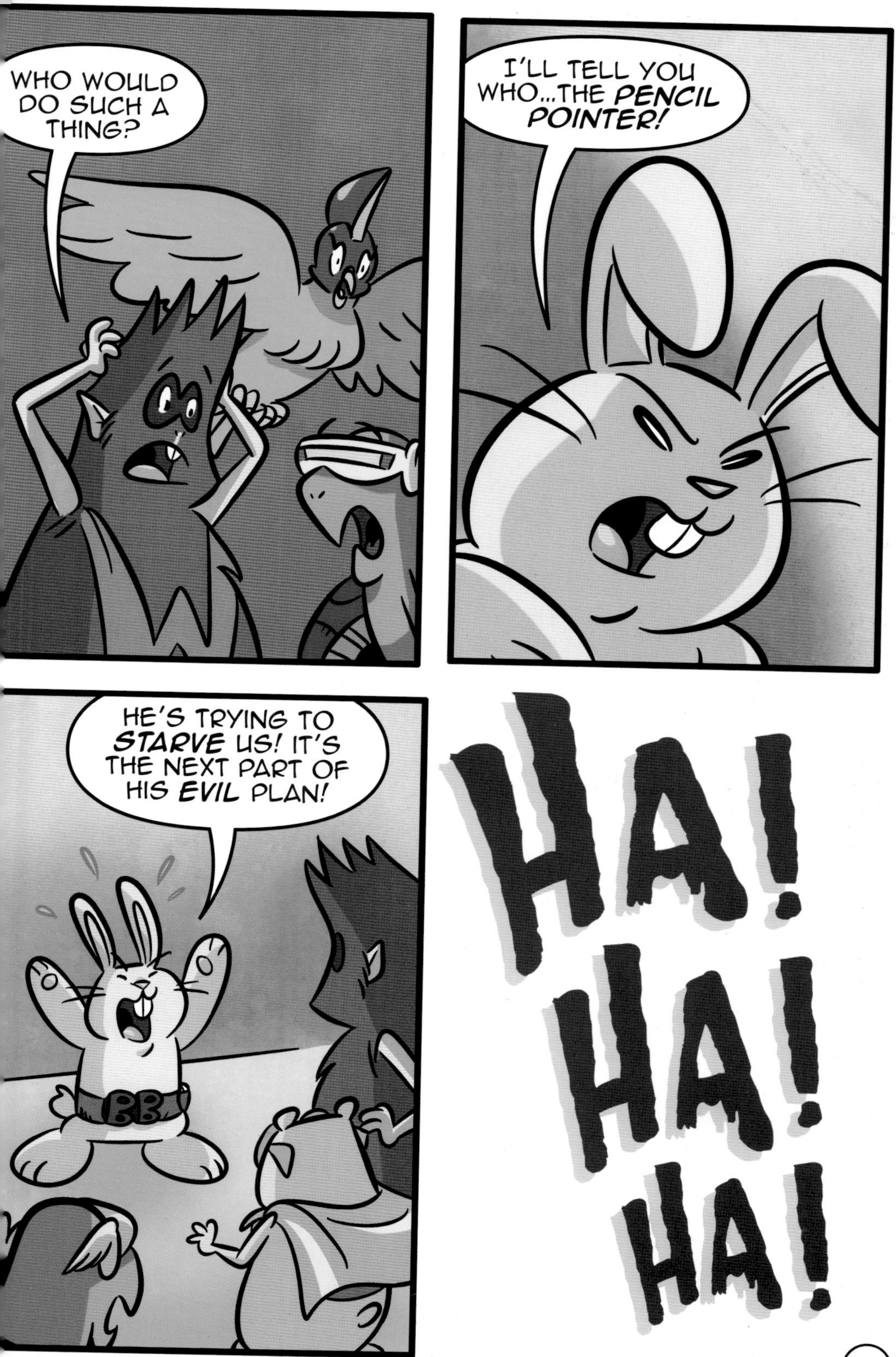
WHO WOULD DO SUCH A THING?
I'LL TELL YOU WHO...THE PENCIL POINTER!
HE'S TRYING TO STARVE US! IT'S THE NEXT PART OF HIS EVIL PLAN!
HA! HA! HA!

TURBO RECOGNIZED THAT *LAUGH.*

I RECOGNIZE THAT LAUGH!

SHOW YOURSELF *WHISKERFACE!*

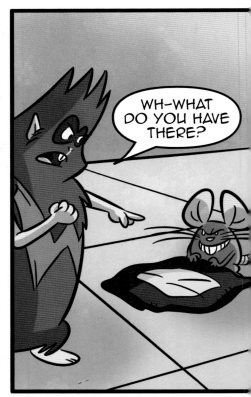

WH—WHAT DO YOU HAVE THERE?

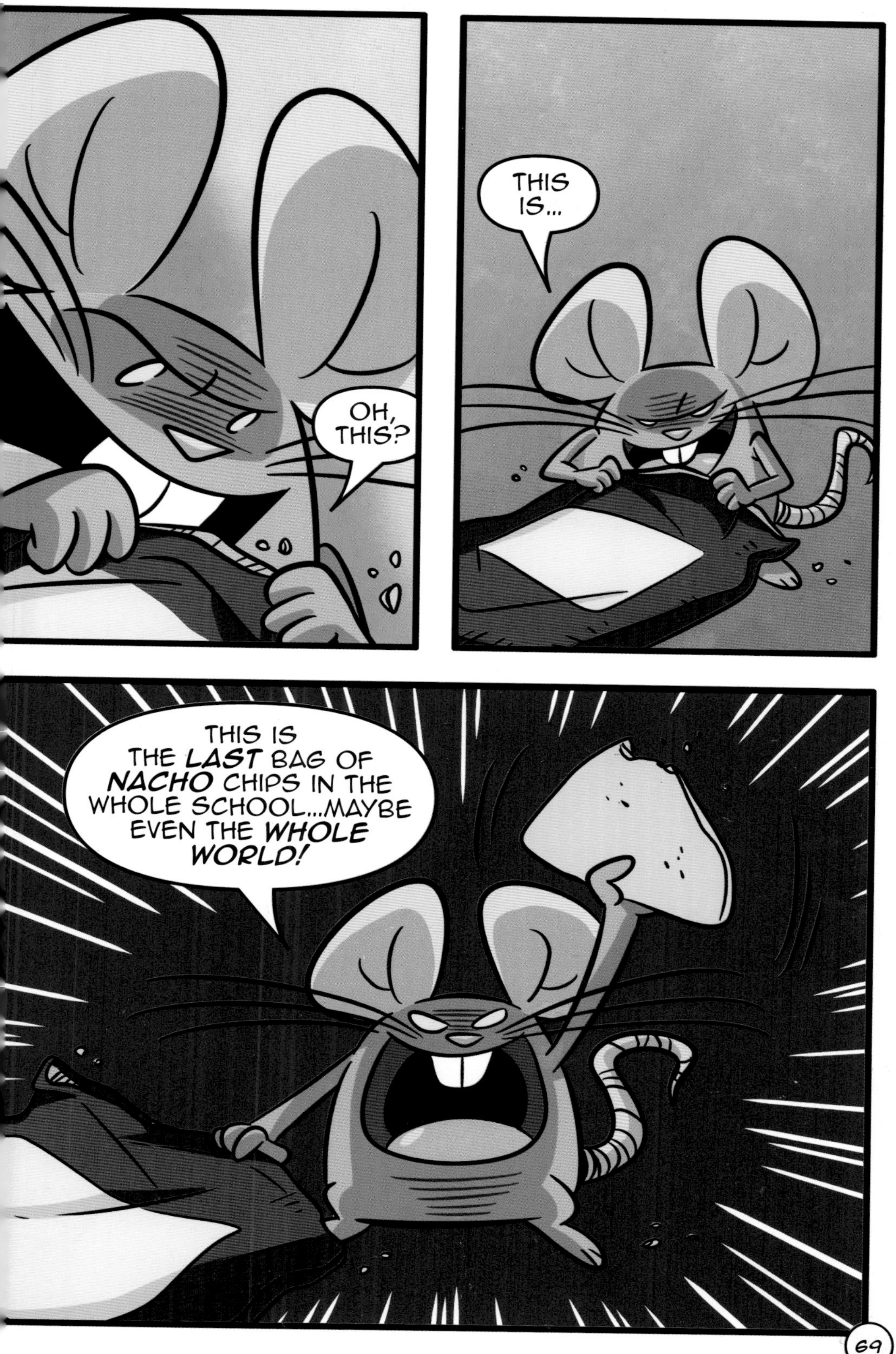
OH, THIS?
THIS IS...
THIS IS THE LAST BAG OF NACHO CHIPS IN THE WHOLE SCHOOL...MAYBE EVEN THE WHOLE WORLD!

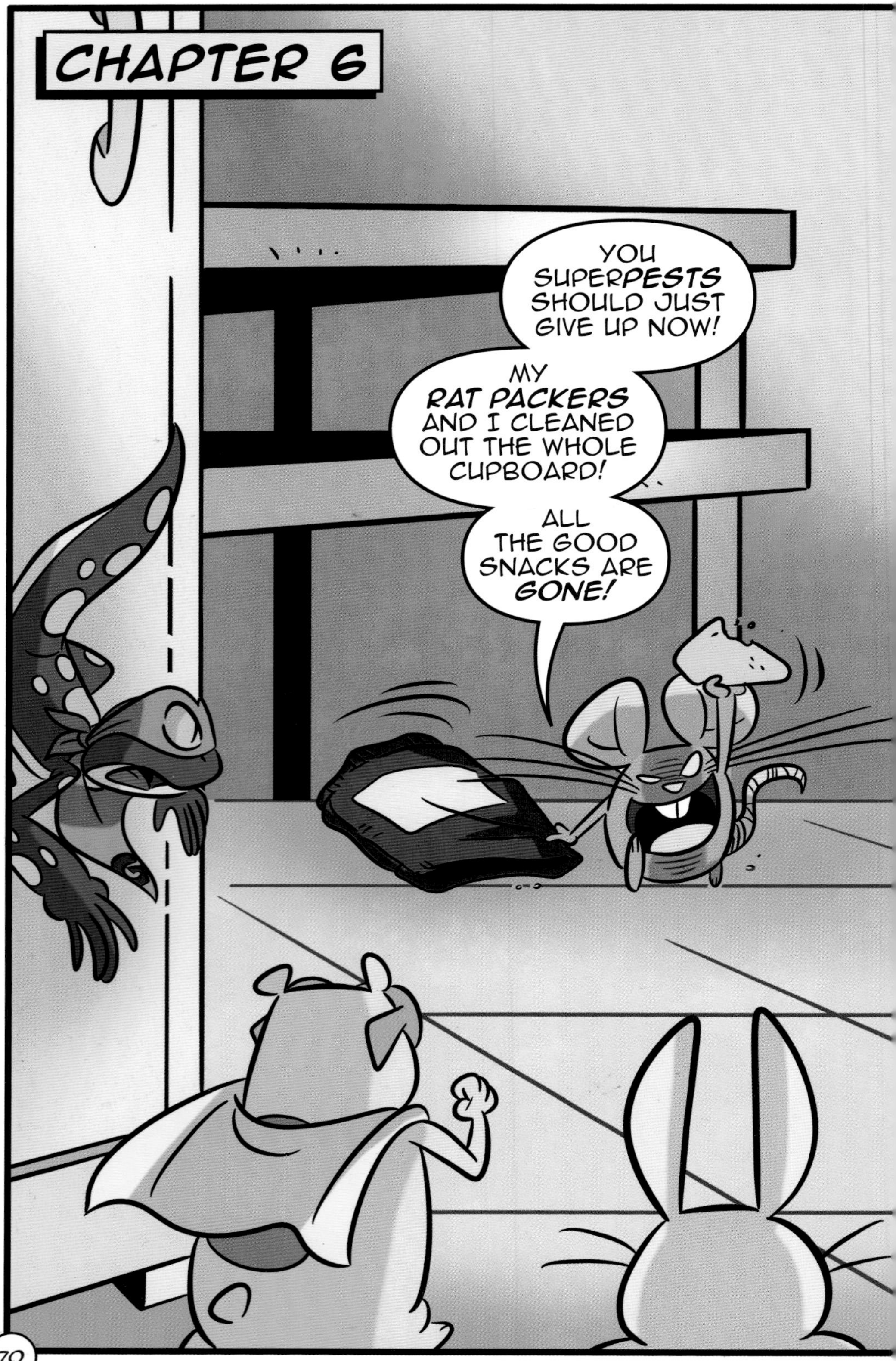
CHAPTER 6
YOU SUPERPESTS SHOULD JUST GIVE UP NOW!
MY RAT PACKERS AND I CLEANED OUT THE WHOLE CUPBOARD!
ALL THE GOOD SNACKS ARE GONE!

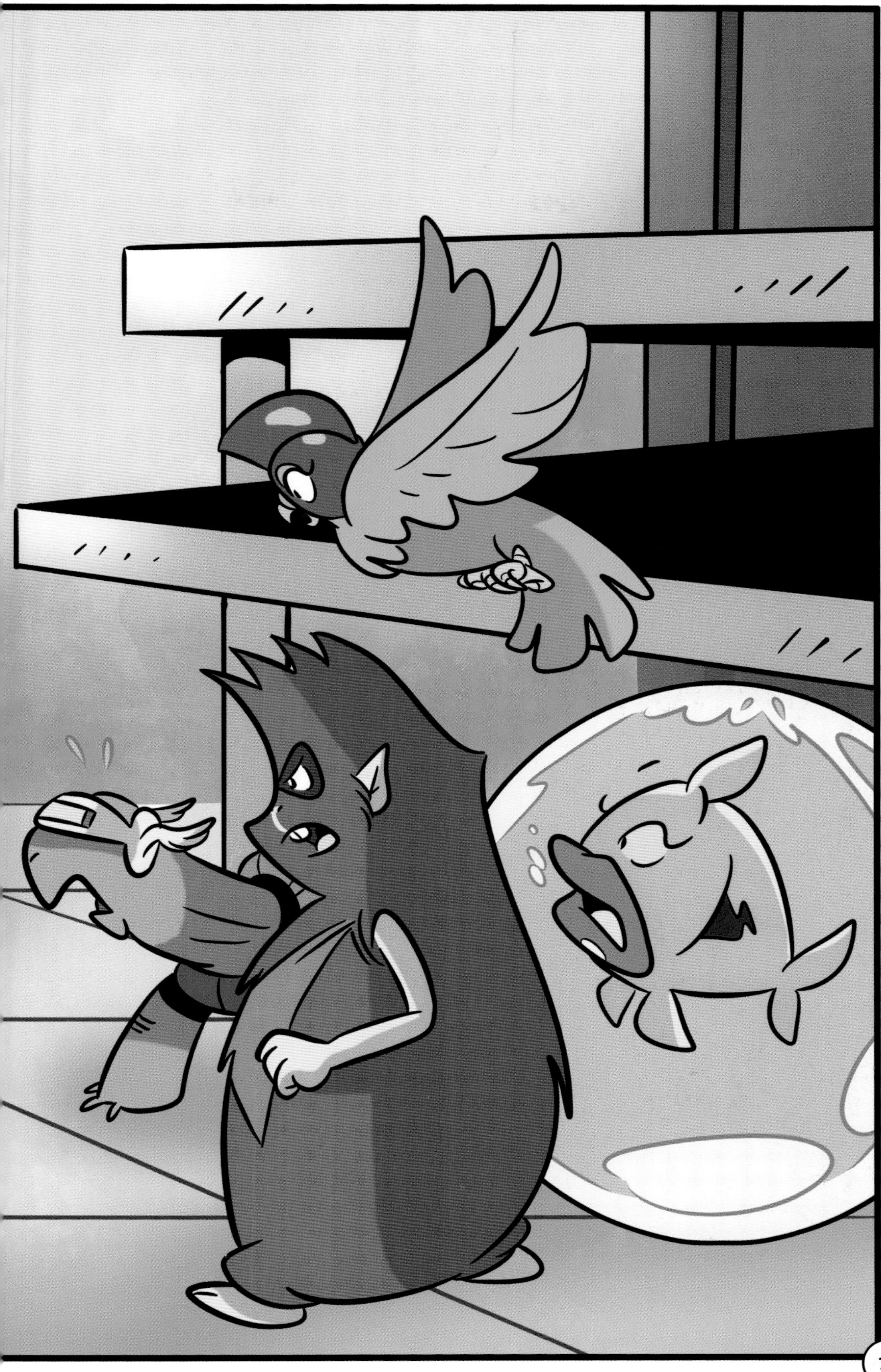

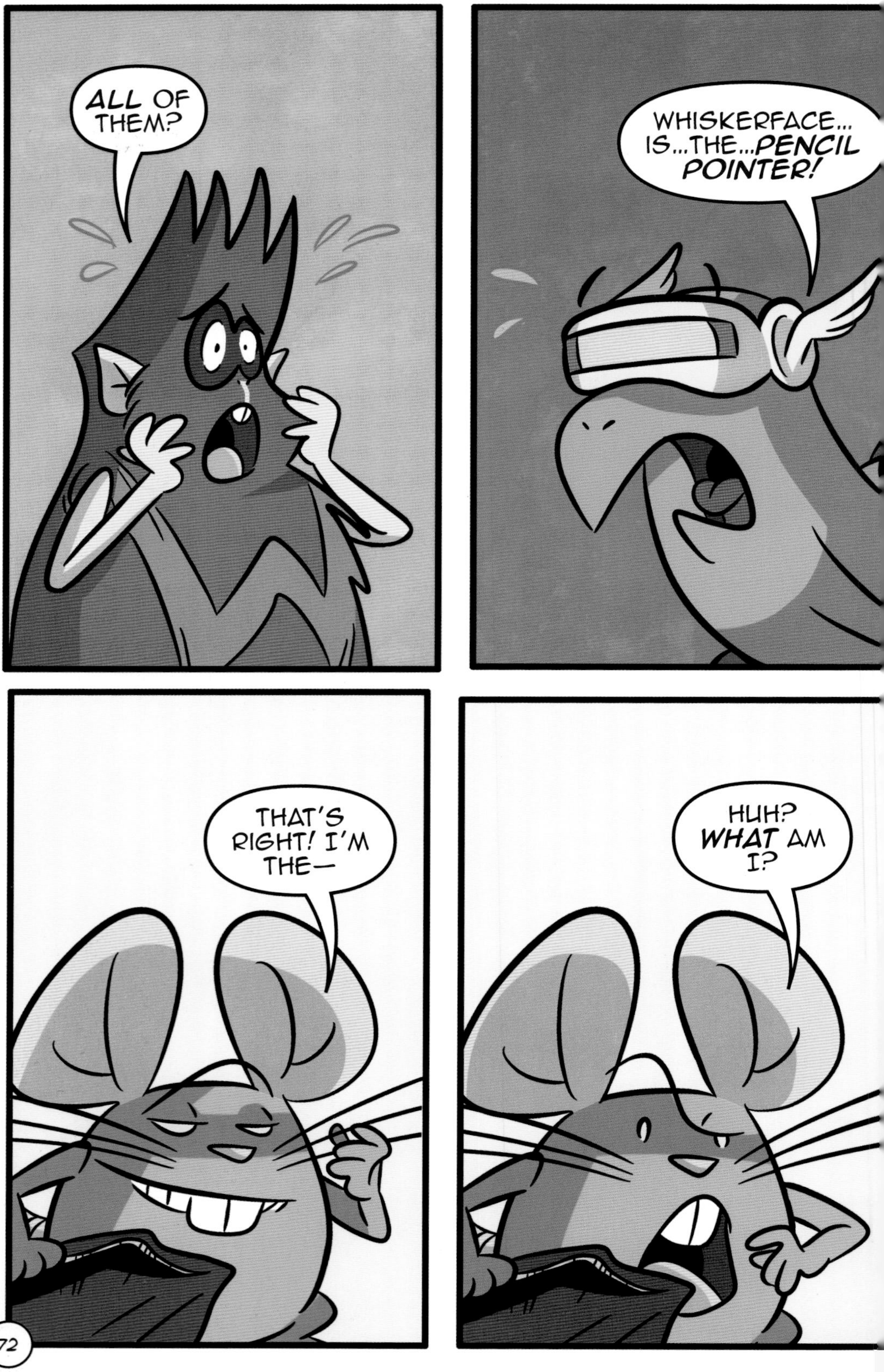
ALL OF THEM?
WHISKERFACE... IS...THE...PENCIL POINTER!
THAT'S RIGHT! I'M THE—
HUH? WHAT AM I?

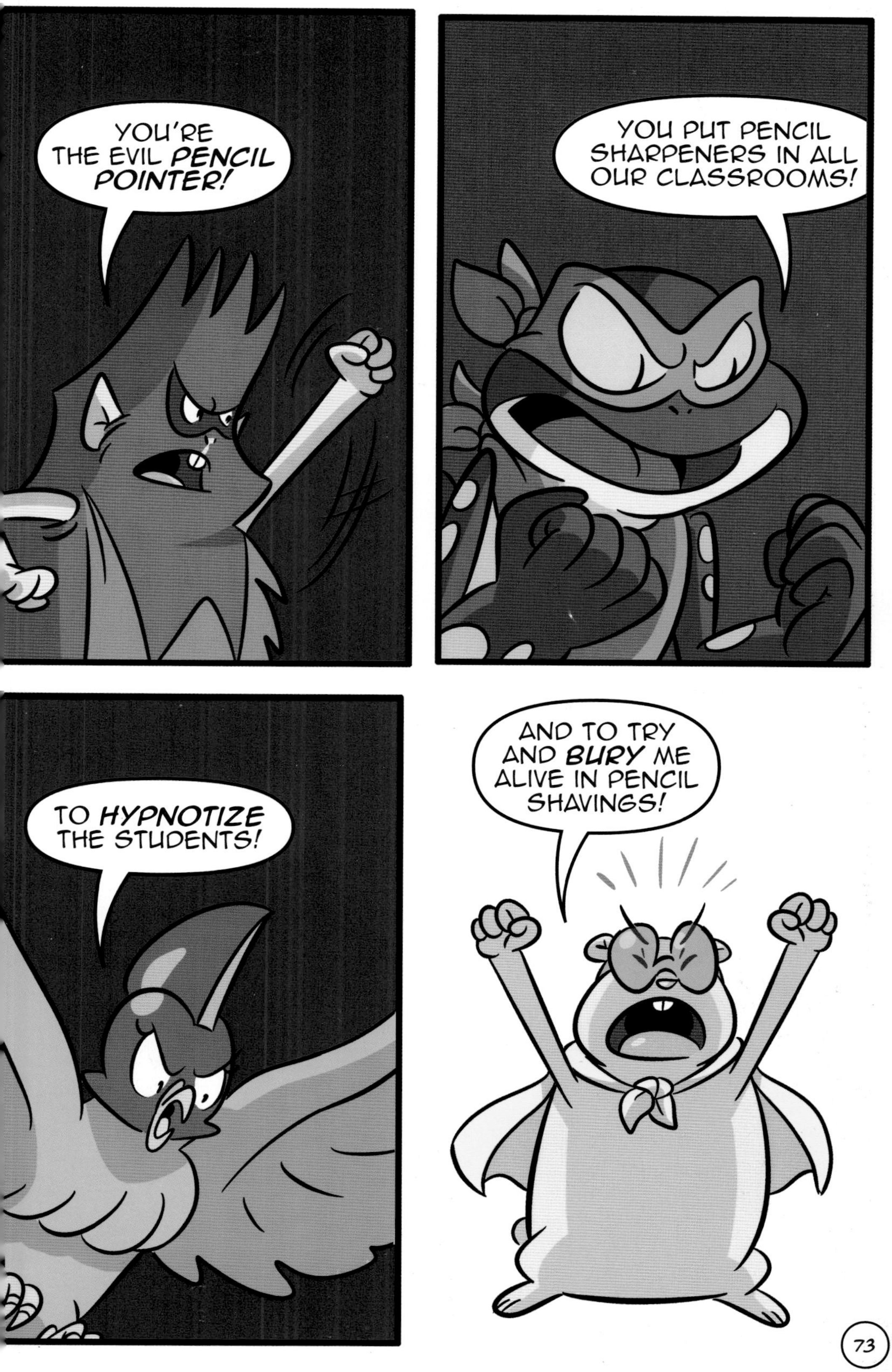
YOU'RE THE EVIL *PENCIL POINTER!*
YOU PUT PENCIL SHARPENERS IN ALL OUR CLASSROOMS!
TO *HYPNOTIZE* THE STUDENTS!
AND TO TRY AND *BURY* ME ALIVE IN PENCIL SHAVINGS!

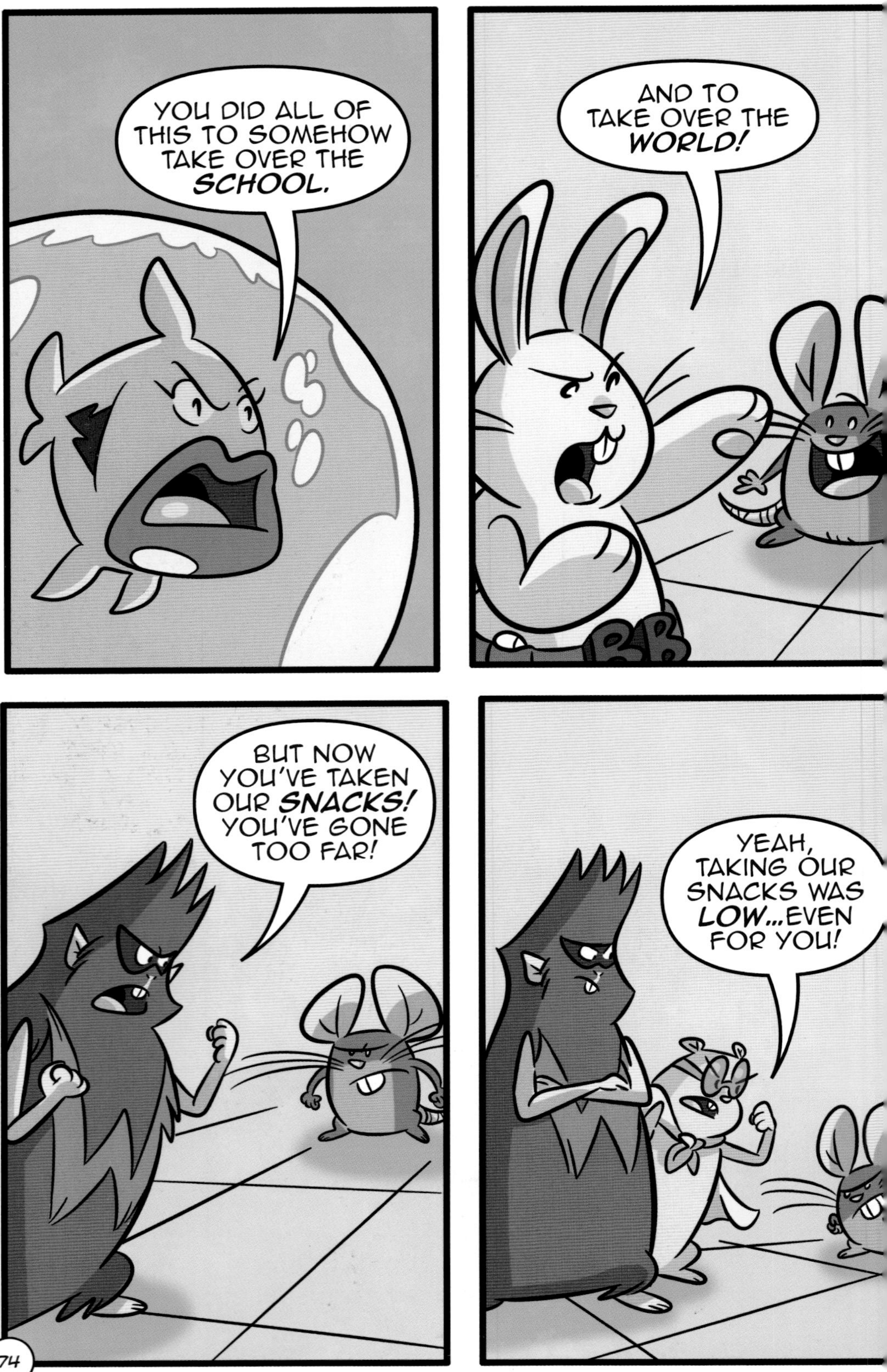
YOU DID ALL OF THIS TO SOMEHOW TAKE OVER THE SCHOOL.
AND TO TAKE OVER THE WORLD!
BB
BUT NOW YOU'VE TAKEN OUR SNACKS! YOU'VE GONE TOO FAR!
YEAH, TAKING OUR SNACKS WAS LOW...EVEN FOR YOU!

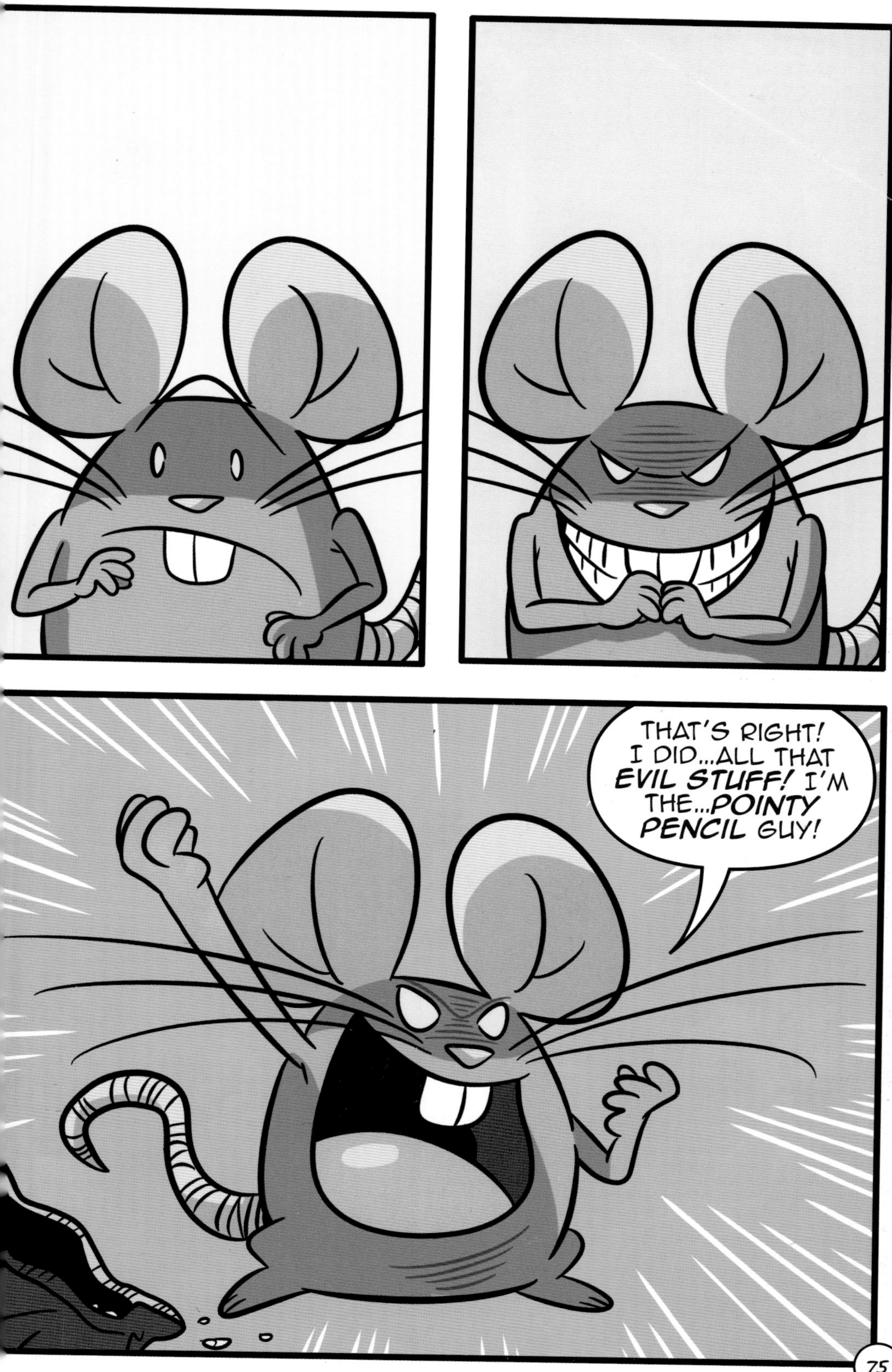
THAT'S RIGHT! I DID...ALL THAT EVIL STUFF! I'M THE...POINTY PENCIL GUY!

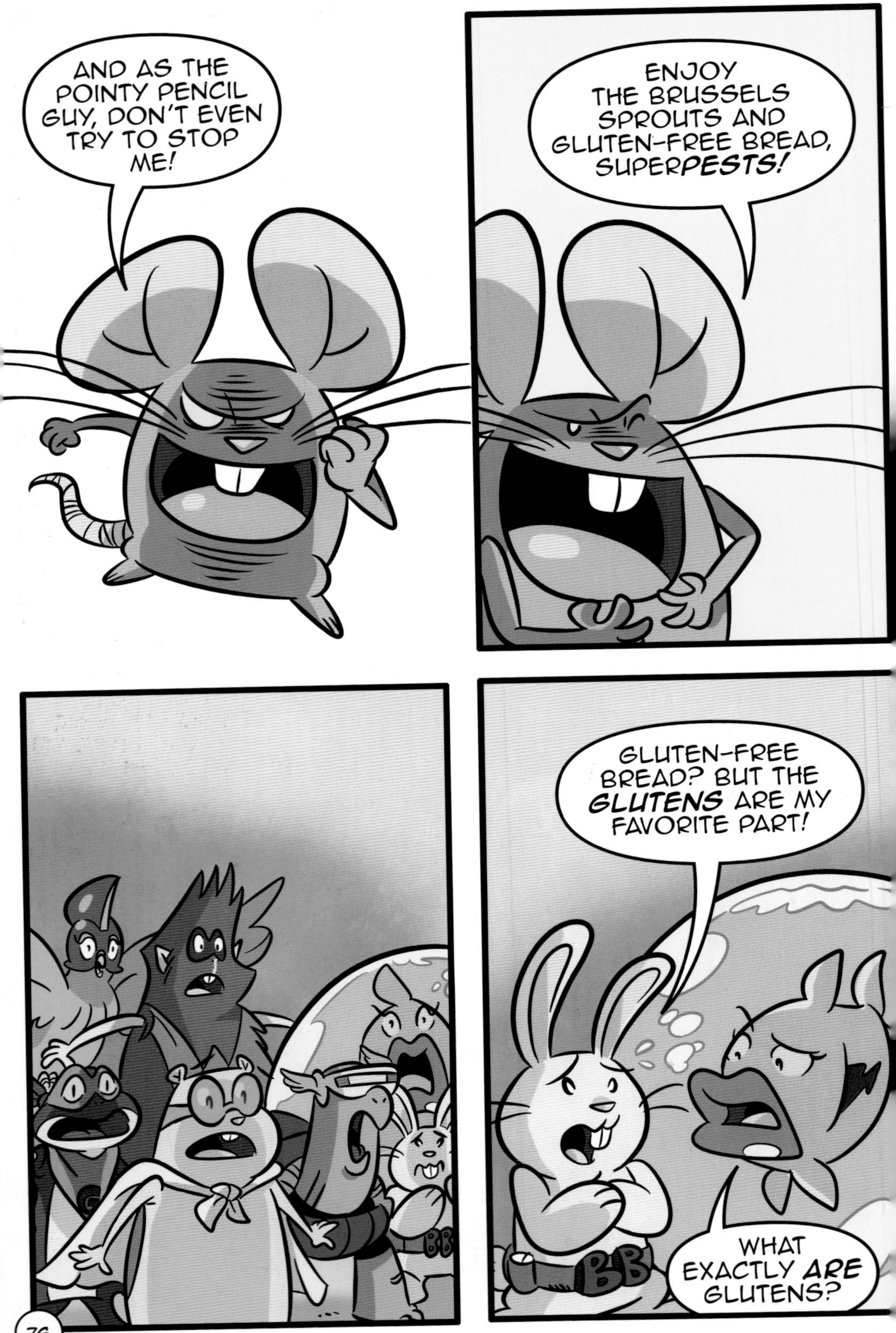
AND AS THE POINTY PENCIL GUY, DON'T EVEN TRY TO STOP ME!
ENJOY THE BRUSSELS SPROUTS AND GLUTEN-FREE BREAD, SUPER*PESTS!*
GLUTEN-FREE BREAD? BUT THE *GLUTENS* ARE MY FAVORITE PART!
WHAT EXACTLY *ARE* GLUTENS?

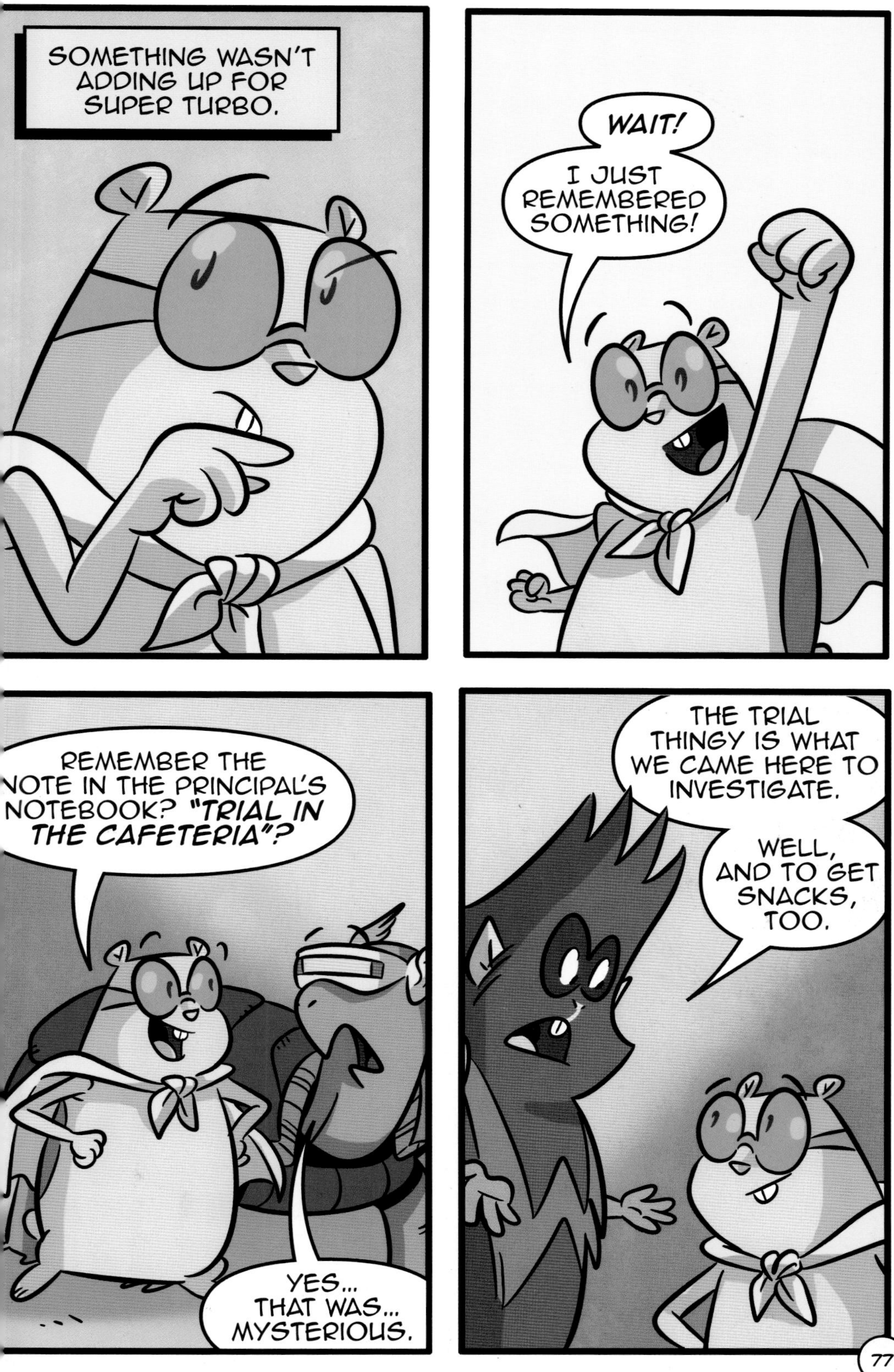

SOMETHING WASN'T ADDING UP FOR SUPER TURBO.
WAIT!
I JUST REMEMBERED SOMETHING!
REMEMBER THE NOTE IN THE PRINCIPAL'S NOTEBOOK? "TRIAL IN THE CAFETERIA"?
YES... THAT WAS... MYSTERIOUS.
THE TRIAL THINGY IS WHAT WE CAME HERE TO INVESTIGATE.
WELL, AND TO GET SNACKS, TOO.

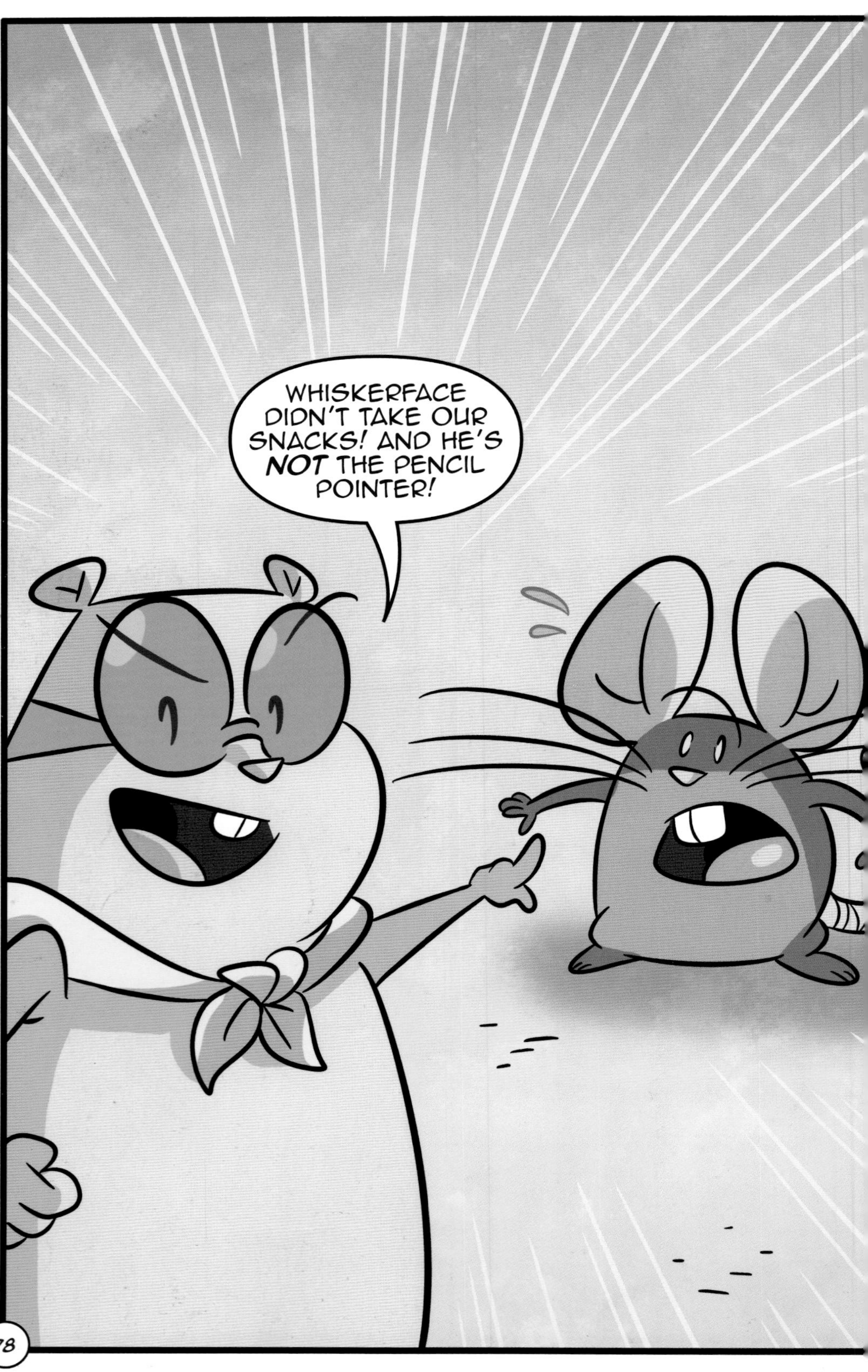
WHISKERFACE DIDN'T TAKE OUR SNACKS! AND HE'S **NOT** THE PENCIL POINTER!

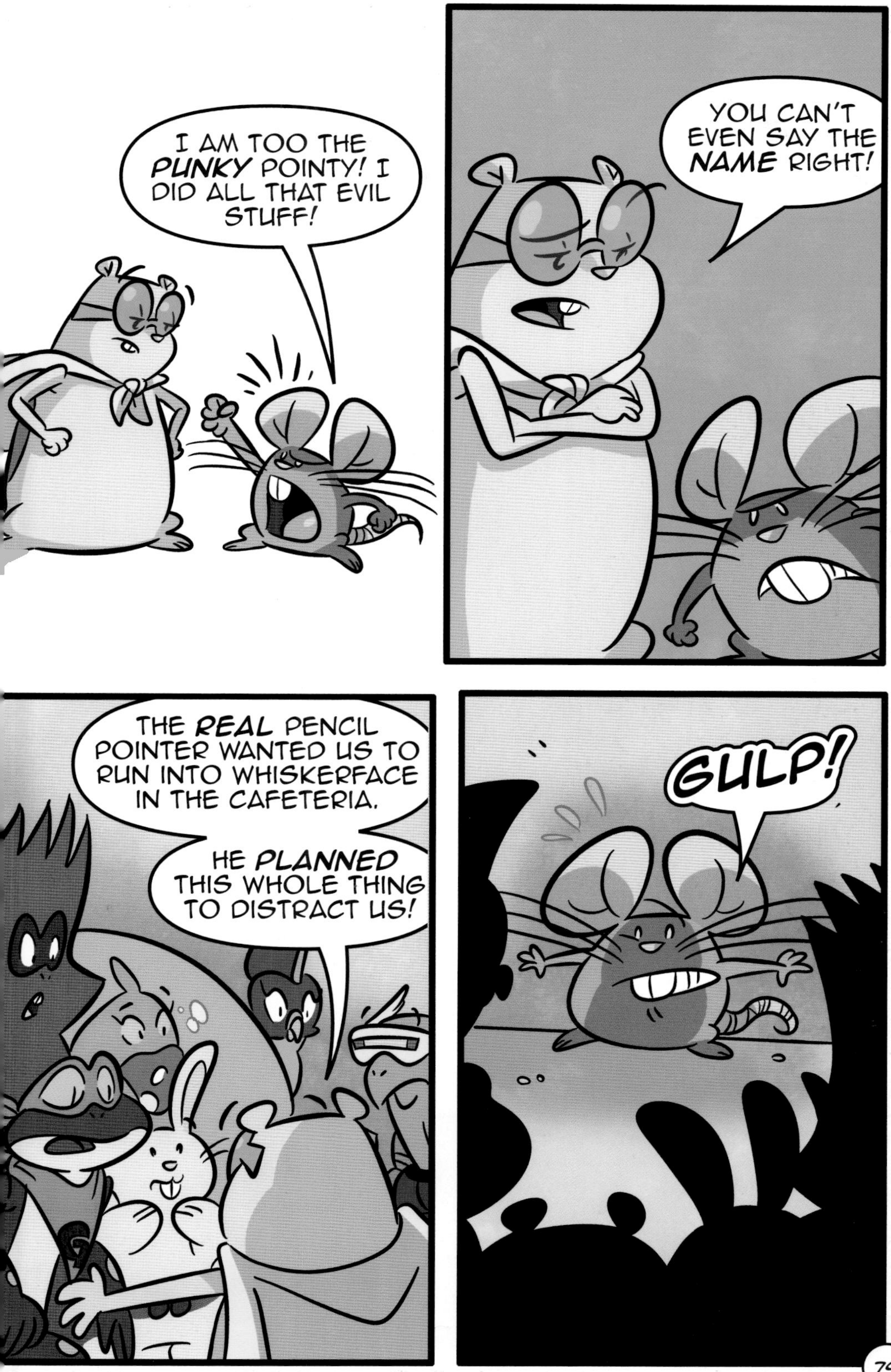
I AM TOO THE PUNKY POINTY! I DID ALL THAT EVIL STUFF!
YOU CAN'T EVEN SAY THE NAME RIGHT!
THE REAL PENCIL POINTER WANTED US TO RUN INTO WHISKERFACE IN THE CAFETERIA.
HE PLANNED THIS WHOLE THING TO DISTRACT US!
GULP!

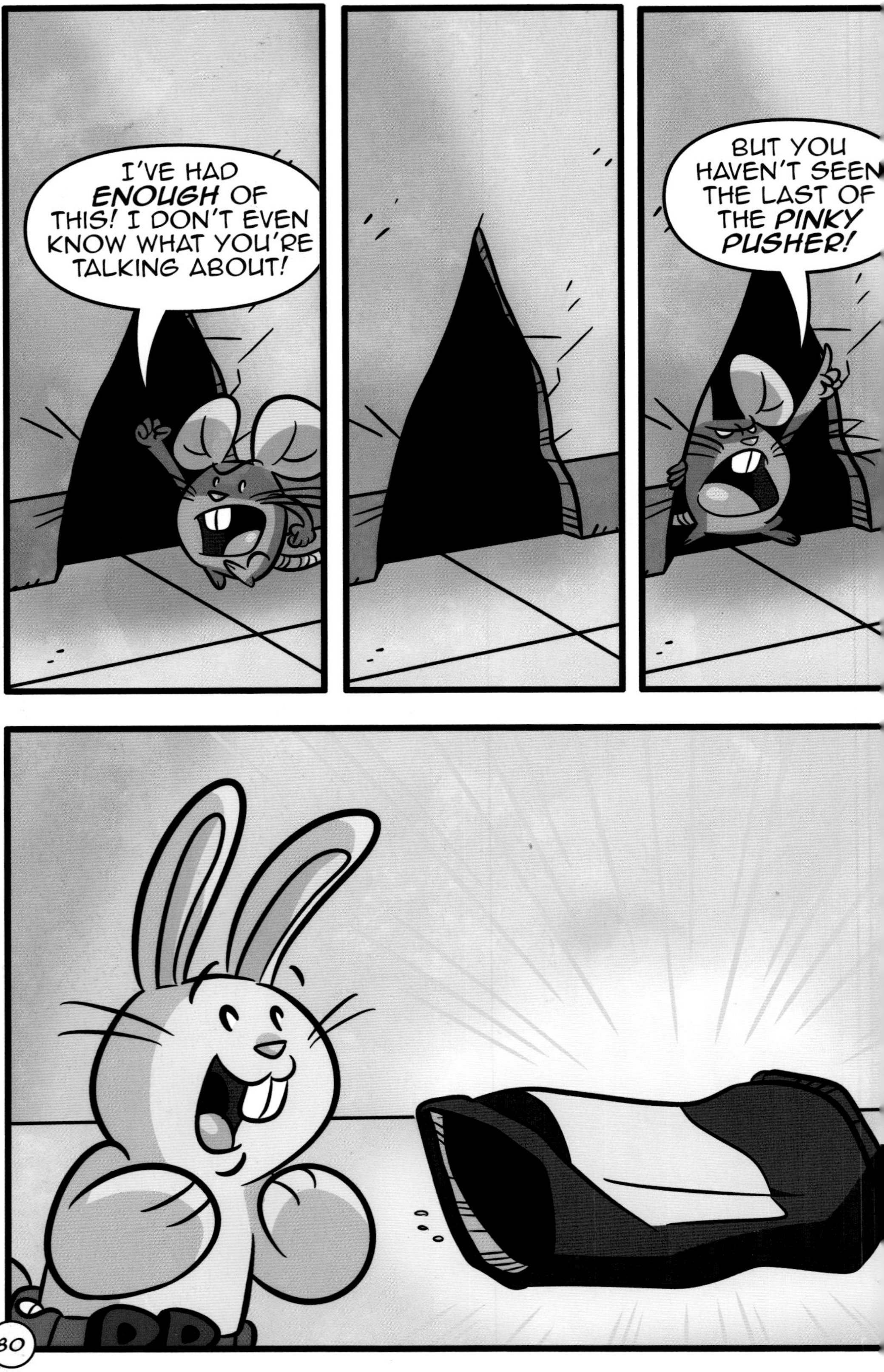
I'VE HAD ENOUGH OF THIS! I DON'T EVEN KNOW WHAT YOU'RE TALKING ABOUT!
BUT YOU HAVEN'T SEEN THE LAST OF THE PINKY PUSHER!

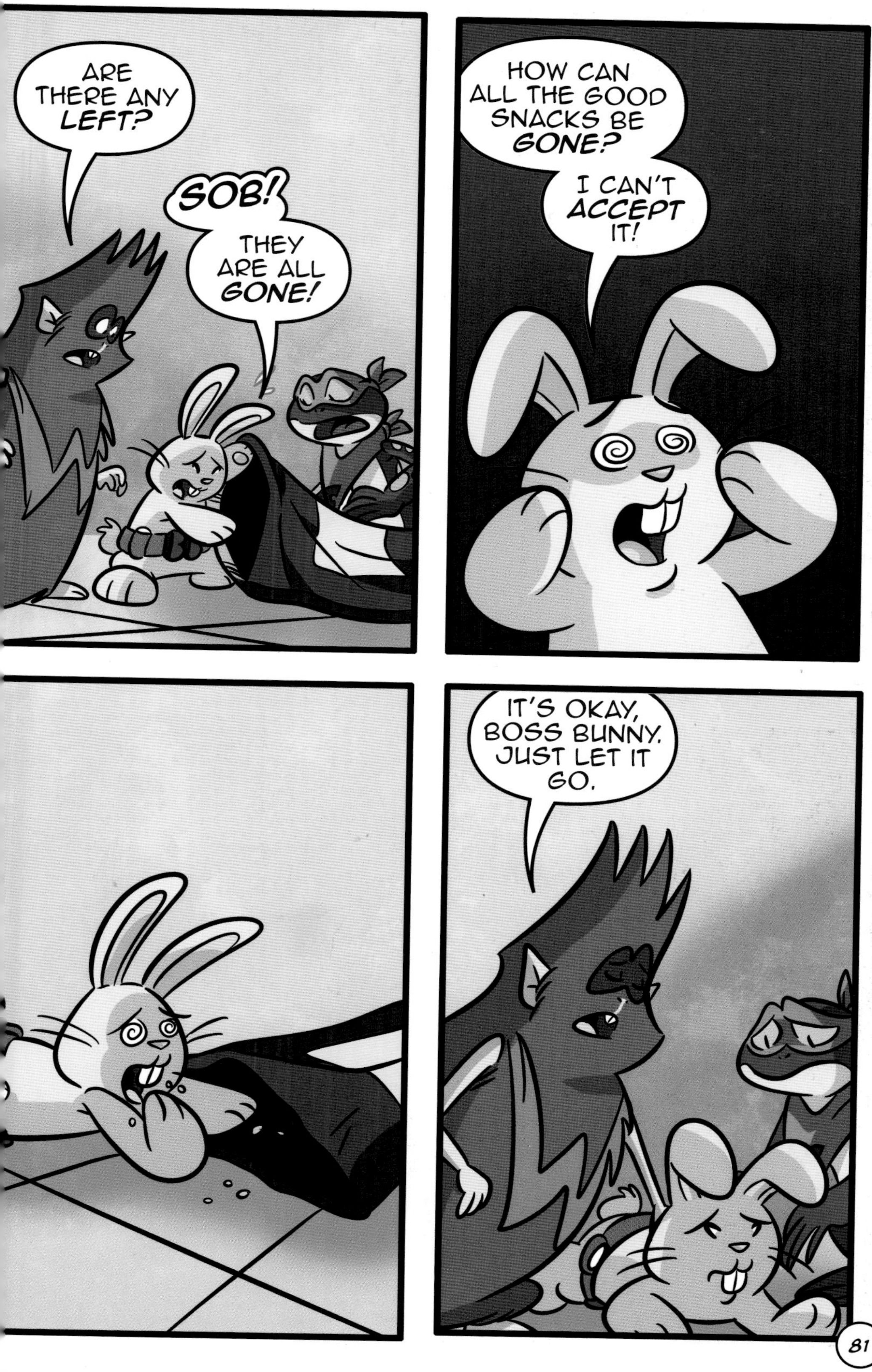
ARE THERE ANY LEFT?
SOB!
THEY ARE ALL GONE!
HOW CAN ALL THE GOOD SNACKS BE GONE?
I CAN'T ACCEPT IT!
IT'S OKAY, BOSS BUNNY. JUST LET IT GO.

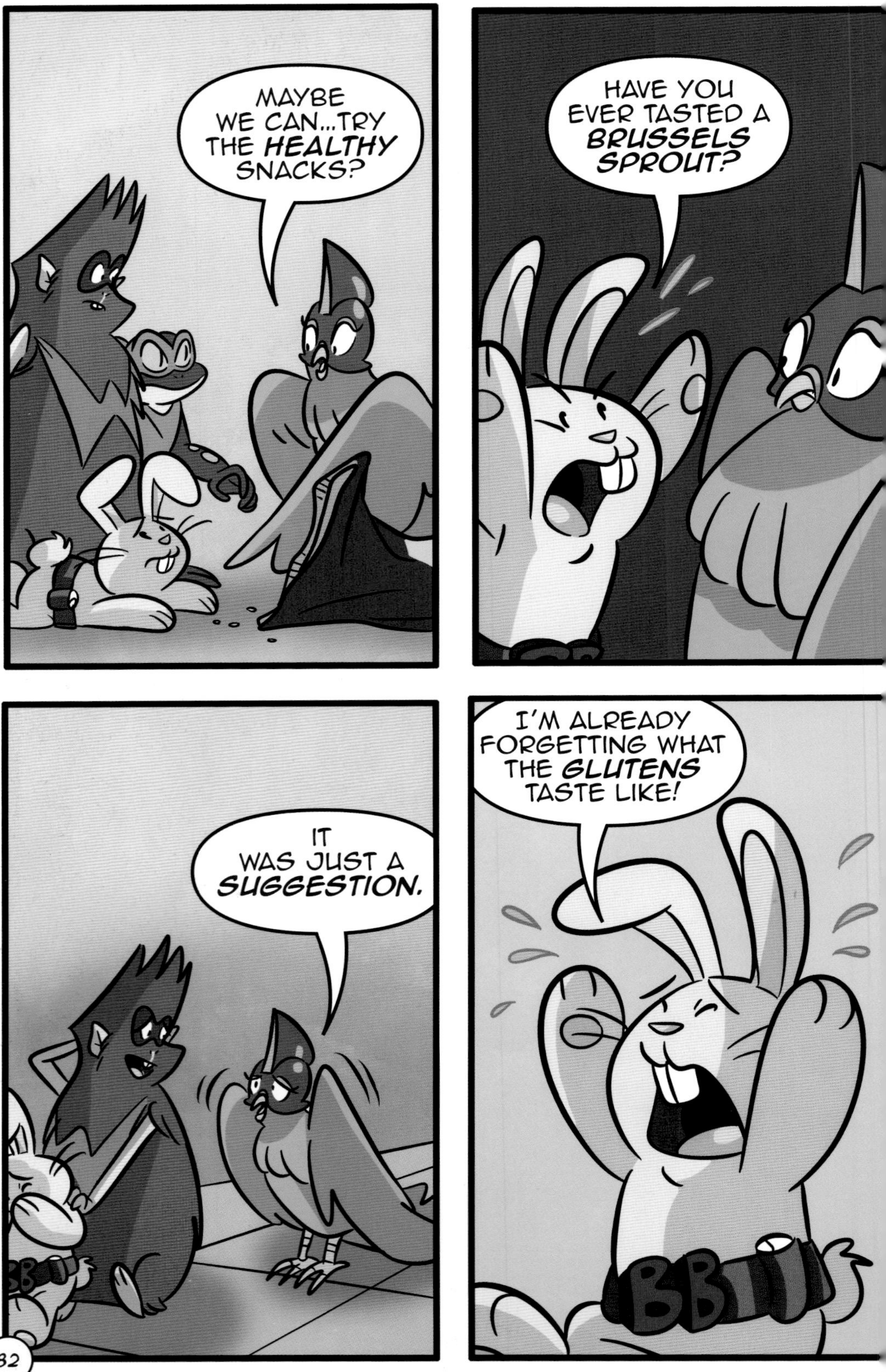
MAYBE WE CAN...TRY THE HEALTHY SNACKS?
HAVE YOU EVER TASTED A BRUSSELS SPROUT?
IT WAS JUST A SUGGESTION.
I'M ALREADY FORGETTING WHAT THE GLUTENS TASTE LIKE!
BB

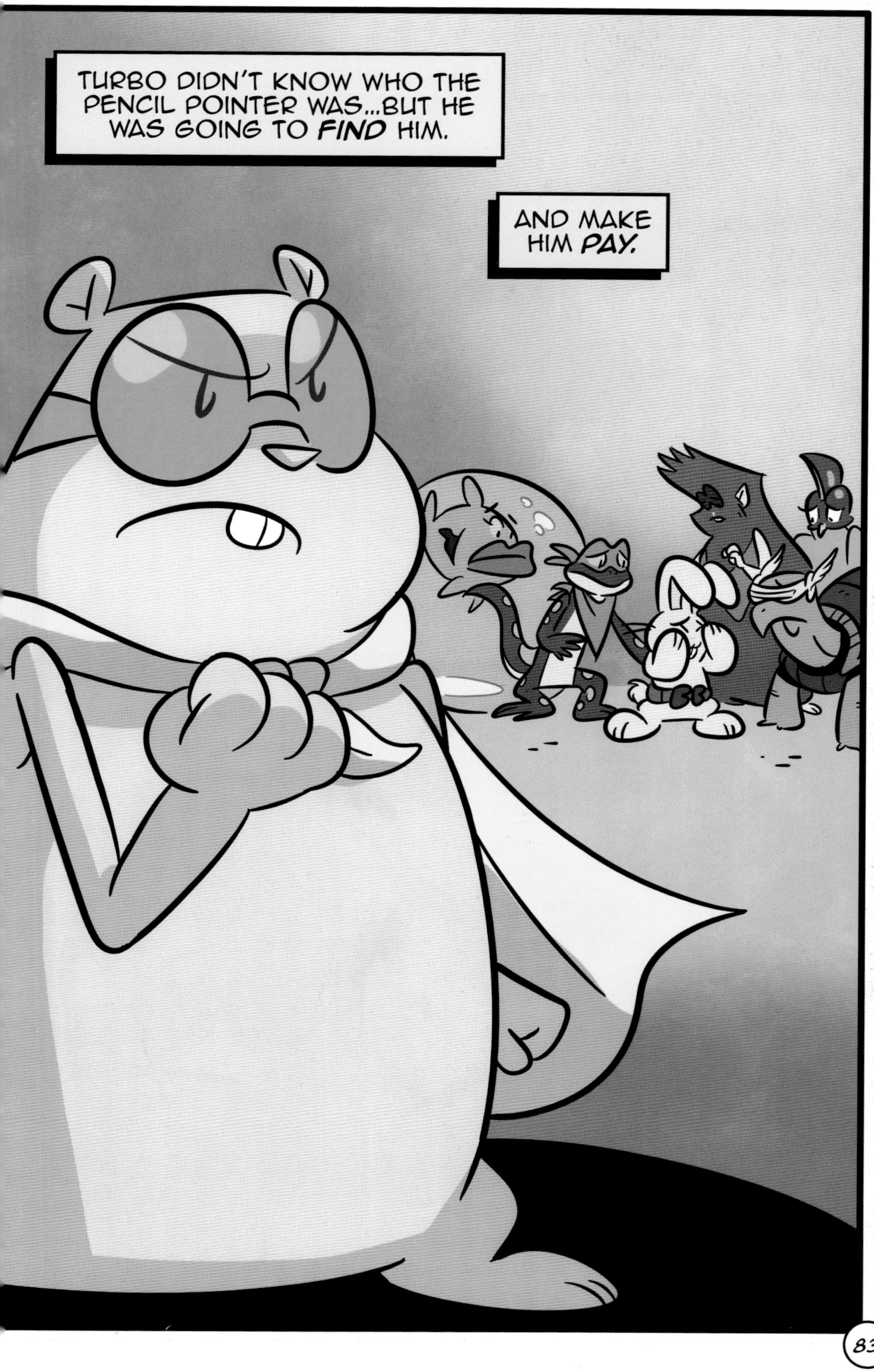
TURBO DIDN'T KNOW WHO THE PENCIL POINTER WAS...BUT HE WAS GOING TO FIND HIM.
AND MAKE HIM PAY.

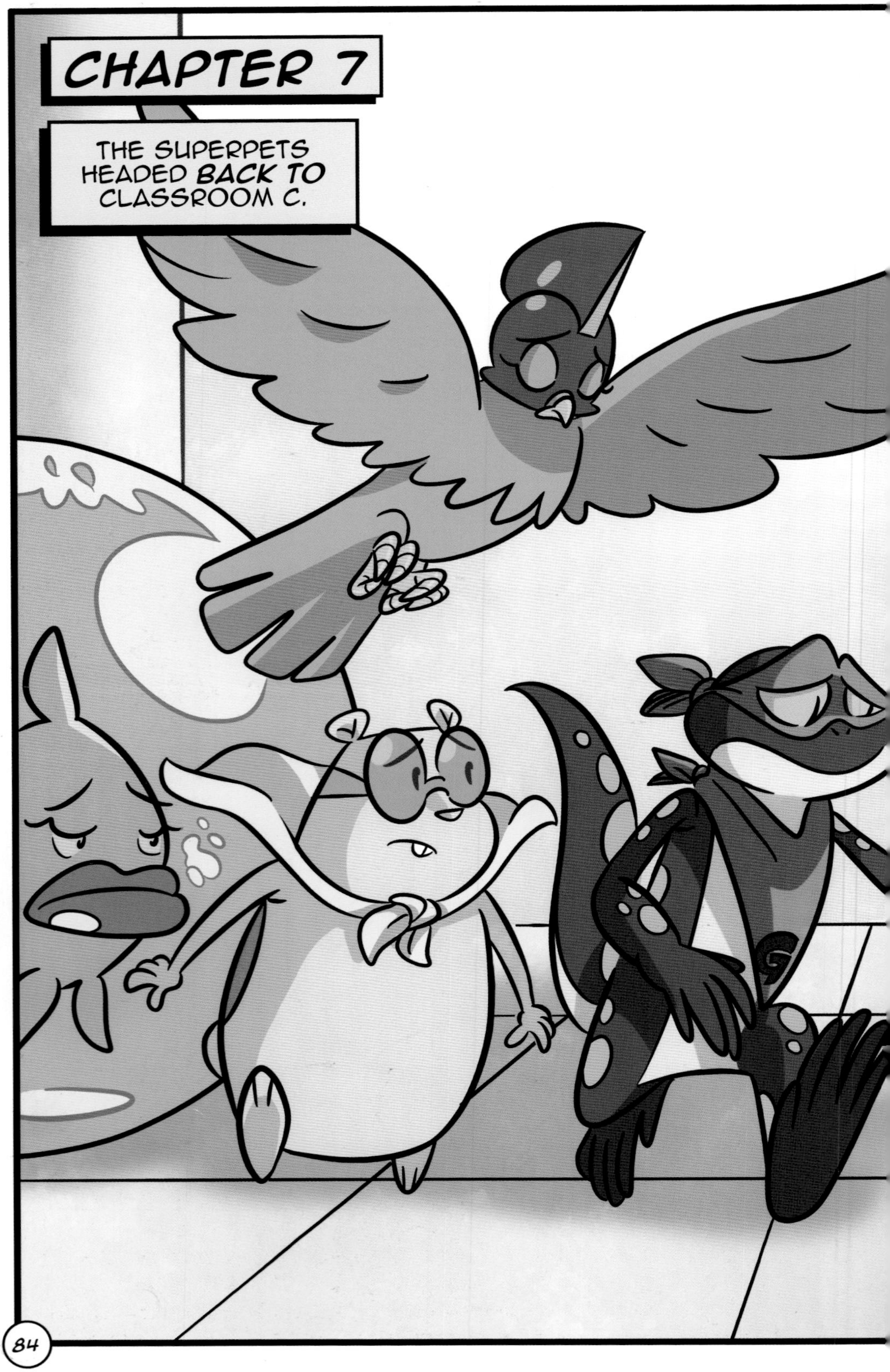
CHAPTER 7
THE SUPERPETS HEADED BACK TO CLASSROOM C.

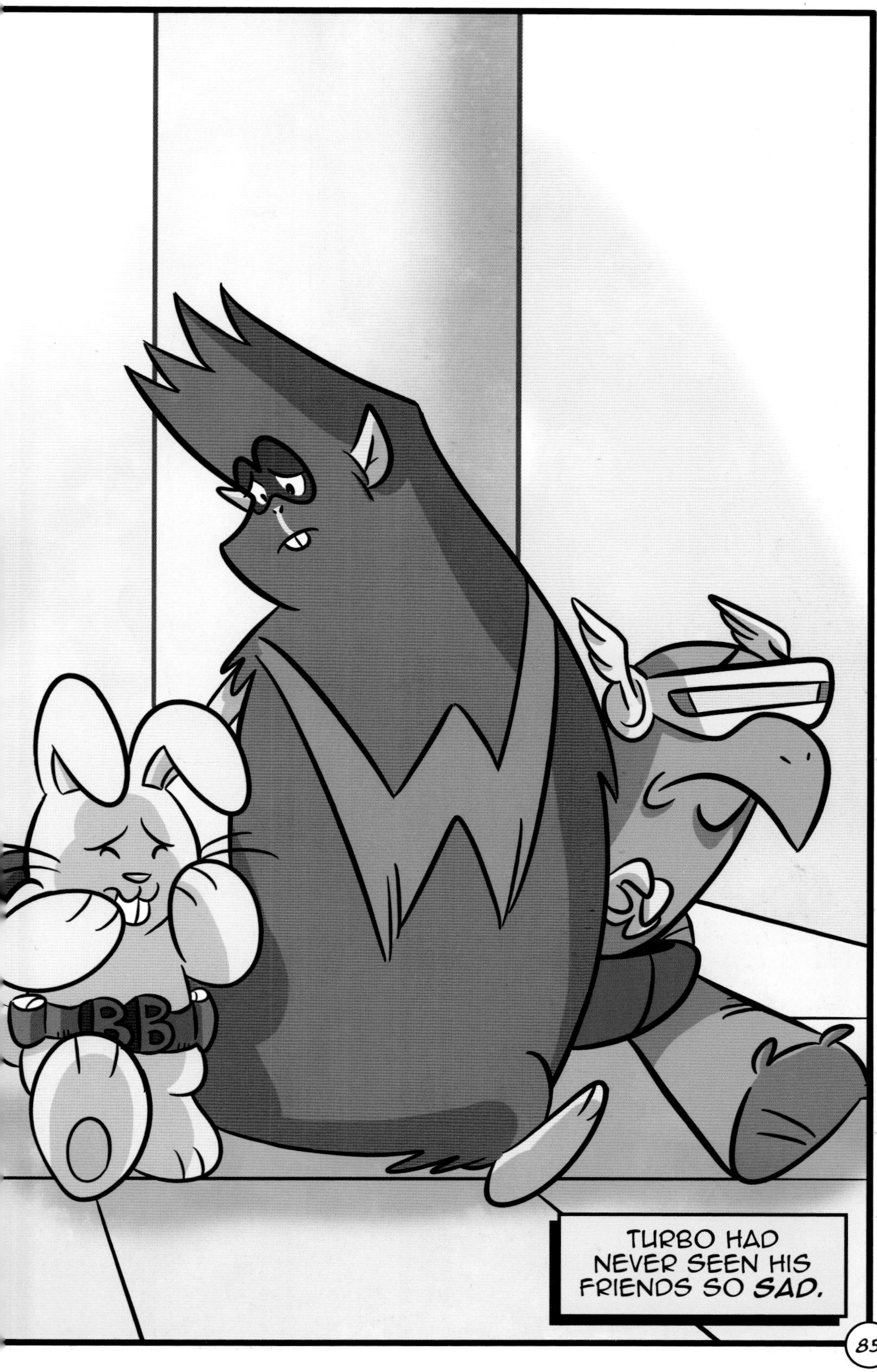
BB
TURBO HAD NEVER SEEN HIS FRIENDS SO *SAD.*

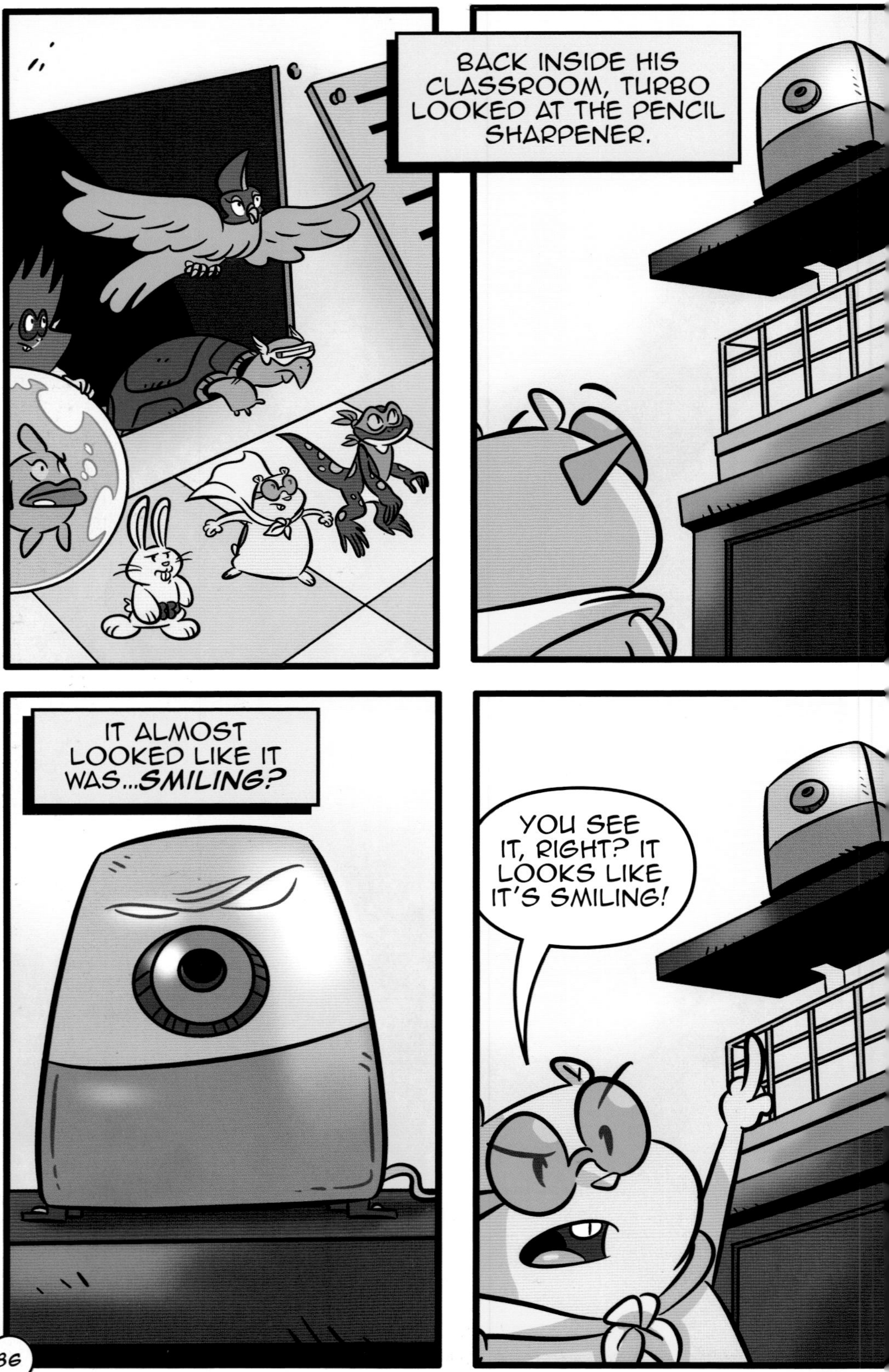
BACK INSIDE HIS CLASSROOM, TURBO LOOKED AT THE PENCIL SHARPENER.
IT ALMOST LOOKED LIKE IT WAS...SMILING?
YOU SEE IT, RIGHT? IT LOOKS LIKE IT'S SMILING!

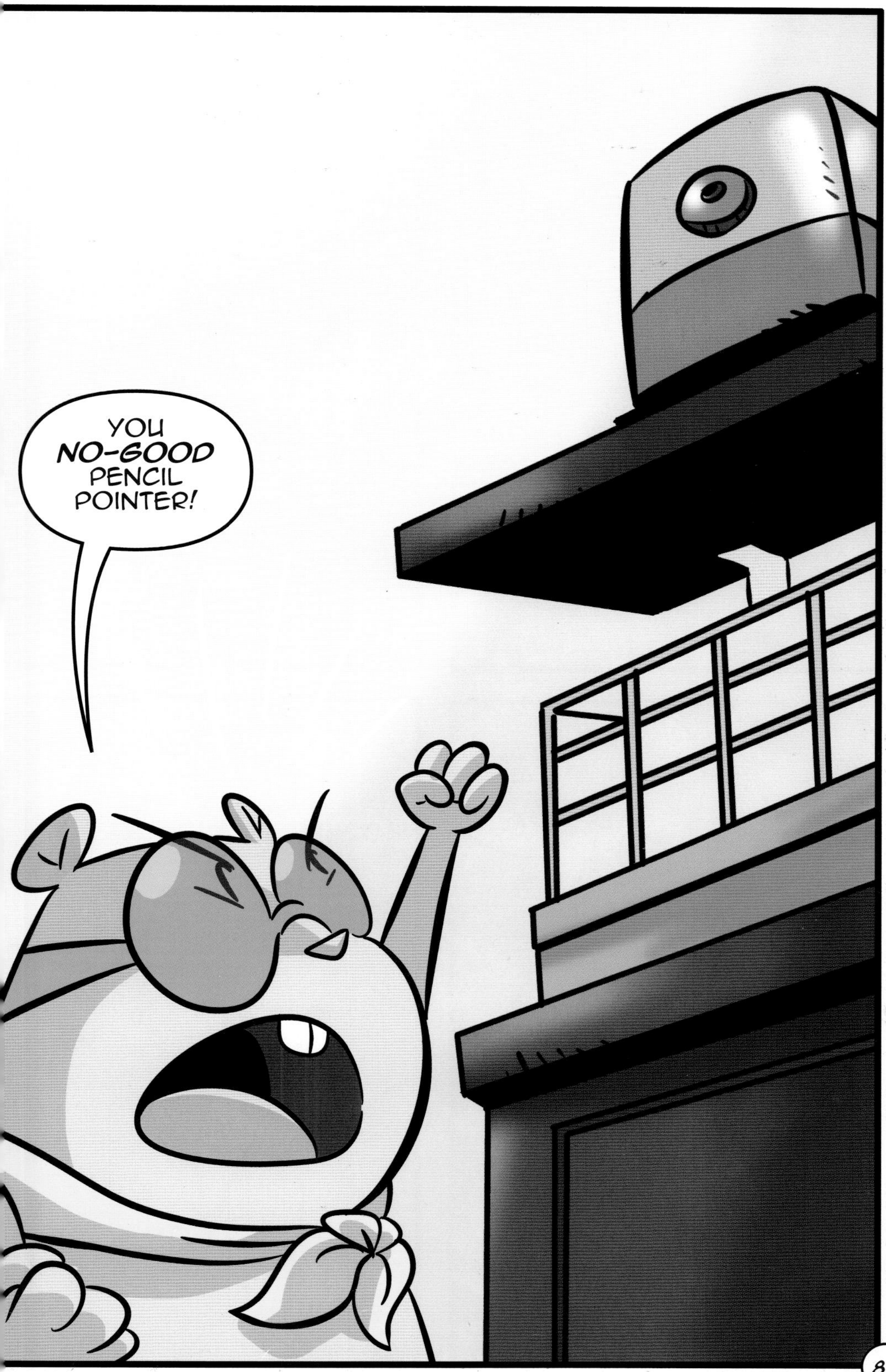
YOU *NO-GOOD* PENCIL POINTER!

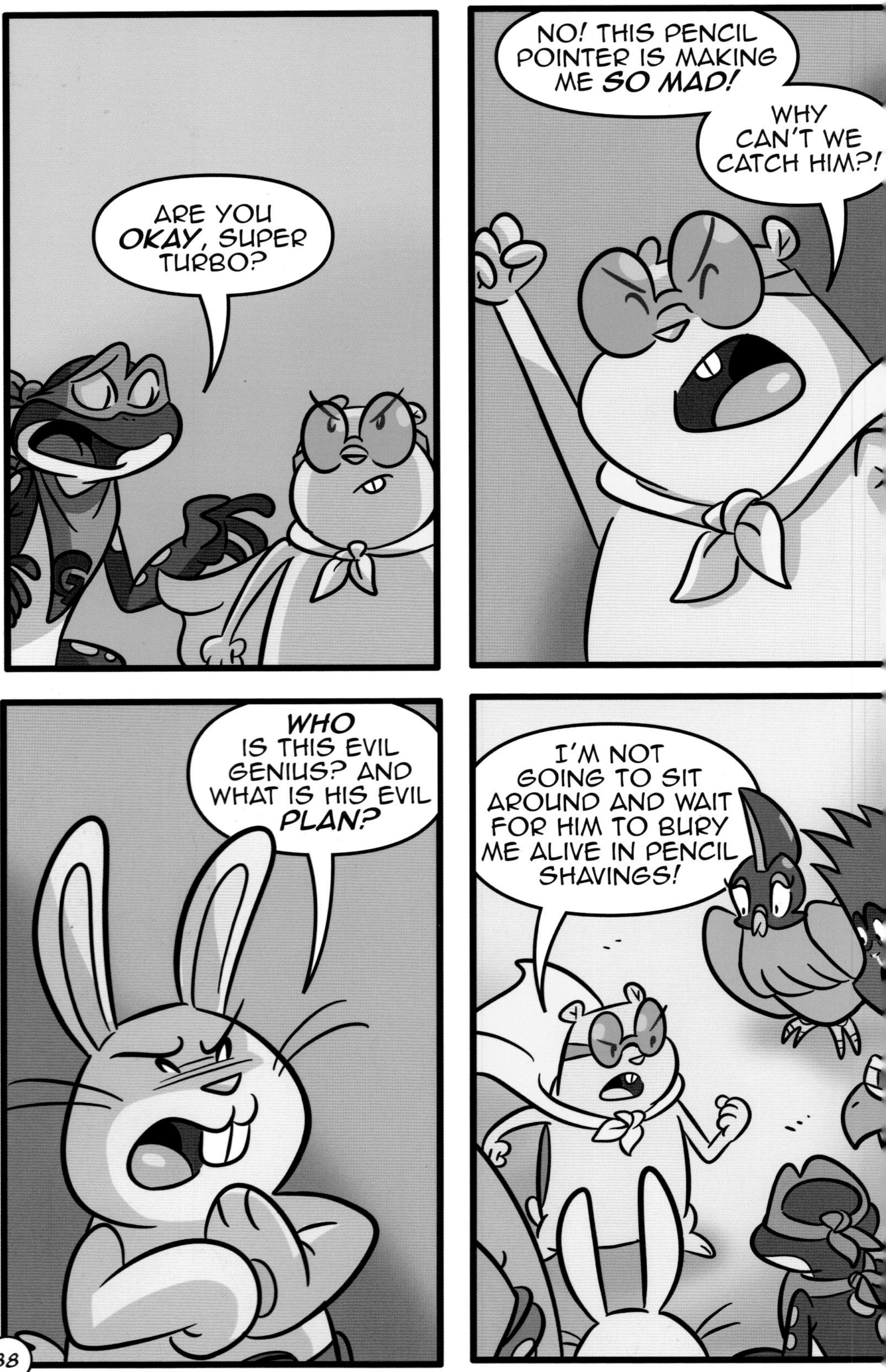
ARE YOU OKAY, SUPER TURBO?
NO! THIS PENCIL POINTER IS MAKING ME SO MAD!
WHY CAN'T WE CATCH HIM?!
WHO IS THIS EVIL GENIUS? AND WHAT IS HIS EVIL PLAN?
I'M NOT GOING TO SIT AROUND AND WAIT FOR HIM TO BURY ME ALIVE IN PENCIL SHAVINGS!

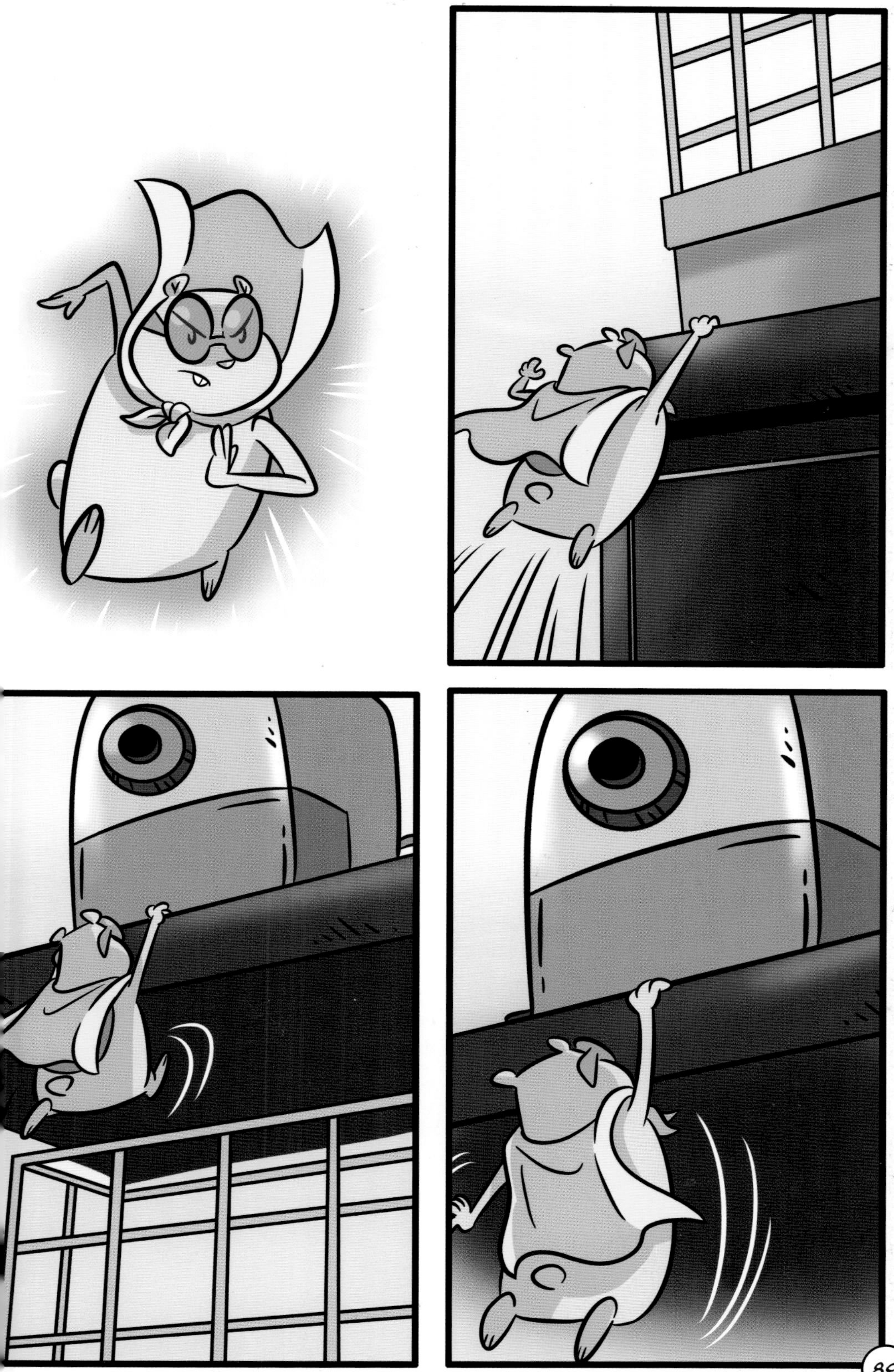

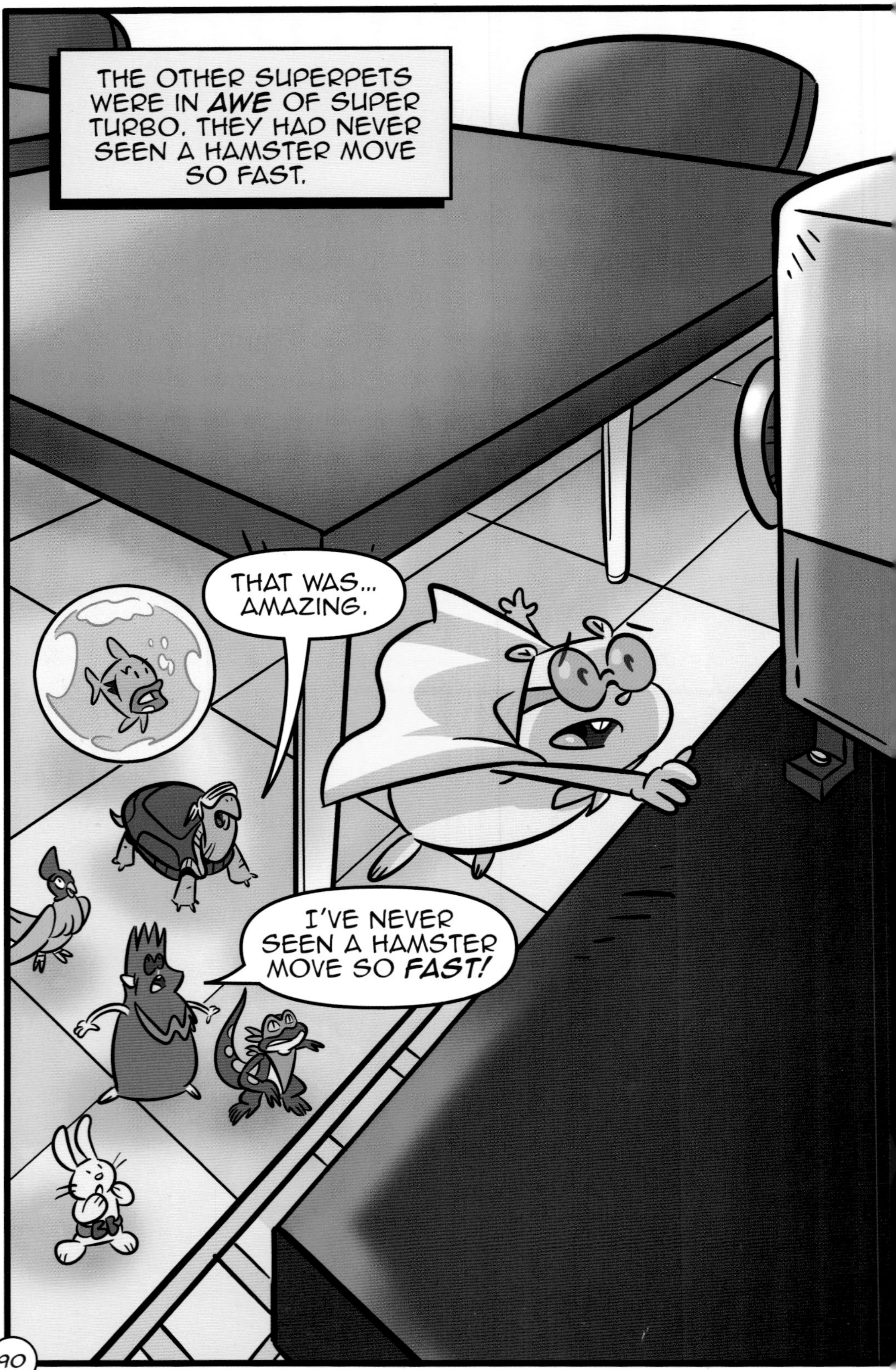
THE OTHER SUPERPETS WERE IN AWE OF SUPER TURBO. THEY HAD NEVER SEEN A HAMSTER MOVE SO FAST.
THAT WAS... AMAZING.
I'VE NEVER SEEN A HAMSTER MOVE SO FAST!

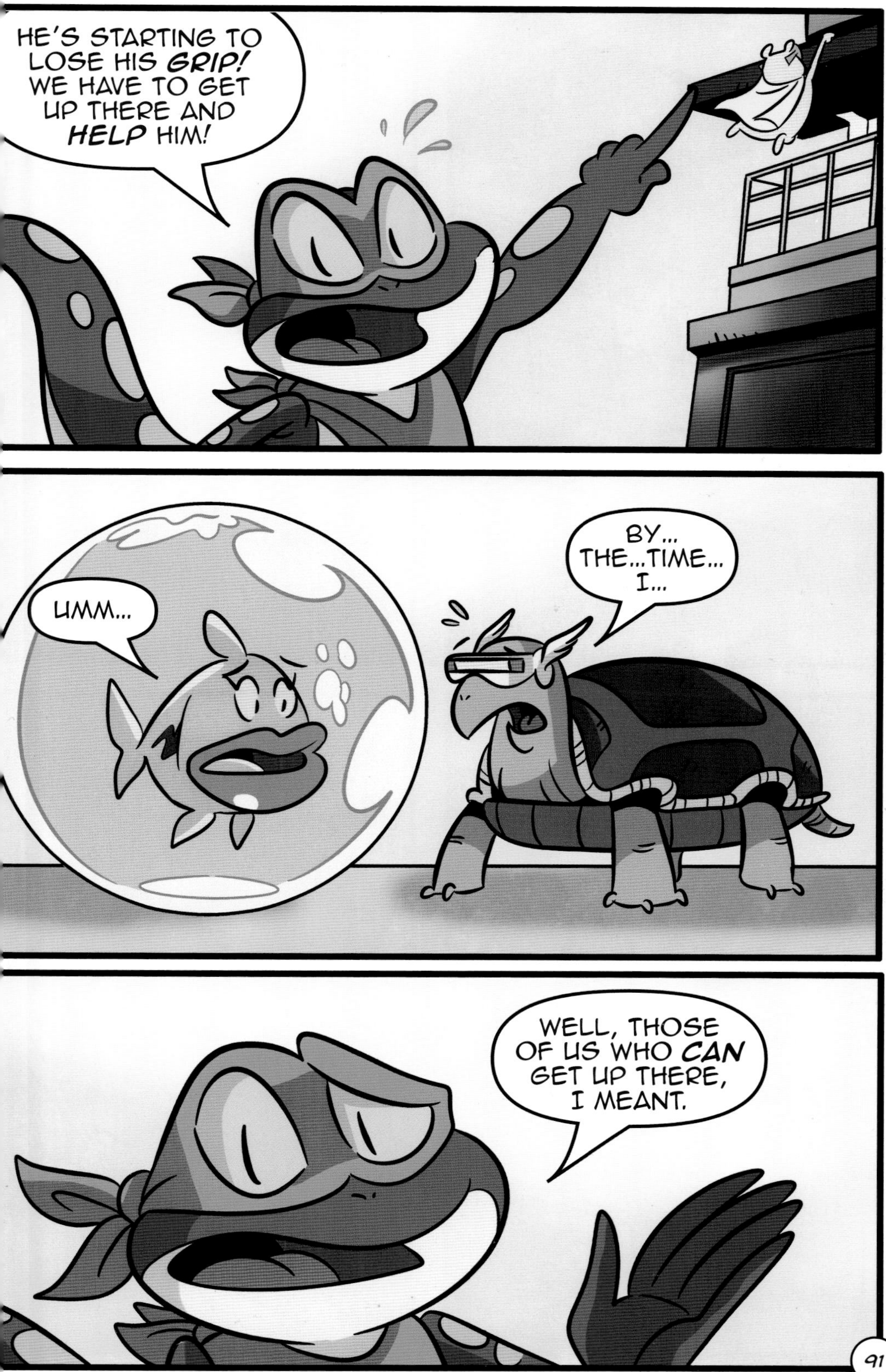
HE'S STARTING TO LOSE HIS GRIP! WE HAVE TO GET UP THERE AND HELP HIM!
UMM...
BY... THE...TIME... I...
WELL, THOSE OF US WHO CAN GET UP THERE, I MEANT.

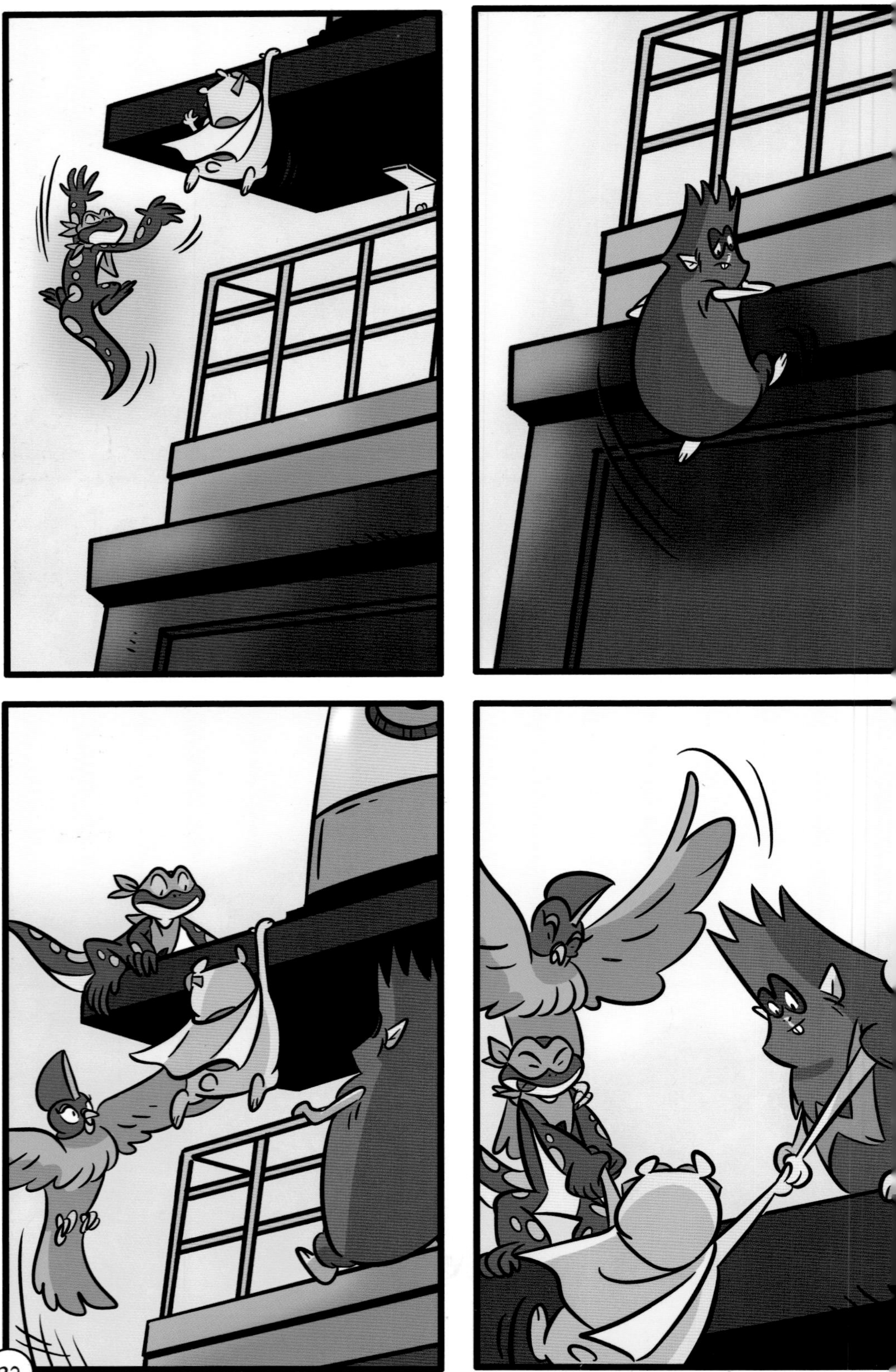

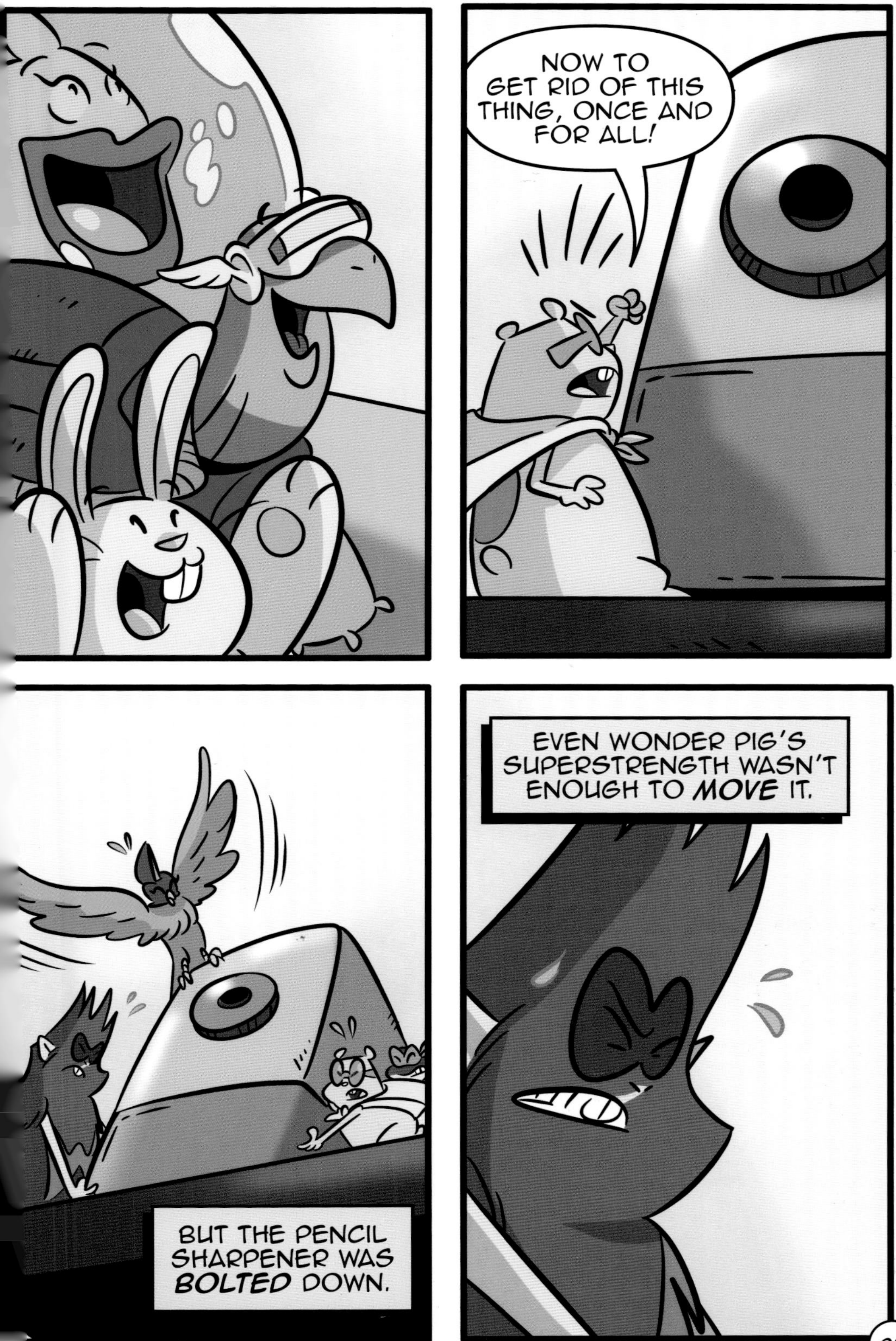
NOW TO GET RID OF THIS THING, ONCE AND FOR ALL!
BUT THE PENCIL SHARPENER WAS BOLTED DOWN.
EVEN WONDER PIG'S SUPERSTRENGTH WASN'T ENOUGH TO MOVE IT.

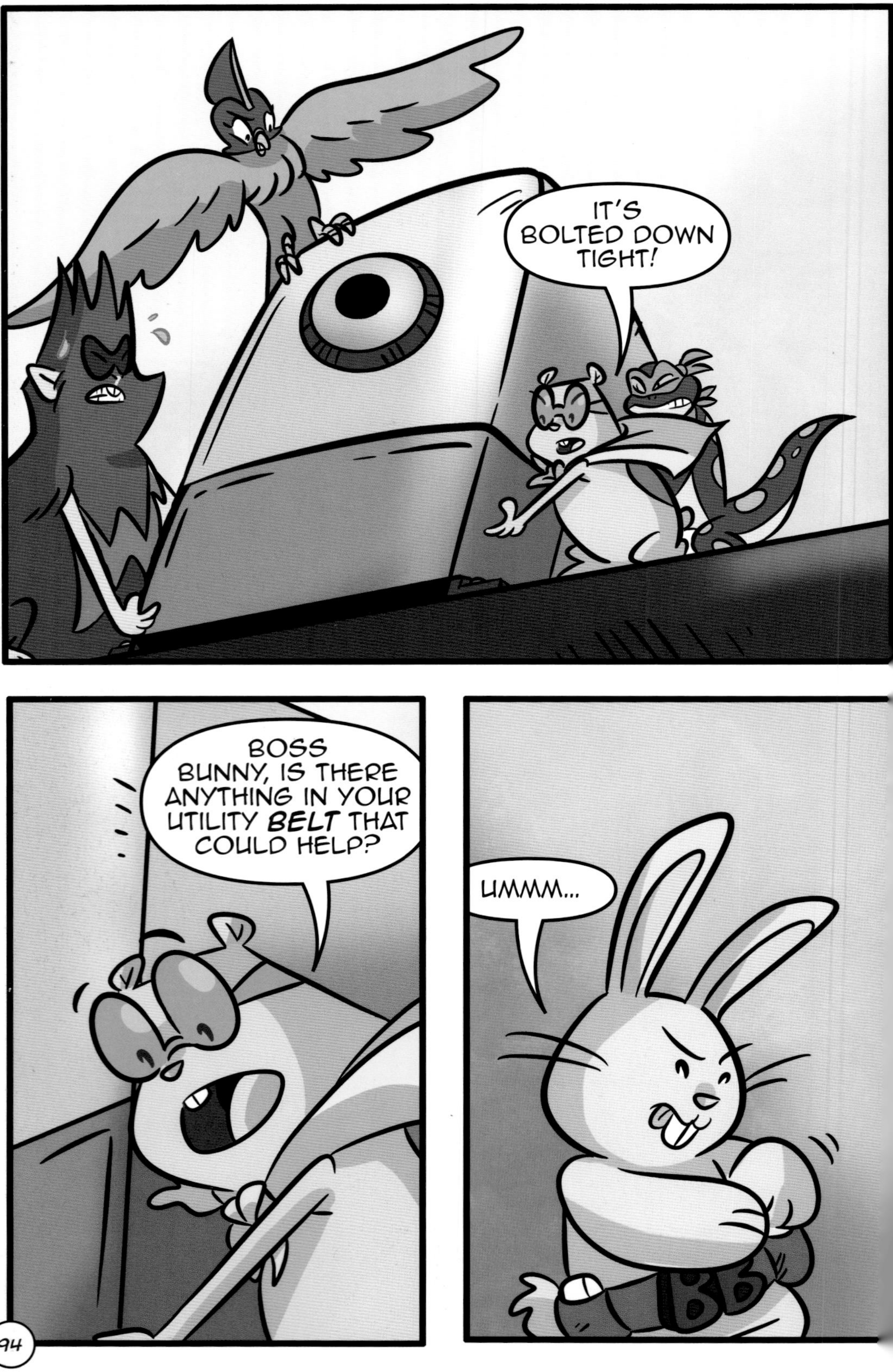

IT'S BOLTED DOWN TIGHT!
BOSS BUNNY, IS THERE ANYTHING IN YOUR UTILITY *BELT* THAT COULD HELP?
UMMM...
BB

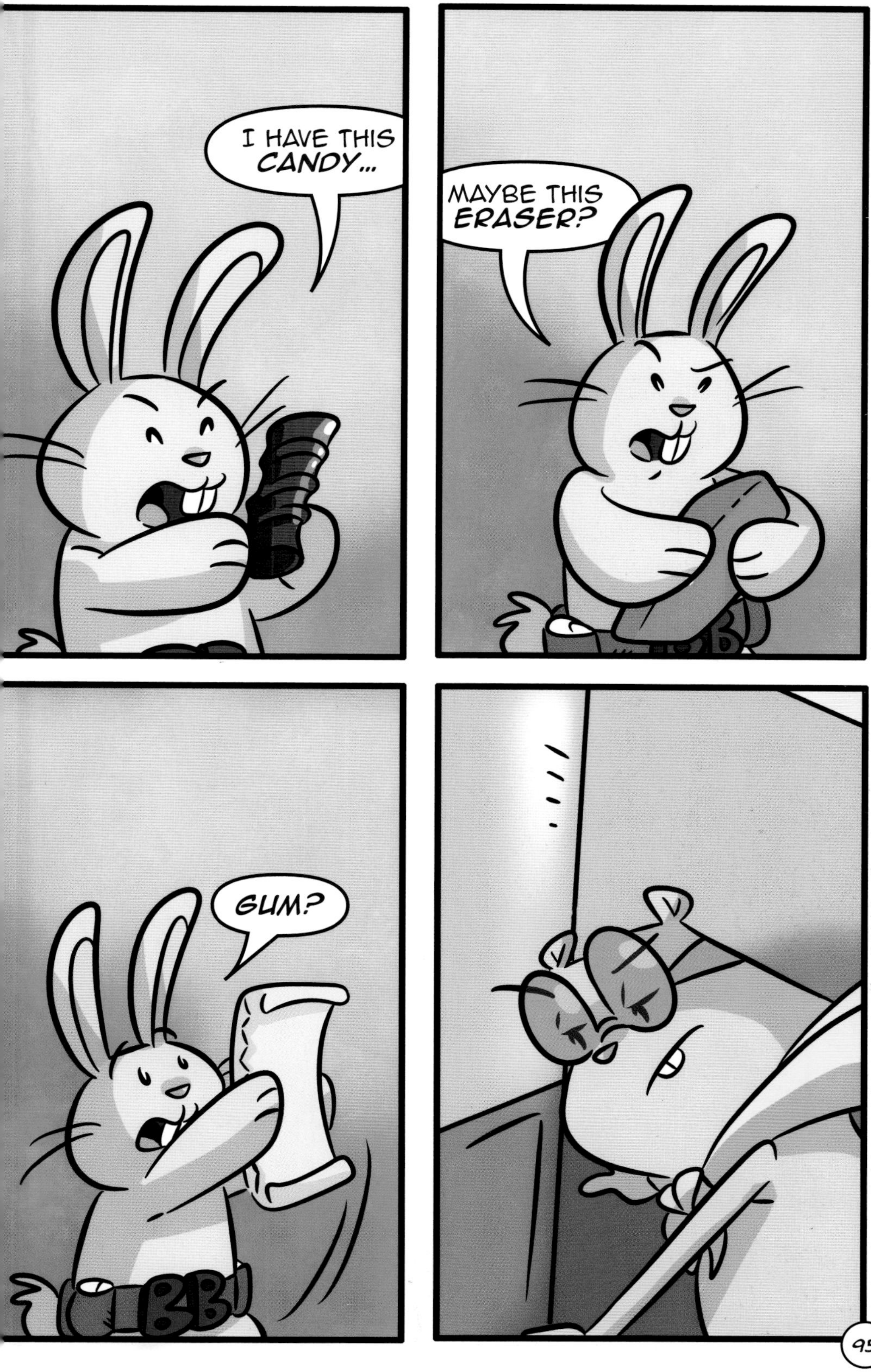
I HAVE THIS CANDY...
MAYBE THIS ERASER?
GUM?
...

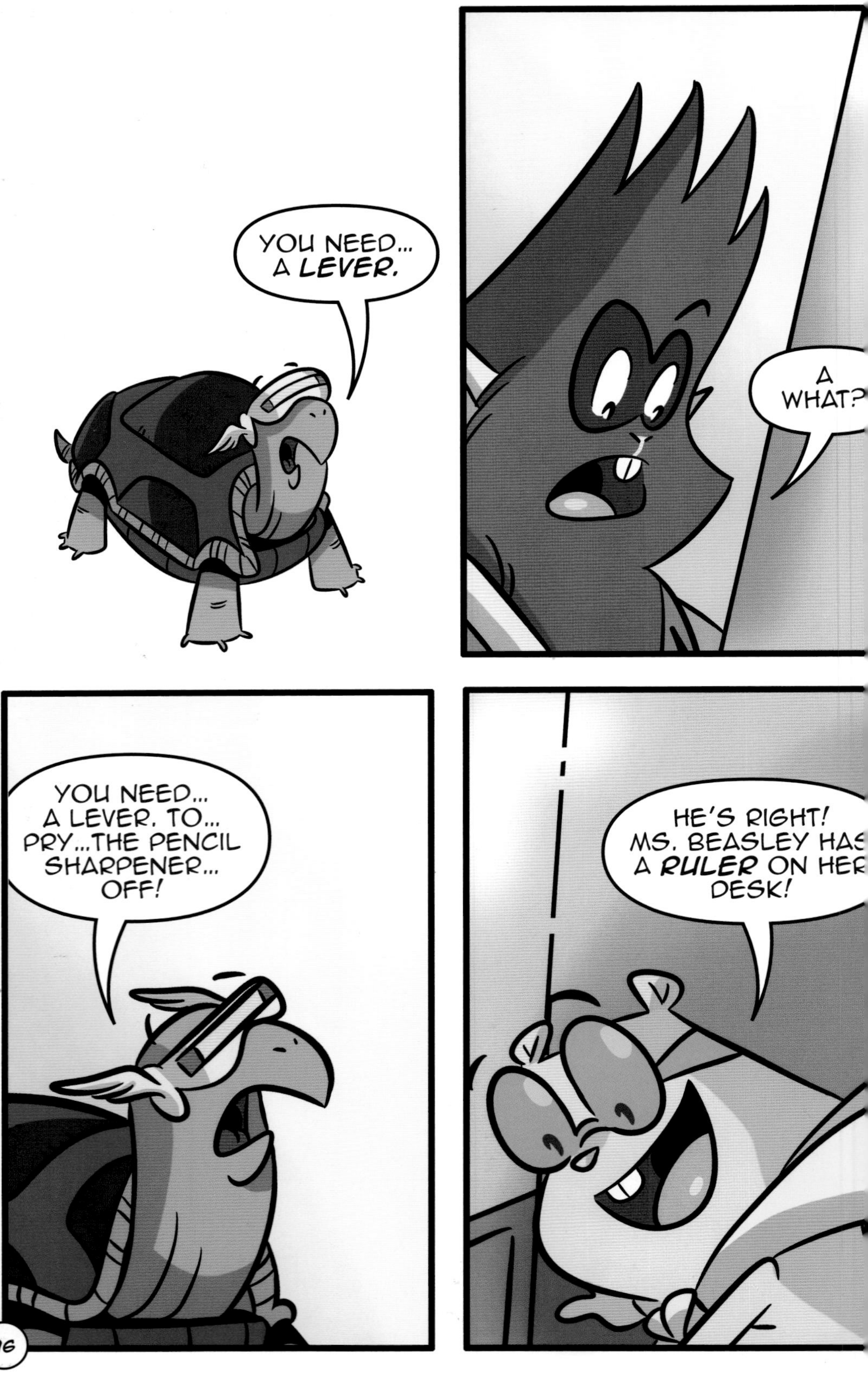
YOU NEED... A LEVER.
A WHAT?
YOU NEED... A LEVER. TO... PRY...THE PENCIL SHARPENER... OFF!
HE'S RIGHT! MS. BEASLEY HAS A RULER ON HER DESK!

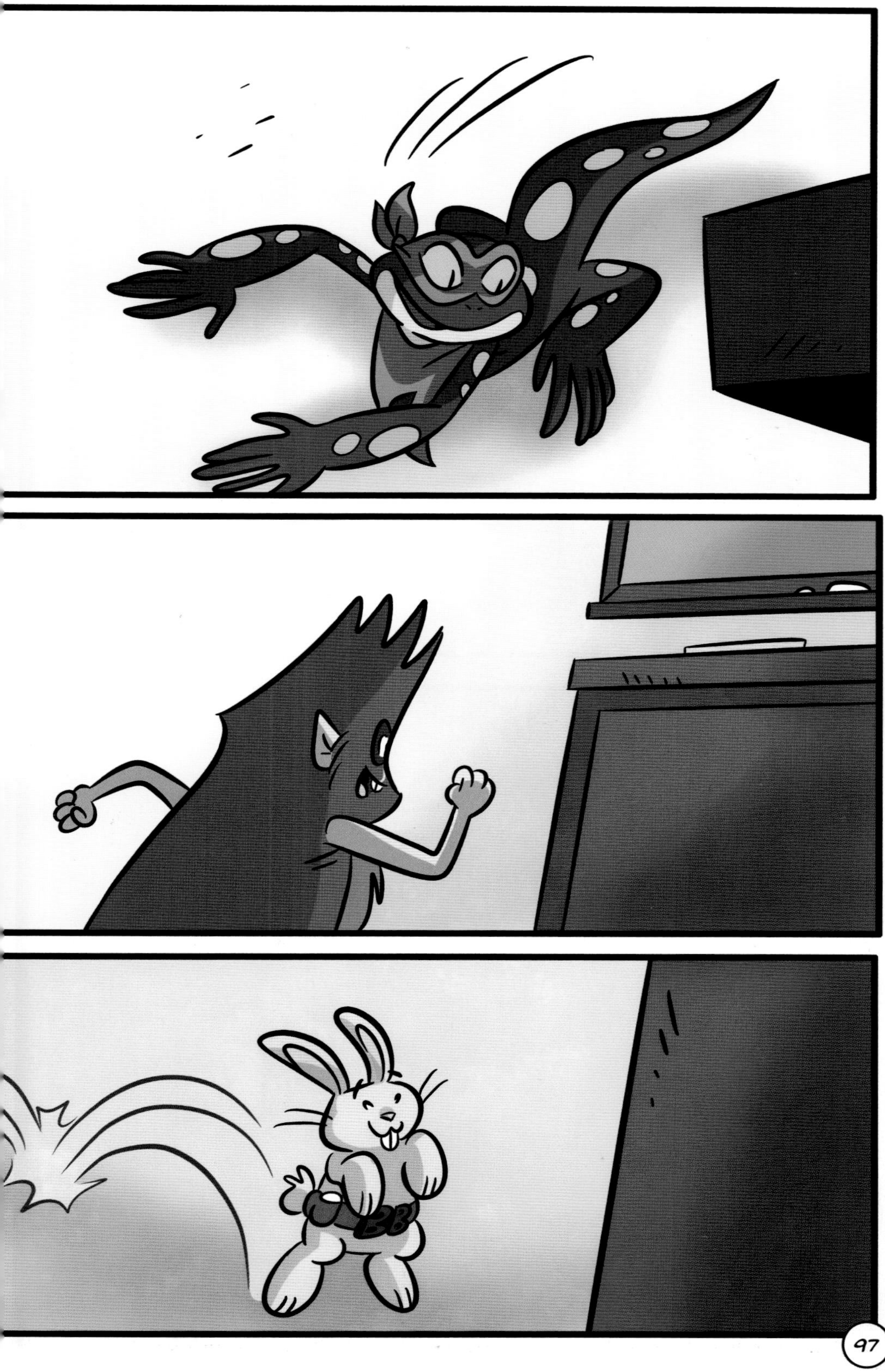

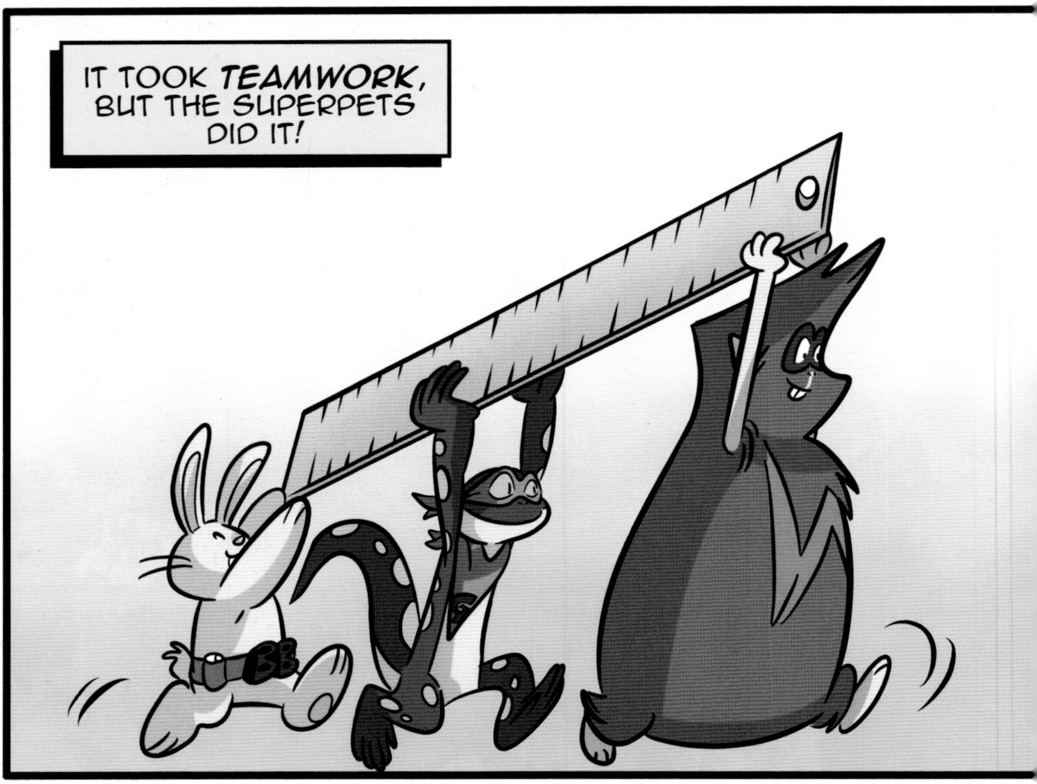
IT TOOK *TEAMWORK*, BUT THE SUPERPETS DID IT!

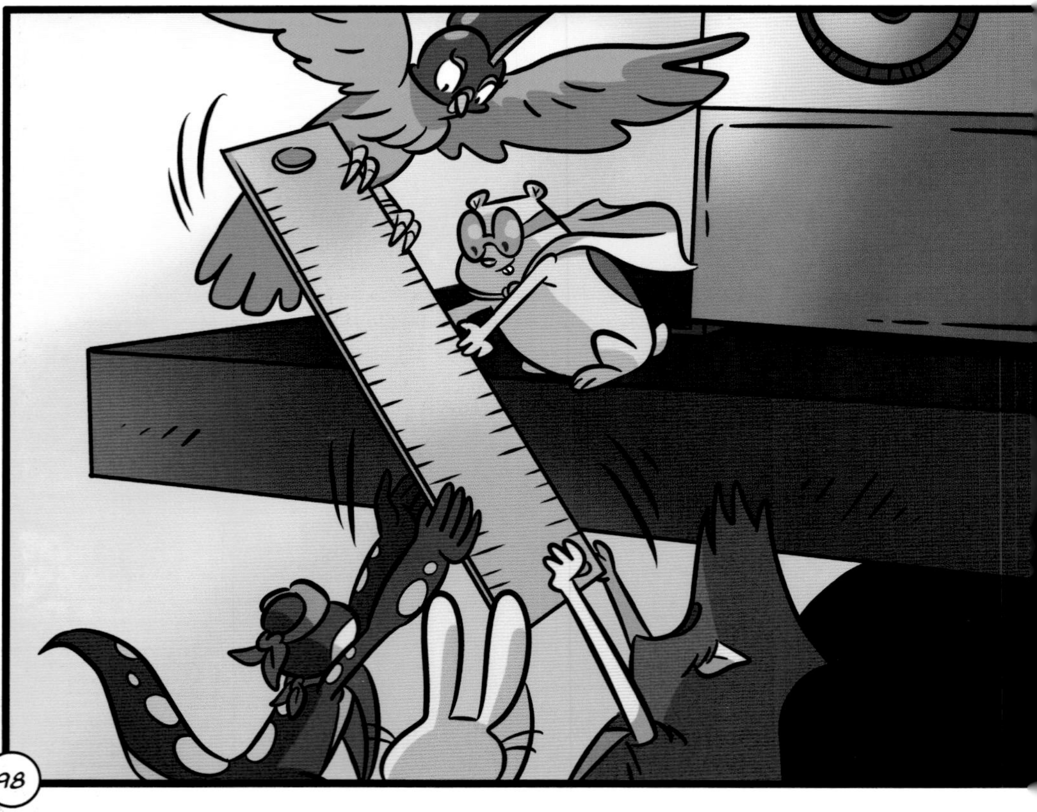

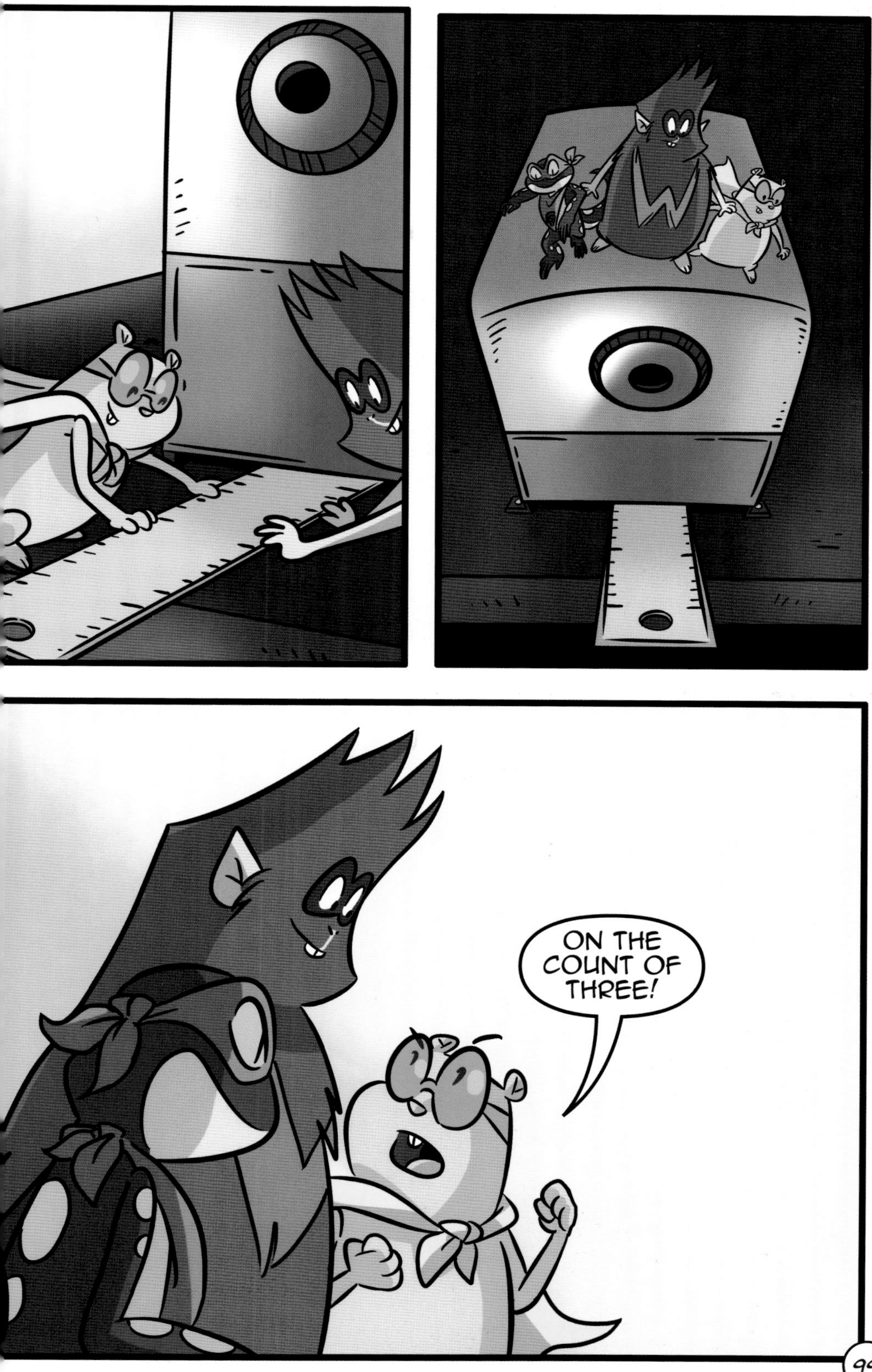
ON THE COUNT OF THREE!

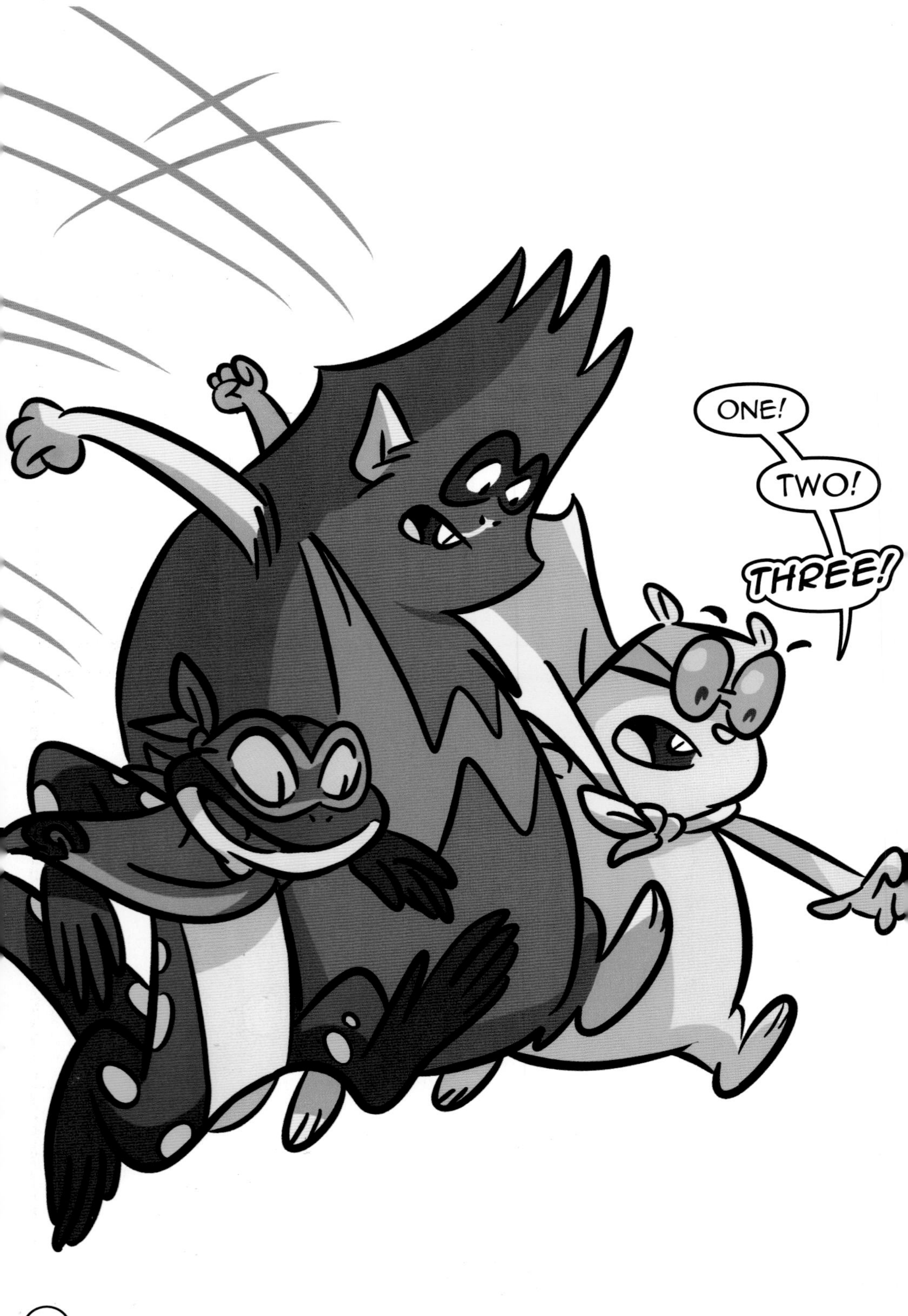
ONE!
TWO!
THREE!

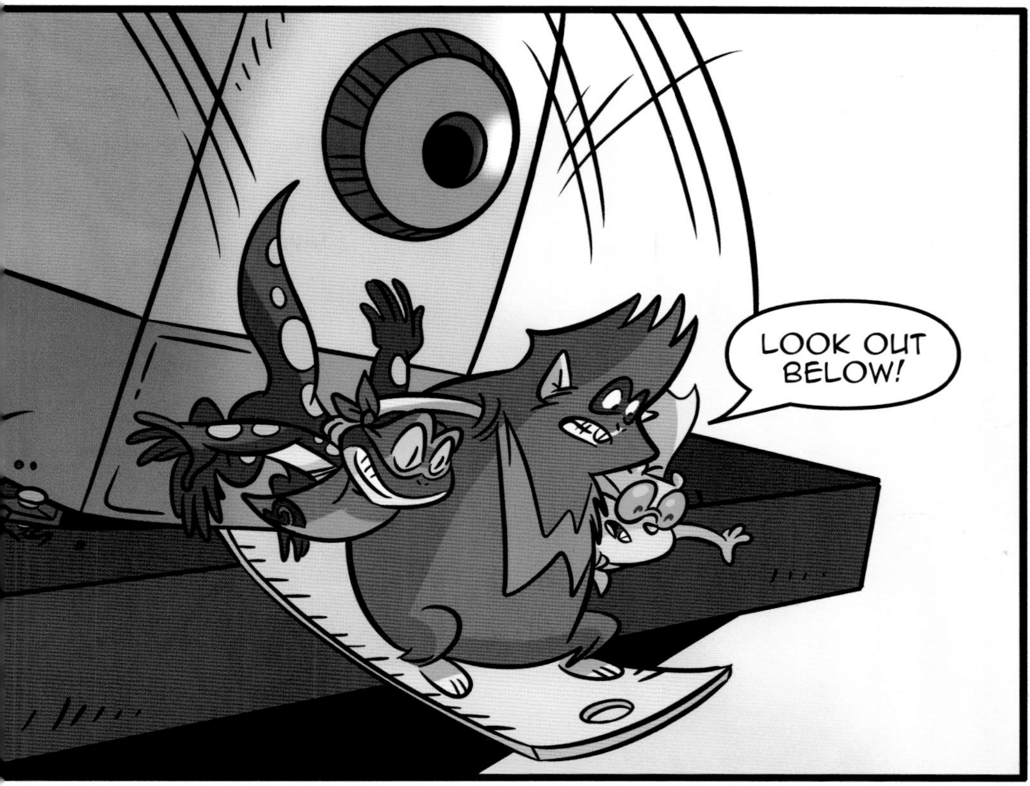
LOOK OUT BELOW!

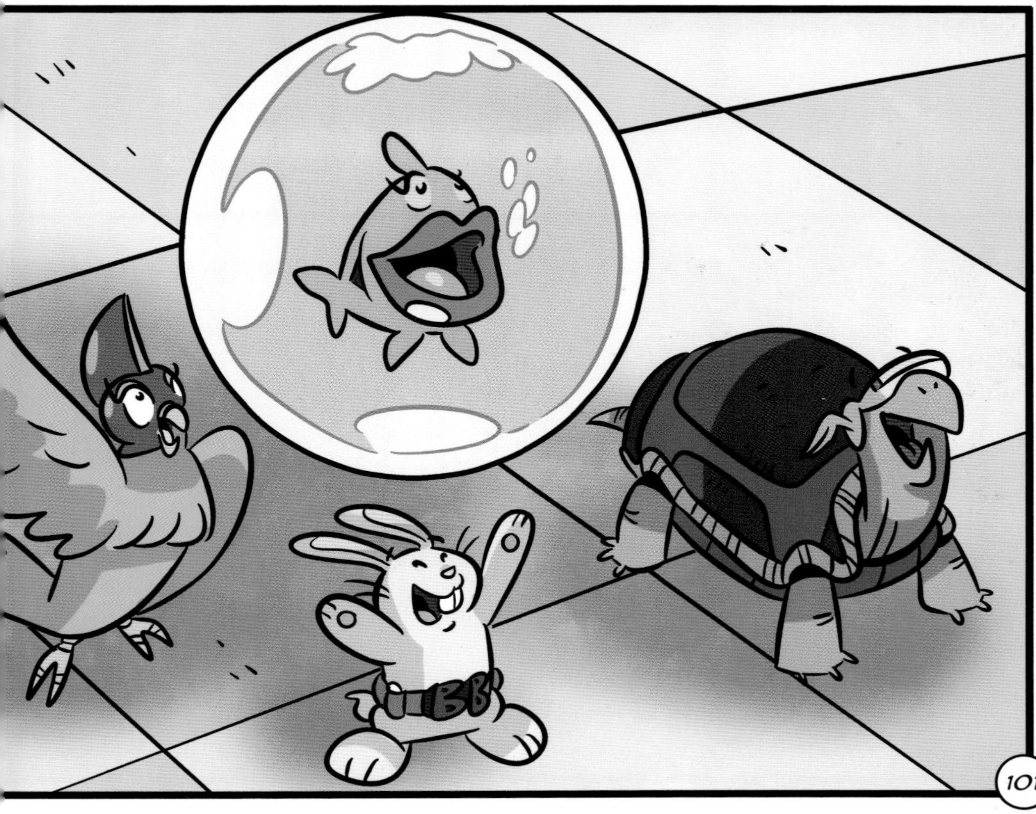

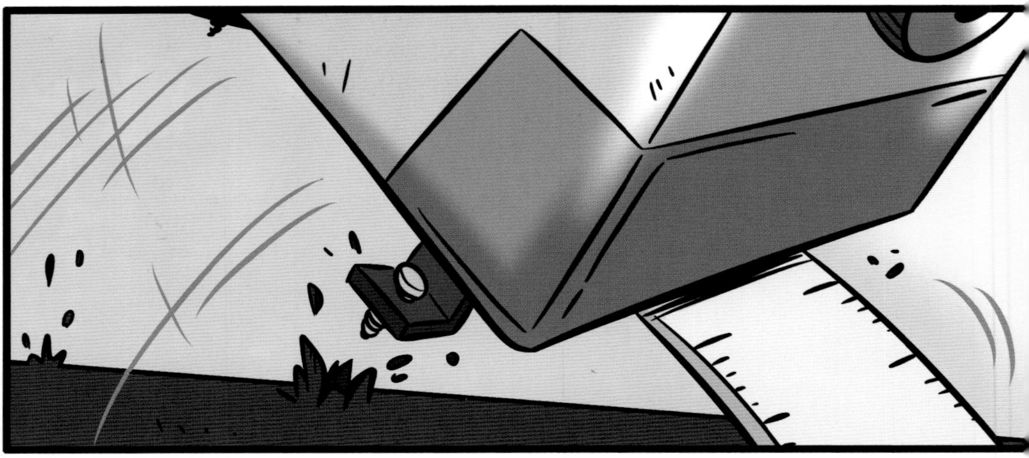

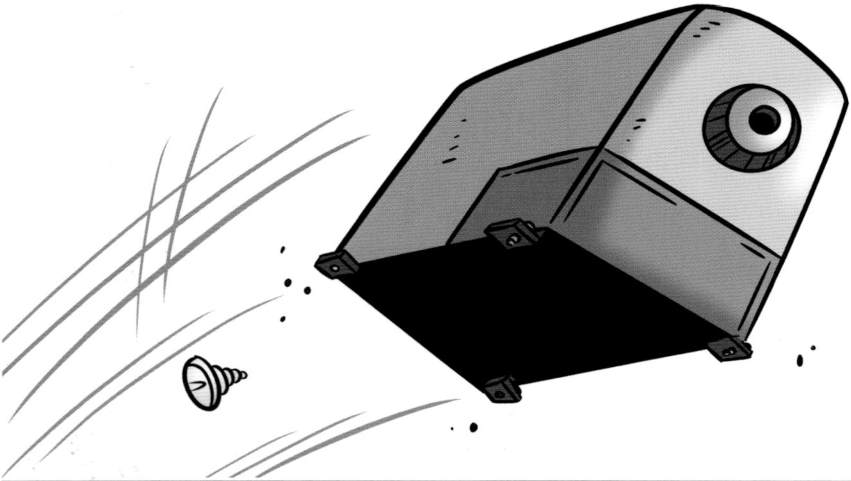

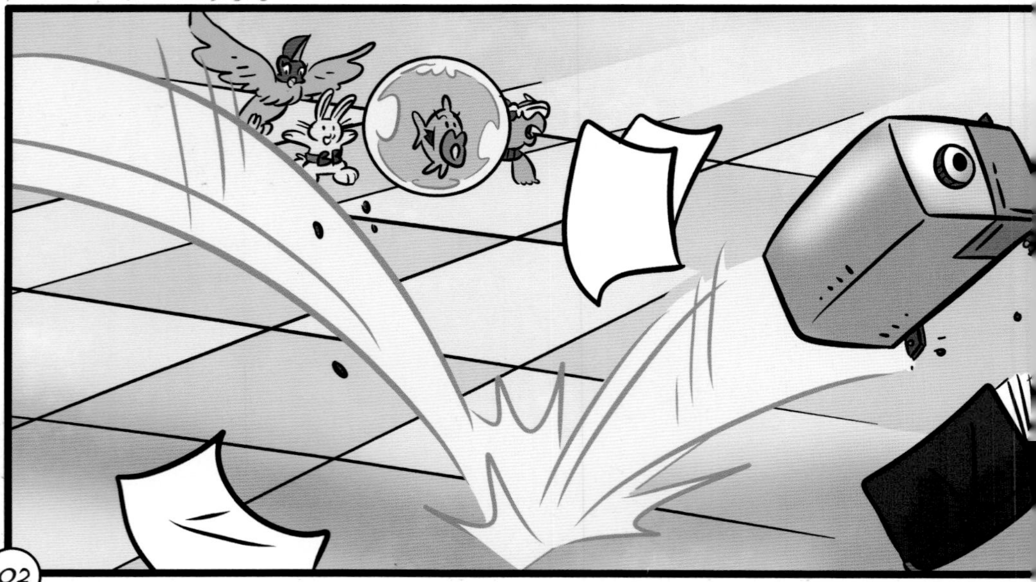

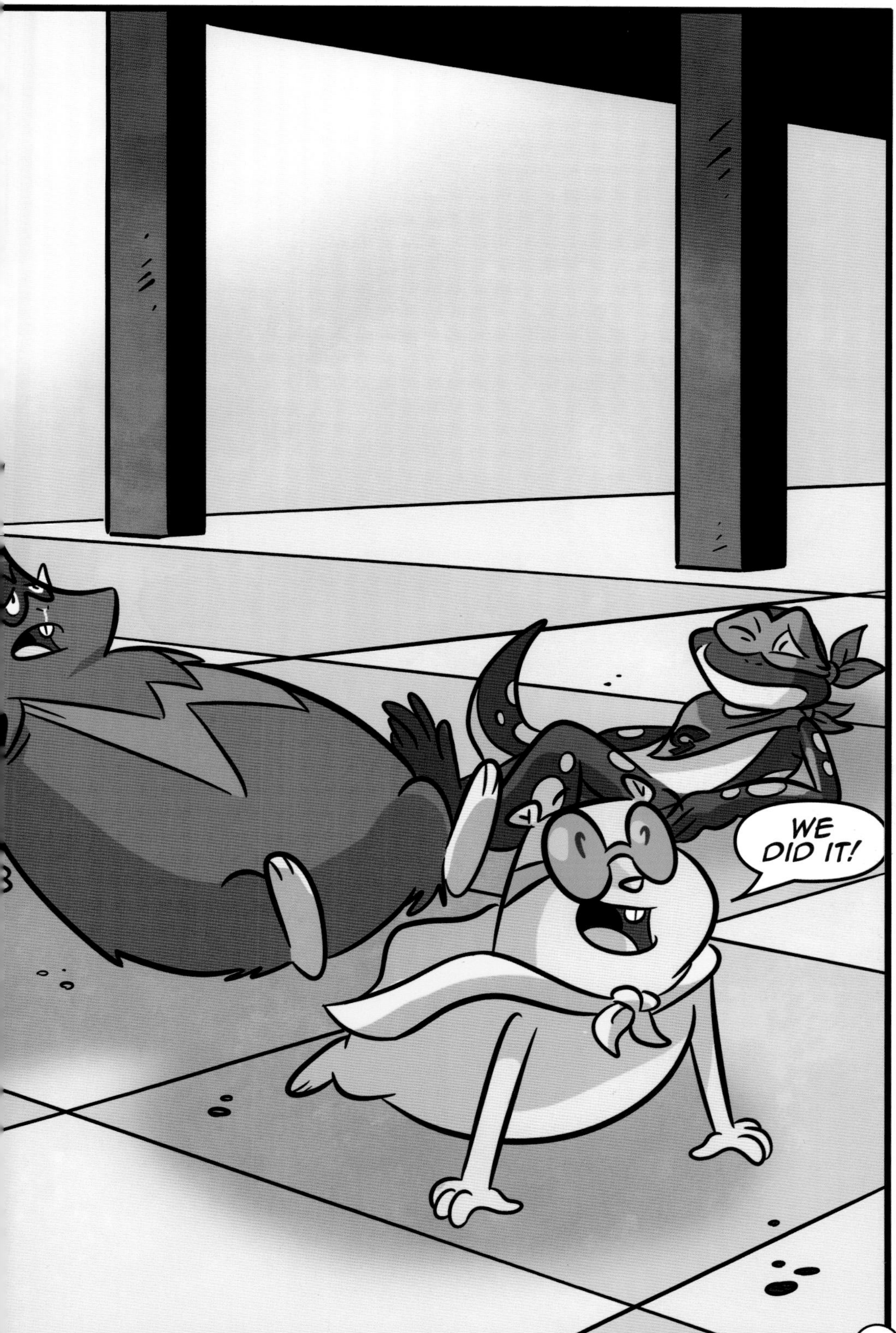
WE DID IT!

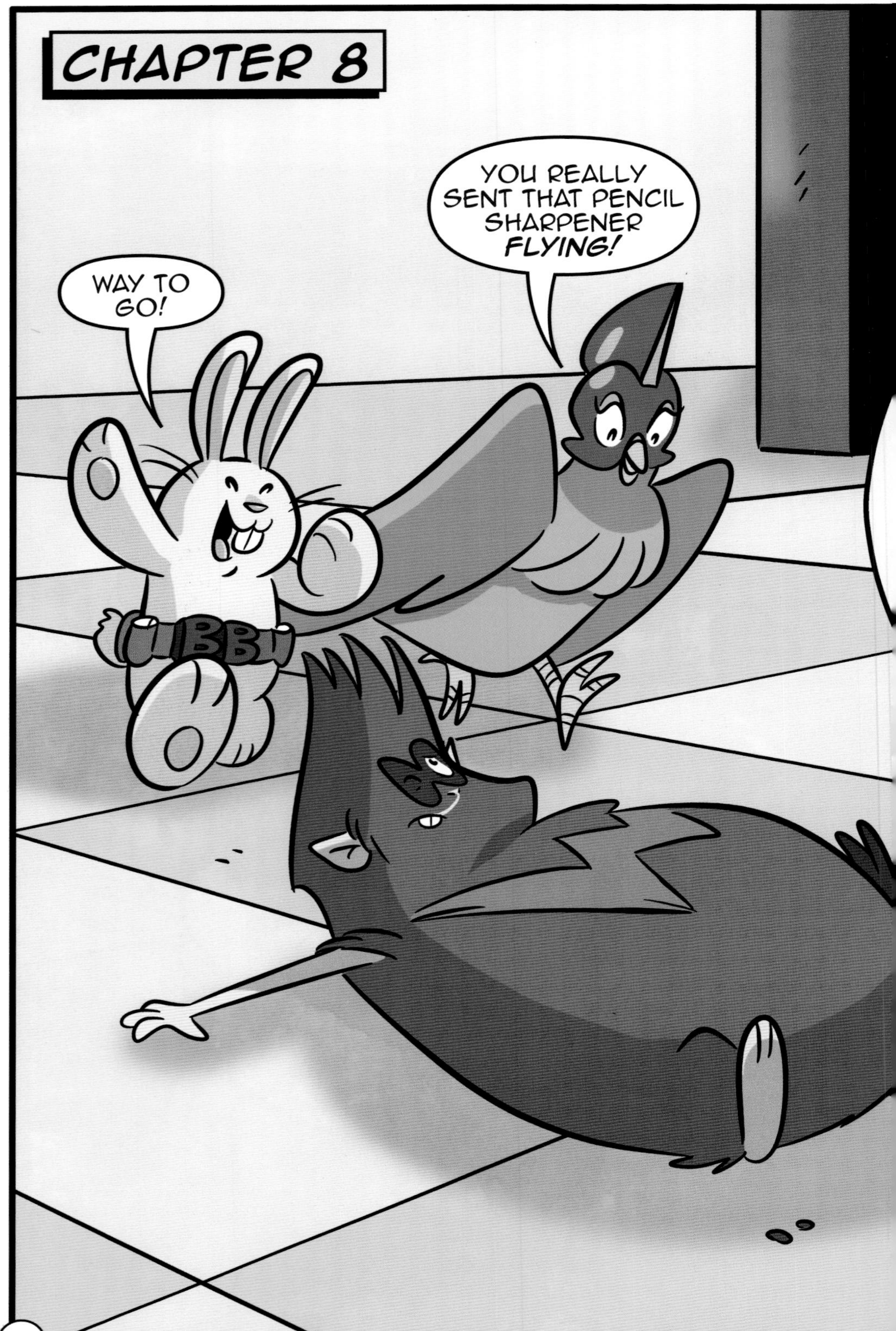
CHAPTER 8
WAY TO GO!
YOU REALLY SENT THAT PENCIL SHARPENER FLYING!

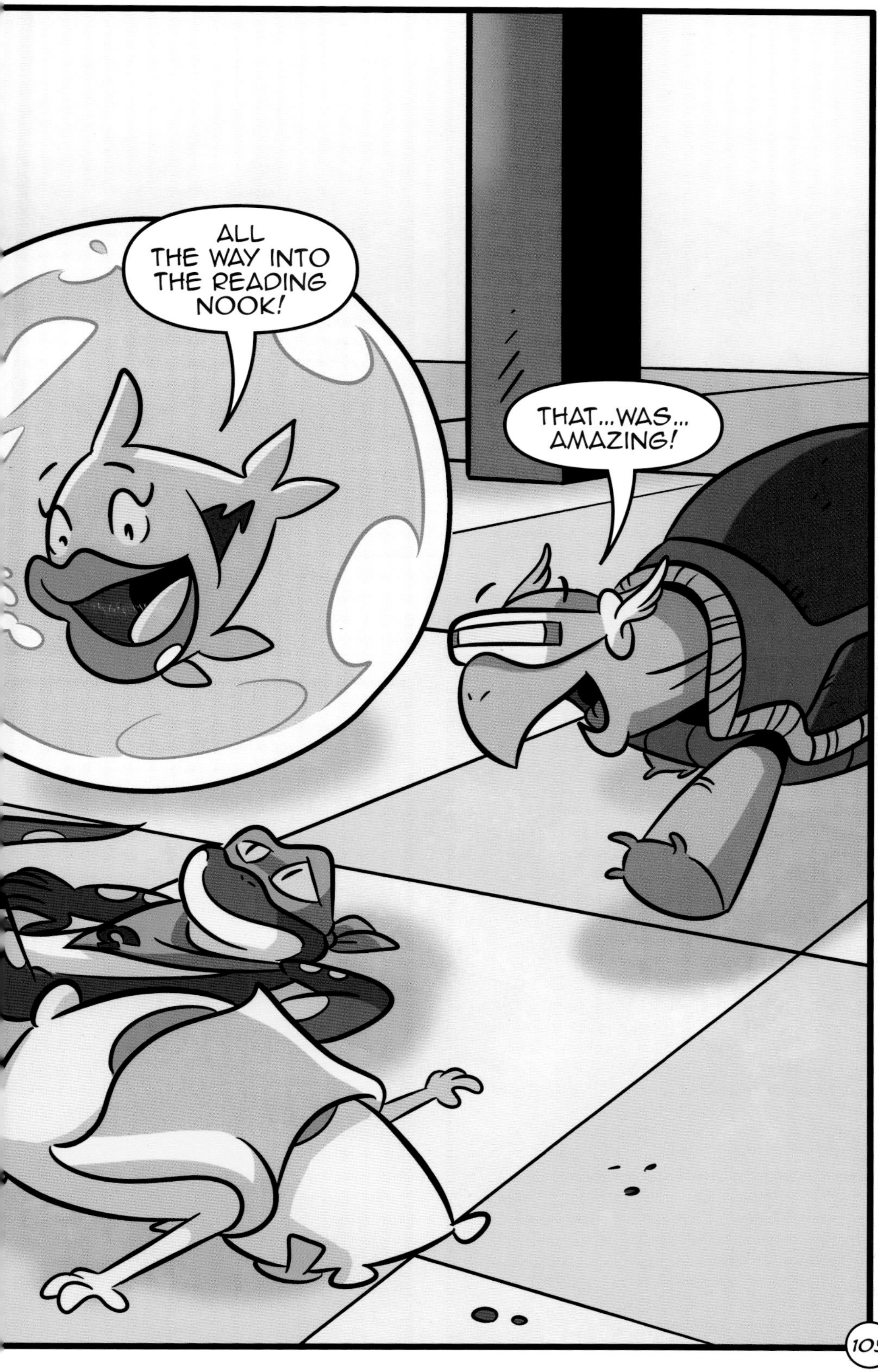
ALL THE WAY INTO THE READING NOOK!
THAT...WAS... AMAZING!

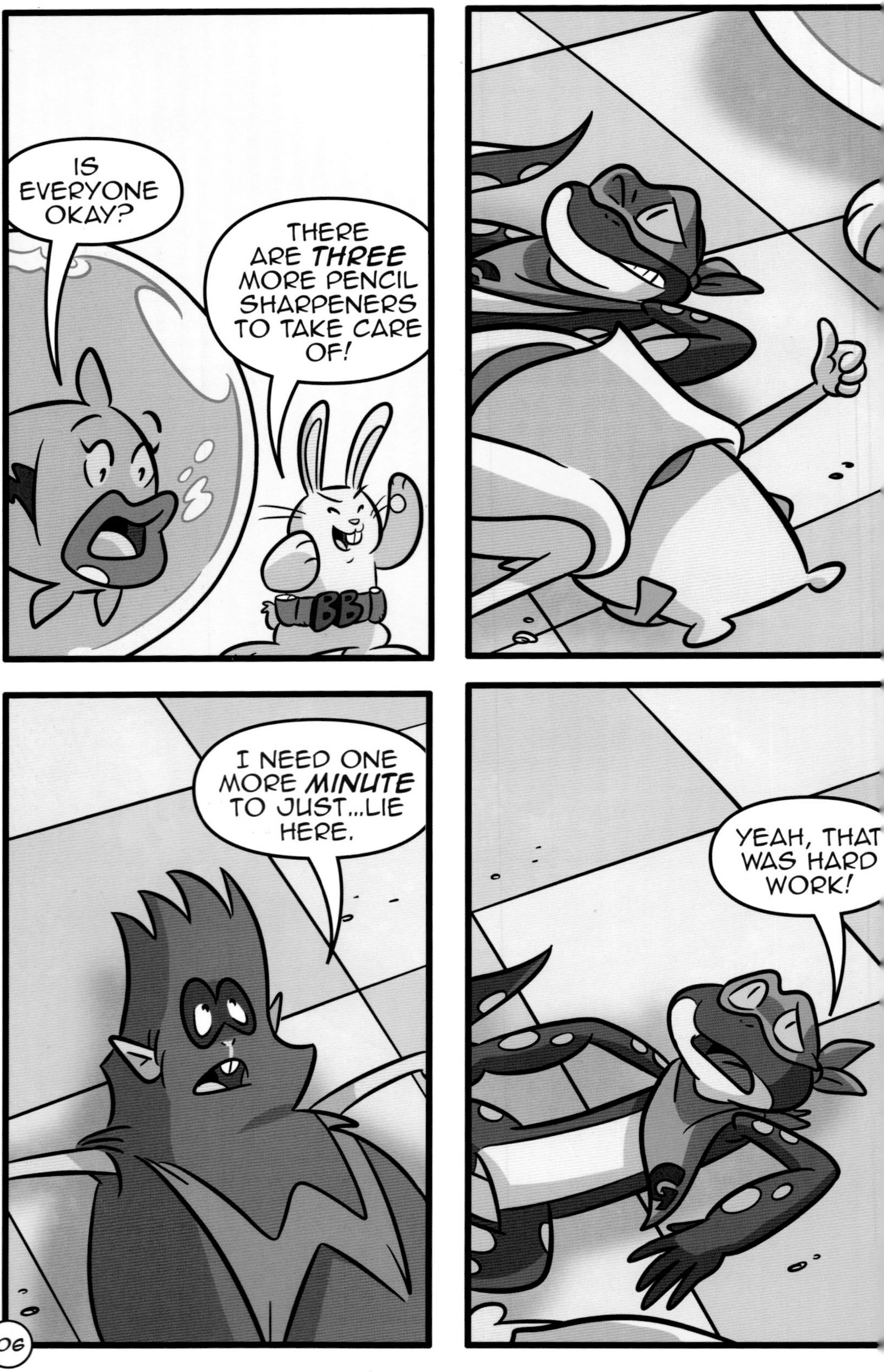
IS EVERYONE OKAY?
THERE ARE THREE MORE PENCIL SHARPENERS TO TAKE CARE OF!
I NEED ONE MORE MINUTE TO JUST...LIE HERE.
YEAH, THAT WAS HARD WORK!

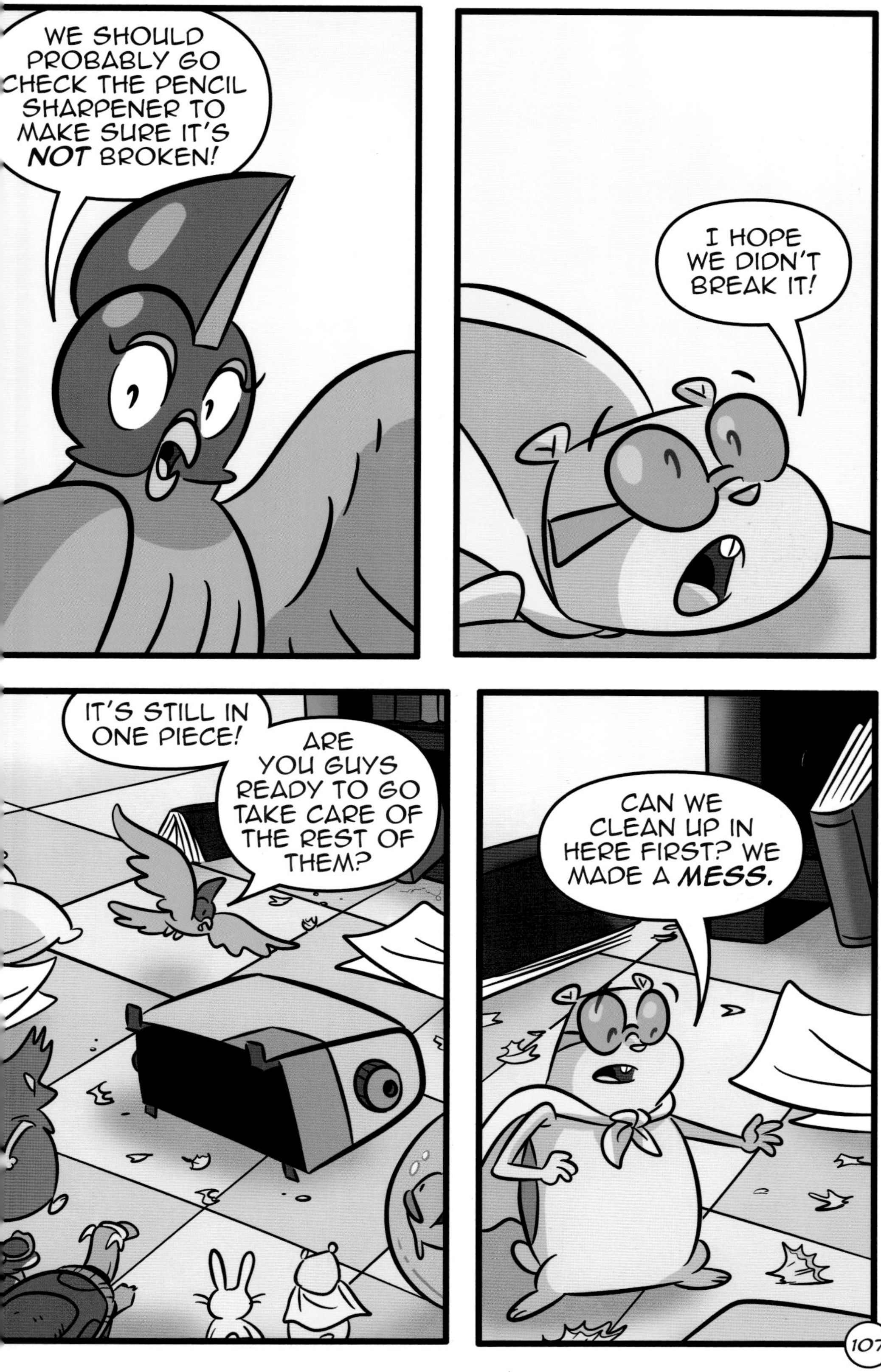
WE SHOULD PROBABLY GO CHECK THE PENCIL SHARPENER TO MAKE SURE IT'S **NOT** BROKEN!
I HOPE WE DIDN'T BREAK IT!
IT'S STILL IN ONE PIECE!
ARE YOU GUYS READY TO GO TAKE CARE OF THE REST OF THEM?
CAN WE CLEAN UP IN HERE FIRST? WE MADE A ***MESS.***

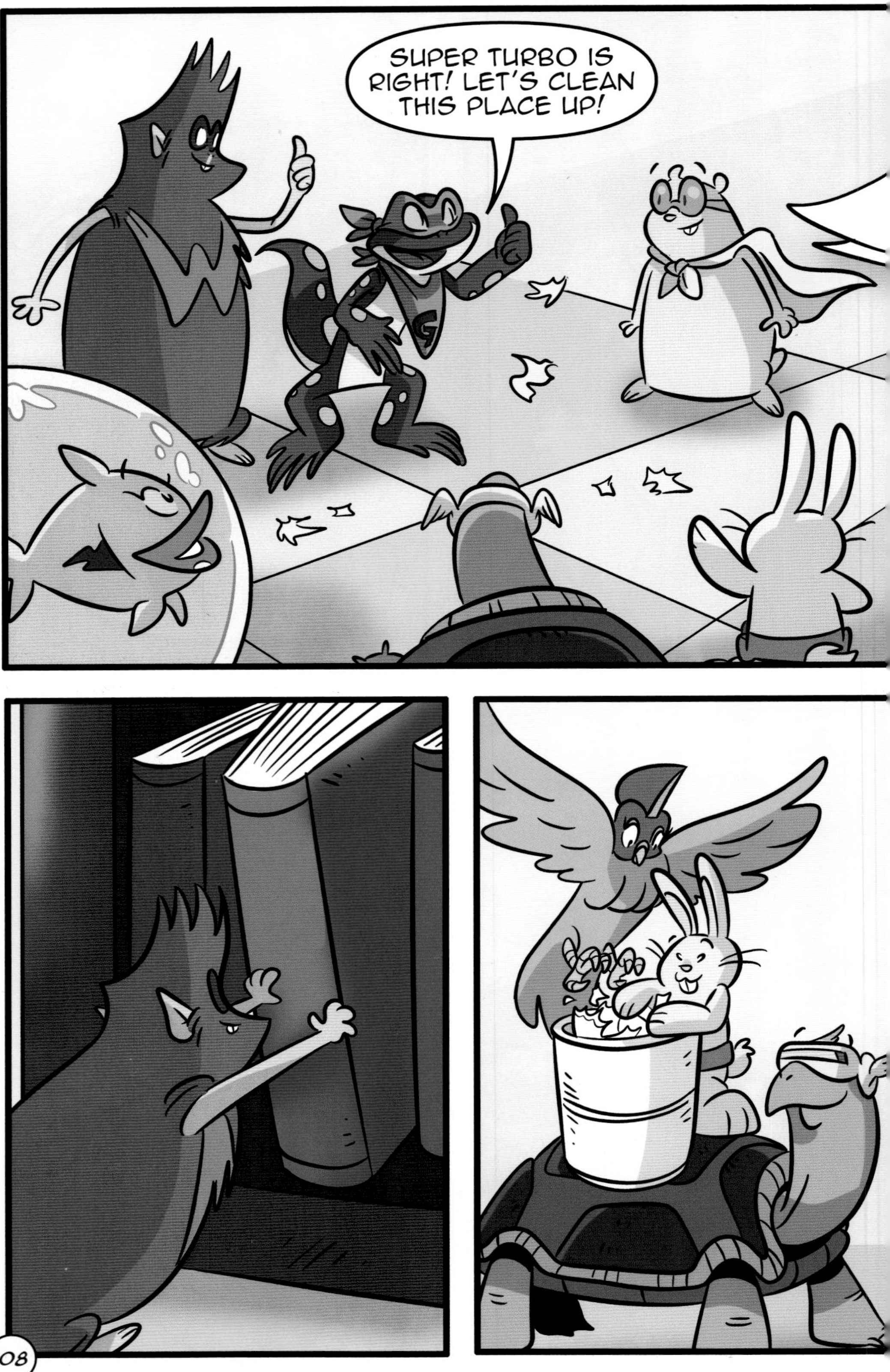
SUPER TURBO IS RIGHT! LET'S CLEAN THIS PLACE UP!

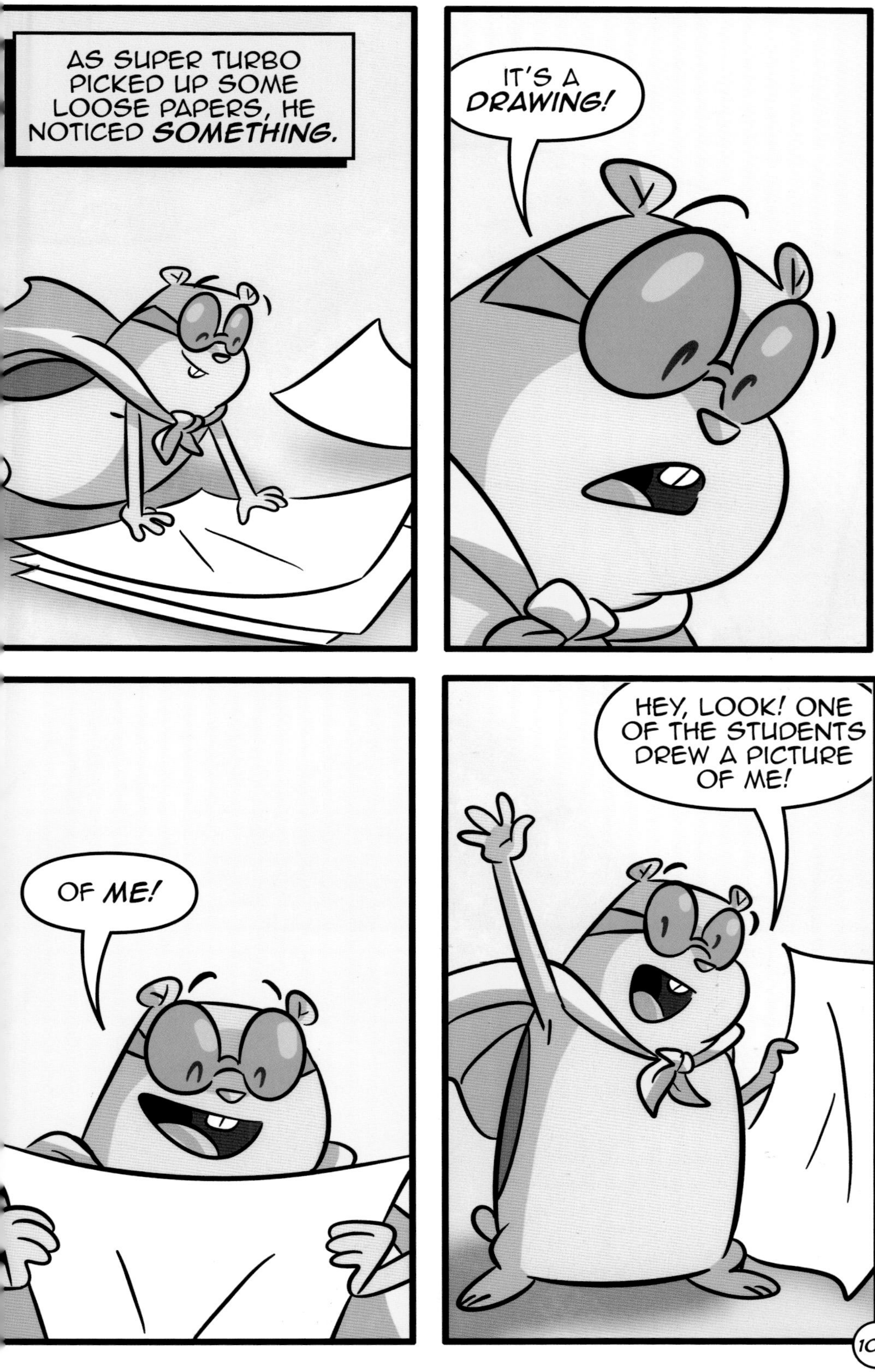
AS SUPER TURBO PICKED UP SOME LOOSE PAPERS, HE NOTICED **SOMETHING.**
IT'S A *DRAWING!*
OF *ME!*
HEY, LOOK! ONE OF THE STUDENTS DREW A PICTURE OF ME!

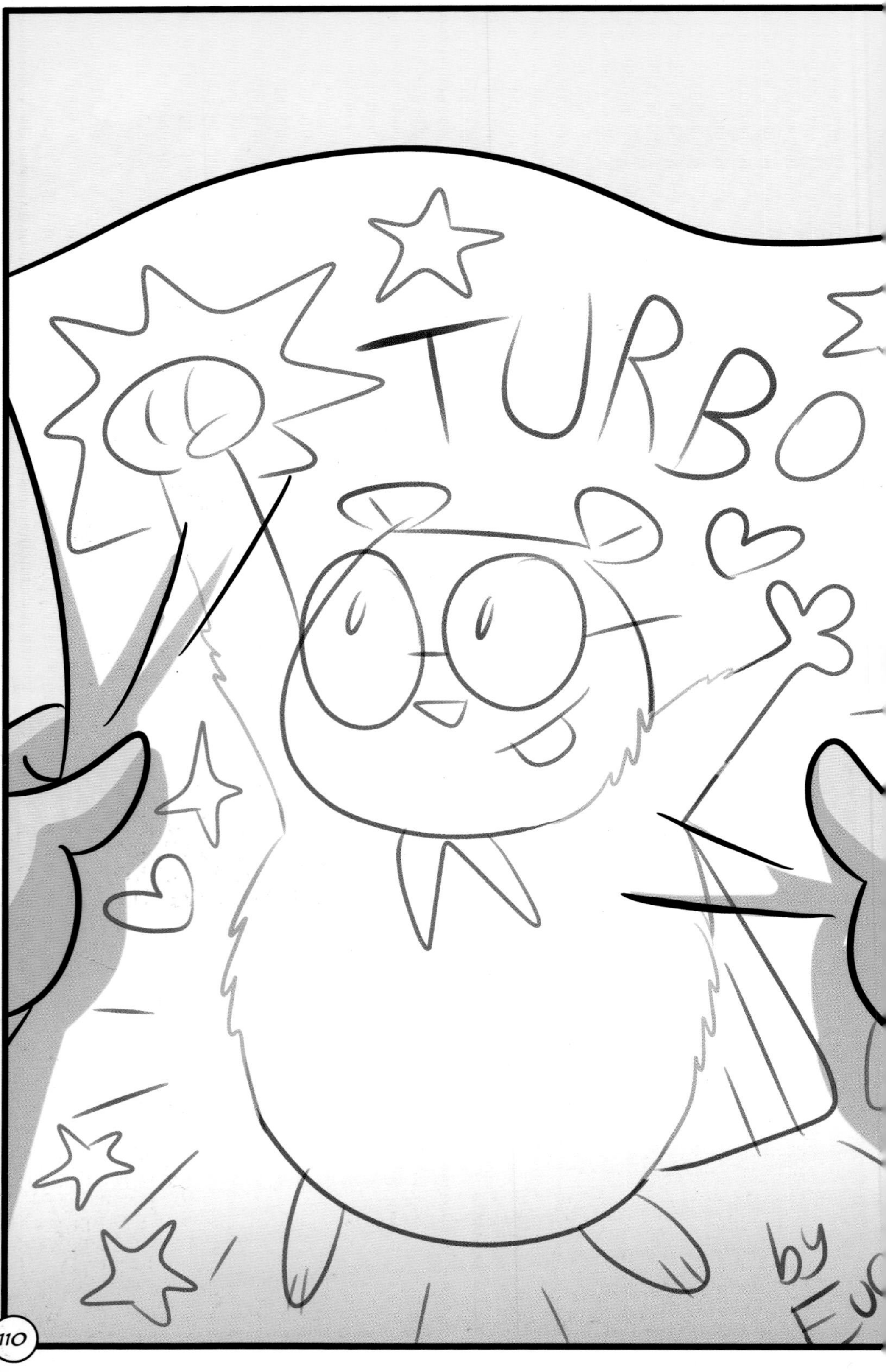
TURBO
by

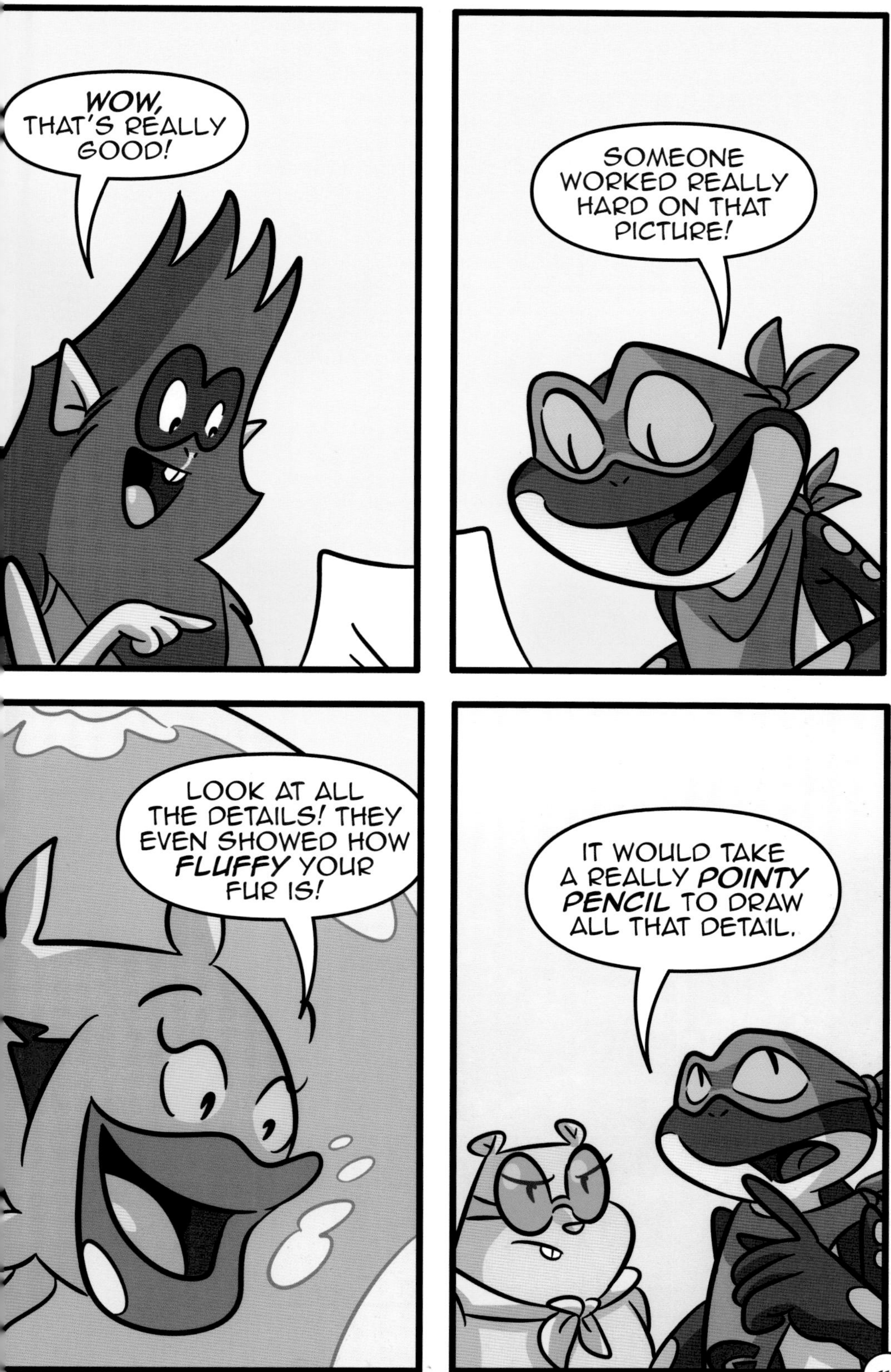
WOW, THAT'S REALLY GOOD!
SOMEONE WORKED REALLY HARD ON THAT PICTURE!
LOOK AT ALL THE DETAILS! THEY EVEN SHOWED HOW FLUFFY YOUR FUR IS!
IT WOULD TAKE A REALLY POINTY PENCIL TO DRAW ALL THAT DETAIL.

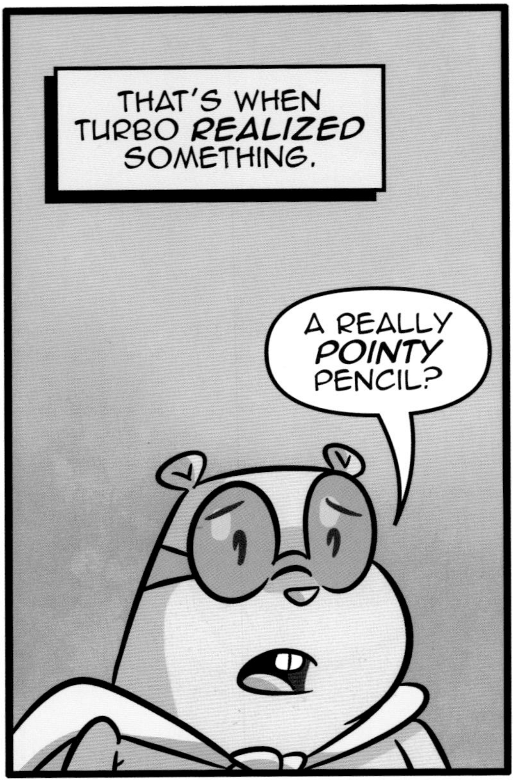
THAT'S WHEN TURBO *REALIZED* SOMETHING.
A REALLY *POINTY* PENCIL?

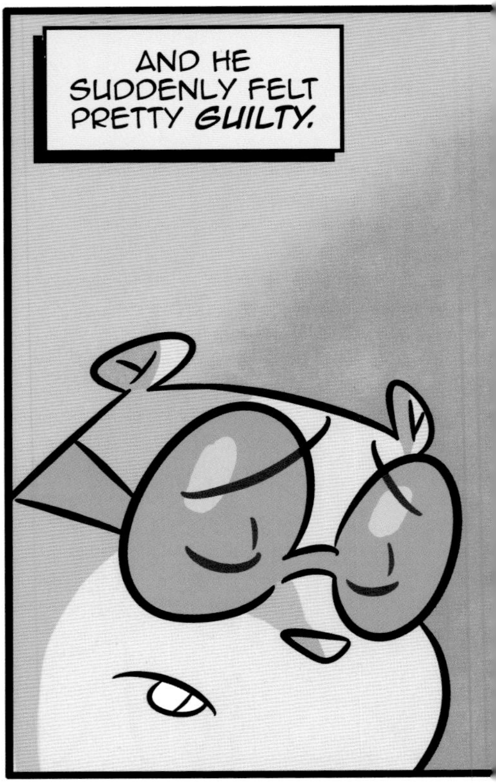
AND HE SUDDENLY FELT PRETTY *GUILTY.*

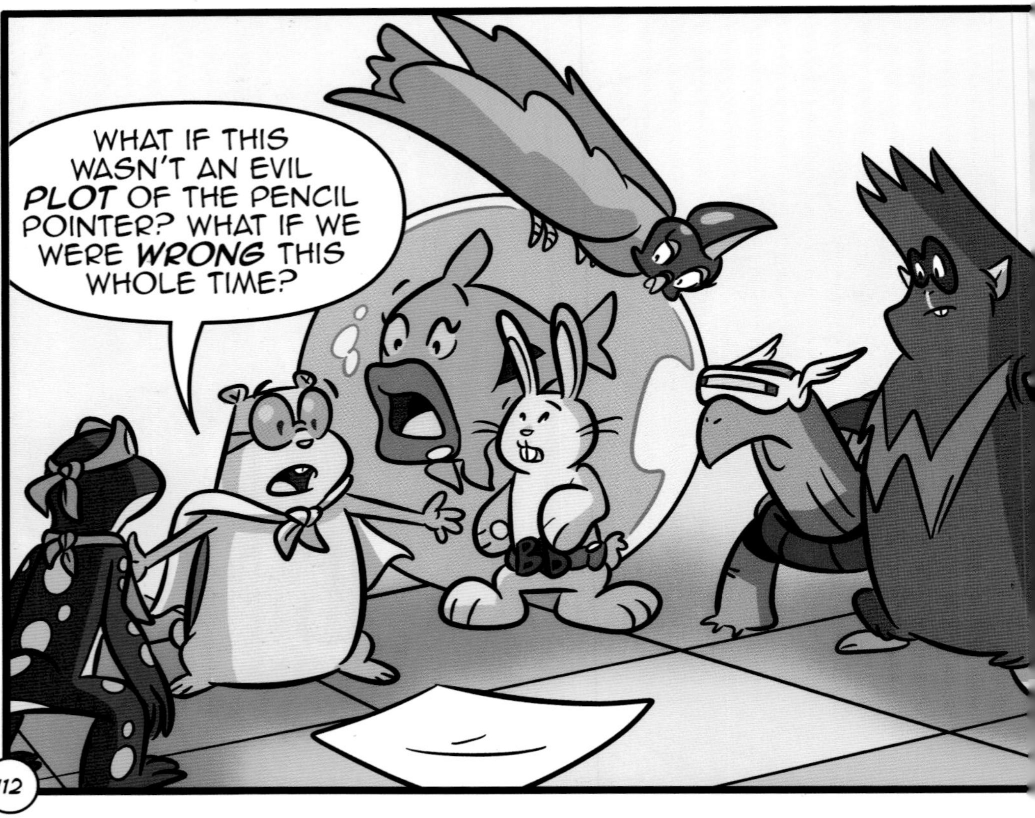
WHAT IF THIS WASN'T AN EVIL *PLOT* OF THE PENCIL POINTER? WHAT IF WE WERE *WRONG* THIS WHOLE TIME?

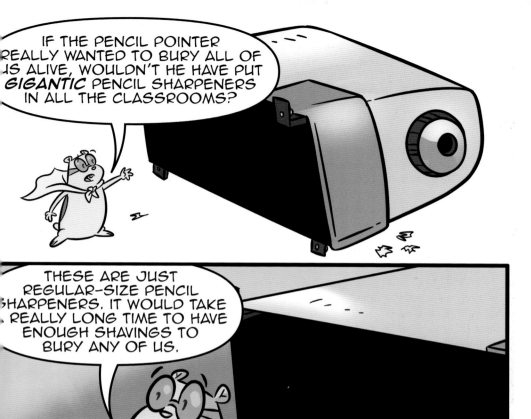

IF THE PENCIL POINTER REALLY WANTED TO BURY ALL OF US ALIVE, WOULDN'T HE HAVE PUT *GIGANTIC* PENCIL SHARPENERS IN ALL THE CLASSROOMS?

THESE ARE JUST REGULAR-SIZE PENCIL SHARPENERS. IT WOULD TAKE A REALLY LONG TIME TO HAVE ENOUGH SHAVINGS TO BURY ANY OF US.

WHAT IF THERE *NEVER* WAS A *PENCIL POINTER?*

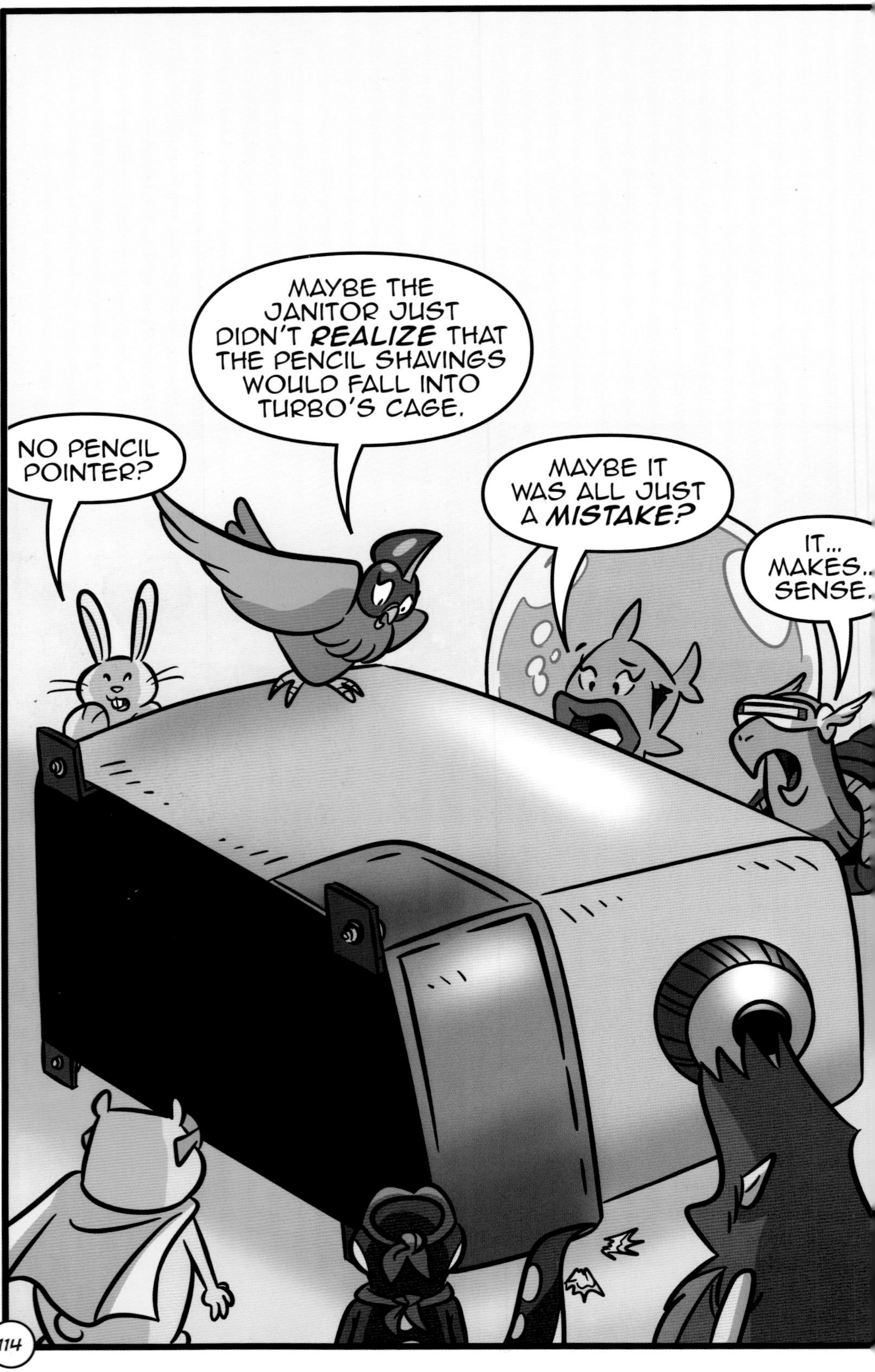
NO PENCIL POINTER?
MAYBE THE JANITOR JUST DIDN'T REALIZE THAT THE PENCIL SHAVINGS WOULD FALL INTO TURBO'S CAGE.
MAYBE IT WAS ALL JUST A MISTAKE?
IT... MAKES... SENSE.

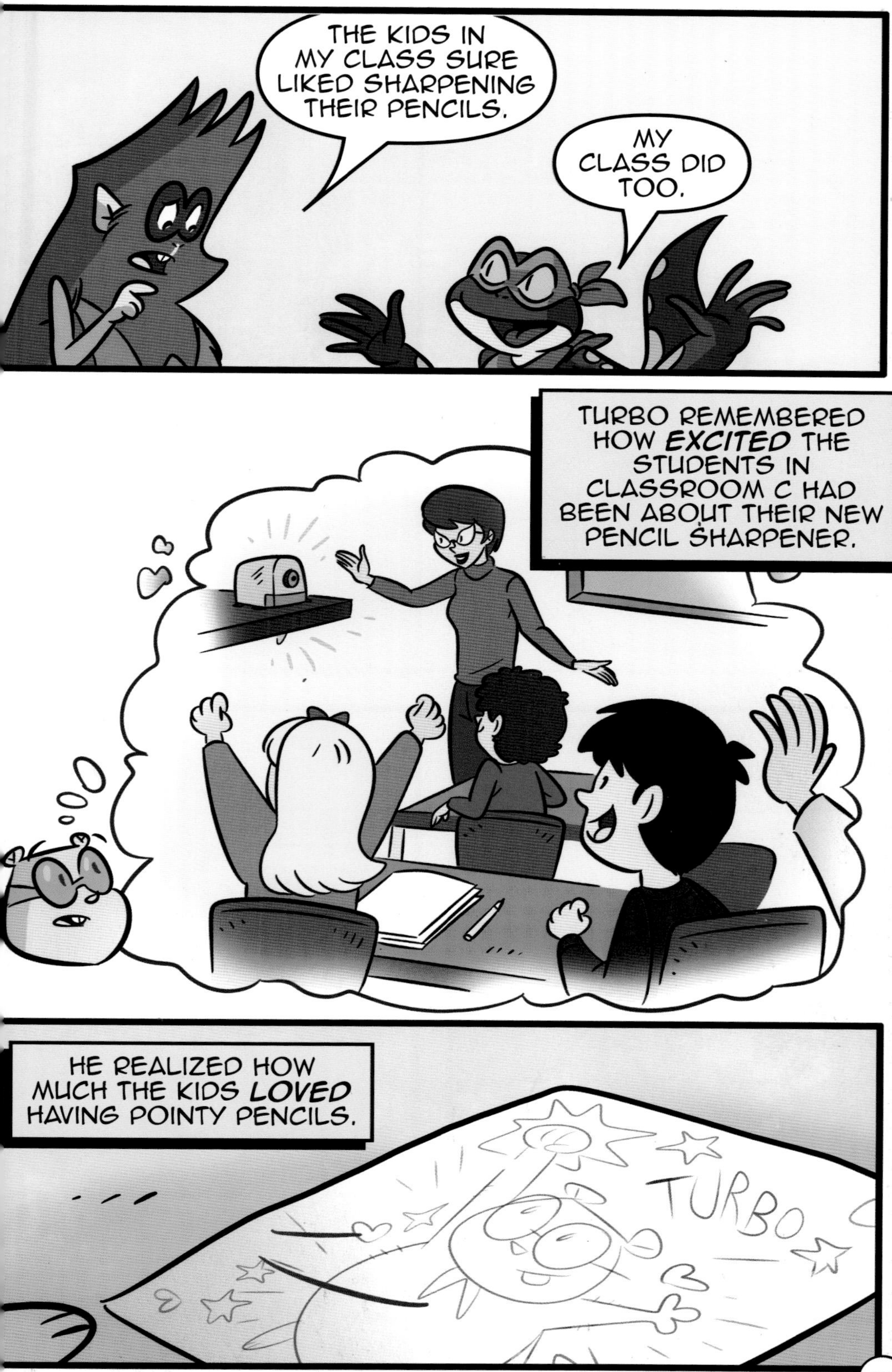
THE KIDS IN MY CLASS SURE LIKED SHARPENING THEIR PENCILS.
MY CLASS DID TOO.
TURBO REMEMBERED HOW ***EXCITED*** THE STUDENTS IN CLASSROOM C HAD BEEN ABOUT THEIR NEW PENCIL SHARPENER.
HE REALIZED HOW MUCH THE KIDS ***LOVED*** HAVING POINTY PENCILS.
...
TURBO

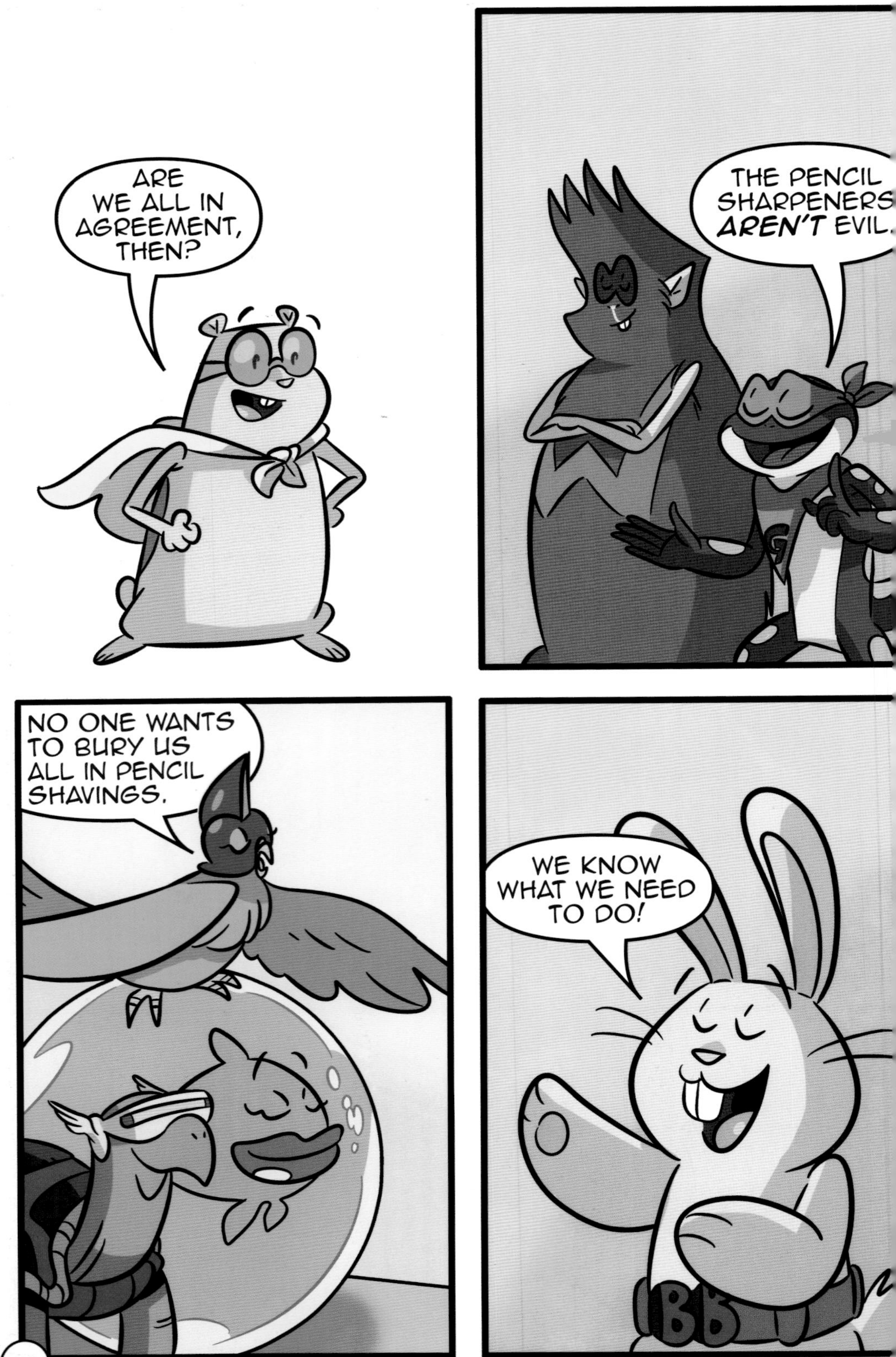
ARE WE ALL IN AGREEMENT, THEN?
THE PENCIL SHARPENERS *AREN'T* EVIL.
NO ONE WANTS TO BURY US ALL IN PENCIL SHAVINGS.
WE KNOW WHAT WE NEED TO DO!

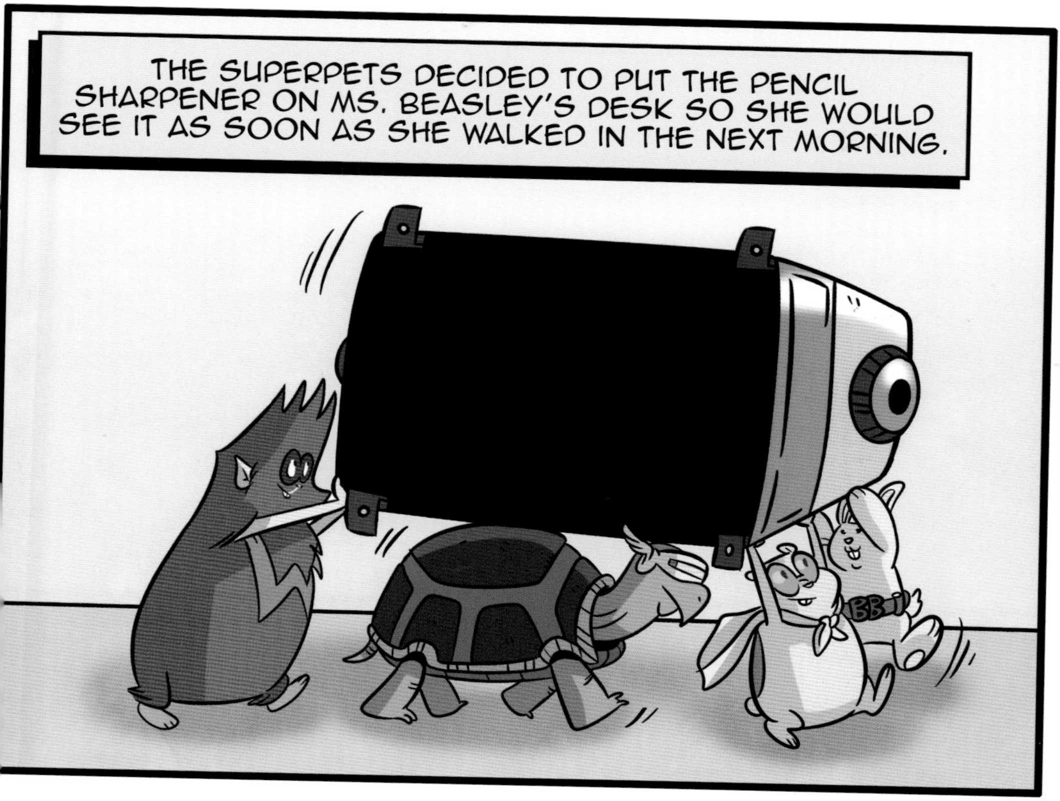
THE SUPERPETS DECIDED TO PUT THE PENCIL SHARPENER ON MS. BEASLEY'S DESK SO SHE WOULD SEE IT AS SOON AS SHE WALKED IN THE NEXT MORNING.
[redacted]

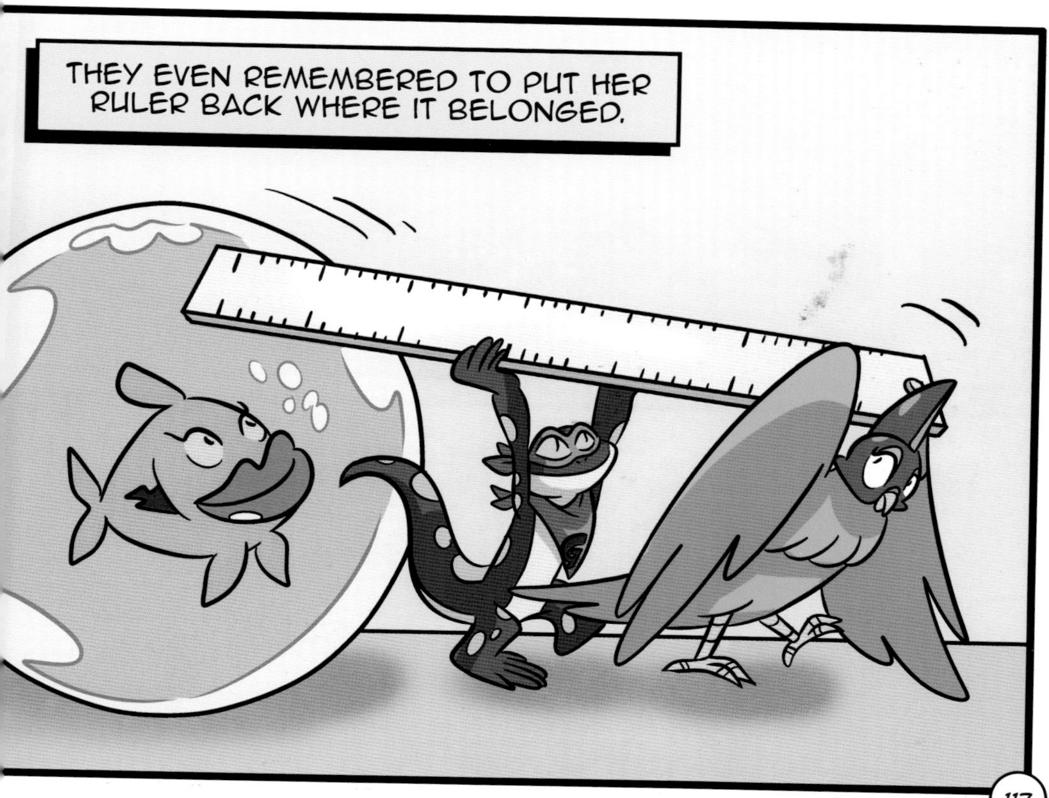
THEY EVEN REMEMBERED TO PUT HER RULER BACK WHERE IT BELONGED.

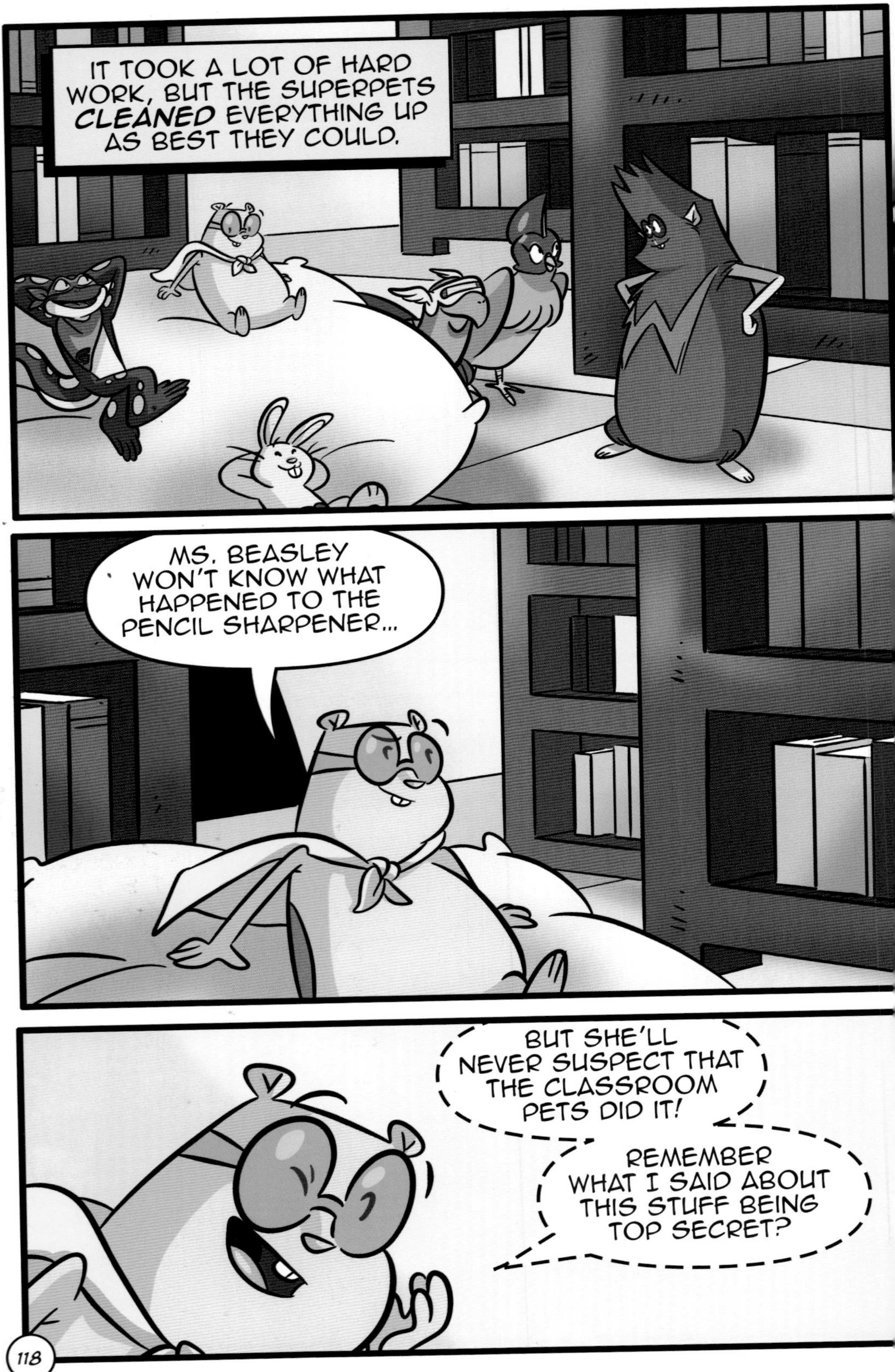
IT TOOK A LOT OF HARD WORK, BUT THE SUPERPETS *CLEANED* EVERYTHING UP AS BEST THEY COULD.
MS. BEASLEY WON'T KNOW WHAT HAPPENED TO THE PENCIL SHARPENER...
BUT SHE'LL NEVER SUSPECT THAT THE CLASSROOM PETS DID IT!
REMEMBER WHAT I SAID ABOUT THIS STUFF BEING TOP SECRET?

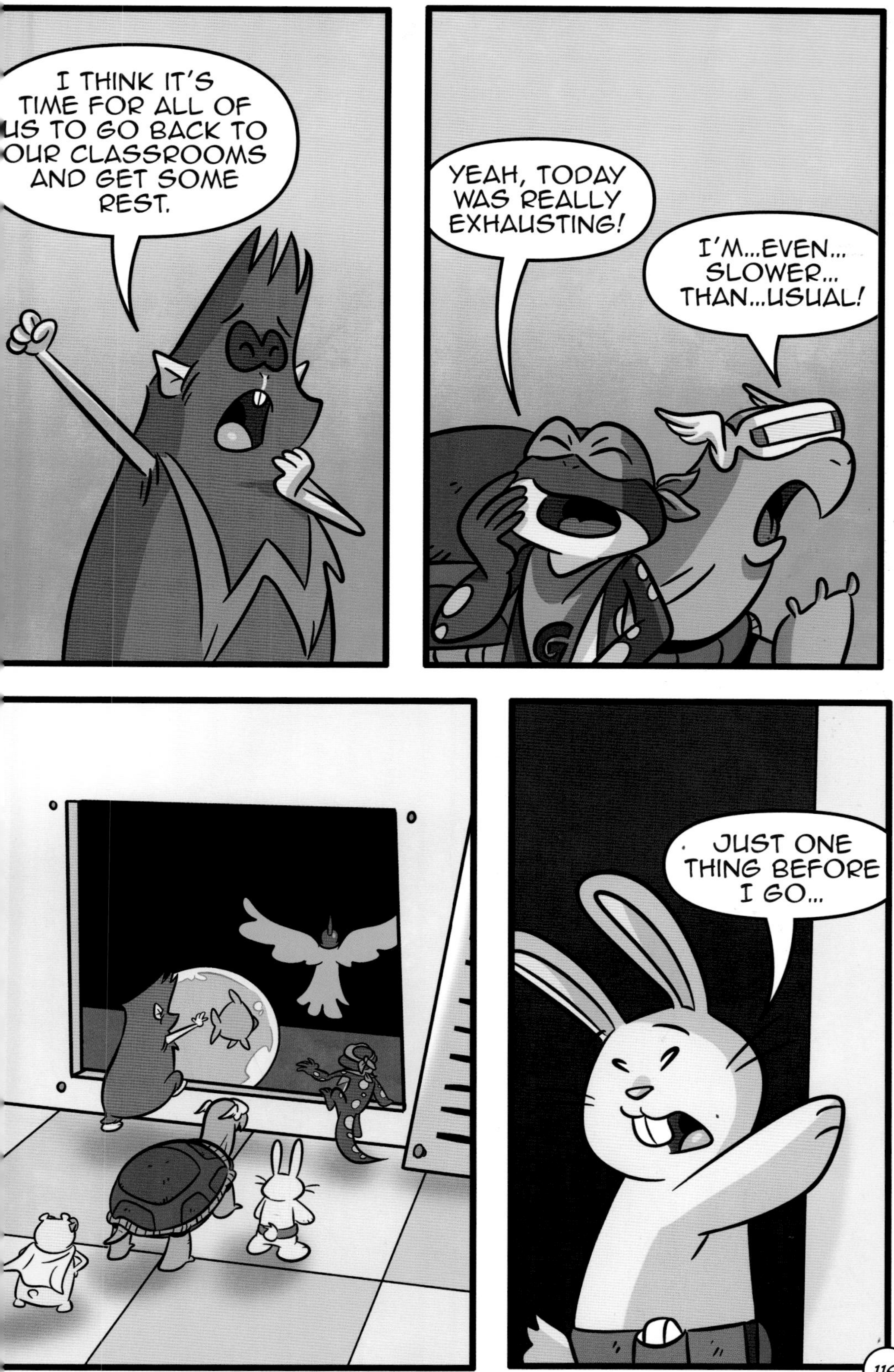
I THINK IT'S TIME FOR ALL OF US TO GO BACK TO OUR CLASSROOMS AND GET SOME REST.
YEAH, TODAY WAS REALLY EXHAUSTING!
I'M...EVEN... SLOWER... THAN...USUAL!
JUST ONE THING BEFORE I GO...

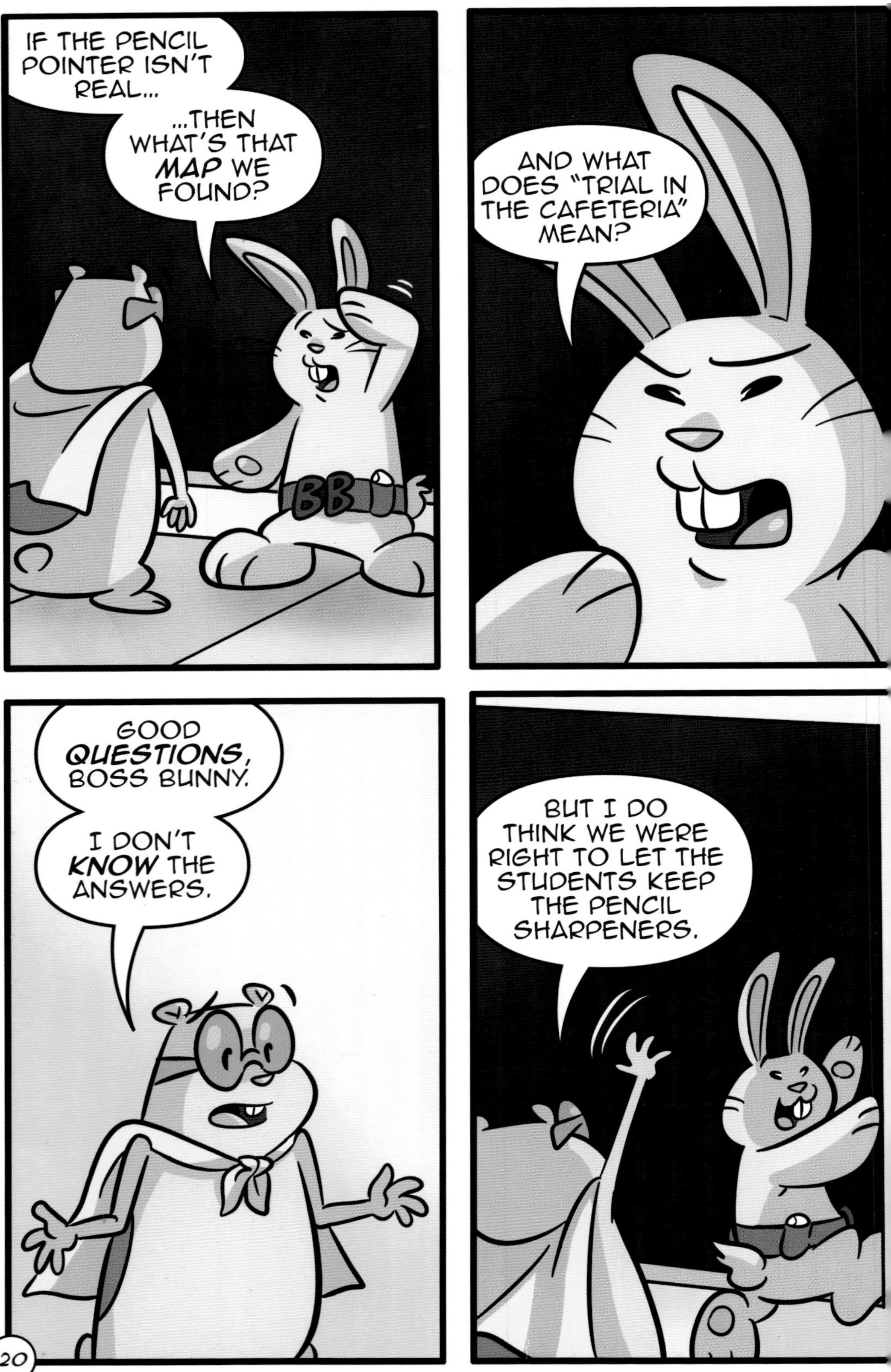
IF THE PENCIL POINTER ISN'T REAL...
...THEN WHAT'S THAT MAP WE FOUND?
AND WHAT DOES "TRIAL IN THE CAFETERIA" MEAN?
BB
GOOD QUESTIONS, BOSS BUNNY.
I DON'T KNOW THE ANSWERS.
BUT I DO THINK WE WERE RIGHT TO LET THE STUDENTS KEEP THE PENCIL SHARPENERS.

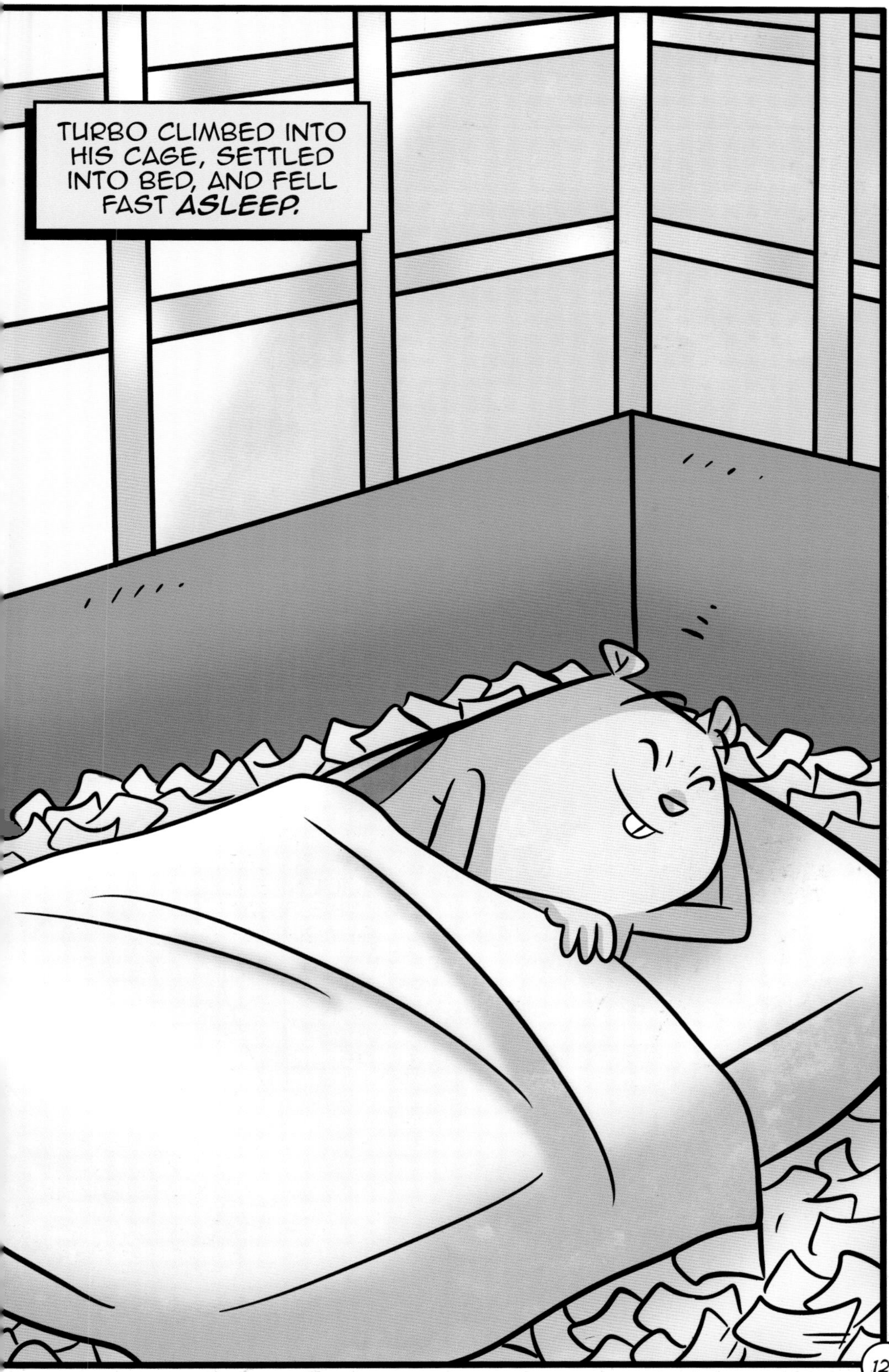
TURBO CLIMBED INTO HIS CAGE, SETTLED INTO BED, AND FELL FAST ASLEEP.

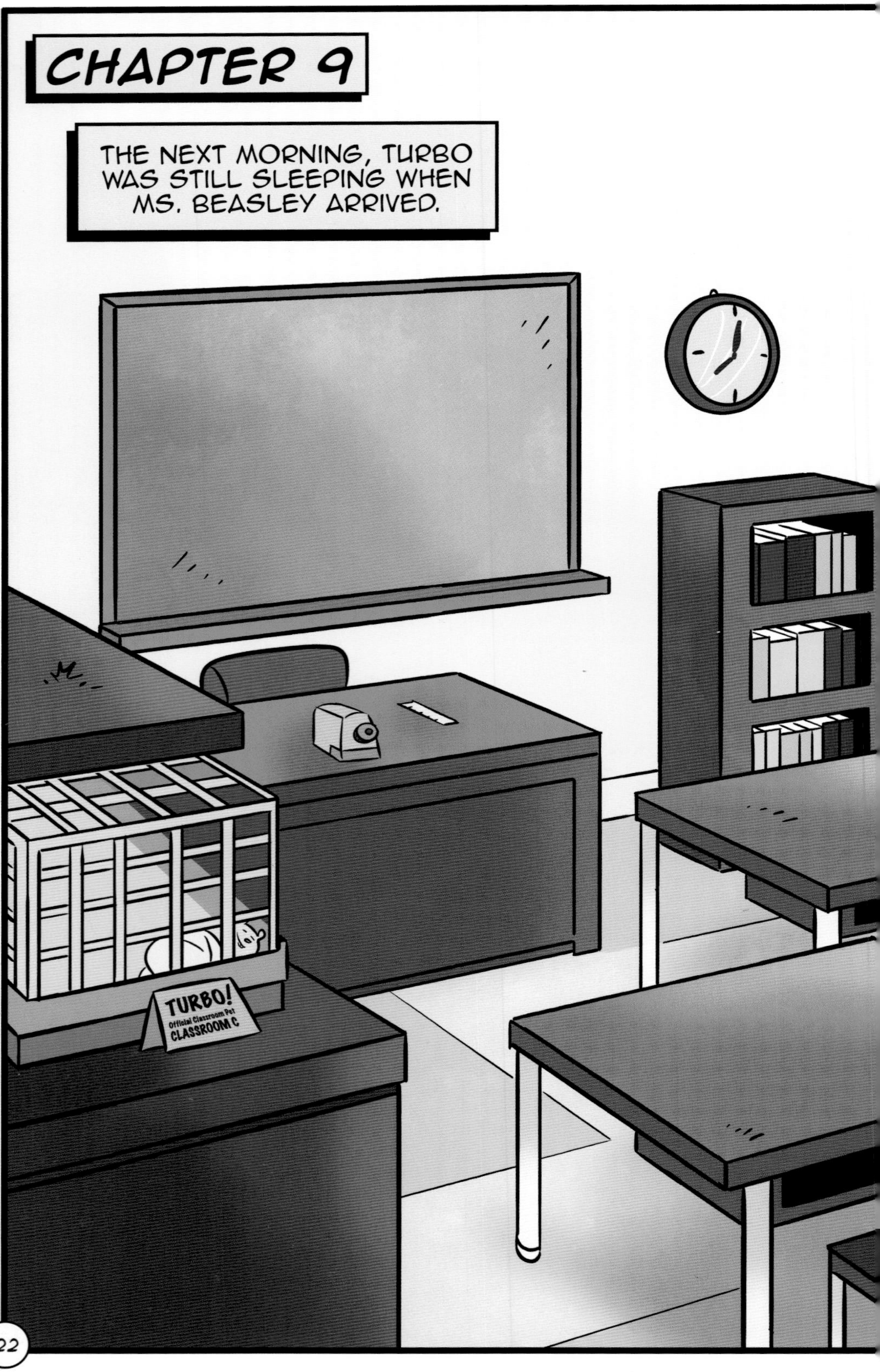
CHAPTER 9
THE NEXT MORNING, TURBO WAS STILL SLEEPING WHEN MS. BEASLEY ARRIVED.
TURBO!
Official Classroom Pet
CLASSROOM C

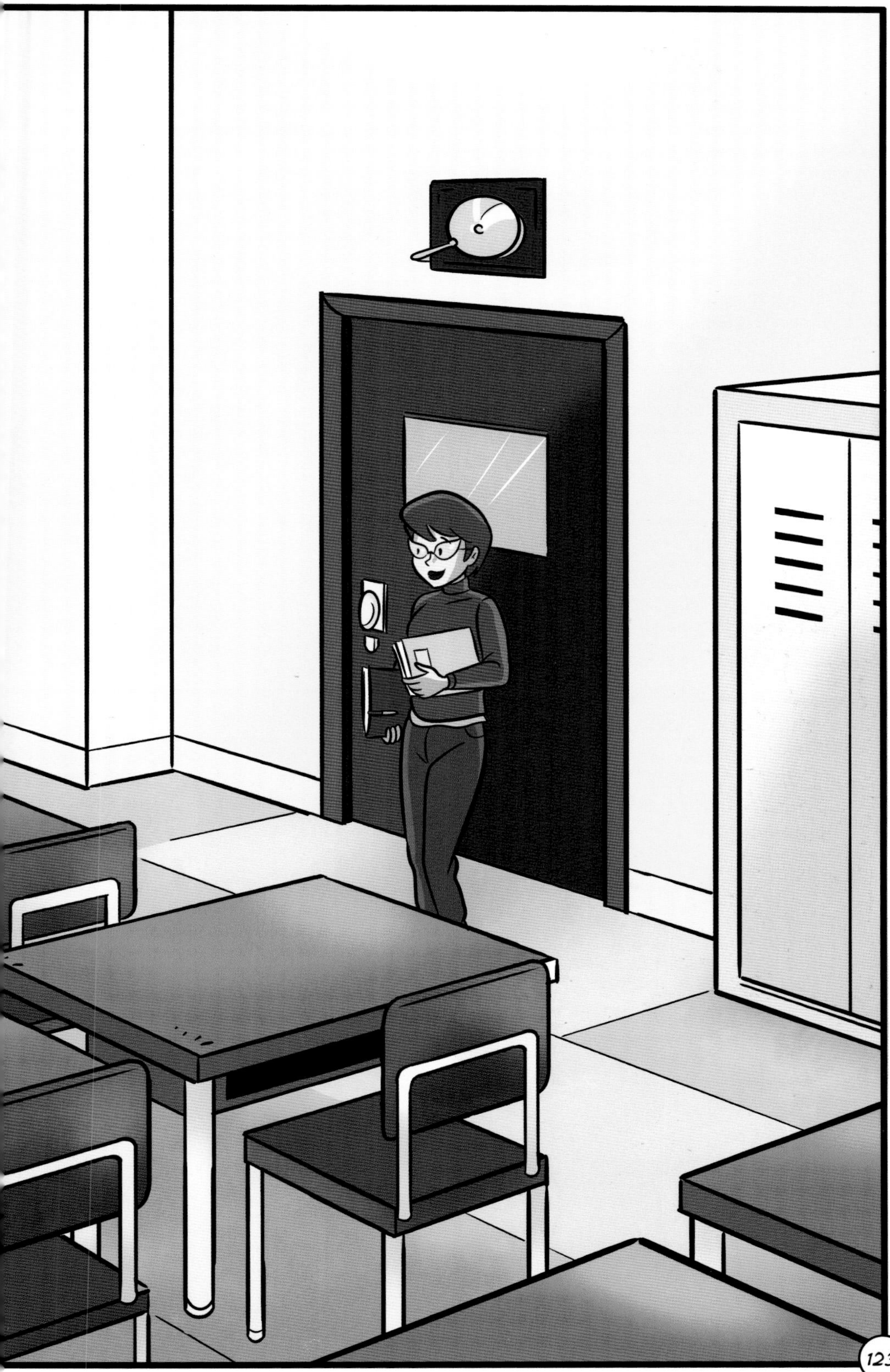

MS. BEASLEY IMMEDIATELY NOTICED THE PENCIL SHARPENER ON HER DESK.

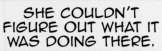

SHE COULDN'T FIGURE OUT WHAT IT WAS DOING THERE.

???

THEN MS. BEASLEY NOTICED *SOMETHING* ELSE.

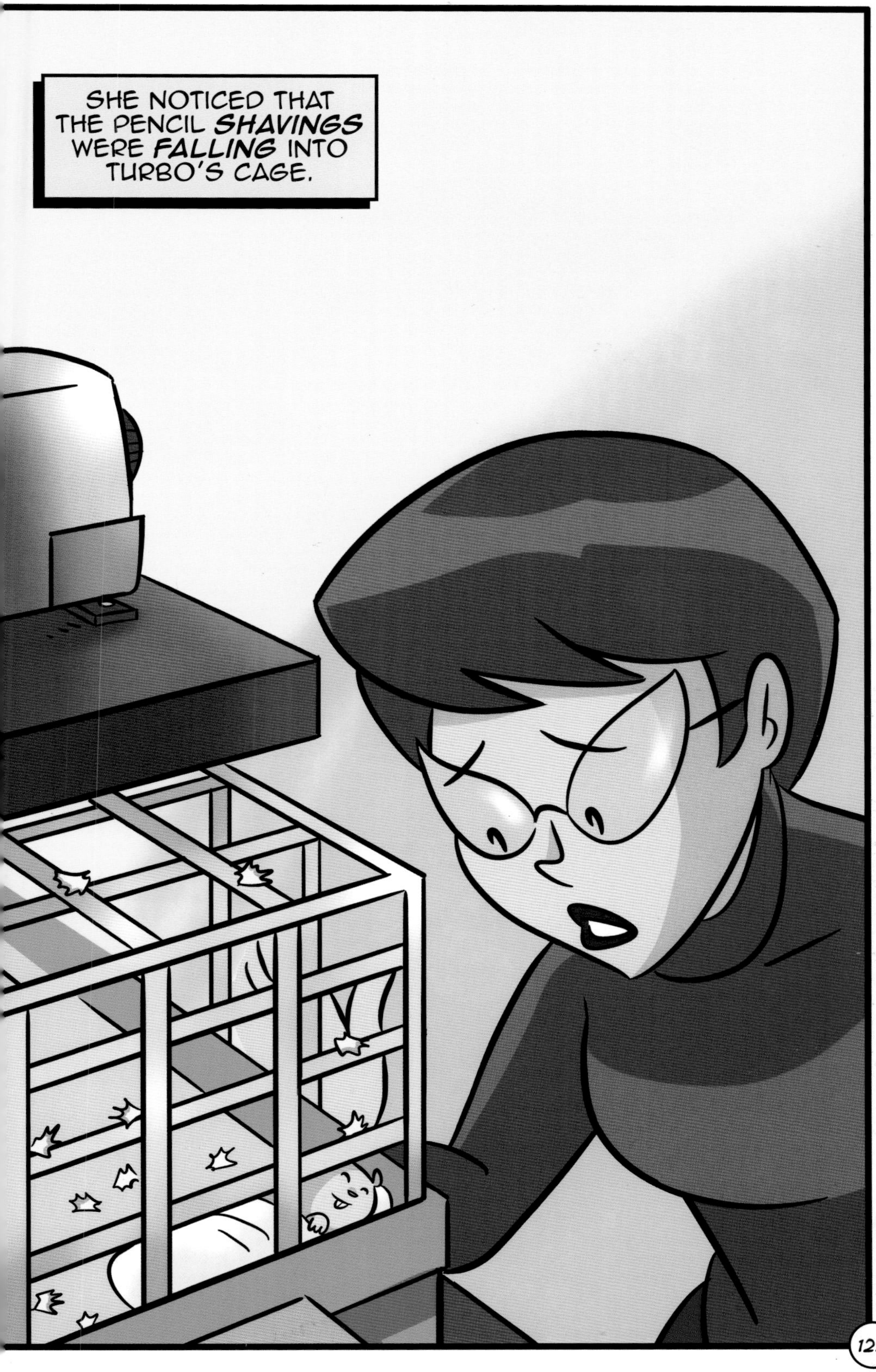
SHE NOTICED THAT THE PENCIL ***SHAVINGS*** WERE ***FALLING*** INTO TURBO'S CAGE.

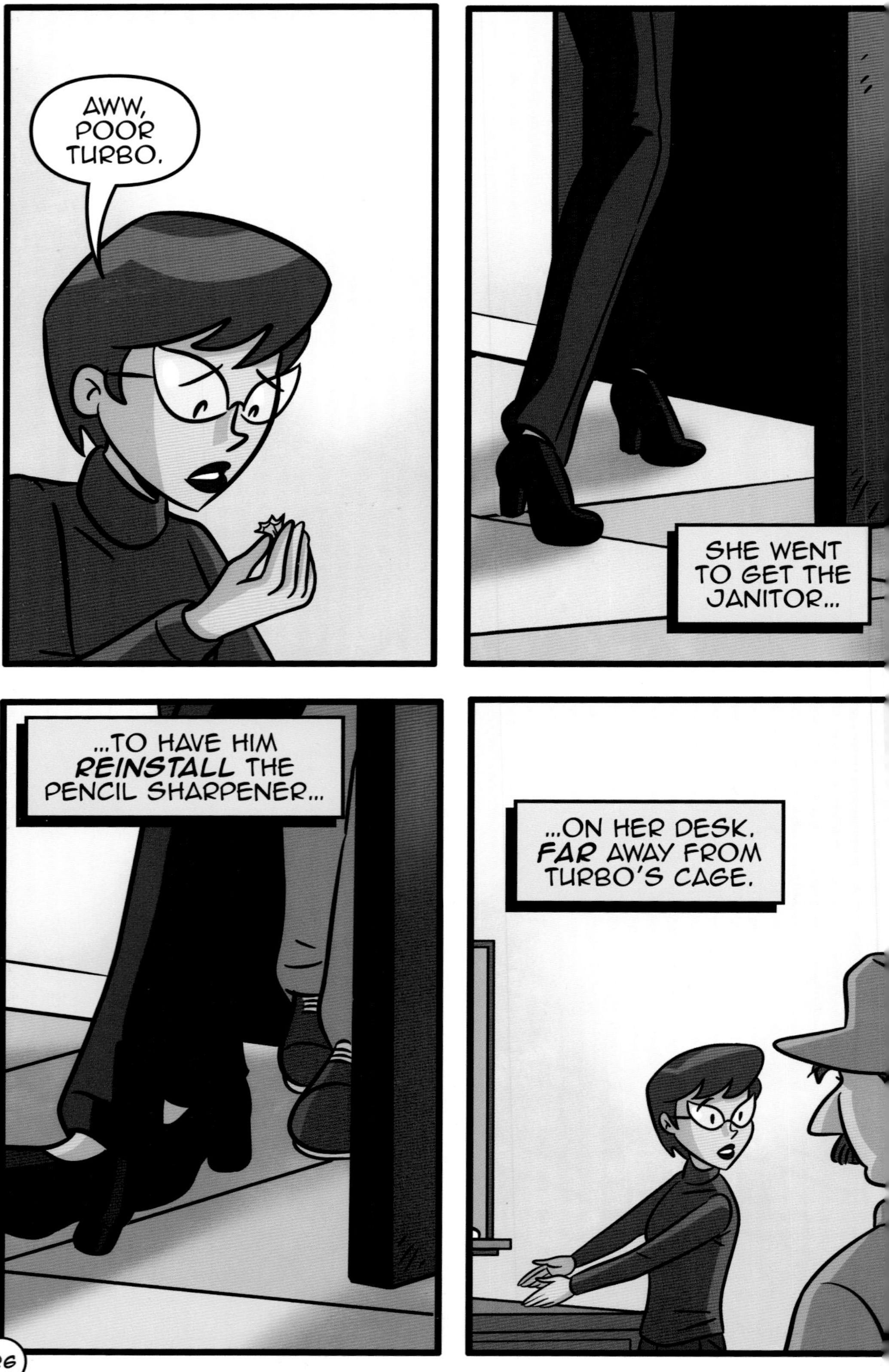
AWW, POOR TURBO.
SHE WENT TO GET THE JANITOR...
...TO HAVE HIM *REINSTALL* THE PENCIL SHARPENER...
...ON HER DESK. *FAR* AWAY FROM TURBO'S CAGE.

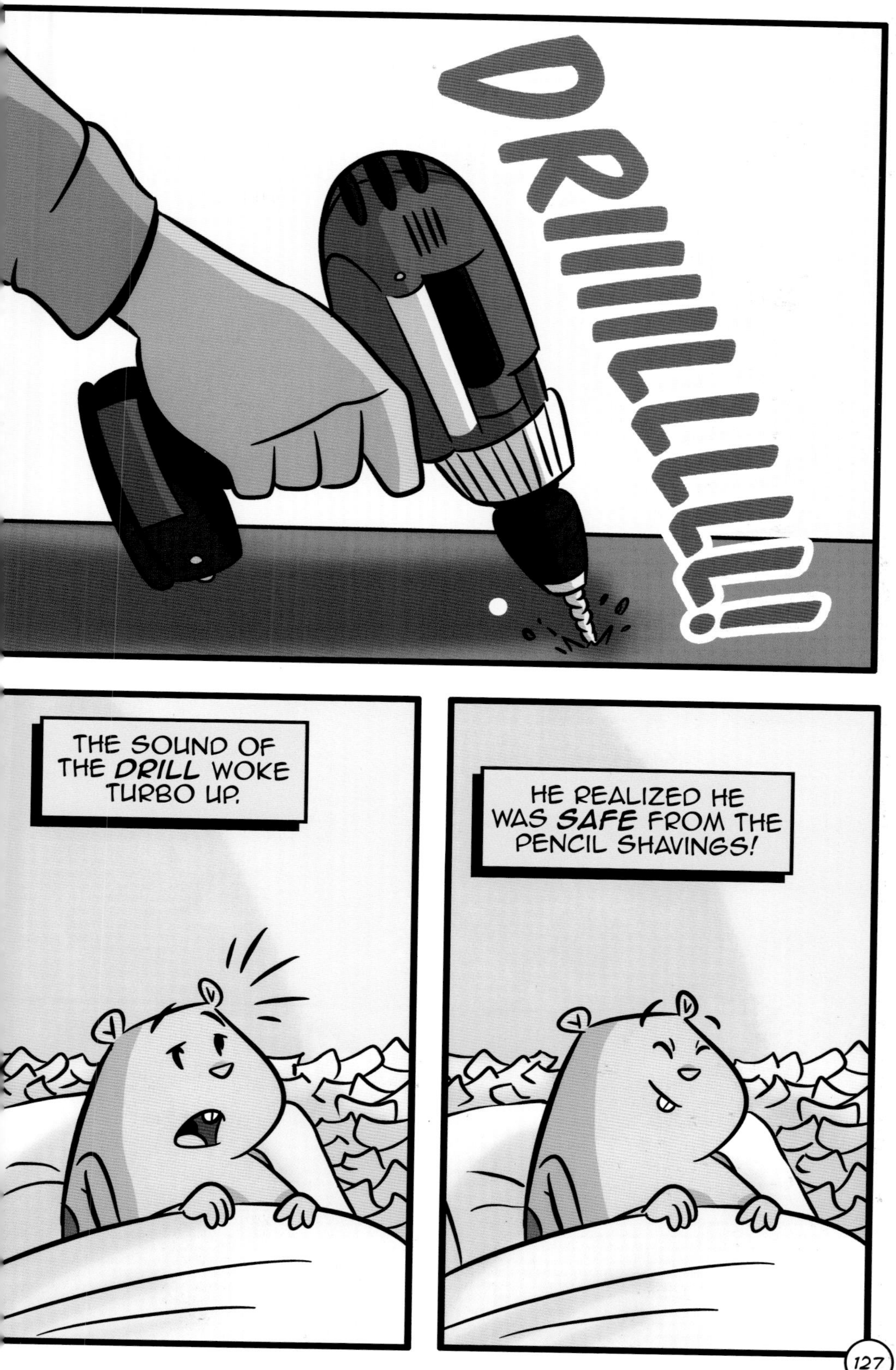
DRIIIILLLL!!
THE SOUND OF THE DRILL WOKE TURBO UP.
HE REALIZED HE WAS SAFE FROM THE PENCIL SHAVINGS!

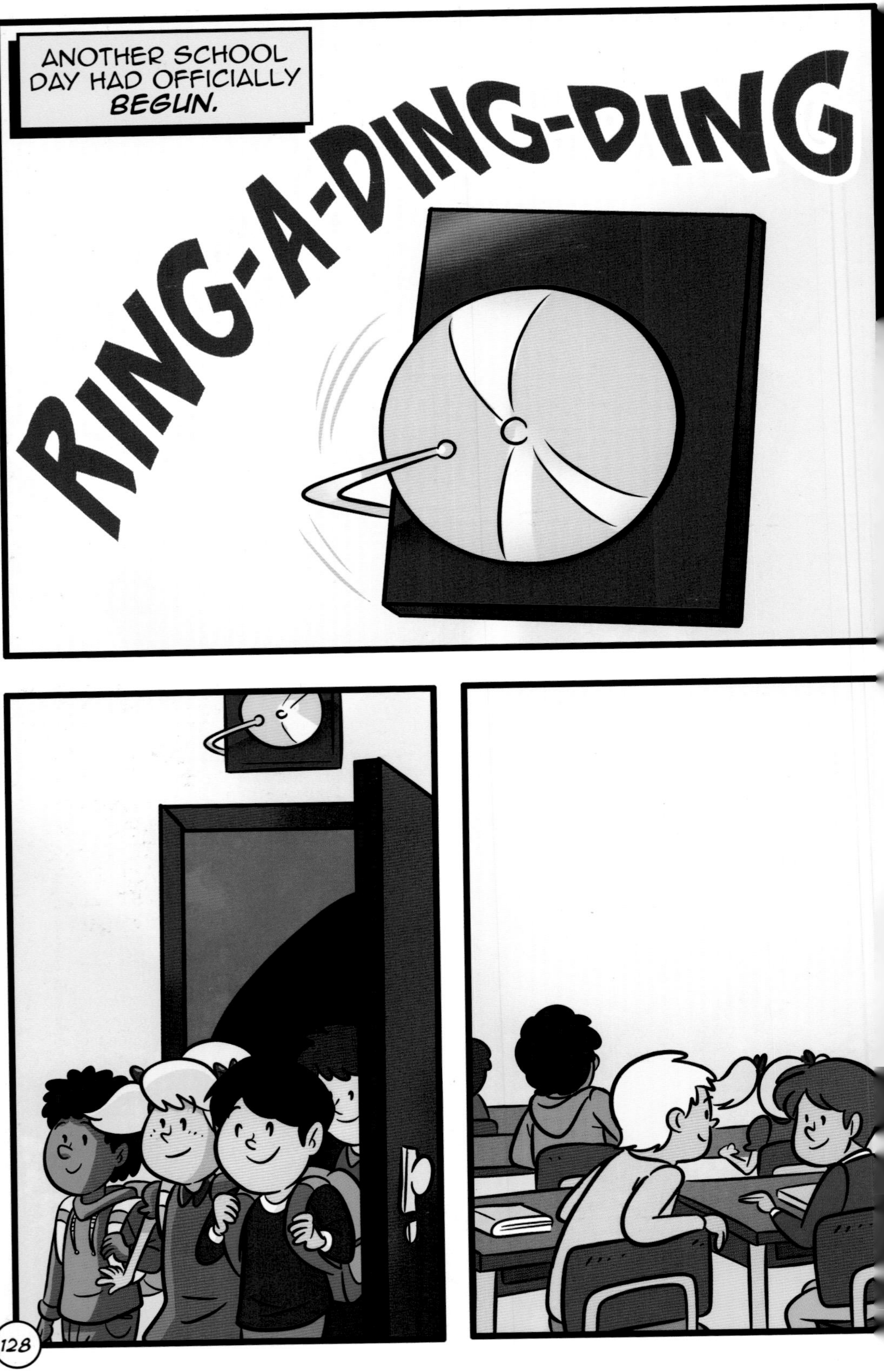

ANOTHER SCHOOL DAY HAD OFFICIALLY *BEGUN.*
RING-A-DING-DING

GOOD MORNING, CLASS! I HAVE A FEW ANNOUNCEMENTS.

FIRST, WE WILL BE STARTING A TRIAL IN THE CAFETERIA TODAY...

AT THE MENTION OF A *TRIAL* IN THE CAFETERIA, TURBO'S EARS PERKED UP.

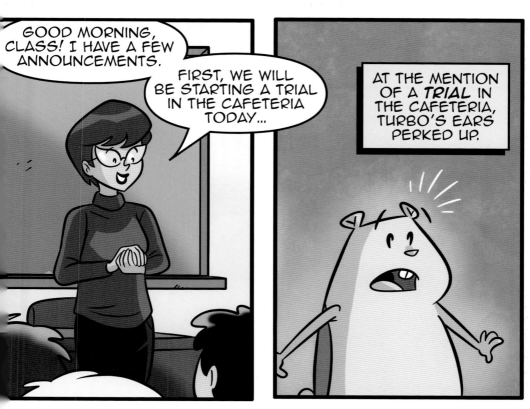

HE RUSHED TO THE EDGE OF HIS CAGE TO HEAR EVERY WORD OF WHAT MS. BEASLEY WAS GOING TO SAY.

WE'RE DOING A TRIAL RUN OF DELICIOUS *HEALTHY SNACKS* IN THE CAFETERIA.

YUMMY THINGS LIKE GLUTEN-FREE BREAD, FRESH FRUIT, AND YOGURT.

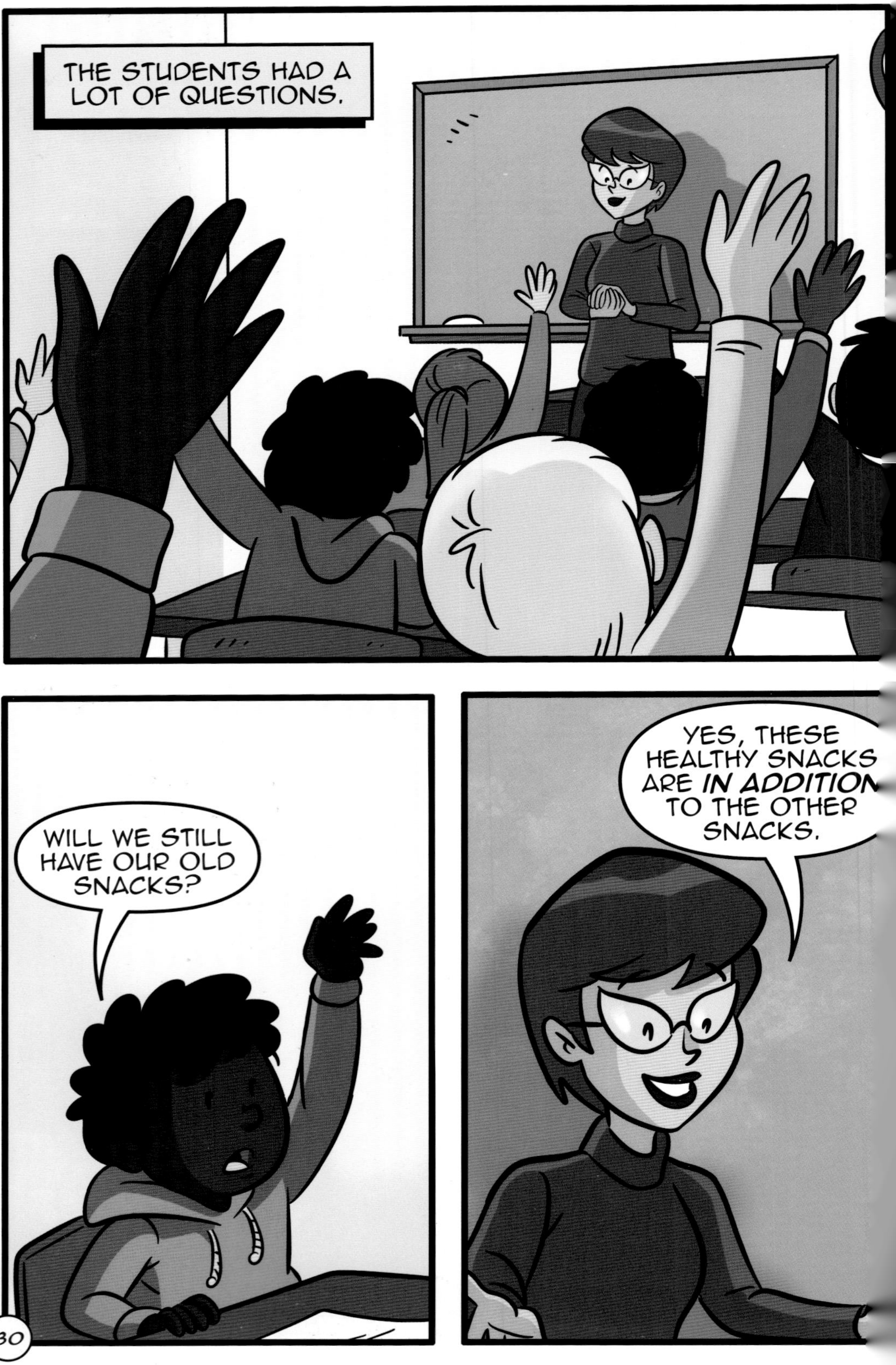
THE STUDENTS HAD A LOT OF QUESTIONS.
WILL WE STILL HAVE OUR OLD SNACKS?
YES, THESE HEALTHY SNACKS ARE *IN ADDITION* TO THE OTHER SNACKS.

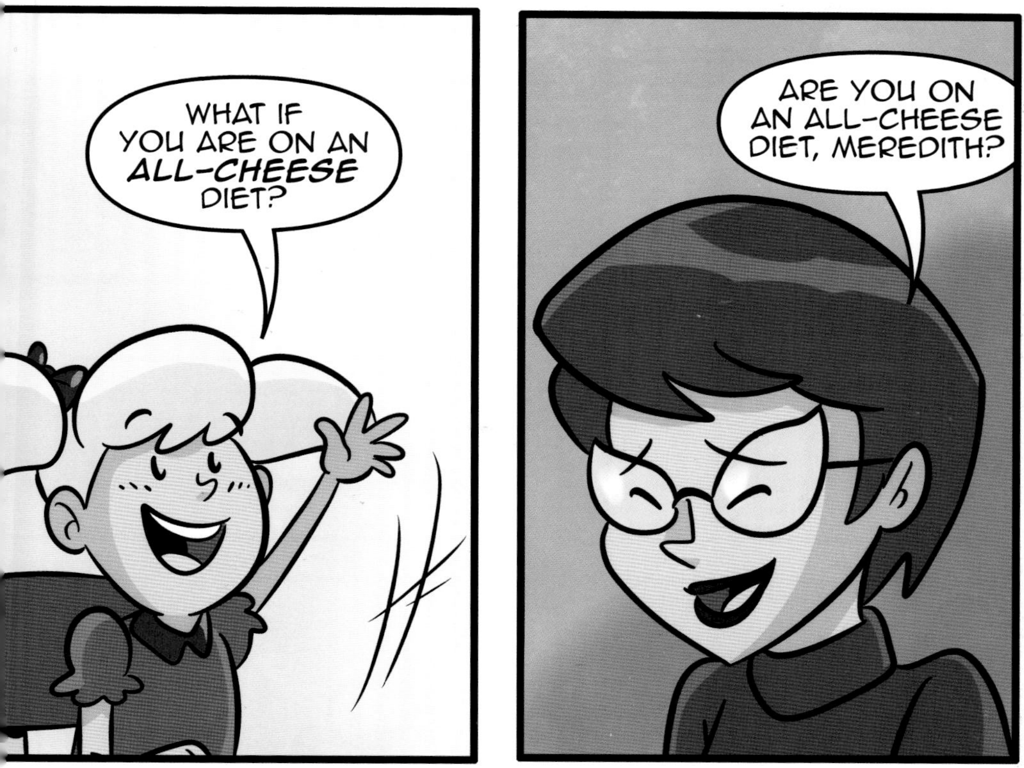
WHAT IF YOU ARE ON AN ***ALL-CHEESE*** DIET?
ARE YOU ON AN ALL-CHEESE DIET, MEREDITH?

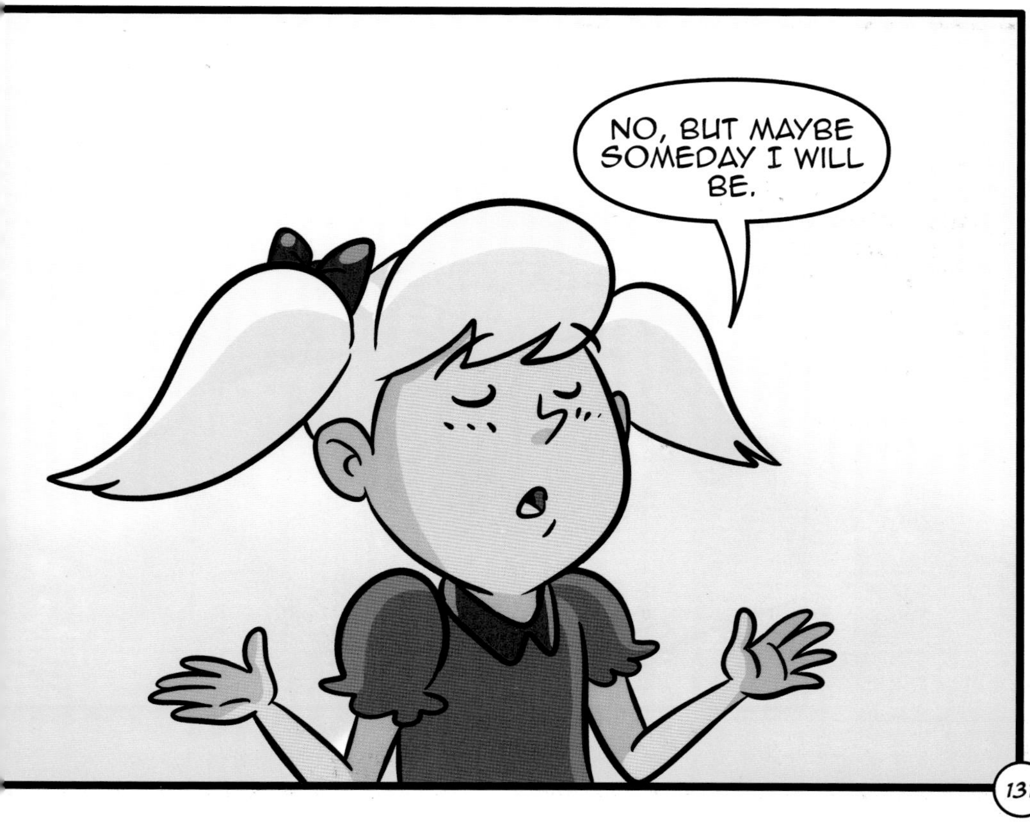
NO, BUT MAYBE SOMEDAY I WILL BE.

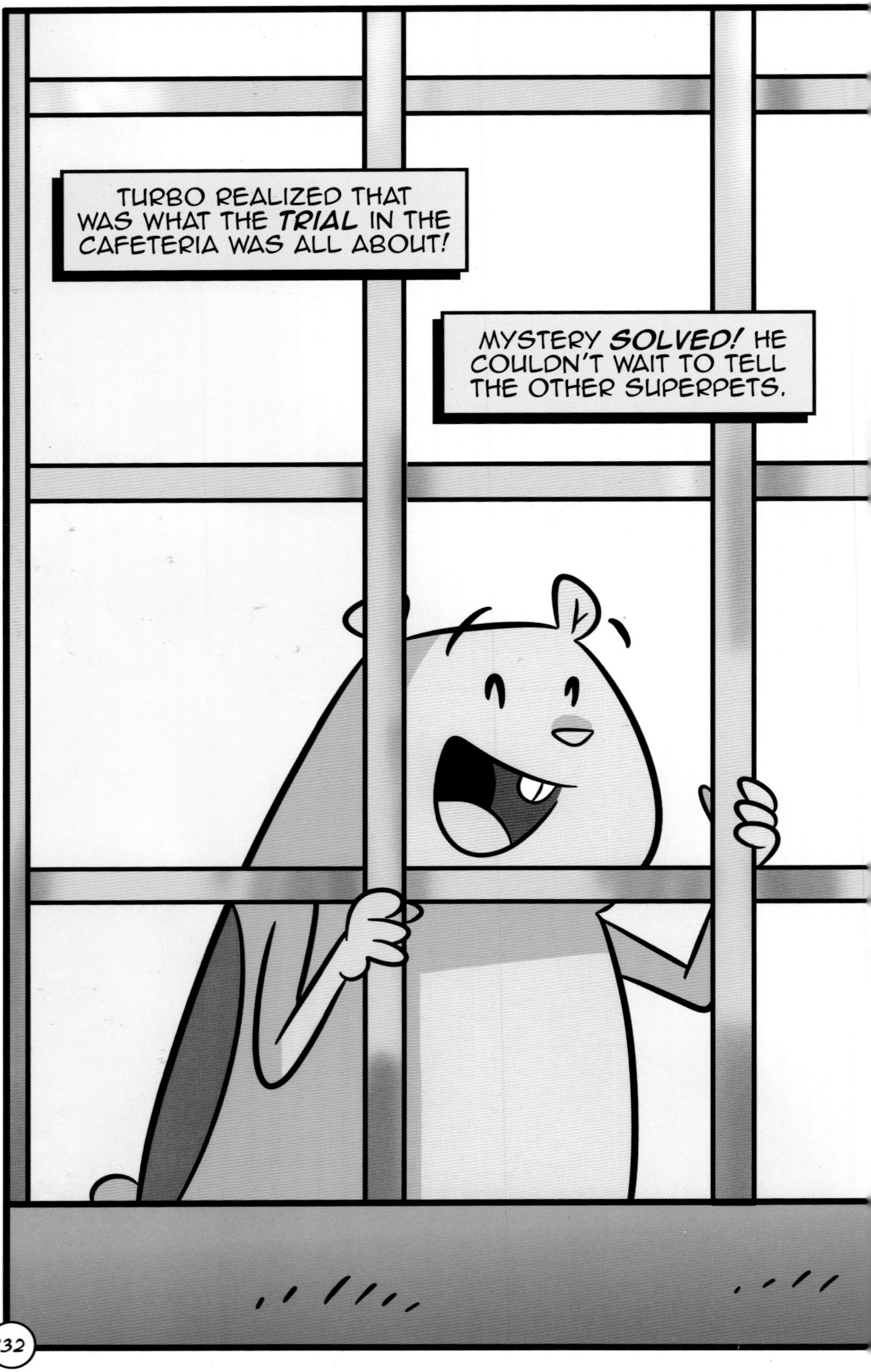
TURBO REALIZED THAT WAS WHAT THE TRIAL IN THE CAFETERIA WAS ALL ABOUT!
MYSTERY SOLVED! HE COULDN'T WAIT TO TELL THE OTHER SUPERPETS.

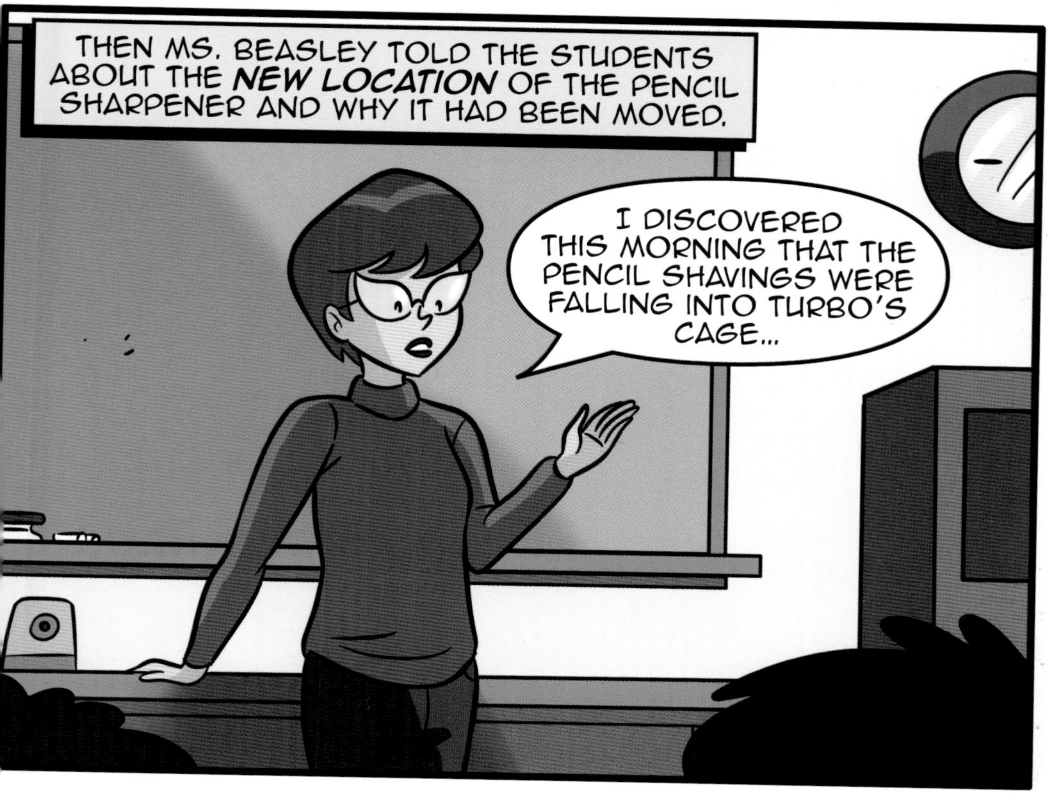
THEN MS. BEASLEY TOLD THE STUDENTS ABOUT THE ***NEW LOCATION*** OF THE PENCIL SHARPENER AND WHY IT HAD BEEN MOVED.
I DISCOVERED THIS MORNING THAT THE PENCIL SHAVINGS WERE FALLING INTO TURBO'S CAGE...

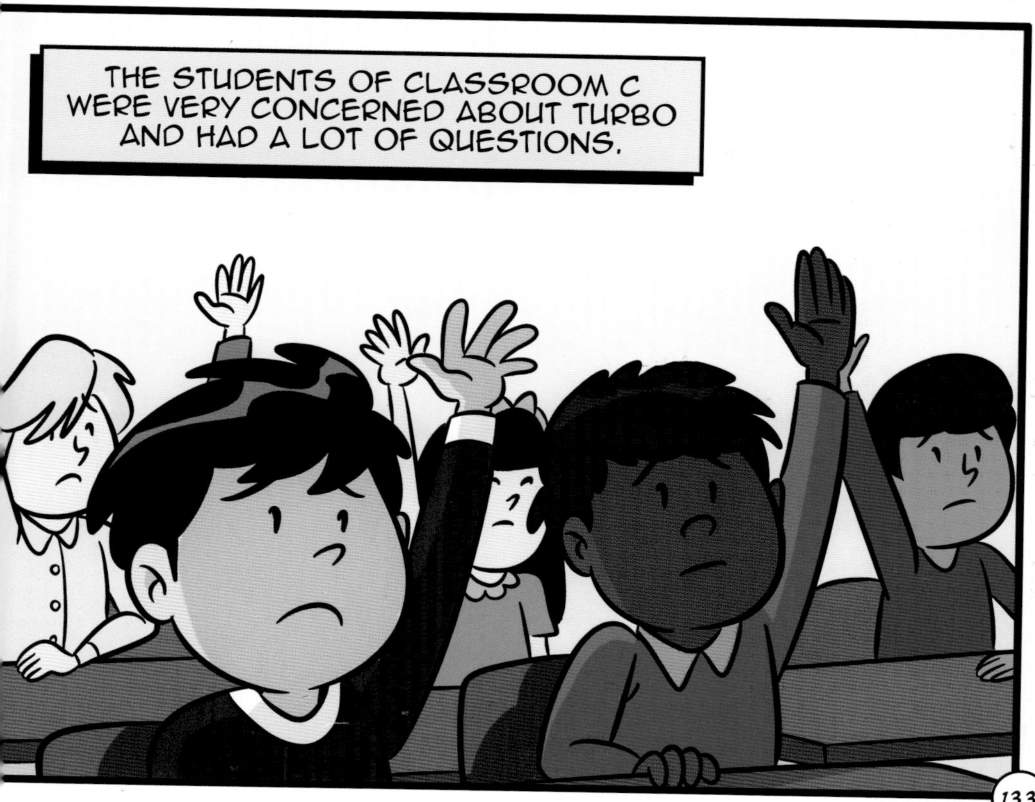
THE STUDENTS OF CLASSROOM C WERE VERY CONCERNED ABOUT TURBO AND HAD A LOT OF QUESTIONS.

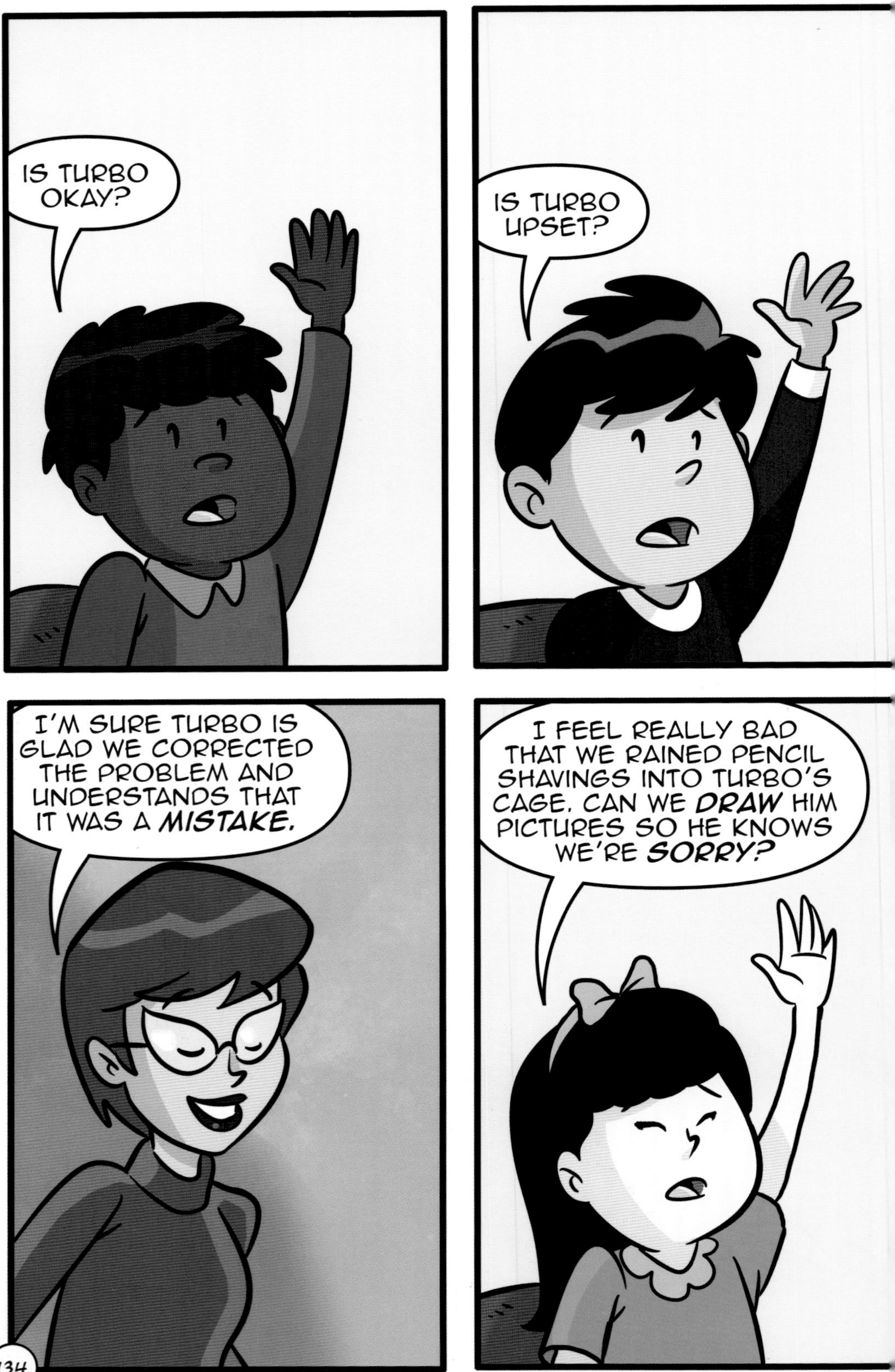
IS TURBO OKAY?
IS TURBO UPSET?
I'M SURE TURBO IS GLAD WE CORRECTED THE PROBLEM AND UNDERSTANDS THAT IT WAS A MISTAKE.
I FEEL REALLY BAD THAT WE RAINED PENCIL SHAVINGS INTO TURBO'S CAGE. CAN WE DRAW HIM PICTURES SO HE KNOWS WE'RE SORRY?

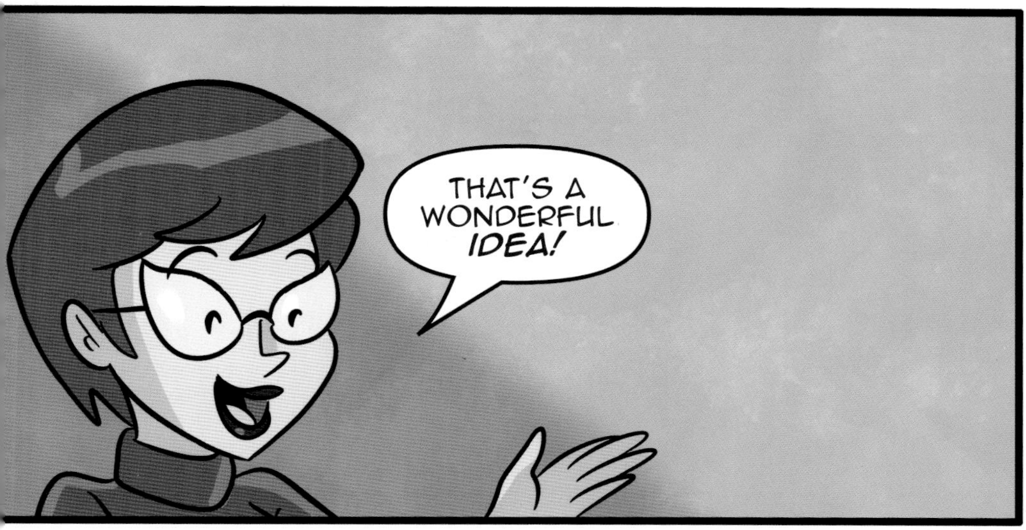
THAT'S A WONDERFUL *IDEA!*

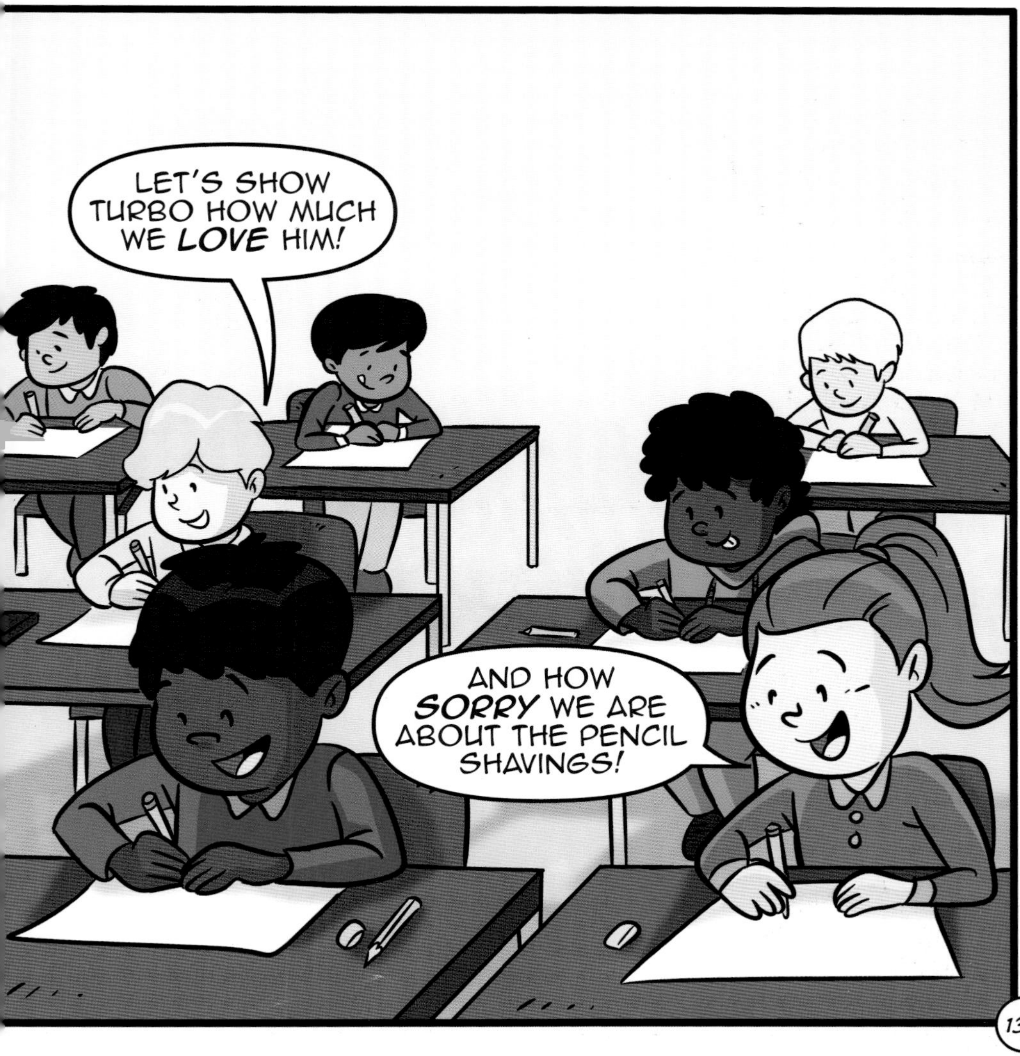
LET'S SHOW TURBO HOW MUCH WE *LOVE* HIM!
AND HOW *SORRY* WE ARE ABOUT THE PENCIL SHAVINGS!

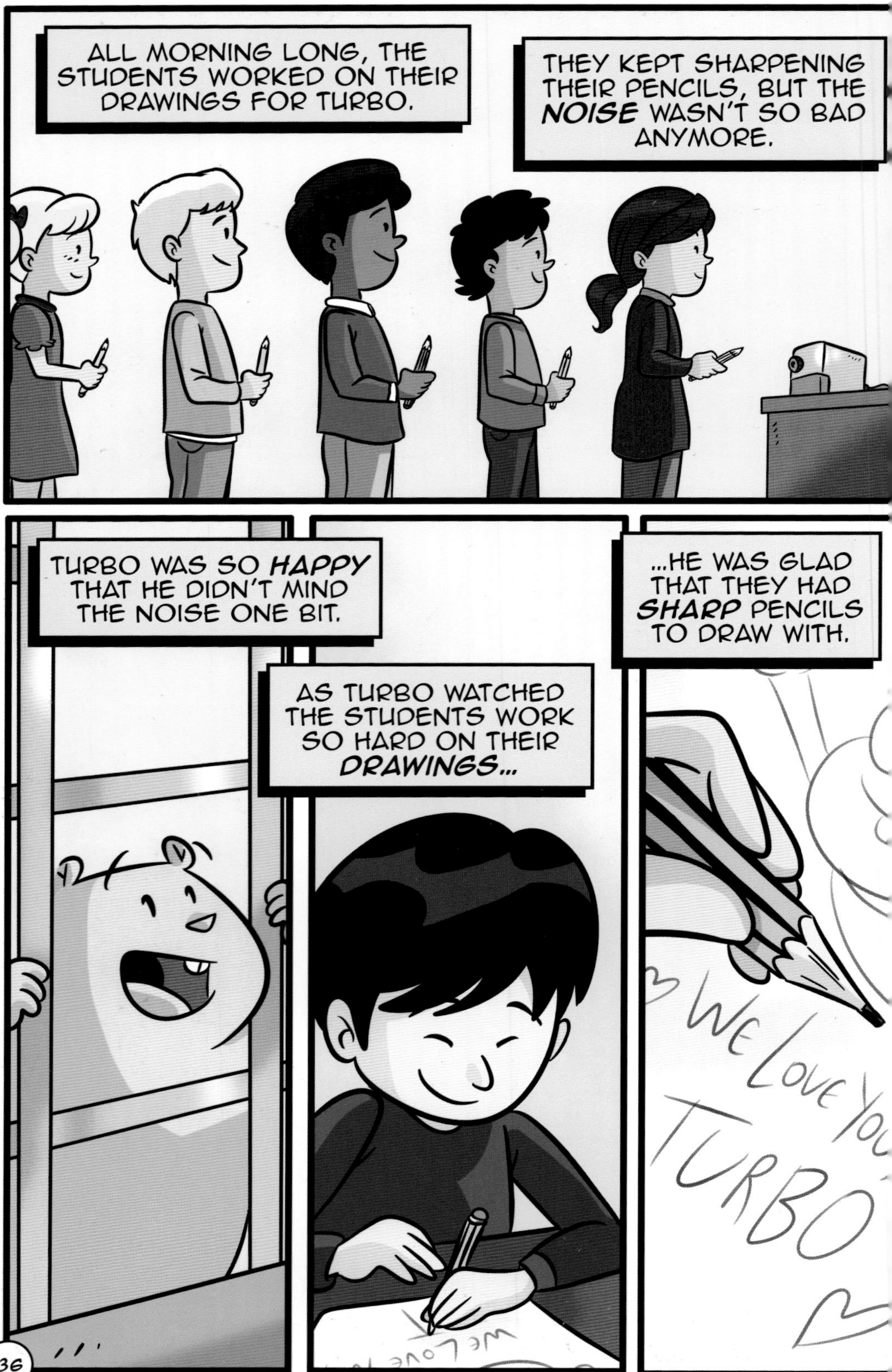
ALL MORNING LONG, THE STUDENTS WORKED ON THEIR DRAWINGS FOR TURBO.
THEY KEPT SHARPENING THEIR PENCILS, BUT THE *NOISE* WASN'T SO BAD ANYMORE.
TURBO WAS SO *HAPPY* THAT HE DIDN'T MIND THE NOISE ONE BIT.
AS TURBO WATCHED THE STUDENTS WORK SO HARD ON THEIR *DRAWINGS*...
...HE WAS GLAD THAT THEY HAD *SHARP* PENCILS TO DRAW WITH.
We Love You
TURBO

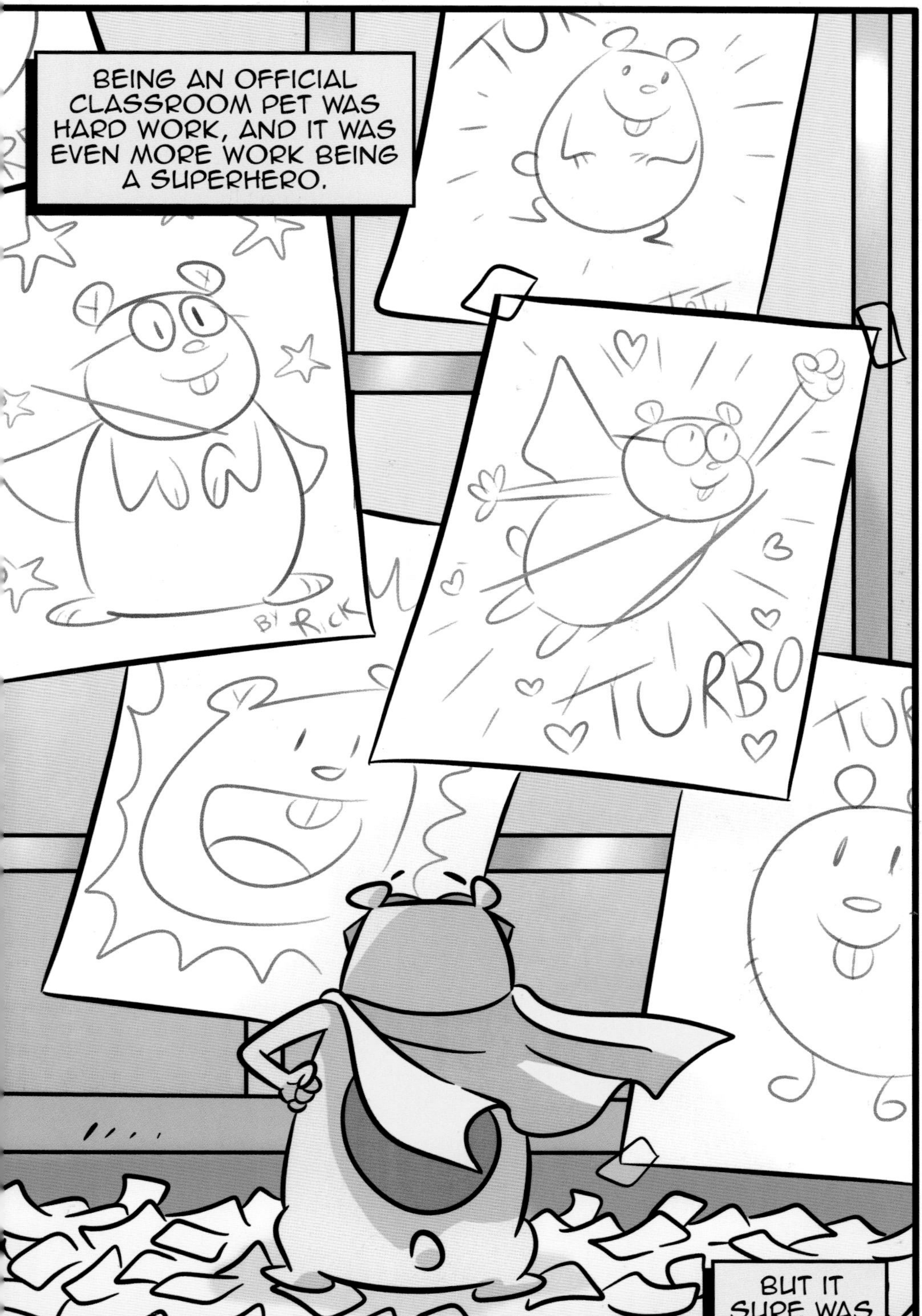
BEING AN OFFICIAL CLASSROOM PET WAS HARD WORK, AND IT WAS EVEN MORE WORK BEING A SUPERHERO.
BY RICK
TURBO
BUT IT SURE WAS WORTH IT.

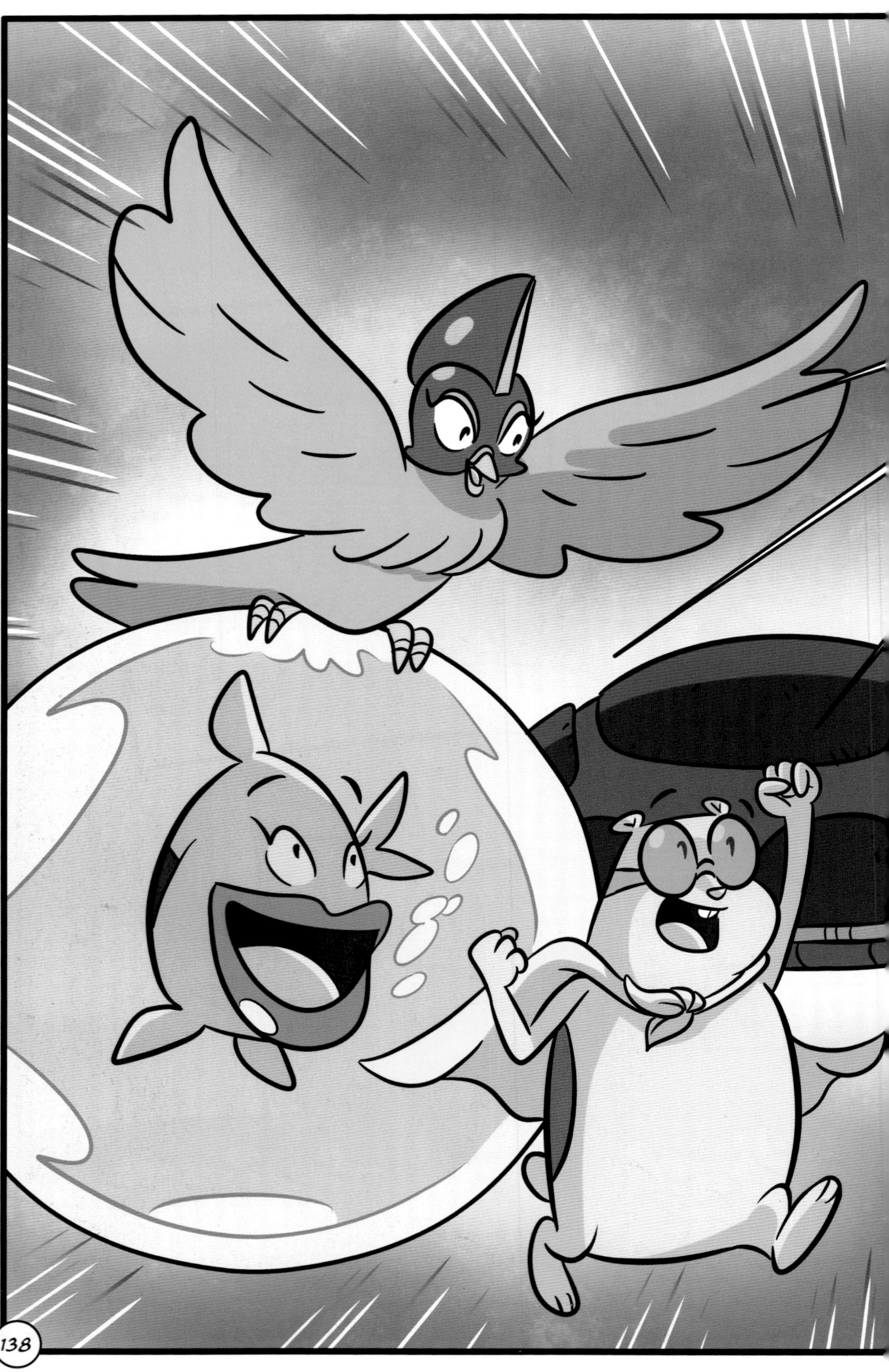

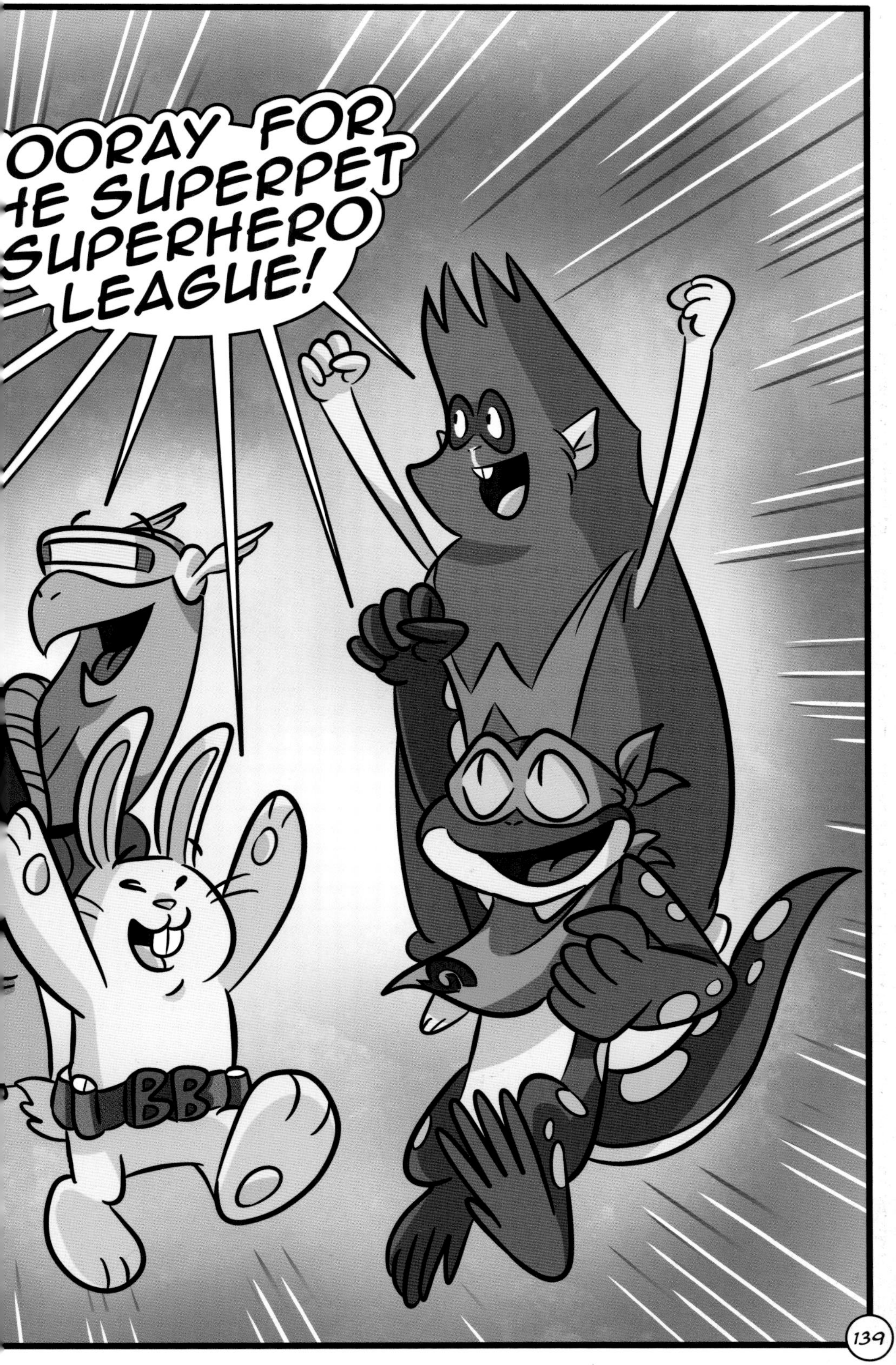
OORAY FOR
HE SUPERPET
SUPERHERO
LEAGUE!

AN'T GET ENOUGH OF TH
PERPET SUPERHERO LEAGU
CHECK OUT THEIR NEXT
ADVENTURE...

Graphic Novel
SUPER TURBO
PROTECTS THE WORLD

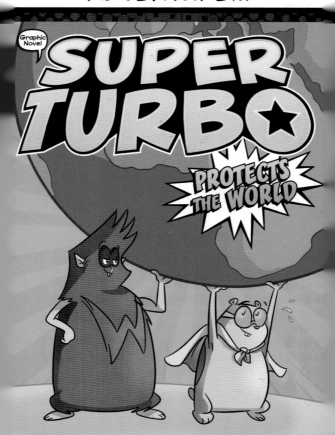

TURN THE PAGE FOR A SNEAK PEEK...

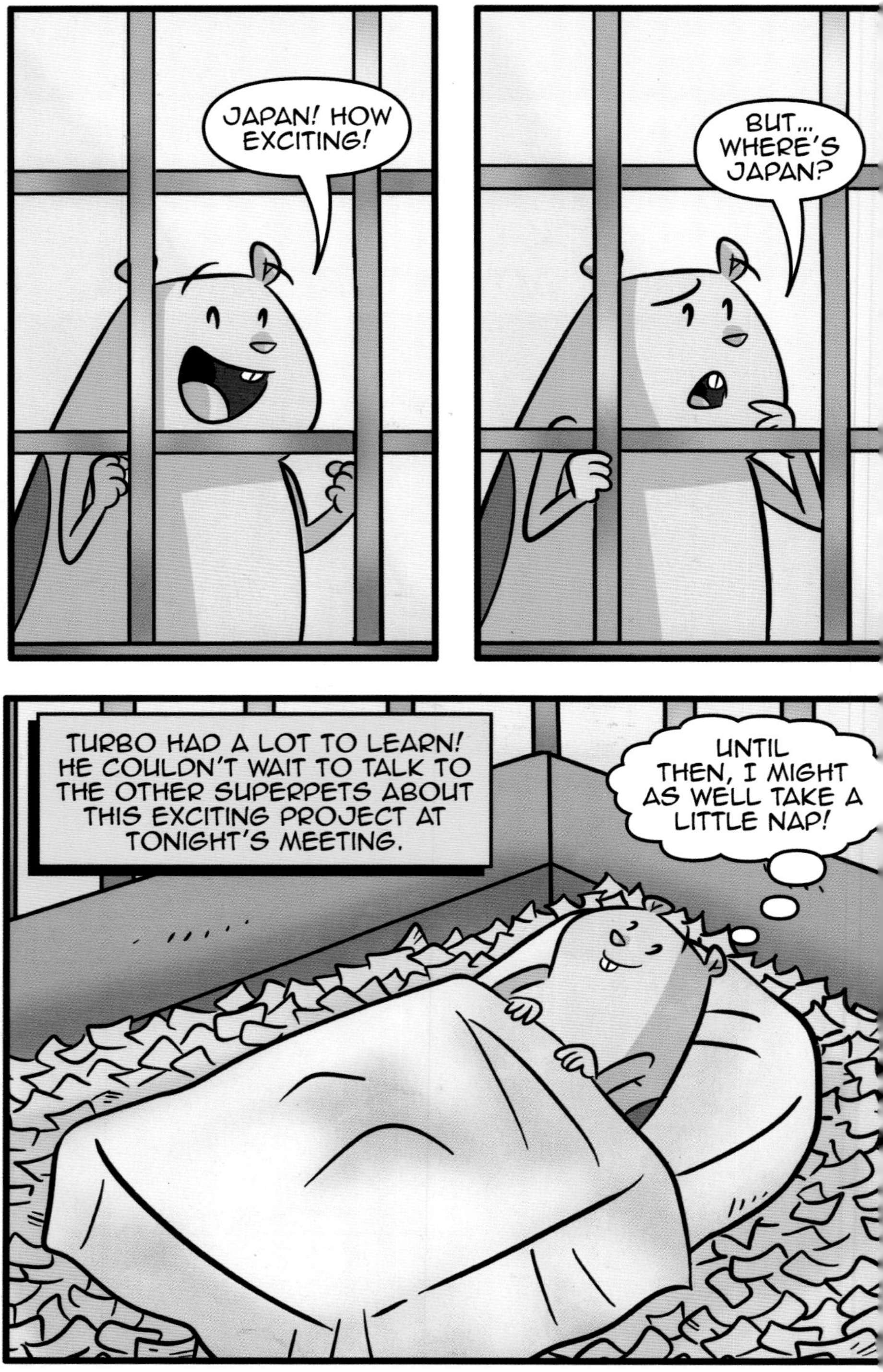
JAPAN! HOW EXCITING!
BUT... WHERE'S JAPAN?
TURBO HAD A LOT TO LEARN! HE COULDN'T WAIT TO TALK TO THE OTHER SUPERPETS ABOUT THIS EXCITING PROJECT AT TONIGHT'S MEETING.
UNTIL THEN, I MIGHT AS WELL TAKE A LITTLE NAP!

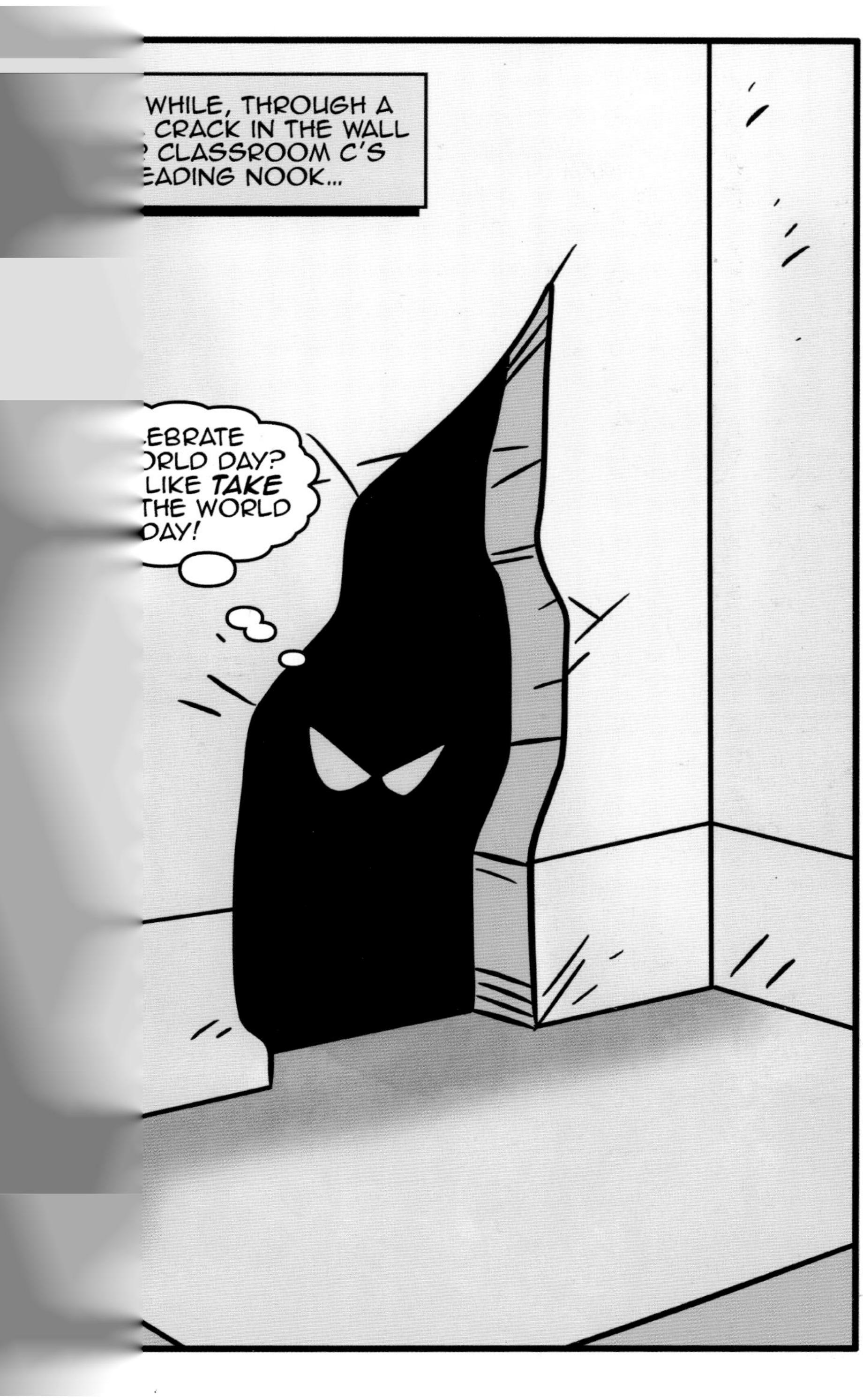
WHILE, THROUGH A
CRACK IN THE WALL
CLASSROOM C'S
EADING NOOK...
EBRATE
ORLD DAY?
LIKE *TAKE*
THE WORLD
DAY!